The Evil Beneath

A Novel

A J Waines

ISBN-13: 9781508648055

Dedicated to the memory of Eleanor Retallack
(1931-2011)
The Queen of Landladies

FACT: There are thirty bridges over the tidal stretch of the river Thames.
FACT: The Thames is tidal for ninety-five miles inland, from the Outer Thames Estuary to Teddington Lock.

Port of London Authority.

prologue

Sunday, September 20th
She had been lying there, facedown in the water long before the tide had turned at 3.04 that morning. Her eyes were staring into the river, her blonde hair first fanning out, then drawing back under her head with the wash of the water, like a pulsating jellyfish. The belt of her raincoat was caught on the branches of an overhanging tree and she'd been hooked, destined to forever flap against the corner of the broken pier with outstretched arms. She wasn't going anywhere now; she was simply bobbing up and down with the rhythm of the water - and she hadn't blinked in a long while.

A male jogger came down the ramp from the main road and ran straight past her. Then a cyclist dipped under the bridge and pedalled at speed with his head down. He, too, passed the bundle tucked under the tree without noticing it. But by 7.15am, the creeping sunrise was opening up the scene for all to see.

Her arms were held away from her body forming the shape of a cross on the water and tiny pieces of weed and broken twigs were caught up in her hair, making her head look like the beginnings of a bird's nest.

An old man with a poodle stopped to stare at the sodden shape in the water, then a woman who had been power-walking joined them, followed by a couple with their arms around each other. Another cyclist, older and slower than the first, joined them. He was the boldest of the group so far. He was wearing black lycra shorts and without taking off his trainers, he began to wade into the river.

In the distance, standing on Hammersmith Bridge, someone was starting to feel pleased with themselves. From that position, you didn't need the binoculars to see a group was starting to form at the water's edge. Where was everybody coming from so early on a Sunday morning? It was like watching wasps gather around a spoonful of raspberry jam.

The cyclist went up to his thighs in the water, getting within a few feet of the body and then turned around shaking his head. He was shouting something to the woman who had been power-walking and she began reaching into her backpack.

The woman's legs were sticking out from beneath the gabardine. They were covered in purple striped tights and she was still wearing both ankle boots. Everything looked intact.

No one would notice the binoculars now trained towards the towpath. She had to arrive at the scene any time now, to get a good view, before the body was bagged up and taken away by the river police.

Take your time, came a whisper from the bridge, we need a certain person to get here before the police tidy everything away.

Another woman, who seemed to have come from nowhere, doubled over and rested her hand against the tree. Someone put their arm around her. You couldn't tell from this distance if she'd been sick.

Then she was there. The chosen one. On her own, walking tentatively towards the water. She'd got the message and she'd responded. All was well with the world. How long would it take her before she realised? Before the shit hit the fan. That was a good image; it had the ring of old Tom and Jerry cartoons.

Was it worth waiting around for that moment or not? She might not make the connection straight away. Some people's brains didn't work as fast as others.

There was a sound of a siren. An ambulance and a squad car pulled up and in a flash, she was lost in the tight little gathering. No point hanging around. The show was over, but the party was just beginning.

An eye for an eye; that's how the saying went. Proper punishment where it was due. And this was going to be one hell of a payback.

Strains of idle humming came from the bridge. It was time to start dreaming of fried eggs and two pieces of toast - and perhaps even some beans on the side. Wasn't that justified?

one | two days earlier

There was a pervasive smell of antiseptic and I couldn't help wondering when the girl lying on the operating couch would notice she had a bystander.

'Up,' said Dr Finely. He was referring to the girls legs. I tried to stay behind her line of sight, as he made sure her thighs were secured into the leg rests. The surgeon's eyes protruded in a way that made me think of a peeping-tom; the kind who steals women's underwear and keeps it under his pillow. There wasn't an ounce of softness or sympathy in his face. Nor, once he'd spoken, was there any in his voice. For him, it was just another tiresome removal.

Glenis and Desiree were laying out forceps and clamps on a stainless steel trolley in the matter of fact way one might lay out fruit on a market stall.

'Waiting for anaesthetic,' he said. Glenis shot round and scuttled towards him holding a kidney shaped dish.

It was a thoroughly ungainly affair; the young girl, no older than seventeen, was naked from the waist down, locked into position with her legs spread apart. I could see the girl's chest rising and falling like an injured rabbit at the roadside as her fingers fluttered in anticipation.

When I'd agreed to take on extra counselling at Fairways Clinic, I'd had no idea that witnessing a live procedure was part of the introductory package. I thought perhaps I'd be given a brochure with discreet diagrams or at most be asked to watch a video, but being in the room when this poor girl was undergoing an abortion seemed a lot to ask of both of us.

'Name?' Dr Finely had said earlier by way of introduction. I'd told him.

'Well, Juliet Grey, don't interfere.' He gave me the kind of look you'd give someone you found rummaging through your wheelie bin. 'Don't do anything to interrupt or influence the proceedings.'

What did he think I was going to do? Push him aside at some point and claim I could make a better job of it?

Dr Finely was lining up various implements on the couch between the girl's legs and he pulled down a plastic sheet; a feeble flap designed to give her some dignity. The 'lunchtime abortion' it was called, with the assurance that the patient would be back to work in an hour or so. Just like popping out of the office for a pint of milk. So convenient.

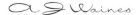

The girl was silent, but watching the surgeon's every move with glistening eyes. Her red tumbleweed hair was tamed into a ponytail and she was pretty, with delicate features. No one in the room had taken the trouble to ask the girl's permission for my presence. I swallowed hard, hoping she would be too distracted to realise she was being observed. With his blue latex gloves in place and the face-mask pulled down over his mouth, Dr Finely swung the overhead light in front of him and began. There were no words of reassurance.

I took a sharp intake of breath. The lights suddenly seemed overly bright, as though I'd walked out into a football stadium. Don't you dare faint, I said to myself, as I took a step back to use the wall for support. The girl squirmed as the surgeon pushed the metal implement, the size of a fat pen, deep into her vagina. Her nostrils flared and she pressed her clenched fists down on to the couch.

As the surgeon introduced another implement, the girl whimpered and reached out her hand. Desiree had her back to the operating table and the other nurse was holding a clamp and tissues. I didn't hesitate. I took one step forward and took hold of the girl's clammy palm.

'It will all be over soon,' I whispered, aware as soon as I said it that I had no idea how long this was going to go on for. 'You're doing really well.'

I gently squeezed the cold hand. I didn't even know her name.

The girl made futile attempts to roll her hips away from the source of the pain and the surgeon looked up and told her to keep still. She began keening quietly.

I kept hold of her hand.

Dr Finely handed a small bloodied tray to Desiree, as Glenis told the girl to pull on her underclothes. It was all over. I let go. The girl, her shoulders shaking, was left to hitch herself down from the couch unaided and find her way back to the recovery room. I thought the clock in the operating room must have stopped; I seemed to have been standing there for far longer than twenty minutes.

Dr Finely stripped off his latex gloves and I assumed I was free to go. As I made a move to leave, he rounded on me, as if I'd just rudely bumped into him on a busy street, his fishy breath blasting straight into my face.

'Ms Grey, what did I say to you about not interfering?' he said, casting the gloves into the bin. He shook his head and took a step forcing me against the operating couch.

I was so startled I couldn't speak. You need to know that this is a rare occurrence for me. I couldn't believe I was being admonished for showing basic human kindness. Who, in their right mind, would deny someone in pain, a comforting hand?

'I was... she was...' I stammered, following him to the door.

'You know how this all works, do you? You've done it all before, have you?'

'Well, I–'

'Perhaps you should have mopped her brow, bought her a sandwich and paid her bus-fare back to the squat she's no doubt living in.'

'I'm not sure–'

His words shot out like flying shards of glass. 'Not in my theatre.' He sliced his hand across his neck in an emphatic gesture. 'You *do not* touch my patient.'

A surge of heat flushed upwards as if my collar was on fire. It wasn't so much the way he made me feel so small that was the issue, it was his total refusal to recognise basic compassion. There was no way I'd done anything wrong. I opened my mouth again, but he'd gone. I turned to the nurses, but they too had moved on and were already preparing for the next patient.

I can't wait to work here, I muttered, wondering if it was too late to tell Human Resources I'd changed my mind. But as I stepped out into the blissfully fresh, cool air, I knew there'd be no reason for me to find myself in the same room as Dr Finely again. As long as there was a distance of at least fifty yards between us, everything should be fine.

Not knowing how long the observation at Fairways would take, I'd kept the rest of the morning free and booked in my private clients at home after lunch. Besides, there was something important I wanted to do before then. I drove over to my flat near Fulham Palace Road in my ancient mini, and parked in a side street. I didn't go inside straight away. Instead, I collected a little bundle from the passenger seat and started walking.

Some late September days felt like they still belonged to summer, but not today. The sun was trying to break through, but the sky was predominantly angry, with charcoal smudged clouds crowding in from the East. It looked like it could rain any minute. I held the parcel carefully in my arms and decided a fierce downpour, under the circumstances, couldn't be more fitting.

When I reached the river, the tide was in, swallowing up the pebble shoreline. I watched the green liquid expand and contract like a robust lung, life-support for the entire city, and opened my package. I didn't have long.

Inside there was a single white rose and a neatly folded piece of notepaper. I lifted the flower to my nose. It had a faint smell of sherbet. Luke would have liked that. Make him think of sweetshops. I trailed the bud down my cheek. It was cool and firm and had started to unfurl; to show itself to the world. A solitary living organism, its stem severed, already on its way towards death.

I leant against the railings, cupping the bud gently in my hand. A woman jogged past me and I could see a couple strolling in my direction in the distance. I needed to be ready. I needed the right moment with no one else around. I waited for them to pass and knew it was time. I could see no one else. My heart trembled. I held the bud out over the handrail, watching the ivory petals; delicate, innocent, vulnerable against the swelling force beneath. I reached right out, held my breath and let it go.

'Happy birthday, Luke,' I whispered. 'Not much of a present, I know...'

I watched the rose swirl and bounce on the water, like a small bird trying to take flight. The tide must have changed, as the water was now heading back out to sea. I ran along the towpath, parallel to the stem for a while, trying to keep track of it as it swirled and twisted, purposeful on its journey. I dodged around people, keeping up with it as it gathered speed before it was sucked away under Putney Bridge. Then I lost sight of it.

'Goodbye, Luke.'

As I caught my breath, I noticed tiny pockmarks on the surface of the water. Grey spots were also spattering the pavement beside me, accompanied by a light hissing sound. People started to hurry for shelter. I stayed where I was. Yes, let it rain. Hard. Give me all you've got.

Luke left us nearly twenty years ago, when he was sixteen. I never forgot his birthday, but finding mental images of him that weren't jaded with overuse was getting harder each year. Like a photograph that creases and fades and finally cracks down the middle. I couldn't imagine him being thirty-five. He was forever locked in a time-capsule; an adolescent with a lopsided smile, five ex-girlfriends behind him (even then) and a quirky desire to playing air-guitar at inappropriate moments. Like the time when Mrs Heppenstall's rabbit died or when Uncle Dan was about to make a speech at cousin Joan's wedding.

I started walking home, feeling like I could breathe again.

The first-floor flat I rented had once been part of a terraced Victorian family house. I crossed the busy road and opened the gate. It was in a reasonable enough area, although it was just around the corner from the place where Jill Dando had been shot in 1999 - one fact I 'forgot' to tell my parents when I moved in. You can get away with omitting any number of pieces of information, I'd discovered, when your parents are as far away as Spain.

There was a message waiting on my answerphone when I got back. It was from Cheryl Hoffman, one of the practitioners at Holistica, a clinic in

Bloomsbury, where I held my supervision sessions. *Ring me – we must do coffee, soon.*

Cheryl was perhaps sixty-five, with thick white hair tied back under a silk scarf. She wore floaty dresses in cerise pinks and cherry reds; layered one over the other so it was difficult to define her exact shape. She had large, masculine-looking hands, but her chunky fingers were weighed down by clusters of gold rings bearing large stones.

What attracted me most about Cheryl was the far-reaching wisdom I saw in the folds of her tanned, leathery skin, and in her eyes, painted with thick kohl like an Egyptian goddess. She gave the impression of having lived an extraordinary life. Whenever she wafted by, I thought of pyramids and pharaohs. It made me want to get to know her better.

'Special day on Friday?' she'd whispered knowingly when I'd last seen her. She claimed to be psychic, although she was officially registered as a homeopath.

'How did you–?'

Before I could ask more, she'd disappeared behind a door marked *Do Not Disturb*.

How could she possibly know about Luke's birthday? Is that what she meant? I'd wanted to find out more, but she was with a client. I'd had to let her go.

I wiped her message and check my list of appointments.

This was my first home without flatmates. When you were on your own I discovered, quirky habits emerged. I had a bit of a thing about creases and once it was just me, I found myself ironing everything – hankies, socks, towels, scarves, even fleece gloves. I loved the smell of hot fabric and there was something symbolic in the purity of pressing out the folds. I could happily while away hours at a weekend making everything smooth – besides, it gave me an excuse to watch soppy black and white films.

My other foible was reading magazines back to front. Don't ask me why. I also hated having hair creep inside my collar and I couldn't bear pictures that weren't hung straight. Friends always told me off for doing regular tours of their flats, scrutinising every frame.

I plumped up the cushions and put a jug of water on the coffee table. Some people thought I was taking a risk working alone as a psychotherapist and inviting strangers into my home. I'd had to learn to be super sharp when I got that first contact from a client and always made sure I spoke to them in person. If I felt the slightest reservation regarding their tone of voice or what they were saying, I would give them the *no-spaces-at-the-moment* spiel. Not that people were always that easy to read. After all, rapists and axe-murderers say 'please' and 'thank you' just like anybody else.

That's where my rape alarm came in. It was always in my pocket when I was working. It was small and discrete and I usually forgot it was there. Thankfully, I'd never had recourse to use it.

Moments later, I heard the doorbell and my sessions got underway. It was a straightforward day, if you considered consoling a woman who had just found out her husband had been frequenting a nightclub dressed as a woman, calling himself Geraldine, straightforward. Or discussing deeply intimate sexual acts with a gay man who was still a virgin at thirty-five. Such were the secrets behind the seemingly humdrum lives of many people. Then my final client scheduled for four o'clock arrived.

'Come in,' I said, opening the front door. 'Juliet Grey.'

Mr Fin was ten minutes late. I decided not to make anything of it as it was his first session. He averted his eyes to start with and brushed past my outstretched hand. He was inordinately tall, perhaps six-feet five. I led him along the corridor to the spare room and pointed to the seat beside the door. He grunted and folded his wiry body into it. In the silence that followed, his dewy brown eyes shifted and were now trying to scorch a hole in mine.

'You told me you hadn't had any counselling before, is that right, Mr Fin?' I asked. When he'd phoned a few days earlier, Mr Fin had sounded meek and lonely. He nodded. His gaunt face was so pale it looked as though it was covered in a layer of talcum-powder. He looked around forty-five, going on sixty.

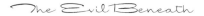

'Okay. So, what has brought–'

'I *know* you,' he said, without the slightest movement.

It wasn't the way my sessions usually started. I tried not to shift in my seat.

'I know that you're thirty-one, that you lived in Norwich before you moved to London, two years ago.' I swallowed hard, but did not interrupt. 'I know that you've been a therapist since 2006 and that your brother died in a fire when you were twelve. He hesitated, but continued to fix his staring eyes on me as if he was hypnotised. 'And that you're not married.'

My insides had taken off on a big-dipper ride, but I didn't want him to see he'd shaken me.

'You know a lot about me,' I said, soothing any alarm out of my voice. After an initial flash of concern, I realised there was nothing he had told me that wasn't publicly available, either through my website or published articles. 'You must have decided that it was important to know something about me.'

He crossed his stick-thin legs, crushing them together. I half-expected to hear a crack as one of them snapped. He didn't speak.

I waited, then tried again. 'What is it you'd like to explore in counselling, Mr Fin?'

'Are you any good at this?'

I didn't like his tone. 'I think that is something you'll have to find out.'

'Aren't you going to ask me questions?'

I was tempted to point out that this is what I'd been doing all along. I tried another one. 'What sort of questions did you expect?'

'About what's wrong with me.' He finally looked away for a second and I realised I'd been holding my breath.

'Wrong with you?' I found myself running my hand over my pocket, checking the rape alarm was there. In a flash I pictured my neighbours. Would the squeal of the alarm get through the walls? Would anyone respond? Would they all be out at work? I made a mental note to remind them about my situation as a matter of urgency.

'Isn't that what you're supposed to find out?' he said.

Mr Fin was going to be a tough cookie, I decided. It was going to take nerves of steel to forge a connection with him and not be intimidated. As I batted back his questions, feeling like I was being pummelled with vicious volleys from a first-rate tennis player, a question of my own rose to the surface and wouldn't go away.

What the heck did he want from me?

two

It was the blue light that woke me during Saturday night. It broke through the white muslin drapes and skimmed the walls of my bedroom in a regular pulse. I went to the window and saw a patrol car right outside, together with a small huddle of people including the couple from the flat downstairs.

I held my breath. My first thought was that someone had been run over, but there was no ambulance and nothing blocking the road. Tony, wearing only a t-shirt and black boxer shorts was gesticulating his way through a complicated mime for the police officers and Jackie, wrapped inside a pink dressing gown, was sitting on the front wall as if she was waiting for a bus. I heard Jackie laugh and knew then it couldn't be too serious. Curiosity got the better of me. I decided to go down and disguise my nosiness with an offer of a hot brew and plateful of custard creams.

'Everything all right?' I asked.

'Didn't you hear me scream?' replied Jackie.

'No - are you okay?' I said, squeezing her arm, looking for an injury.

'We've had a nasty shock - a burglar.' Tony looped one arm around his wife's shoulder. 'Crazy guy,' said Tony. 'Got into our flat at the back, but as he was starting to rummage through our stuff his mobile phone went off!'

'All I heard was the William Tell overture and then a loud crash,' said Jackie.

'He must have realised he'd cocked it up and made a run for it.'

'Have they caught him?' I asked.

'Not yet. By the time we knew what had happened, he'd legged it out of the French windows and over the fence into next doors' garden. I wasn't going after him.'

Tony was around five feet six, with thickening belts of flesh around his waist. He didn't look the type to routinely scramble over fences. I glanced down at his bare feet. They must have been numb with cold by now.

I ran inside to boil a kettle and found myself thinking about my weird session that afternoon with Mr Fin. I wasn't sure what to make of him. He'd complained that my clothes were too casual and that I wasn't old enough. Honestly. What was he trying to do? Deflect from his own issues? Challenge me? Frighten me? By the time he left, I was sure he wouldn't be coming back, but he surprised me by insisting on coming again at the same time next week.

I was torn between the challenge he presented and a reluctance to return to the lion's den. But, I had a say in this, too. It was simple. If he continued to be hostile, I'd discontinue the sessions.

I braced myself against the night chill and handed out the steaming mugs and biscuits. A few more people had joined the group beside the police car, but no one had anything to add. No one had seen a thing. I went back inside acutely aware that I was on my own.

As I switched off the bedside lamp, I noticed there was a text message on my mobile phone:

> *At first light go to Hammersmith Bridge. There is something there you'll be interested in. No later than 7.15am.*

As I read, I felt a fierce pummelling in my ribcage. The number had been blocked. I had no idea who it was from. Someone must have punched in the wrong one. I switched it off.

I pulled the duvet over me, but I kept seeing the message in white letters in the black space under my eyelids. Hammersmith Bridge. It wasn't far along the towpath from here. I was bemused. It meant nothing to me. What on earth could possibly be of interest there at seven in the morning?

I turned over, hoping to shake the stupid message out of my head. I needed to get to sleep. It was well after 3am. I plumped up the pillow and let out a loud sigh.

Within half an hour, I was wide awake again, mulling over the meaning of the message. I put on the bedside lamp and switched the phone back on to read it one more time. I knew curiosity was one of my biggest strengths, but it could also be my downfall. Surely, though, going down to the bridge to have a look would do no harm? If it was a misdialled text or a stupid prank, it was no big deal. I could go for a run along the towpath. I'd been meaning to do something about my fitness.

The jogging idea swung it and by 6.30am, I was dressed. I gulped down a glass of orange juice and then taking my keys from the hall table, quietly let myself out. Even if this was a silly game, at least I'd get a decent run out of it. I checked the message once more before slipping the phone into my pocket. It was precise about the time - *no later than 7.15am*. The weird thing was, if I hadn't been woken by the incident downstairs, I would have completely missed it. Daybreak would have come and gone without me.

The street lights were on and it still felt like nighttime, although lower parts of the sky were starting to turn a pale grey, as though they had been rubbed with an eraser. To make sure I got to the bridge by first light I needed to drive down to the river. Surprisingly, my mini fired up first time. The starter motor had been on the blink for weeks and I kept meaning to get it fixed. I left it near the Wetland Centre in Barnes and broke into a slow jog as soon as the footpath joined the towpath.

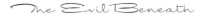

I hadn't gone far before I started to get a stitch. Then I twisted my ankle on scattered stones on the path. Suddenly the whole idea seemed ridiculous: launching myself into rigorous exercise without any preparation. I hadn't jogged for months and my last block of yoga classes had clashed with the new job at Fairways. Besides, there was no one else around and no one knew where I was. The thought that I might be in danger slipped into my consciousness. Bad move. I checked my watch: 6.50am. It would be light soon. It seemed feeble to go back now.

I heard panting behind me and a bulldog shot out of the bushes and brushed past me, followed by a woman wearing an orange bandana and a whistle around her neck, trying to keep up.

'Too much bloody energy,' called out the woman, as she staggered by.

I smiled. There were people around after all.

When I passed the penthouse blocks of Harrod's Village, I could see the shape of the bridge ahead. The darkness was lifting now and although there was no burning sunrise, there was a shift from the earlier monotones. Blues and yellows were breaking through. Rather a magnificent time to be out and about, I decided, as I ran down the slope that dipped under Hammersmith Bridge.

At this point I slowed down, as a small gathering was forming by the water's edge. People were pointing at something in the water and then turning away. A woman was propping herself up against a large tree, the branches of which, swung out over the water. As I got nearer, I could see leaves and sticks forming clumps under the tree. At first, I couldn't see exactly what was trapped in the weeds; it looked like a floating bin bag or a thick log covered in dark moss. I looked closer. Then an icy chill crept under my skin.

It was a coat.

I shuffled another step closer and heard someone being sick.

By now it was light enough to see clearly and all of a sudden I knew what people were looking at. The body was face down. It looked, from the build and the amount of hair floating on the surface, like it was a woman.

There was no question about it. She was dead.

A gurgle of vomit rose in my throat and I held my chest, snatching to get my breath, wanting to look away, but also drawn to the sodden shape. I could hear a man behind me saying he'd called the police.

For a moment I stood aimlessly staring at it, as it - she - rocked gently with the lull of the water. I didn't dare think about her final moments. Nothing gentle about that. I didn't dare imagine what her face must look like. I kept thinking she must be so cold lying there, except of course by now she wouldn't be able to feel a thing.

Suddenly the sound of people commiserating and gasping around me became too loud, the soapy smell of the Thames too pungent. I didn't want to be there. This was some awful tragedy and the shock and grief belonged to other people, not to me. Then I remembered the message:

> *At first light go to Hammersmith Bridge. There is something there you'll be interested in. No later than 7.15am.*

I looked down at my watch: it was 7.19.

Dawn was breaking and here I was at the bridge. I'd been invited to come to this exact spot, at this exact time for what, exactly? To see this wretched dead woman in the water? *Is this what I'm supposed to be 'interested' in? What on earth did it have to do with me?*

I twisted round searching for anyone who might be watching me, but everyone seemed preoccupied with what was in the water. Two people turned away from the bank, leaving a space for me to squeeze through to the edge of the water. Perhaps just one closer look, I said to myself. I looked down at the feeble shape rocking backwards and forwards. That was close enough - my stomach couldn't take any more.

Three police officers emerged from under the bridge telling everyone to stand back, followed by a pair of paramedics and the group of onlookers started to break up. I was jostled to one side and could no longer see the body, only the yellow and black shapes hovering over it. I needed to see the face. It occurred to me that this could be why I'd been sent here: *NoGodPlease* - I might know this person.

A paramedic carrying a box crossed in front of me and I made use of the space she created to follow in her wake. I leant against the tree, out of the way of the emergency services, but with a view of the body. I could hear myself hyperventilating as I stared at the bundle. The paramedic held the limp wrist for a moment, but it was obvious that life had long since departed. She noted something on a clip-board and knelt down. It took two of them to untangle her from the scrub and turn the woman over. I held my breath. Every muscle inside me was urging me to move away, but I knew I had to hold my ground. The last thing I wanted to do was look at her face, but I had to see who see was. I needed to set my mind at rest that this had nothing to do with me.

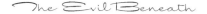

It wasn't a pretty sight. The woman's flesh was off-white and glutinous, with small leaves and weed caught around her nostrils. Her eyes were open, staring up at a sky she'd never see again.

I forced myself to look, swallowing back surges of nausea, trying not to heave. I made myself search for signs of recognition, but as I scanned her bloated features, no lights were going on. I did not recognise this woman. That was all I needed to know. A wave of vertigo forced me to lean back into the tree and I pressed my hand against my chest in an instinctive gesture of sorrow and relief. I found myself drifting away from the group and sat down at the edge of the bridge. I'd seen enough.

And yet - there was something else. Something I wasn't seeing, but I couldn't make my brain join the dots.

Every muscle in my body wanted to move away, but I was riveted to the spot. If I left, I might never know what was trying to get through to me. It was like looking at random letters upside down, feeling sure they make a word. It could be important. It could be the reason I was sent there.

Perhaps more than most, I knew how the brain could distort images left to fester in the memory. An impulse was telling me I had to capture this scene exactly as it was. On the spur of the moment I pulled out my phone. I had to take a photograph. Revulsion gnawed at me, but I had to take an image of this scene away with me, so I could reflect on it in my own time. It was the only way I could be sure.

More people were appearing all the time; from the bridge, the road and both directions along the towpath. Police officers were more occupied keeping the surge of new onlookers at bay than they were with the group already collected at the scene. With my phone held low, hoping no one would spot it, I edged as close to the river as I could get without getting my trainers wet. I tried to focus on the abstract shapes as they appeared on the screen without putting them together. I took two shots and with my eyes lowered to avoid any outraged stares, elbowed my way to an unoccupied patch of grass.

I wanted to cry, throw up and curl into a ball all at once. What I had just done filled me with disgust. Right there and then, I had no hesitation in making the call. If I'd thought it through, I'd probably have chosen someone else, but as soon as my composure was sufficiently restored, I punched Andrew's number into my phone.

True to form, he had a hangover.

'Bloody hell, Jules - what time is it?'

I didn't even occur to me until then that he might not have been alone, but it was too late.

'Sorry, Andrew, but something awful has happened...'

I got no further before the tears came. I tried to stay coherent to explain what had happened, but the sobs swallowed up my words. Finally he interrupted me.

'Where are you?'

'Just under Hammersmith Bridge - the Barnes side.'

'What on earth are you doing there?'

'Long story. I got a text message and then when I got here–'

'I'll come and find you,' he said, stifling a yawn.

In spite of Andrew's past failings, I knew I could count on him at a time like this.

As I waited on the bridge, I wondered what he'd been doing lately. Probably sitting in his studio with a blank canvas in front of him thirsting for his next drink. What I felt most wasn't frustration, but sadness. Alcoholics went through such torment to keep the truth from others, but mostly from themselves. Andrew used to hide bottles amongst his paints, lie about how much he'd knocked back that day and try to convince himself that what he was doing was normal. The worst thing he feared was that without a drink, he wouldn't be able to paint. Like many artists, he was convinced that the moment he swilled that whisky down the plughole, his muse would drain away with it. Drink was his friend, his ally, his supporter, but mostly Andrew believed it had a symbiotic relationship with his gifts. Take it away and he would dry up completely.

I might have been able to tolerate his artistic reliance on drink, if it hadn't brought about such a profound Jekyll and Hyde effect. It was like going out with two different men and not knowing which one would be standing there when I answered the door.

It wasn't long before I spotted him walking over the bridge. Lovely Andrew, with his penetrating green eyes and long artistic fingers. I felt just the same as I did when we first met. My palms started to feel moist and I couldn't help wondering if my hair looked a mess. I went to meet him and we stopped about a foot from each other, both caught in a moment of awkwardness, not knowing what form of greeting was appropriate.

'Thank you so much. I know it's early.' I pulled on his jacket sleeve, with an affectionate tug.

'And a Sunday,' he reminded me, coming along-side and leaning on the handrail of the bridge.

He was around six-feet tall, slim with dark blonde hair he liked to keep highlighted. It looked in need of a trim and a curl rolled over his left eye. He brushed it away and I saw his eyes were still lazy with sleep. His energy was set to different levels than most people's, with only two speeds for living: full-on or off. He didn't seem to have an in-between. Nothing flew at half-mast in Andrew's life.

We walked down to the crime scene.

'You said you had a message to come here.'

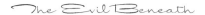

'Yes - have a look at this.' I pulled out the phone from my running top.

He handed it back and rubbed his head. 'What time was the message left?' he asked.

'I didn't think of that.' I pressed a few buttons. '9.30pm - I forgot to check it before I went to bed.'

'You've got to tell the police,' he said. 'Someone knew about this...'

'But, it's all so vague and I can't even be sure the text was meant for me.' As he walked close beside me, I detected his distinctive sugary smell. The one that played havoc with my blood pressure. I also noticed a series of scratches on his neck, like the doodle of an angry child. They looked fresh. 'What's happened here?' I said, reaching up towards his collar. I knew Andrew didn't have a cat, nor would he take any interest in one.

'Nothing,' he said, pulling away. 'Leave it.'

'I was only–'

'Well don't.'

There was an awkward moment when I was torn between pursuing it and apologising. Instead, he changed the subject.

'Look, there's a police officer over there, go and say something.' He nudged me in the back. I shivered, but didn't move forward. The officer was talking to people and taking down notes. 'Someone meant for you to come here,' said Andrew. 'They knew something was going to happen. Maybe the woman was dead even before the text was sent to you.'

'But, what does it have to do with me?'

'You get a good look at her?'

'Yeah. But, it's very hard to tell. She was... you know...in a bad way.'

'Not one of your clients?'

I shook my head.

'Nothing about her clothes? What was she wearing?'

I stared at the sandy towpath for a moment. I couldn't bring myself to tell him I'd taken pictures.

'You know, I can't remember...a sort of long anorak, I think...dark...not wearing jeans...tights of some sort.'

Andrew shrugged. 'What does that tell us?'

'I don't know... she was youngish? She had money?'

'Come on, you're the queen of detection.' He jogged my arm.

'I didn't see it...her...well enough.'

The officer turned and looked like he was heading back to the patrol car.

'You're not going to say anything are you?' he said.

'Not yet, no. Anyway, it can't help her now and I'm sure it's all a mistake.'

Andrew put his hands on his hips and I almost looped my arm through. 'There'll probably be a photo and a name in the local rag in a day or so,' he said. 'Perhaps that might shed some light on it.'

'That's true.'

'Then you'll know for sure if it has anything to do with you.' I squeezed my lip. 'I wonder what happened...' he said. 'If it was suicide.' He leant over the bridge. 'Or maybe, she was killed first and then dumped down-stream. She could have travelled a long way with the incoming tide.' Andrew was watching the water, as if trying to judge how fast it might be flowing.

'Stop it!' I snapped. 'Either way, I want to know what it could possibly have to do with me.'

'It's really creepy, Jules, that someone contacted you about it.' He put his arm around me, as we walked back to the bridge. It didn't occur to me to duck away. He was being a good friend when I needed one, that's all. 'Fancy some breakfast?' he said, pointing over the bridge. 'I know for a fact that the pub across there does a mean breakfast.'

I was tempted to add that they also served a mean Scotch whisky, but it felt unfair to be sarcastic when he'd come all this way.

I tutted. 'Typical,' I said. 'An awful business like this and all you can think about is food.'

'It's a bloke thing,' he said.

three

Having slept on it, I knew Andrew was right. First thing, I handed in my phone at the police station on Shepherds Bush Road so they could trace the text. I'd downloaded both photos, printed off copies and made sure I deleted them, first.

I was making poor progress through a bowl of cornflakes when an officer, DI Roxland, rang my landline and gave the impression he thought the anonymous text and the incident at the bridge were a coincidence. Every part of me wanted to agree with him.

I was due at Holistica all morning, offering others supervision this time, so I didn't have a chance to look at the pictures properly straight away. I left them on the kitchen table and headed out. By leaving them in plain view, there was no way I would be able to avoid them when I returned.

Clive, the clinic receptionist, buzzed me inside.

'Dying of boredom here, darling,' said Clive, swinging his bare feet onto the desk. He was busying himself straightening leaflets and waiting for the phone to ring. Clive was petite with bed-head blonde hair and a pre-pubescent face. I was convinced he used eyeliner to hatch in the appearance of stubble to make it clear which gender he was. He was in his early twenties, but looked about sixteen. I wondered whether if I'd had his cheekbones, they'd work the same magic on me. The phone rang and he switched on his ever-so-helpful and slightly camp tone to answer it.

All my supervisees that day mentioned the fatality; they'd heard it on the news or seen the front page of *London Daily*. Just before I left, I heard Cheryl Hoffman talking about it in the cloakroom.

'At least she didn't drown...' she said.

I thought I'd misheard her, but by the time I'd taken in what she'd said, she'd gone.

It took me back to the time when Cheryl and I had our first proper chat; a supervisee hadn't shown up and she'd invited me to her room to share a tuna sandwich. I learnt straightaway that Cheryl wasn't the sort to bother with small talk; two minutes in and we were talking about New Age philosophy, interpreting dreams and whether I believed in an afterlife. I said I wasn't sure. I didn't mention Luke.

'Ever heard of the Academy for Psychic Development,' she said. 'It's near Sloane Square?' She saw my head shake. 'I do readings there and run a class. You should come.'

I said I'd think about it. I wasn't exactly sure what she meant by being psychic and we didn't have time that day to go into it further. My father would have called anything of that sort 'poppy-cock' and my mother would have warned me against getting involved. 'It's dangerous to meddle with evil forces,' she would have said. Luke would have laughed: 'It's all a con trick.' I remained undecided. I'd had no personal experiences to pull me either way.

It was my second meeting with Cheryl, shortly after our first encounter, that unnerved me. She'd left a note in my pigeon-hole suggesting we meet at the local wine bar at the end of the day. We'd settled in a corner with two large glasses of Rioja and she started by telling me about her family. I'm ashamed to say I found myself drifting off, having listened to people's life-stories all morning and undergone a heated discussion with my own supervisor, in the afternoon. I rubbed my eyes and found Cheryl looking at me, waiting for me to respond.

'Sorry?' I replied. 'Can you say that again?'

'I said, I know about the sadness in your life.'

'Oh.' I rolled the stem of the wine glass between my fingers. She'd caught me by surprise. She reached over and took my hand. I wanted to pull away, but her eyes were like pulsating bright lights, paralysing me. 'I'm getting some sadness about a boy,' she said. 'In the family. I get the feeling he's not with us anymore.' She waited for me to say something.

I paused, struggling to understand her words as if she was speaking a foreign language. I didn't blink for a moment. I cleared my throat.

'That's right - he's not.'

'I feel very hot,' Cheryl continued. 'Like I can't breathe.' She started rocking slightly. 'There are flames.'

I snapped my hand away, not happy about the way this was going. She seemed to know about Luke, the fire. As she spoke, I saw harrowing visions of that fateful night, a collage of flashbacks interspersed with tortuous scenes of my own making: the burning building, looking up and finding Luke missing, flashes and blasts forcing us back, crackling flames tearing out of exploded windows, smoke, water, steam belching into the night air, Luke's pyjamas on fire, his skin blistering as the rest of us grabbed each other and watched transfixed. His death was still raw, still able to churn up my insides, even though the accident was nearly twenty years ago. I didn't want to talk about it with a virtual stranger.

Cheryl's face had turned pink. Perhaps she was reacting to the red wine. Maybe it *was* too hot in there. I grabbed a menu and started wafting it at her, hoping she'd laugh and draw her uninvited reading to an abrupt conclusion.

'Am I right?' she said, quietly.

'Yes, you're right,' I said, looking down for my bag. 'He died in a fire.' I wanted to close the subject for good and leave. 'I don't want to talk about it.'

'Terrible business,' said Cheryl, her head titled to one side in sympathy. 'Must have been awful when you found out it was wasn't an accident.'

I was taken aback. *What was she saying?* No, she'd got that bit wrong.

'It was... it was an accident.'

'That's not–'

I shot to my feet, making the wooden chair squeal on the tiled floor and held up my hand.

'Sorry, Cheryl. We're going to have to leave it right there!'

Thankfully, she'd let it drop and I hadn't spoken to her properly since. It was after that time that I noticed other practitioners at the clinic avoiding her. Had she tried similar antics with my colleagues? I'd been starting to think it would be wise for me to follow suit.

Cheryl's chilling words had played over and over in my head ever since, but she must have been mistaken. At the time of the fire, there had been no suspicious circumstances; there was never any question that someone had started it deliberately. An electrical fault was what the police had told us. Something to do with the toaster; a common cause of domestic fires. Even if her psychic conviction was right and there had been a question-mark over the case, there's no way I could find out more, so long after the event. No - Luke's accident was beyond further scrutiny.

But I couldn't say the same about the woman in the water.

Back at the flat, I sat at the kitchen table for twenty minutes staring at the photos. Nothing. I made a bowl of pasta and came back to them; watched a mindless TV sitcom and came back to them. I made a cup of coffee, put some music on and sat in front of them again. It was like waiting for a mechanical toy to come to life when it hasn't been wound up properly. Nothing was happening. There was something about the woman in the river that was familiar and yet I couldn't place her. Was it to do with the shape she made in the water? Did she remind me of someone?

Perhaps sleeping on it would help. Maybe in the morning, my brain would have a fresh take on the whole thing. I didn't know if it was going to work, but I did know there was definitely something there. I just couldn't see it yet.

There was a queue of women waiting to see me the following morning as I arrived at Fairways, the abortion clinic in Brixton where I'd recently taken on a few shifts. I had stuffed the photos into my bag before I left, but had to put them out of my mind immediately and switch into listening mode.

The first client was ushered into my tiny counselling room by her mother. Aysha looked like she was African Caribbean and had earphones pressed into her ears, which were already weighed down by large gold earrings. Her heavy breasts made her look over eighteen, but her eyes said she was much younger. Turned out she was fourteen. I knew she hadn't switched off the music, because she continually twitched her shoulders to the beat. She also chewed in time to it. I gave the mother a stare, but Mrs Turner had a faraway look that suggested she'd long since stopped trying to tell her daughter what to do.

'Can I ask you if you've taken a pregnancy test, Aysha?'

'Yes.' It was her mother who answered.

'And when was your last period?'

'She can't remember.'

Her mother continued to do all the talking and Aysha did the chewing. That was about as much as I was going to get out of her. We stumbled around with dates, until it became clear the girl was probably around eighteen weeks pregnant. That was late. It meant she'd need a general anaesthetic, but if she left it much longer, a more complicated procedure would be necessary. Either way, it wasn't going to be pleasant. Leave it too long, of course, and she would be too late for a legal termination altogether. I tried to reinforce the urgency of the situation, but it was like trying to score from the penalty spot with a ping-pong ball.

I ran through the required form, with the mother answering all the questions. At one point Aysha pulled the gum out of her mouth and twirled it around her index finger. I thought she'd removed it to say something, but it went straight back in again.

At the end of our short interview, as I held open the door, Aysha spoke for the first time.

'I know what happens,' she said, with a look verging on loathing. 'I dun it all before.'

I sank down on the padded window seat once they'd gone, and rested my head against the frosted glass. I couldn't help wondering what kind of life was in store for that girl. She was already caked in make-up, with a low-cut top and barely-there miniskirt and probably had no trouble getting into nightclubs. What had happened to her childhood? What had happened to swooning over pop-stars and fantasies of becoming a ballerina? I'd seen only one client and I was already wiped out.

My brain was crying out for a strong coffee. I went to the machine in the reception and came away with a poor substitute for one, then invited the next girl through.

By 3.30, the stream of clients began to tail off and I saw the chance for a break. I stayed in my room and pulled out the photographs. I'd been hoping for a spare moment to study them again. *What is it I'm supposed to know? What connection do I have with any of this?*

The two pictures were of the same scene: the water, the tangle of weed and the woman's body, one slightly closer than the other. I focused on the close-up and scrutinised every detail. I tried to be dispassionate, tried to look with the clinical eyes of a pathologist, but I could almost feel the chill in the water, feel it seeping into my clothes making me heavy and unable to keep my head up. I wanted to shut my eyes, turn away, tear the pictures into tiny pieces, but I forced myself to stare, the pictures blurring as tears formed a glassy film over my eyes. Focusing like this was tortuous, but I had to find out why I'd been targeted. *Who are you? What am I missing?* I had to know.

I sprang to my feet as the door opened.

'Sorry, Juliet.' It was Dina. She was one of the receptionists, in her early twenties with cropped yellow hair and a ring through her nose. Her expression had a worn look about it that indicated she'd had enough of this kind of work. I tried not to look startled and laid the photos facedown on my desk. 'You've got two latecomers left over from lunchtime. Shall I send the first one through?'

Annoyed at the interruption, I put the pictures back in my bag and cleared my throat. I'd have to come back to them later.

At the end of the day, as I left the room to head home, I could hear Dina laughing.

'I nearly ran off with it, sorry,' said Dina. She was pulling a jacket from her shoulders and handing it over to the other receptionist.

'It's easily done - they're practically the same,' said Amanda, slipping her arms through the sleeves. 'See you tomorrow.'

As I left the building, I could have kicked myself. *I'd got it.* I knew exactly what connected me with the photographs. It had been staring me in the face all the time.

The coat, the blouse, the tights, the boots.

The dead woman in the water was wearing my clothes.

four

As soon as I got back from Fairways, I banged on Jackie's door. Given that I was trying to move on from Andrew, she was the only other person to hand I could think of. She answered the door, chewing, holding something behind her back. Her long mousy hair was dripping onto the carpet. It looked like well-used rope and I wanted to reach across and squeeze more water out of it. I'd clearly caught her in the middle of getting ready to go out, but I decided my need was greater than hers. She cautiously invited me in, perhaps convinced of the urgency by the lack of colour in my cheeks.

I garbled my way through what had happened; the text message, the body under the bridge, the photographs.

'It was only when the receptionist at work nearly ran off with Amanda's jacket by mistake that I realised,' I said. 'The clothes she was wearing - they all used to be mine.'

'*Yours* - how can that be?' She was sitting on the edge of the sofa finishing off a doughnut.

'She must have bought them. I remember taking a bag of clothes to a charity shop a few months back. There was a blue gabardine that was past its best and some woolly tights my Aunt Libby bought me. And the ankle boots, with a distinctive buckle - they'd been giving me blisters for months, so they went in the bag as well.'

'And are you absolutely sure they're yours and not just duplicates from M&S or something?'

'No. I'm certain.'

'Have you called the police?'

'They were sceptical at first. But they asked me to see the body.'

'They let you look at the dead woman, just like that?' Jackie was licking her fingers and her expression fell from relish to revulsion.

'She hasn't been identified yet, so the police are looking for any leads they can get. Once I saw her on the trolley, I knew for definite she was wearing my old blouse. I'd altered the neckline by hand. I recognised my own wonky stitching.'

'Maybe this woman just happened to buy several garments that you took in...maybe they were all on the same rail.'

'Don't you think that's a bit unlikely? The entire outfit she was wearing, down to the boots, belonged to me.'

'It's sick.' She wiped her greasy hands down the front of her cardigan. Perhaps she wasn't going out after all. 'Together with the text message, don't you think it's all a bit suspicious?'

'The police told me to keep an eye open for anything unusual. That's all. I've got the number of the officer I'm supposed to contact...' I pulled out my purse and read from a small card. 'DCI Madison. I've got to ask for him directly if anything else happens. I should get my phone back in a day or so; they're still checking the SIM card.'

'Can they track down the person who sent you the text?'

'I think so. The number was withheld, but they have amazing forensic technology these days.'

Jackie turned to face me. 'This isn't connected with that burglar we had, is it?'

'I don't know.' I hadn't thought of that.

There was a hiatus as I pursued my own internal chilling fantasy. The look on her face suggested she was doing the same.

'Are you still seeing that bloke?' she said, unexpectedly. 'The blonde guy?'

I wondered why she'd changed the subject. Perhaps she was checking I had others to offload to, so I wouldn't be tapping on their door every five minutes.

'No.' I got up to go.

'Shame,' she said. 'He seemed a nice guy.'

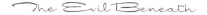

I gave her a noncommittal look. I'd never told anyone that there had been three in our relationship: Andrew, me and Johnnie Walker.

I was too early to get an evening meal ready. I was tempted to have a nap on the sofa, when my landline phone rang. I checked the caller-display and saw that it was Andrew. Even though my hand was already on the receiver, I decided on the fourth ring to let the answer-machine take the call. I turned the volume down. I wasn't ready to hear his voice. Everything had been clear when I'd ended the relationship two months ago; I knew I couldn't cope with his drinking anymore and that was that. Now I'd gone and muddied everything up again. *Why had I called him when I'd seen the body at the bridge? Why hadn't I considered the consequences?*

I made a cup of tea and curled up on the sofa. I started a crossword, but got stuck on 'three across'. I found myself drifting back to the day I'd met him. I was in an art shop in Notting Hill, looking for a stylish notebook to use as a journal and Andrew was in front of me in the queue, buying charcoal. I noticed the way his blonde hair curled inside the collar of his t-shirt.

As I left the shop, he was pinning a flyer on the notice-board. It was for an exhibition of his paintings and when he noticed me glance at it, he invited me to the opening.

'You don't look the kind of person who would turn down a free glass of champagne,' he said. He was dressed as though he'd come straight from his studio, wearing crumpled shorts, with a purple t-shirt covered in streaks of paint. I knew enough about art to know that his trainers were spattered like a Pollock painting and told him so.

'Do your pictures look anything like this?' I'd asked him, waving vaguely at his clothes.

He'd pulled at the front of his t-shirt as he replied. 'Actually, this is better. This is what should be pinned up in the gallery.'

I let him see me smirk and stopped to read the description of the exhibition on the flyer, realising I didn't want our brief encounter to end:

> *Andrew Wishbourne is a colourist of the highest calibre, whose instinct for whimsy and subtlety echoes the reverberating palettes of the Abstract Expressionists.*

High-powered stuff.

'You're good then?' I said.

He turned his nose up and put his hands in his pockets, swinging his hips slightly like a small child.

'Will you come?' He'd won me over already, but I didn't want him to know it was so easy.

'I'll check my diary, ' I said, as he held the door open for me.

'Actually, it's a glass of Cava,' he said, 'but it is free - and there might be crisps, if you get there early enough.'

Ironic that his opening gambit should involve an attempt to lure *me* with the promise of alcohol.

Andrew claimed later that I was never his type; not being blonde, buxom or leggy. I wasn't exactly the opposite either. One cup-size or two short of buxom perhaps, but I was slim and despite being five-feet-four, my leg-to-body ratio was higher than most women's. Besides, brunettes get their fair share of attention, especially if their hair is sleek and glossy like mine.

At his private viewing, he'd made a point of breaking away from other people to come and talk to me. He invited me to a firework display on Primrose Hill. And that was that. From the start, he was romantic and spontaneous. He showed me sunsets and bought me flowers and I was in awe of his unstructured life-style that included modelling and being a film extra, as well as work on his own canvases. I couldn't believe how someone so good-looking and fun to be with wasn't already hooked up with someone. Then, with time, the reason began to bleed through to the surface.

You'd think, as a psychotherapist, I, of all people would have been able to reach him. But nothing worked. 'I'm *not* an alcoholic, Jules - I can go for days without a drink,' he always claimed.

I looked at the phone. I couldn't deny it; I missed him. But, I knew nothing would have changed. The bottle of amber-coloured liquid would still be in arm's reach. It had been unfair of me to turn to him in my hour. I couldn't pick him up and then put him down again, whenever I felt like it. I owed him more than that.

I pulled the throw around me, but I didn't feel any warmer. I couldn't get the image of the body in the water, dressed in my own clothes, out of my head.

Did she get hold of the clothes, herself, before she died or did someone dress her in them after her death? Either way, it left me drowning in my own feeling of bewilderment and dread.

five

It wasn't until I'd washed up after an early tea that I realised a text message had come through earlier that afternoon. I glanced at the screen and saw that the number was withheld. A hot flush crossed over my chest as the words came up:

> *Eleven feet and three inches were added before 1940.*

That was all there was. Just over two weeks after the first message.

Eleven feet and three inches were added to what? And what did 1940 have to do with me? I tried Mack, my best friend from Norwich, but reached her voicemail. Kelly wasn't answering her phone either. I didn't want to worry my parents. When you're a million miles away living in Spain, you don't want to hear that your daughter's in a panic. Support suddenly felt like it was thin on the ground. I was beginning to feel like a dandelion clock where all the fluffy seeds have been blown away. Within the last year, Robbie, one of my best friends had emigrated to New Zealand, Pete was studying in America, Kelly had just had a baby and Laura had been swept off her feet by a new boyfriend and had disappeared into the ether. Who else was there?

I glanced at my watch. I didn't have time to try anyone else, anyway. I was running late and at fifty pounds an hour, I didn't want to waste any more time getting to Chelsea. I jumped on a bus, rather than risk pumping up my blood-pressure trying to get the car started. Every set of traffic lights was against us as the double-decker stuttered along Fulham Palace Road. I was out of breath when Miriam opened the door. Without a word, she invited me to a small room on the first floor.

There was a glass of water on a table by my chair and the ubiquitous box of tissues within reach. I knew the rules. Knew how it went: identical chairs, at a slight angle to each other; nothing personal in the room such as photographs or soft toys. Silence. Just like the set-up at my flat. In the eight months that I had been coming here, I'd never glimpsed any other family member and I wondered if this room had once been a bedroom for a daughter or son who had long since flown the nest.

Miriam had shoulder-length grey hair, clipped with diamante grips at the sides. It was the hairstyle of a teenager in the 1970's and it didn't look

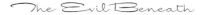

right on a woman in her fifties. I put my judgement down to not being sure whether I liked her or not. Or, perhaps it was the reluctance to sit in the client's chair, when most of the time, I'm far more comfortable sitting in the other one.

The relationship with a therapist is a peculiar one: it's not a friendship, and yet Miriam gets to know my darkest secrets; it's not equal, because I pay her and she doesn't talk about herself. All sorts of inner struggles came to the surface during my weekly sessions: struggles about power, honesty, trust. A therapist is only ever on your side as long as you're paying them, then you never see them again. It made the whole set-up feel fake. Did my clients think in such a complicated way about me?

Miriam rested her hands in her lap and in line with every other session, waited for me to speak.

'Sorry, I'm late,' I said. 'It wasn't about a reluctance to come.'

I knew that having been trained in the Freudian school of psychotherapy, Miriam would be ready to pounce on my lateness and interpret it as some sort of subconscious resistance. I didn't want to waste time on that. 'Something delayed me. Upset me.'

'Go on,' said Miriam, her face impassive.

'I had another message on my phone. I don't know what it means and I'm really scared someone else is going to get killed.'

'Okay, slow down. What did the message say?'

I explained. Miriam seemed to consider the obscure words. 'And this is from the same person?'

'I don't know. The police may be able to check that out - they checked it before, but didn't tell me anything. I need to call them after this.'

'You feel responsible?'

'I don't want there to be another death like last time.'

'You think someone is playing games with you?'

'It's starting to look that way.'

'What have you been dreaming about lately, Juliet?'

The question seemed ludicrous. Why do Freudians have to pay so much attention to the hours we know so little about? Wasn't there enough to go on, drawing on the sixteen hours a day we are awake?

'I can't remember.'

'And when you say that to me, who are you *really* angry with?'

Miriam was on form, tonight. Nothing was getting past her.

'I don't know. Me, perhaps. I contacted Andrew and I shouldn't have.'

'You still love him?'

'Yes - terribly - the sober Andrew. But, I can't live with the person he becomes when he's...' I could feel tears making their way towards my cheek and reached for the cardboard box. 'He won't do anything about it. He won't acknowledge that he's got a problem.'

'We're talking about him now, not you. Let's come back to you.'

'Okay,' I said, louder than I meant to. 'I'm upset, lonely and frightened.'

'And how old do you feel, right now, with those feelings you've described?'

'How old?' I was thrown for a moment. 'I don't know. A child. Eleven, twelve years old maybe.'

'And what was it that happened to you - when you were eleven or twelve?'

Not that old chestnut again. 'Luke, you mean?'

Miriam tilted her hands up, as if to say: *you tell me*.

'You know I was twelve when Luke died in the fire. But this isn't about that, about him.' Suddenly the words Cheryl had said in the wine bar flashed through my mind. When she'd given me her impromptu reading, she'd sounded convinced that the fire hadn't been an accident. Maybe Miriam and I could explore that sometime. But not now. Now, there were more urgent things going on. 'I'm not sure how talking about what happened to Luke can help with what's happening right now.'

'Most of my clients say that. They can't see patterns replaying themselves from the past into the present. I'm wondering why you're blocking this.'

'I'm not. I just don't want to talk about it today, that's all.' I pulled at a loose thread on the cuff of my cardigan. 'I'm confused and upset by another text message and I'd like your support.'

'And what it is you think I can do to help?'

'Take it seriously for a start.'

'Go on...'

'I'm frightened about what might happen to another victim. I'm concerned that this text is like the last one - a kind of warning or clue to another death.' I gave in to sobbing. 'I don't know why it has anything to do with me.'

'What do *you* think you should do?'

'Curl into a ball and hope it will all go away.'

I caught the beginning of Miriam's smile. Perhaps she was human after all.

'Do you need a break from seeing clients for a while? Are you feeling too responsible for other people?'

I thought about it. 'I don't think so. I'm usually good at making a professional separation from my clients. I'm not burnt out. I think the best thing is to tell the police, like I did after the first message. Pass the responsibility on to them. It might be nothing, but...' My words fizzled out. I barely seemed to have the energy to finish my sentences. 'I'm powerless to do anything.'

'Perhaps that's what this is really about, Juliet. You are such a competent and practical person, who always knows what to do. Maybe you're feeling particularly vulnerable and confused about this, because for once, things are outside your control and you can't see what you're supposed to do. And that's a very uncomfortable position for you to be in.'

Sounded about right. I couldn't speak for a moment. When I did, I could feel my chin wobbling. 'People seem to think that because I'm a therapist I'm immune to feelings - they think I sail along in life unaffected by the calamities and ordeals that knock other people for six.'

She folded her arms. 'Perhaps that's because you don't reveal your real self to many people...they assume you're coping just fine.'

'So, it's my fault?' I stared down at my nails.

'You might just want to think about it, that's all. If you don't let people in, they can't see you, can't reach you.'

'It's hard. After what happened to Luke, I had to build a brick wall around me. My father turned into this solitary and distant person I couldn't talk to anymore and Mum just seemed to be crying all the time. I didn't want to burden her. I felt completely alone. I couldn't trust people to be there for me. To make everything alright.'

'And you daren't take the risk with the people in your life, now?'

'It's hard,' I said again, burying my nose in a tissue.

'Well - you're doing it now. How does it feel?'

I looked up and let out a brief sputter of laughter. 'Good. Perhaps I should think about making a few more friends and start letting those people I'm already fond of get closer.'

Normally, I left Miriam's sessions in a mist of confusion and frustration. It made a refreshing change to come away feeling lighter than an hour earlier, knowing I'd made progress. Miriam had helped me see that the text messages and whatever followed were neither my fault nor my responsibility. With that in the forefront of my mind, I pulled out the scrap of paper with DCI Madison's number on it and made the call.

It was 9pm by the time I got off the bus at the stop opposite my flat. I was pulling out my keys by the front gate, when I realised I'd forgotten to pick up a pint of milk. I was about to backtrack to the local Deli, when I remembered it was closed for refurbishment. As it was a mild October evening, I headed for Putney Bridge; there were plenty of late-night grocers on the high street and I fancied some fresh air.

As I rounded the edge of the park, I had a flashback to the day I decided to become a psychotherapist. It was six years ago and was one of those instant decisions that come out of the blue, but change your life forever. Frank, my boss at Capricorn Healthcare, had queried my sales figures and, for the fourth month in a row, told me I was under-performing. I'd returned to my desk, bewildered. *What was I doing wrong?*

Surely, my personality was perfect for selling insurance - I had flair, creativity, I was outgoing and good with people. 'You know what your problem is, don't you?' said Laura, who occupied the booth next to me and was always handing out good advice and stale digestives. Laura had the knack of getting straight to the point. She'd also had the highest sales figures in our team for the past nine months. 'You're too good at listening,' she said. 'If you're listening, you're not *selling*.' She gave me a pained smile and went back to her buzzing headset.

In that moment, it was as if a silent tornado had swept through the room. *I was in the wrong job.* It was as simple as that. I couldn't believe how I'd missed the obvious for so long. I resigned the same day and had enrolled on a course in psychotherapy by the end of the week. It was the best thing I'd ever done.

Counselling had been waiting in the wings for years. I simply hadn't spotted it. Ever since I realised that after eight years I still wasn't coping with Luke's death. I'd struggled since he'd gone, with periods of sombre questioning and existential loneliness. *Where was he? Was he living some parallel life somewhere without us? Why had he been taken away?* My sorry state had culminated in a nasty accident on the High Street where I'd collided with a bus, because my eyes were flooded with tears for the third time that morning. The months of counselling that followed had probably prevented a more serious crash, as well as saving my sanity.

Twenty-eight was fairly young for that profession, but I took to it immediately. Psychotherapy was like being a detective and I'd always loved mysteries. I regarded myself as the most 'private' of Private Detectives; drawing out hidden meanings and subconscious motives that could shock even the clients themselves. It was all about noticing, listening and finding clues.

I cut across the grass to the embankment walkway that runs along the north side of the Thames. Before the incident at Hammersmith Bridge, a solitary stroll here meant a peaceful, reflective time to listen to the river lapping against the banks and take in the damp musty smells. Not anymore. Once I arrived at the riverside, I realised that things had changed. Despite there being good lighting along this stretch and a regular stream of joggers, I felt a frisson of doubt about my personal safety that I'd never had there before. I hated that feeling. It robbed me of my freedom; that feeling of being able to go anywhere at any time, and I wasn't sure I'd be able to get it back.

Several boats, moored in the centre of the river, bobbed gently as the tide came in. I stood and leant over the railing, determined to spend as much time here as I wanted without being forced by my new-found fears, to move on. At this time in the evening, the water looked inky black with a green hue. The mud banks were gradually disappearing as the water crept higher, imperceptive to the passing glance, but resolute in its purpose. I stared down at the cold wash of foam and blinked hard to try to remove the image of the body I'd seen at Hammersmith Bridge. It didn't work and my stomach clenched as I remembered the woman's arms, spread out like the wings of a dead bird and her head, pressed up against coarse tangles of branches. I wondered if the police had found out who she was, by now - and how she'd died. Someone, somewhere was waiting for her to come home.

I looked up to the right, following the line of the water, but Hammersmith Bridge was out of sight due to the sweep of the river. I rested my head on my arms. *Would the strange text I'd received that afternoon turn out to be just as ominous as the first?*

I was still caught up in my internal monologue when I heard a twig snap behind me. I turned round, expecting a dog, but there was nothing there. No need to get jumpy, I said to myself. A sweet-wrapper danced across my path and was swept by a small gust over the edge and into the water. *Someone knew she was going to die. How much of a fight did the woman put up, before someone took her life? Was she pushed off the bridge, alive? What were her thoughts in those final moments before her life came to an end?*

I turned to go and as I did, a flash of grey slid behind the bush beside me. It didn't look like a dog; it looked more like the elbow of an anorak. My pulse notched up a gear. I looked both ways on the path, but there was no one else in sight. I strode out towards Putney Bridge, head down, staring at the path ahead of me. *Keep walking, keep moving; other people will appear any minute.*

Only, no other people did appear. I had taken several steps, when I heard another rustle in the bushes. There was definitely someone there. I didn't know whether to stop and confront whoever it was or continue to ignore it. I broke into a run, instead. Thank goodness I'm wearing flat boots and not high heels, I thought, realising I'd need to bear in mind my footwear, whenever I went out from now on.

I got to the spot where the park opened out on the left. By now, I was wishing I'd paid more attention to my fitness in recent months, but with a surge of relief, I saw there were people about: a woman walking three dogs; a man jogging towards me and a couple, laughing, with their arms around each other. Safe people. I slowed down to a walk.

More people were coming down from the bridge. I dared to turn and look behind me. A tall figure in the background was walking in the opposite direction. I could just make out shades of grey as he passed under a street light. Had he been the one lurking in the bushes beside me? I felt bolder, now that others were filling out the area and started retracing my steps. He was nearly out of sight and I didn't want to lose him. I made a shortcut and ended up on the path about fifty yards behind him.

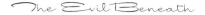

He turned a corner and I lost him behind a hedge, so I broke into a run, trying to keep my heels off the tarmac, so as not to draw attention to myself. He came back into view. He had his hands in his anorak pockets and was walking purposefully towards a side road that led to Fulham Palace Road. He stopped at the end of a line of parked cars and pulled something out of his pocket. I slowed to a walk, realising that now he'd stopped, I would shortly catch him up.

I hadn't thought this through at all. *What was I doing chasing after a strange man who could have been following me?* There were no other turns to take, other than back the way I'd come.

Before I had chance to make a decision, the man looked up in my direction. For a moment, he just stood there. The traffic hummed. A car tooted. It was my client, Mr Fin. I swallowed hard, not sure what to do. If I turned back now, it would look like I wanted to avoid him. As his therapist, that was neither appropriate nor professional.

He didn't acknowledge me, but an uncomfortable frown creased his forehead. He dropped his car-keys and was straightening up again. I was ten feet away from him. In the counselling room, the ability to think on one's feet was a prerequisite and thankfully, I'd had a lot of practice. I pulled the hair back from my face and smiled.

'I thought it was you, Mr Fin,' I said, trying to filter the tremble out of my voice. 'I didn't want you to think I'd ignored you.'

He looked at his shoes, then fiddled with the zip on his anorak. 'Oh... I... actually...didn't see you.'

'I won't stay and chat. I'm sure you understand. It muddies the water if we stand and chat.' It didn't come out as I'd intended. I knew he was going to take it as a form of rejection.

'I'm not interested,' he said. He turned his back and walked around to the driver's door.

'Not interested?'

He looked up as he opened the door. 'I'm not interested in having any kind of chat with you.'

My smile was still there, but I knew it wasn't sitting right.

'Good. That's...fine. That's absolutely fine.'

Mr Fin's car was parked between a concrete bollard and a Range Rover. It was so tightly wedged that the bumpers were overlapping. I watched him get in and start the engine, then I turned away. I didn't want to stand and stare as he tried to manage the tricky exit manoeuvre. For a second, I felt sorry for him - a sad, lonely man - but it didn't last long. Goosebumps skittered down my spine like a daddy-long-legs and I knew there was something not quite right about him. I couldn't put my finger on it, but it sent me a clear message: I mustn't let down my guard. I heard the grating of gears and cringed, keeping my head down, walking away.

six

When I turned into the car-park at Fairways Clinic after lunch, I very nearly drove straight out again. There was a crowd blocking the front entrance. About thirty people or more were holding banners and placards. I found a space at the far side and stayed in the car, punching in the clinic number on my phone. I could hear the corresponding handset ringing inside the building.

'I see we've got company this afternoon,' I said. 'I'm in the car-park - is everyone all right?'

'We're all okay,' said Amanda. Her voice was far from steady. 'Dina's called the police.'

'How long ago?'

'About ten minutes. They started growing in numbers about twenty-five minutes ago.'

'They're allowed to protest,' I said. 'But the police will pounce if they're stopping anyone from coming in or if there's any intimidation.'

'I know. It's happened before. Last year we had the same thing - Pro-Life demonstrators. We got paint thrown on our cars. Are you coming in?'

I hesitated. 'Yes. If I don't appear soon, I'm in trouble.' I laughed, but it wasn't sincere.

I craned my neck to look at the gathering of people and rolled down the window a couple of inches. They were chanting the phrase *Save their lives* over and over. Several had t-shirts with *Say No to Abortion* in black letters on the front and an old bedsheet stretched between two poles had the words *Protect the Embryo* painted across it. One man was holding a rough painting of a gravestone, which read *Here lies the Unborn Child*.

The front door of the clinic opened and a young woman tentatively slid out, her head down. A man stepped forward, shouting at her, pushing a leaflet into her hand. She lifted up her arms to protect her face, letting the leaflet fall, and pressed her way through the tight-knit crowd. Once free, she ran towards the gate and disappeared. I watched two women approach the gate from the street and stop dead. They looked at each other, exchanged a few words and then did a U-turn off the premises.

'This isn't fair,' I said out loud, still inside the car.

I got out, clutching my bag close to my chest. There might be women coming today who have been raped or who have been told by their GP that their lives are in danger, if they went through with their pregnancy. They shouldn't be bullied; they must decide for themselves. I was preparing my speech just in case I needed it.

As I approached the group, a woman rounded on me.

'You should be ashamed of yourself!'

Others were booing and an elderly woman thrust a leaflet into my face.

'You don't know what these women go through,' I shouted, but my voice was drowned out by the chanting and jeering. I elbowed my way towards the main entrance and was reaching out to open the door when a man pushed me in the back. I fell against the glass door, hitting my forehead. I tried to turn round, but the man was pressing against me, his chin in my hair. I managed to wriggle away from him, but he pulled my coat and wrenched me round to face him. He looked like he'd been in a fight. There was an open cut in his eyebrow and a bruise under his eye.

'You murderer!' he hissed. I could smell alcohol and stale tobacco on his breath. I tried to turn away, but the weight of the mob held me so tightly that I couldn't move. 'You'll pay for this,' he said, spittle flying into my face. The door behind me shook and I heard someone banging hard from the inside.

Suddenly the group opened out, like melting ice rolling away. Three policeman were heading my way.

'You all right?' said one of the officers.

I was wiping away the man's saliva with a tissue. 'Yes. I just need to get inside.'

The police officer instructed the man to stand aside and I managed to pull open the door. I half-fell through and stumbled into Dina's arms. I was still reeling from my unnerving encounter with Mr Fin - the last thing I needed was another one.

'Shit! Are you okay, Juliet?'

'Yeah. Just shaken.' I straightened my coat, leaning against the reception desk as pin-pricks of white stars began to spin across my vision. 'Any chance of a glass of water?'

I flopped into a nearby chair and Amanda put a plastic cup in my hand.

'No one hurt you?' she asked, leaning beside me, stroking back my hair.

'I'm okay. Not a nice welcome, is it?' I didn't want to create any more drama, especially as there were two young women waiting for me in the reception area, pretending to read magazines. 'I'll get started as soon as I've been to the bathroom.'

The bathroom was actually a single disabled cubicle, with a mirror and padded seat. I wasn't seeing anybody until I'd soaked my face with water to get rid of the threatening bloke's saliva. I scrubbed with a rough paper towel, managing to turn my cheeks a raw pink colour, but I didn't feel clean.

The demonstration broke up shortly after I started seeing clients, but images of the angry bloke's dirty and bloody face, pressing right up against mine, distracted me at regular intervals throughout the afternoon. His threatening words were still fresh and vivid in my mind as I left the building and walked back to my car: *You'll pay for this.*

As soon as I got home, I got straight into the bath. It still felt as though the remains of sticky spittle were eating into my skin. I hoped that hot water and plenty of sweet-smelling bath salts might cleanse it away, but even after I'd scrubbed with two different soaps, I still hadn't managed to shift the sullied feeling.

I settled on the sofa with my latest novel, hoping the words would take me somewhere else. When my brother died, books were my hiding place. My solace and protection. I loved the raw, fresh smell of sawn timber when opening a new book. But more than the promise of a good story, books taught me how to survive on my own. My parents were too preoccupied with their own grief to notice that I had gone into my shell. They didn't realise that I cried myself to sleep or went to sit in Luke's room in the middle of the night.

Luke died because he went back into the house to find Pippin, our dog. He pulled himself free from my father's arms, dodged the fireman who was directing a heavy hose at the windows and disappeared into the black fog. We never saw him again.

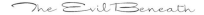

At twelve years old, books like Frances Hodgson Burnett's *The Secret Garden* had wrapped a comforting blanket around me and held me safe, while my parents paced the room beneath me. As I held the book close in the light of my bedside lamp, I would hear my mother sobbing and my father opening and closing drawers in his study, as if searching for something to bring Luke back. For me, books had been my private life-raft; the words on the page a reliable constant in a world where things could change dramatically and forever.

This evening, however, I couldn't concentrate.

I switched on the *London News*, interested to see if there was any mention of the demonstration before I started chopping vegetables. There wasn't. When I lived in Norwich, the local roundup might have covered such an event, but in London, the stakes were higher. I was about to leave the room, when a shot of Richmond Bridge filled the screen.

'The body of a girl was found this morning under Richmond Bridge, in Surrey,' said a female reporter, standing beside a boat. 'Police have yet to make an identification.'

I could see blue and white tape, wrapped around poles at the edge of the water. It looked just like the crime scene at Hammersmith.

I was on my feet. All thoughts of making supper were instantly extinguished, as I swayed from side to side in my dressing gown. The shot cut to the familiar set-up. Uniformed officers with microphones behind a long table, answering questions. Detective Chief Superintendent Rollinson, presumably representing the police in the Richmond area, was speaking:

'We have no reason to connect this death to any other crime at the present time, but, of course, we are exploring all avenues in our efforts to find out what happened.'

'How old is the girl?' called out a reporter.

'We believe the girl to have been in her teens,' replied DCS Rollinson. 'She was found by a fisherman first thing this morning. We're not able to release any more information until we've made an identification.'

'Have you identified the other woman yet? At Hammersmith Bridge?' called another voice.

'We have no reason to link this death to the body found downriver, over two weeks ago. We are, however, appealing to anyone who might have any information about the woman found at Hammersmith Bridge, to come forward.' He held up a detailed charcoal drawing of the woman's face. He went on to give further details about her height, weight and what she was wearing.

A voice from the back of the press conference called out: 'Do we have a serial killer on our hands, sir?'

Rollinson looked like he hadn't heard the question and pushed his papers together, as he stood up. 'That's all we have for now, I'm afraid. We'll keep you posted.'

My mind was racing in several directions at once as I switched off the television. *Was this connected to the second text message I'd been sent? Was this teenage girl also going to be wearing my clothes?*

I sank back onto the sofa, my head spinning, as I tried to slow myself down and decide what I should do. I'd spoken to DI Roxland again about the second text message; he'd been grateful, but his voice betrayed a certain tone in it - the kind normally reserved for small children who make outrageous claims. I wondered if they'd bothered to trace the message. *Did it have any connection to this death?* Without being consciously aware of it, I'd crossed my fingers, twice, on both hands. *Please let it be nothing to do with me.* But, even my most optimistic streak couldn't convince me. It was another body under a bridge - surely it had to be connected to the other one.

I pulled myself to the edge of the sofa. What I needed most was more information and the only way I was going to get that was through calling the police station again. DCI Madison picked up the phone, this time. I didn't expect to reach him in person; I must have been lucky. Of the officers I'd come across so far, he was not only the most approachable, but the only one who seemed to be on the same wavelength.

What he suggested didn't fill me with enthusiasm.

He wanted me to see the second body.

Because it was a river death, the Marine Policing Unit had taken the body to the mortuary at Wapping Police Station for identification. I needed to get there before they got started with the post-mortem, so I had to cancel my clients for Wednesday morning. Everyone else's problems were going to have to wait.

I showed my identification at the front desk and then followed the attendant along a bare corridor, until we reached a small booth on the left. Inside, one wall was a wide glass window with a view of a larger space on the other side. It was cold and there was a nasty smell that reminded me of dissecting frogs at school.

'We can't let you get too close to the body. Cross-contamination...' said the attendant rubbing his fingers together, as if this explained what he meant. On the other side of the glass, a door opened and a covered trolley was wheeled in. My knees went rubbery and I wondered whether I was going to stay upright.

'Ready?' asked the attendant.

I wasn't, but gave the faintest nod.

In turn, he nodded through the window and a figure, masked and gowned on the other side, pulled down the sheet covering the girl's face. I craned forward in the cautious way one looks over the edge of a cliff, holding on to the thin ledge that ran under the window.

I took a sharp intake of breath and covered my mouth. I recognised her at once. I didn't feel too well. I looked around the room for a wastepaper bin: I might be needing it.

'Take your time,' said the attendant, with a well-practised sympathy he must use every day for relatives taking those fateful steps towards the glass.

'She's stopped chewing...' I said in a whisper.

'Sorry?'

I stared at the large hoop earrings and the unmistakable double-stud in her nose.

'Yes, I know her. I can't remember her second name, but she's recently been to see me at the clinic where I work. I'll have a record...'

'Okay. Can you take one more look to be sure.' He tapped the glass.

I forced myself to look again. I was sure. It was Aysha, the girl whose mother had answered all the questions, while she'd sat listening to her iPod. She wouldn't be responding to any more music, no matter how loud it was.

'Which clinic was it?' the attendant asked.

'Fairways in Wimbledon. She came for a termination.'

'And you work there?' I nodded. 'This will be useful for the police,' he added. Just before the trolley was wheeled away, I raised my arm. The figure on the other side took her hand off the grip bar.

'Can I see what she's wearing?' I said to the assistant on my side of the glass.

He didn't look fazed by my request - presumably he'd received far stranger demands in his time. He clicked a button by the window and spoke into a small box, asking for the covering sheet to be pulled right back. I avoided Aysha's face this time and took a good look at her clothes. Tight halter-neck top, thick gold belt, ribbed mini-skirt, bare legs. The same kind of outfit she'd worn when she came to the clinic. Certainly none of these items had ever belonged to me. I let out a low breath and allowed myself to be guided back into the corridor.

The acrid smell was strong enough to take the skin off the inside of my nostrils. As soon as I was outside, I drew in the welcome air as if I'd been holding my breath under water. I pulled out a bottle from my bag and took several long swigs of juice to swill away the sickly taste that had turned the inside of my mouth into a foul-smelling pit - and headed back.

DCI Madison sounded pleased to hear from me.

'You said in your message that you think you know the girl we found at Richmond Bridge?'

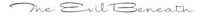

'Yes. I've been over to the clinic and got her records. I've got them in front of me. There's not much, but her name is Aysha Turner and there's an address and telephone number.' I read out the details. 'She had a termination last Friday at Fairways.'

'That's really helpful. No one has come forward yet to identify her. You said her mother was with her when you saw her?'

'Yeah. The long-suffering type. Looked like Aysha had already put her through enough turmoil for one life-time. She's probably used to Aysha not coming home.'

'Listen - the Senior Investigating Officer wants to see you. Asap.' He pronounced it like it was a word. 'Can you bring the clinic records with you - this afternoon? We've had the PM results from the first woman at Hammersmith and there could be a connection. In fact, can you bring all your recent records from the clinic? Is that too much for you to manage?'

I laughed. 'I've only been there a few weeks, so there isn't much paperwork. I'll go back and see what I can find.'

seven

DCI Madison showed me to a seat in a small office inside the police station on Shepherds Bush Road. It smelt of stale coffee. As he poured me a mug, I took a surreptitious look at him. We'd spoken on the phone a few times, but until then we hadn't met in person. His hair was thick and dark brown, cut short with a clean side parting and his eyes were the kind of blue that made me think of outdoor swimming pools. Tall and charismatic, he looked like a hybrid between an airline pilot and an Italian waiter. The kind of pilot who would wink at you as you boarded the plane. The kind of waiter who would give you extra parmesan on your spaghetti bolognaise.

'This is a bit awkward,' he said. 'The SIO wants to formally interview you before we go any further..'

I pushed the mug away. 'I'm a *suspect*?' I felt my eyes bulging, my jaw sag. 'You should have warned me.'

'It's standard procedure.' He shifted in his seat. His voice was cooler this afternoon, his words clipped. None of the matey tone he'd used with me so far.

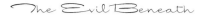

I shrugged. It didn't seem like I had much choice.

'We need to go to another room. Follow me.' I almost expected him to pull out a pair of handcuffs.

'Don't I need a lawyer, or something?'

He marched ahead of me. 'Not at this stage. You're not under arrest.'

'I should think not!'

We moved to a stuffy windowless room with a black table in the centre, with three spindly wooden chairs not designed for sitting on parked around it and a tape-recorder, to one side. There was one-way glass along the wall. DCI Madison tried to placate me with another cup of coffee. I declined. Before I had a chance to sit, the door flew open.

Borough Commander Katherine Lorriman sliced the air with her arms as she breezed in. The SIO looked the part, with her navy-blue trouser suit, thick leather belt and flat shoes. Her thin lips had no trace of lipstick, but her no-nonsense approach was tempered by tiny pearl studs in her ears. DCI Madison introduced us all for the tape and BC Lorriman got straight to the point.

'Ms Grey, you seem to be the common denominator. We need to find out why.'

That was *my* burning question, too, but I wasn't the one who could answer it.

'You've had one text message telling you to go to the scene of the first death. Then hours after you get a second message, we find ourselves with another dead body under a bridge...' She stared at me as if expecting me to explain. As if somehow I was behind it all. 'It's a bit of a coincidence, Ms Grey.'

'Listen,' I said. 'I'm terrified by this whole thing. I haven't a clue what's going on or why I've being singled out, like this.' The temperature seemed to have suddenly risen in the room. I was finding it hard to breathe.

'You say the first woman was wearing your old clothes?'

'Yes, that's right.'

'We understand you've only recently started working at Fairways Clinic?'

'Yes.'

'It deals solely with abortions, right?'

I nodded.

'Where do you stand, personally, with regard to abortion, Ms Grey?'

'Me? I'm impartial.' I didn't hesitate. 'I have to be, as a counsellor. I just help women explore all the options. Give them a non-judgemental space to check how they really feel about being pregnant.'

She stabbed her pen into the wad of notes in front of her, as if spearing a small fish. 'Have you ever expressed views against abortion? Ever been in doubt?'

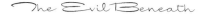

'No, never. I've never been opposed to it. Never felt like that.'

The room was thick with an accusing tone, as thick as the smoke we would have generated had we all been heavy smokers. DCI Madison turned to me, his eyes lowered in apology.

'We've had a minor breakthrough with the first victim.' He was trying his best to diffuse the situation.

'The woman at Hammersmith Bridge?' I said.

'She was American. It took us a while to track her down - her husband didn't report her missing.'

BC Lorriman butted in. 'Her name was Pamela Mendosa. She'd had a recent termination at Fairways. You've just identified the second victim as Aysha Turner, who had a termination there last week - so, you see, we have the same link to Fairways...and to you.'

So, they'd both had been to Fairways. Both had an abortion there.

I shook my head in frustration. 'You really think I'm involved?' Her gaze was fixed on me, her hands folded together, as if she was a judge about to pronounce her sentence. 'Why would I draw attention to myself by sending obscure text messages to my own phone?' I said. The room was starting to move of its own accord. I hadn't eaten for a while and felt my hands shaking, my chest fluttering.

'That's what we're keen to find out. It's very personal, Ms Grey. Everything seems to point back to you.' The Borough Commander leaned over the table at me. She looked like she was about to breathe fire into my face. 'Where were you in the early hours of Sunday, 20th September and yesterday, Tuesday, 6th October?'

I thought for a second. 'At home. Asleep.'

'Can anyone vouch for that?'

My eyes flickered to DCI Madison.

'No. I was alone.'

'We'll need to do some background checks into your history, Ms Grey, I'd like to–'

I cut her off.

'Wait a minute,' I said. I was on my feet. 'The night before the first woman was found at Hammersmith Bridge, there was a break-in, downstairs.' I was almost laughing with relief. 'Your officers can vouch for me! The police came along sometime between two and three in the morning. Fulham Palace Road. I gave them cups of tea!'

BC Lorriman gave DCI Madison a sideways glance.

'Right,' she said, pulling her papers towards her. 'We'll need to look into that.'

DCI Madison took over, his voice softened now. It seemed I had slipped back into the category of helping-them-with-their-enquiries, instead of being about-to-be-arrested.

'We'll need to speak to your colleagues at Fairways and Holistica ,' he said. 'Is there anything else we need to check out? Any clubs you're a member of? Fitness classes? Church?'

'Not really.' I began to see what a paltry social life I'd managed to cultivate recently. Miriam was right. I needed more friends, but now wasn't the time to find a salsa class or join the Ramblers.

'Well - whatever - DCI Madison will take all the details,' she said, as she rose to leave. He informed the tape that the interview was terminated and the SIO left the room without another word.

There was a pause, as if we were both waiting for her footsteps to recede.

'I'm sorry about that.' He said it as though he meant it. 'She takes a hard line, but she gets results.' I blew out a weary breath and sank back into the chair. 'Got to be done, I'm afraid. Looks like you're out of the frame now, but I do need to ask you a few more questions.'

My stomach gurgled and I realised how hungry I was.

'Not without a decent sandwich,' I said.

'Fair enough. Let's get out of here and go back to my office.'

The chicken was tough, the bread was dry, the lettuce was soggy, but it did the job.

'The first woman you saw at Hammersmith Bridge, Pamela Mendosa, she was...strangled,' he said, graciously allowing me to finish my last mouthful before informing me. A small involuntary sound slipped out of my mouth and I pressed my fingers over my lips. 'Her husband had been abroad for three months, so the baby wasn't his.'

'No one missed her?'

'Husband wasn't in regular contact.' He checked his notes. 'On an archaeological site in Indonesia. They'd had a row before he left, apparently. When she didn't answer his emails, he didn't worry too much. He's still there, so he's not a direct suspect.'

I was mulling it over. 'She'd had a termination at Fairways. I don't recognise her name. Pamela something?'

'Mendosa.' He pulled out a pen. 'Did you bring your records from the clinic?'

I lifted a manila file onto the desk. 'I've spoken to the other counsellors and I've got a list of everyone who's had a termination there in the last six months.' I had a look down the extensive list. 'Oh, yeah, here it is - Pamela Mendosa. Had a termination at Fairways on September 14th. Three weeks ago.' I ran my finger across the page. 'She didn't see me for counselling, though. It says here she was down to see my colleague, Helen Boxer.'

'Okay. We'll be in touch with her and see what she can tell us.'

I took a sip of coffee. It was lukewarm and tasted like dust. I tried to turn my grimace into a silent comment on the case. 'Can you think of any personal reason why London bridges or the Thames should have any connection with you?' he said.

I leant on the table with my chin in my hand and stared into space.

'No.'

'Nothing connected to your parents, your family at all?'

I shook my head. 'My parents moved to Spain in 1996, when I was eighteen - mainly for my Dad's bronchitis. We used to live in Norwich. My brother was killed in a fire when I was twelve. There's nothing in my parent's lives that I can think of that might have any bearing on this...Dad's quite well-off, he's a property developer. He never lived in London, as far as I know.'

As DCI Madison added to his notes, I stared at the flip-over calendar on his desk and the surreal nature of the situation got the better of me. Here I was, sitting in the DCI's private office, assisting the police with an investigation and viewing dead bodies as if this was normal life. It sent a shiver up my spine; an odd combination of intrigue and revulsion, with a smattering of excitement sprinkled over the top for good measure. Like a mountainous ice-cream that starts off tasting delicious, but you know will eventually make you sick.

'And your mother?' he said.

'Mum was a social worker, before they both retired. She grew up in Cambridge.'

'You can't think of anyone your parents might have upset, or any disputes?'

'Not a thing. Not during my life time. There's no London connection at all that I can think of. I've only been here two years.'

'Might be worth checking things out with your parents as soon as you can.'

I wondered how I could do that without giving them cause for concern. I also wondered if my parents had got hold of any British newspapers recently. At some stage they were going to read about the murders and realise how close they were to where I was living. At least, as far as I knew, my name had never been associated with the killings outside of the police.

'And you, personally?'

'Sorry?' I was miles away.

'Have you had any problems with anyone? Ex-boyfriends, disgruntled clients?'

I thought about Andrew. Just because he had a problem with drink didn't make him a killer. I dismissed him, then remembered the odd scratches I'd seen on his neck when he met me at Hammersmith Bridge. He'd certainly been jumpy about them. Could they have been defence wounds? Did the victim claw at him in her bid to escape some frantic attack? The whole idea was ridiculous. Not

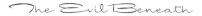

Andrew. I didn't want the police to waste valuable time. Mr Fin? He was creepy alright. Had he been following me the other evening? I thought about it and dismissed him too. I was just being jumpy. Mr Fin looked decidedly ill and frail; there's no way I could see him having the strength to lift a watering can, never mind corner a woman, strangle her, then drag her body down to the river.

'I don't think so.'

There was a tap at the door and a young female officer popped her head in.

'Sorry, sir, the results of the PM on the Richmond Bridge murder are here.' The WPC's blonde hair was tied up in bunches, making her look like a cheer-leader. She gave me a glance, as if silently asking whether she should continue. DCI Madison nodded. 'Aysha Turner was strangled, sir, like the other one... and they can confirm she had a recent termination.'

She handed the DCI the report and left. At that moment I regretted having bolted down the chicken sandwich. I wanted to go home. Pretend none of this was happening. I wanted to be tucked up under a blanket on my sofa, watching this sort of havoc at a safe distance on television.

DCI Madison closed his file and stood up. He offered to take me home and I was glad to accept. My car was playing up so I'd caught the bus over, but I didn't feel like being in a crowd right now. As he opened the passenger door for me, I noticed he had no ring on his wedding finger. I guessed he was probably the right side of forty, although his healthy tan and trim frame could be concealing a few extra years.

As we drove back, I asked him something that had been playing on my mind since the discovery of the first body.

'Do you think I'm in danger?'

'You?' I caught the ever-so-swift reorientation of his eyes, as they shifted from my face back to the road.

'Yes. You know, the text message sending me to Hammersmith Bridge the night before the first...' I swallowed, '...murder...and the fact that the first woman was wearing *my* clothes...and I definitely had contact with the second victim...'

We pulled up outside my flat. He rested his hands on the steering wheel.

'I know this must all feel a bit too close to home, for you.' He thought for a moment. 'I'd like to say you're not in any danger, but that would be flippant. At this stage, we really don't know what's going on. Someone has killed twice, and we cannot deny that there are links to you: through the text, the clothes, the clinic where you work.' I could see he was struggling to tread the fine line between caution and scare-mongering, but when he put it like that, he made me recognise how impotent I felt. I was a helpless fly caught in a giant spider's web. I found myself gripping the car seat even though we weren't going anywhere. 'You've not been threatened, have you?' he said.

I stared out of the window for a second, trying to think.

'Not unless you count the guy at the demonstration outside Fairways, the other day.'

'What?' He turned to me, letting go of the wheel.

'Yeah. I was shaken at the time, but I didn't think much of it. You expect that sort of thing when you work somewhere like Fairways.' I tracked back to that day. 'He certainly looked rough, nasty...and angry...and said I was a murderer and I'd pay for it....'

'We need to follow this up.' He rammed the gearstick into first and the tyres squealed as we swung into a U-turn and took off, back the way we'd come.

I felt the colour drain from my face. *How could I have dismissed it?* So busy putting up on a brave face, I'd almost convinced myself it was nothing. I was glad I was sitting down. I'm not sure my legs would have supported me at this stage. 'Is it him? Do you think he's connected? Am I at risk?'

'Let's see who we're dealing with, first. You'll have to give another statement. We'll need some sort of e-fit, as well, if you can.'

It was turning into a long day.

I left the police station on foot, insisting I needed some fresh air, but after a few strides along Shepherds Bush Road, I crossed over and went into the library. It was well past evening meal time, but I wasn't hungry. Instead, what felt like a bundle of eels was causing a commotion in my stomach, making me jittery and goading me to make some progress. I had been running the second text message through my mind, wondering if it had any link to Aysha's murder. I knew the message now off by heart:

> *Eleven feet and three inches were added before 1940.*

Once inside the library, the significance of my quest hit me. If I did find a link, it meant it wasn't some random text. It meant there was yet another connection between me and both bodies in the water. It meant, once again, that I'd been specifically targeted. Part of me didn't want to face that possibility. Go home and let the fine and capable DCI Madison handle this case, said a sensible voice inside my head. But a stubborn and inquisitive one got the better of me.

There was a vacant computer terminal at the far end, near the periodicals, so I booked it for thirty minutes. I didn't know where to start, so I requested a search for the exact phrase: *eleven feet and three inches* to see where it would take me. There were eight results, including reference to a street sign in Wisconsin and the combined height of Santa's helpers in an entry about Christmas. There were no results with any link to London.

Then I typed *eleven feet three inches*, missing out the *and*. Over thirty thousand hits came up, so I narrowed it down to the UK pages only. This brought up over three hundred hits. Better - but wading through all of those was going to take ages, especially as I didn't really know what I was looking for. I went back to the blank screen and rested my chin in my hand.

I added *Richmond Bridge* and began trawling through individual entries, before adding *history* to the search. I was about to give up, when the last item on the page caught my eye. It was a timeline for Richmond Bridge. I selected 1940, but found nothing relating to the message.

I closed my eyes and let my mind go still for a moment. It was easy to focus in here: apart from the odd cough and dropped pencil, everyone seemed to be respecting the library rule of silence.

The message I'd been sent said *before 1940*, so I punched in 1939 and found a small item written for a tourist information service that stated that Richmond Bridge had been widened between 1937 and 1939. It didn't say by how much. My allotted time at the computer was about to finish, so I made a note of the site and signed out, knowing I could always use my laptop at home to check again later.

I wandered over to the shelves and decided to try one last thing. The section marked 'British history' was at the far end by the window. I tracked through the titles until I came across a section on London. Squatting down, I found three books that looked promising, scooped them up and carried them over to a table. The first two were full of photographs and written in a coffee-table style, but the third had a full chapter on the history of Richmond Bridge. I skim-read for several pages, before what felt like a firework exploded in my chest. I read the paragraph twice and then took the book over to the photocopier.

DCI Madison will want to see this, I said to myself. Here it was in black and white: a reference to how the Richmond Bridge was widened by eleven feet and three inches between 1937 and 1939. Remarkable. And even more remarkable that I'd tracked it down - if I said so myself.

It was only once I'd got outside and had started walking towards the river, that I started to feel queasy. The devastating truth of the matter struck me like a blow with a sledgehammer: someone *had* sent me a clue pointing to the location of the second murder - extraordinarily enigmatic though it had been. *Why?*

I felt my steps veer to the right. The pavement seemed to be tipping away from me, my eyes were having trouble staying in focus, my head was heavy, like a ball on a chain. I had the proof: someone *was* sending me messages about these savage murders.

I wondered if, whoever it was, knew I was telling the police everything I knew. I took a swift look behind me as I joined the path along the Thames, away from the thunder of the traffic. *Was it sensible to be walking in this quiet spot? What if the killer was watching me right now?* I screwed my hands into fists and turned back towards the bridge.

Was the killer going to prevent me from leading my life? Was I going to have to modify my every step?

I needed to tell DCI Madison what I'd discovered at the library. I ran the words of the second message through my mind again:

> *Eleven feet and three inches were added before 1940.*

Richmond Bridge. *How on earth was I expected to work out the location, from such a flimsy piece of information? Could I have prevented it?* I shivered as a more troubling thought took hold of me: *was I next?*

eight

I watched the hand of the clock click on to the hour. I'd give it fifteen minutes before I gave up on him. I'd just about to put some washing on, when the doorbell rang.

Mr Fin had been subdued and only barely unpleasant in our second session, so I'd decided to keep the appointments going for the time being, but since our awkward encounter at the park, it wouldn't have surprised me if he hadn't shown up again. Was it him lurking in the bushes the other night? Up to that point he'd been just a sad guy, with a self-esteem problem and a chip on his shoulder. I couldn't be absolutely sure, but seeing him in that area at all had been something of a coincidence and there had been too many of those lately.

I took two quick sips of water, wishing it was gin, as Mr Fin's gangly shape coiled into his seat. This was going to be awkward. He stared at me with those hard eyes that tried to drill their way into mine. It was so unnerving I wanted to avoid eye-contact altogether, but I was supposed to be the trained professional here. I tried to focus on the bridge of his nose and forced my voice to sound warm and welcoming.

'Good to see you again, Mr Fin. Where would you like to start?'

Mr Fin acted as if he hadn't heard me and started picking at his nails. I was grateful that he had at least dropped his gaze.

I heard the clock tick thirty times or more. I broke the ice. 'Is it hard to know what to talk about, today?' I wasn't the kind of therapist who waited indefinitely in silence. I didn't have the patience.

'I nearly didn't turn up,' he said. His voice was raspy and thin. I assumed he must be getting over a cold. 'I didn't know if I wanted to see you.'

'To see me?'

'After the other day.'

'Right.'

He lifted his eyes towards mine again and I felt a chilling unease.

'After I saw you.'

I sat still, waiting for him to continue. He changed tack. 'Hot in here, isn't it?'

I was relieved. For once, he'd been the one to back off. 'There's no heating on,' I said. 'Shall I open a window?' I knew I should press him following his previous statement, but the opportunity to deflect was too good to refuse.

'Don't bother.' He thrust out his bottom lip and sat back, in a way that suggested he knew something I didn't. I waited, forcing my hands to stay still in my lap. The sound of the clock ricocheted around the room.

'Do you have a boyfriend?' he asked.

'I'm wondering why you want to know that,' I said.

'Can't you snap out of therapist-mode for one minute and talk to me like a normal person?' He gripped the arms of the seat, looking for a moment like an emaciated wolf about to pounce. I took my time; kept my voice steady.

'That's what you're paying me for. Not for a friendly chat with someone, but for the experience of a psychotherapist.'

'You might be too smart for your own good,' he said, tilting his head to one side.

I didn't want to rise to that one.

'Are you finding these sessions at all helpful, Mr Fin?'

'Only when you speak to me like a real human being and not like just another one of your patients.'

'Is that what you find happens, Mr Fin? That people don't speak to you like you are a real person?'

He looked down at his lap and wrapped his fingers together into a tight ball. I kept my eyes on his face and realised that a lone tear had escaped from the corner of his eye. It hung there for a while, before he brushed it away.

'Rivers of tears,' he said. 'Rivers of tears.'

I waited, barely breathing.

'There will be more, won't there?' he said.

'More tears?' I asked, leaning forward, finding his voice difficult to hear.

'We'll have to wait and see,' he said.

After the session had finished, I went straight to the window and flung it open. I leant right out, looking down to the back yards below. The breeze was divine. I needed it to flush Mr Fin and his oddly threatening behaviour out of my hair, off my skin, out of my clothes. Some clients did this. They seemed to get right inside me and when it felt menacing, it was exceedingly unpleasant. I went straight to the bathroom and started running the shower.

As the water poured over me, I couldn't help fix on various words Mr Fin had used. He'd referred to a river of tears. *What was he getting at? Did he mean his own tears, there and then in the session, or did he mean something more ominous? Should I break client confidentiality and explain my concerns to the police? Or had I heard the word 'river' and overreacted? Was I getting paranoid and linking everything I came across to the murders?*

When I was towelling myself down, the phone rang. I thought it might be DCI Madison, following my message that the anonymous text I'd been sent was indeed an obscure clue to the Richmond Bridge. Without checking the caller ID, I picked it up.

'Oh, hi, it's you,' I said.

'I was checking up on how you were and whether you'd heard anything more...about the... you know, river incidents.' I grimaced at the familiar way Andrew's words were rolling into one another.

'I'm okay. Not much to report. Look, I can't talk now, Andrew, I've got someone here.' The lie came more easily than I expected.

'Moved on already, have we?' His tone was sharp, agitated.

'It's not like that.' I took a breath. 'Even if...look Andrew, we're not together... you and I, so–'

The line went dead. I dropped a cushion on to my lap and wrapped my arms around it. If I had any doubts that I was doing the right thing, that call was sufficient to set my mind at rest. Andrew was history.

Before I went to bed, I switched on my laptop, on the off-chance that there might be an email from Robbie, my mate who'd moved to New Zealand. There were four new messages, but his name wasn't attached to any of them. Three should have gone straight into my spam box and the fourth was untitled. It came from an address I didn't recognise, using what looked like random numbers and letters. I opened it:

Sorry. Don't think I gave you enough to go on last time. We'll both have to try harder.

I grasped the lid of the laptop, scoring deep ruts into my palms. There was no name, but there was an attachment. I opened it and a drawing filled the screen. It was an old etching of a bridge, with several arches reaching across a large expanse of water.

There were low buildings and boats to the right-hand side, but no other indications: no date, no title, no name of the artist and more importantly, no name of the bridge.

I swore under my breath and picked up the phone.

DCI Madison's voice was sleepy and slow. I knew he was off-duty, but he'd insisted I call him on his private number if anything major came up, no matter what time it was.

'I'm sorry to wake you, but I think this is important. It's Juliet Grey and I've had another message.'

I pictured him sitting bolt upright in bed. 'What is it? What have you got?'

'It's an email this time. I've just checked my computer and there's a picture of a bridge and a message that seems to refer to the last text.'

I quoted the exact words.

'Oh, God,' he said.

'Shall I forward it straight over to you?'

'You've got my email address. Does it say which bridge it is?'

I paused. 'No, it doesn't. The drawing is so old, I don't recognise it at all. No usual London landmarks, as far as I can tell.'

'Okay. Send it over.'

I hit send. 'It's done.'

'I just hope we can work this one out, before...' Silence. 'When was the email sent, Juliet? Today?'

I checked the screen and gasped. 'No. It was two days ago. Oh, no...I'm really sorry. I didn't know.'

'It's okay. It's not your fault. Someone is using you in a despicable way.' He rang back once he'd opened the attachment. 'It's obviously another bridge, but I don't know which one it is, either.'

'No - the drawing is so ancient.'

'There are thirty bridges over the tidal part of the Thames,' he said. 'We're going to have to get an expert in. Someone who might be able to work out the clues you've been getting. Track down which bridge the killer is referring to before...'

'You think there will be more deaths?'

He didn't hesitate. 'It's starting to look that way.'

I'd tossed around both nights over the weekend, unable to get to sleep, drifting into half-dream states that weren't the least bit restful. During Sunday night, I woke abruptly, my throat cutting like blades when I swallowed, my forehead burning. I made a hot-lemon drink, took it back to bed and knelt on my pillow in front of the framed photo of Luke I always kept above my bed. It was taken around two months before he died; the last one I had of him. He was at that gawky, self-conscious stage; crossing back and forth between boy and man. I often talked to him in bed; usually silly things about my day, but at times, sharing inner thoughts I never told anyone else.

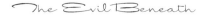

I'm scared, Luke. I wish you were here. Something awful is happening and I don't know what's going on.

DCI Madison rang as I was getting dressed. He was out of breath, on the move. 'Sorry it's early. We've been in touch with the London Blue-badge guides.

There's one guy who leads walks for tourists and is supposed to be the number one expert on London bridges.'

'That's brilliant.'

'Not all good news. We've sent him your email, but he hasn't got back to us yet. Not answering his phone. We've also sent it to various other experts: Museum of London, university professors, archaeologists, Tate Britain...even the BBC.'

'You should get *something*.'

'I hope so. The email came from a library, by the way. Someone created a new email account just for this one message. We're trying to trace them from the library card, but I've got a horrible feeling we'll find it was stolen. He might also have accessed other sites and left a trail, but it's a long shot.'

I could hear phones ringing and people calling out in the background, before he rang off. I pressed the print button on my laptop.

I've got a long shot of my own, I said out loud.

nine

Two heads are better than one, I thought, as I drove over to Holistica later that morning. I was lucky. When I rang, Cheryl said she had a gap of forty-five minutes. I didn't tell her what it was about. I wanted her to approach the situation without any fore-warning.

I burst into her room and gave her a garbled summary of the situation. She'd started out open and relaxed, but by the time I'd finished her shoulders had risen and her forehead resembled the lid of a roll-top desk.

'I'm not sure I'm sufficiently gifted to do this,' she said, perching on the edge of her desk, then straightening up again.

'Can't you at least give it a try? I've got something here that could lead us to the next bridge... it could help prevent another of these terrible murders in the Thames.' I held up the plastic folder with a copy of the etching.

'This is police business. I can't be expected–'

My voice rose in pitch. 'This is *everybody's* business, Cheryl. I've been staring at this etching for hours but I'm not getting anywhere. Please can you give it just a few minutes? Then I'll drop it. I promise.'

I was thrown by Cheryl's reaction, but I had a strange feeling that the prevarication was fake for some reason. Cheryl shrugged and took the plastic folder from my hand.

'Ten minutes and that's it.'

It was then that I remembered something odd the day after the first murder at Hammersmith Bridge. It made me think she might know more than she was letting on.

'Just after the first woman was killed, Cheryl, you said something - do you remember? Here, in the clinic?'

She narrowed her eyes and shook her head.

'You said something about the woman not drowning. I wondered how you knew.'

'Did I? I don't remember.' Her tone was terse.

'But - you sounded certain - you said straight out, "at least she didn't drown". Did you have a...premonition..?'

'Now you mention it, I do remember getting a vague feeling...of doom...that day...'

'About that woman found near the bridge?'

'Yes - but I've never had anything since.'

'You sure?'

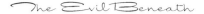

'Absolutely.' She looked at her watch and moved away.

My hands were shaking. I knew time wasn't on my side. The email had been sitting inside my laptop for two days.

She sat behind her desk and closed her eyes. I waited.

'I'm getting a strong smell of fish and a group of men...in a boat...they're singing...and...' Cheryl hesitated. 'I'm way back in time, here,' she said. 'It's London...I'm getting images of men who look Victorian... top hat, frock coat, walking cane...'

I could feel my face burning with impatience. *Come on!* I wanted to shout: *Where is it? Which bridge is it, Cheryl?* Instead I forced myself to breathe deeply and stand still.

Cheryl then rattled on about a woman called Nancy, who worked in one of the houses by the river. She seemed to have got side-tracked into a Dickensian theme. I was starting to feel desperate. I stared at her, expectantly, my hopes pinned on some final revelation.

'I'd say this was mid to late nineteenth century,' she concluded, opening her eyes. The room felt remarkably quiet all of a sudden. There was nothing else. She handed me the etching and apologised, saying her mind was blank and she wasn't picking up anything else. 'It's like that sometimes,' she said.

'You don't know which bridge it is?' I bleated.

She shook her head.

Dead end.

My stomach hit the floor. I reached for the door handle.

'My last patient finishes in an hour. Have a coffee in the place across the road and I'll find you,' she said. It was a request not a suggestion.

I had nowhere else to be. If there was any inkling it might be worth my while, I had to hang around.

She joined me as I was starting my third cappuccino.

'I'm sorry about the etching,' she said. 'Sometimes it's hard to come up with answers to order.'

'Sorry I put you on the spot. It was all I could think of.'

I hoped DCI Madison had had more luck with his 'experts'.

She smiled. 'It came to me later, when I was with the next person. It happens like that sometimes.'

'You got it? The bridge?' I froze, sending the froth dribbling down my cup.

'It's Battersea Bridge.'

'You sure?' I grabbed my phone.

Cheryl didn't hesitate. 'Yes.'

I got up and took her hand. 'Thank you so much. It really might be a matter of life and death.' I was about to move away, when Cheryl blocked my path.

'What I said about your brother the other week. The fire. I know I'm right. It wasn't an accident. You might need to think about that.'

'Yes, yes, I will,' I said, pushing past her, punching in the number.

The phone rang and rang until finally I heard DCI Madison's familiar voice.

'You didn't get my message?' he said.

'No. Not yet. I've just–'

'We've found another one...a woman's body...' I was unable to suppress a sob. 'I'll speak to you later,' he said. 'Got to go.'

'Just one thing. Where was it?'

'Battersea Bridge,' he said. 'Jogger found her about two hours ago. The Blue-badge guy phoned through about half an hour ago. He'd identified the right bridge from your etching, but it was already too late. Listen, I'll call you later.'

I slipped the phone back into my bag and cried all the way home.

'Thanks for coming in again,' said DCI Madison. We were back in his office at Shepherds Bush the morning after the third victim had been found. I was starting to feel like I worked there. He introduced me: 'This is DI Roxland - you've spoken before I believe.'

I remembered DI Roxland only too well from various patronising encounters over the phone. He had a damp hand and his face was too shiny. It made him look the sort to do train-spotting in his spare time. He was at that age where it had become necessary to keep ear, eyebrow and nasal hair at bay, but sadly such gentility had passed him by.

There was a tap on the door and a man was ushered in.

'Juliet, this is Derek Moorcroft. He's our bridge man.' DCI Madison invited him to sit. The man looked jet-lagged, even though he'd only driven over from Oxford. 'Thanks for coming,' said the DCI, addressing both of us. 'I know this is extremely unpleasant.'

Derek Moorcroft was going seriously bald and his screwed up eyes had a permanent look of someone having just got out of bed. He had the kind of face you would instantly forget, even if you'd been trapped for an hour in a lift with him.

'I'll help in any way I can,' he said. His voice was unexpectedly high-pitched, as if he'd been practising for a Punch and Judy show.

DCI Madison sat back. 'I know it's rather unorthodox getting civilians to help out in this way, but we're trying to make the most of our resources.'

Derek seemed more interested in the plate of biscuits on the DCI's desk than on what he was saying.

'As you know, Juliet, Mr Moorcroft was able to identify the bridge from the picture you were sent in the email.' DCI Madison rolled a pencil on the desk. 'But, sadly, due to technical difficulties with his computer, we didn't get to know about it in time. We haven't identified the woman yet.'

Derek bowed his head.

'Not your fault, Mr Moorcroft.'

'Call me Derek.'

'If this is going to carry on, God forbid,' said DCI Madison, 'we need to make sure we're in a much better position than we were before.'

'That's if the killer uses another bridge as his place of discovery,' I said.

'That is the assumption. That's been the pattern, so far - although, obviously we need to be open to the idea that the killer's methods might change.'

'Can't you set up cameras on all the bridges or get your officers to keep watch?' said Derek, blithely.

I had to turn a sharp intake of breath into a cough. *Honestly*. Even *I* knew police resources wouldn't stretch to one bridge, let alone thirty of them. DCI Madison put him straight.

'Are the women...killed beforehand and left under the bridges or are they attacked where they're found?' I asked.

'The post-mortems show that the three victims we've found so far were killed somewhere else, then taken down to the water. There is no internal evidence of any water intake prior to death and there's no evidence of a struggle at the scene. The boots of the women show no mud or shale, although obviously running water plays havoc with evidence. All of the spots can be easily viewed from the bridge or road, so it's unlikely the killer would risk being caught during the attack. He'd want to get the body into the water as quickly and silently as possible.'

There was silence, except for the sound of Derek crunching on a butter-crinkle.

'Hammersmith, Richmond, Battersea - is there any link between those particular bridges?' I asked. All the questions keeping me awake at night were pouring out all at once.

DCI Madison raised his eyebrows in Derek's direction.

'I've had your report and I can't see any obvious links, but I haven't had much time..' He dunked his biscuit. 'Richmond Bridge was opened in 1777. The other two were opened at the end of the nineteenth century. There are two hundred and fourteen bridges in total, over the full length of the Thames, which is tidal, of course, as far as Teddington and there are forty-five locks on the non-tidal...' Half of his biscuit broke away and disappeared into his coffee.

Derek was clearly on a roll and I hoped the DCI would rein him in.

'That's very useful, Derek,' he said. 'If you could get down in writing anything that *links* these bridges for us... that would be a great help.'

Nicely done.

DI Roxland spoke for the first time. 'We need to keep the media at bay with all this,' he said. He glanced at Derek and I in turn. 'If the press approach you about any of this - it's strictly "no comment" - you got it?' Roxland gave me a weak smile which brought a bubble of spittle with it. I decided to leave my last biscuit.

The DCI turned to me. 'Anything new and get it straight over to Derek...as well as telling us, of course. You've got my personal number.'

I nodded. Derek's sleepy eyes came to life. He couldn't have had this much interest in his work for a long time.

'Time is a big factor. We need to try to identify the right bridge before the killer gets there.'

'What if the killer sends the messages *after* the murders have already taken place?' I asked.

'So far, it's been the other way around. We're pinning everything on the fact that the killer will use the same routine.'

'The same M.O?' said Derek, rubbing his hands together. He was actually enjoying this. Too much TV crime and not enough social life, although I need talk.

'What about the email? Did you trace it?' I asked.

'Kensington library,' he said, shaking his head. 'Over a hundred computers available to the public there. He used a stolen library card, like we thought, and he didn't log on to any other sites. We're looking at CCTV footage to see what we can find...but to be honest, it doesn't look good. Too many people around.'

'And no one saw anything untoward near the bridges - no cars parked in the early hours near the water?' I said.

'No - nothing. We're looking into the possibility that the bodies were driven down to the water, then put in a boat and carried on along the river to the bridges.'

'A boat?' I said. 'I hadn't thought of that. So obvious.'

'It might be the way the bodies are transported, without being seen - and placed in position, without leaving evidence on the bank. We're looking for a vehicle that has a boat-rack or a trailer. We're trawling through the CCTV footage on that, too.'

DCI Madison got to his feet. 'Okay - that's all for now.' As he opened the door to guide Derek and DI Roxland out, he raised his arm to indicate I should stay where I was.

When he returned I knew the atmosphere had changed.

'There's something else,' he said.

I didn't like his ominous tone. I wasn't sure I could handle any more bad news.

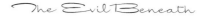

'We found an embroidered handkerchief on the second girl - Aysha's body. In one of her pockets.' I was surprised. Aysha didn't look the kind of girl to carry tissues, never mind an old-fashioned handkerchief. He pulled a plastic evidence bag from a drawer and placed it on the desk. 'It had some initials stitched onto it.'

He slid it towards me and I held it up.

I gasped. 'J.L.G.,' I said in a whisper. 'This is mine. Mum's been buying them as a Christmas stocking filler ever since I was about six years old.'

'We thought it might be. Especially after you identified your clothes on the first woman.'

I shoved it back to him. I didn't want it to be mine. It was contaminated and involved in something ghastly.

'The L is for your middle name?'

'Lucy,' I said, grimly.

'We were wondering where she might have got it from.'

'Yes, so am I.'

'Could she have taken it when you saw her at Fairways Clinic, when you had your appointment with her before the termination?'

I blew out a gusty breath. 'I'll have to think about that.'

'Or, maybe she found it on the floor?'

'Yeah, yeah.' I got the picture, I just couldn't remember whether I'd had a handkerchief with me.

Another idea crossed my mind. 'Maybe she didn't take it at all. Maybe the killer just bought one with those initials.'

'We did wonder about that. We found no match with the DNA samples you gave us.'

It was hardly a cause for celebration. The hanky was still another ghastly link between me and these despicable murders.

'By the way, we're going to be tracing all your emails and calls from now on.'

'You're tapping my phone?'

'Not me personally, but yes, the police will be monitoring all your communications from now on.' He looked sheepish.

'Big Brother...' A wave of nausea gripped my stomach and I rubbed my belly. This ordeal wasn't going away any time soon.

'I know...I'm sorry, but it's necessary.'

He got up from his chair and for a moment he looked like he was going to give me a hug. 'Listen, probably shouldn't ask this, but are you free tomorrow tonight?'

'Tomorrow night? To look at more evidence?'

'No. Not exactly.' DCI Madison rubbed his nose. 'I was thinking of something...off-duty...my way of saying thanks, I suppose.'

He'd caught me entirely off guard, but suddenly my chest felt warm, as if a hot-water bottle had found its way inside my jacket.

'Oh. Is that protocol?'

'Not strictly, but you're giving us such a lot of your time and...'

'Yes, that would be lovely,' I said, before he could change his mind. 'Is Derek coming?' I tried to hide a smile.

He grinned, his hands in his pockets. 'Er, no. I forgot to ask.'

'Right, then.' I stood fiddling with the buckle on my bag, feeling like a school girl.

'Is dinner, okay?' he said, toying with some papers on the desk.

'Perfect. One thing, though. I can't go for dinner with you and keep calling you Detective Chief Inspector Madison.'

'No, you can't.' He held out his hand. 'I'm Brad - Bradley Madison.'

Great name. That would do nicely.

'Pleased to meet you, Brad - I'm Juliet.'

The smile stayed on my face until I'd left the police station. Until I remembered how I'd come to meet DCI Madison in the first place. No matter how distracted I might be by his banter and good looks, it was something evil that had brought us together. Something evil that was going to be lurking in the shadows behind us every step of the way.

ten

Lynn Jessop had started sessions a few weeks ago. I was surprised when she told me she was forty-nine; the deep furrows in her forehead made her look ten years older. Her hair was drab and thin and her chin stood out from her face like a half-opened drawer. She must have been around five feet seven, with a broad frame, but years of suffering or low self-worth had bowed her shoulders, making her look like she was in a permanent state of apologising for herself.

It was a difficult case: she was the mother of a teenage boy who was being bullied at school. The boy was coming home bruised, but didn't want to involve the teachers. There appeared to be no father on the scene and Lynn was feeling powerless to stop her son being picked on. In some ways, I wondered if counselling was going to make much difference. Proper intervention at the school seemed the obvious solution; the offenders needed to be identified; the teachers needed to nip it in the bud, but the boy didn't want to tell anyone and Lynn was abiding by her son's wishes for the time being.

'Do you know what it's like to wake up every day knowing your son is being traumatised and not be able to do anything about it?' said Lynn. She was pulling strands of hair from behind her ear as she rocked backwards and forwards. It occurred to me she might be self-harming.

'It must be awful for you. Not being able to do anything about it.' Tread carefully, I thought. Build trust.

'I've been following him to school - he's thirteen and refuses to let me walk with him - but nothing's happened to him on those days.'

'When do you think the bullying is taking place?'

'He won't talk about it. He comes home with cuts and bruises. Or his rucksack is scorched or soaking wet. Every week there's something - but I can't be there all the time to watch over him.' Lynn buried her face in an already wet tissue.

'No, of course, you can't. Have you reported it to the school?'

'He won't let me tell the school. I told the police, but they won't do anything.'

'What would *you* like to do?'

'Go to the headmistress and find out who is doing this. Make the teachers put a stop to it. Get the boys punished.' She sat back, looking exhausted.

I managed to check the clock as I took a sip of water. Only twenty minutes had gone. How was it that time could race past like a Bugatti one moment and then crawl by like a bicycle with a flat tyre, the next?

Lynn looked how I felt: wrung out with worry and lack of sleep. I found myself being distracted by images of the bodies again; daytime replays of the nightmares I'd been trying to forget. I realised Lynn was speaking.

'...don't you think?'

'Sorry, Lynn, I missed that last bit.' Damn. Unprofessional.

Lynn looked at the floor.

'Now, not even *you* are listening.' There was a quiver of anger in her voice.

'Lynn? Does it hurt when you pull on your hair like that? I've noticed...'

Lynn looked at the small clump of grey hair tangled around her fingers, as if she had no idea how it had got there.

'I didn't realise...' She wiped her hands on her skirt sending the clump on to the carpet.

'This is difficult to ask, Lynn, but have you been hurting yourself at all?'

Silence. Enough time for me to realise I'd pushed too hard, too soon.

'I think I'd better go, now.'

Lynn stood up, her bag clutched over her stomach. I stood too. 'We still have time left...' I said. Lynn ignored me and opened the door, leaving it open as she went to the stairs.

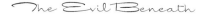

I heard the front door snap shut and sat down. I kicked off my shoes, pulled my knees up to my chest and hugged them. Maybe my therapist was right. Maybe there was too much going on in my own life for me to be able to offer emotional support for my clients; I certainly wasn't doing enough for Lynn.

The restaurant was dimly lit and crowded and I hovered inside the door, scanning the tables for Brad. A hand fell on my shoulder from behind and I jumped.

'Sorry...' said Brad, 'shouldn't have done that...'

'Probably not,' I said, turning around. He was wearing low-rise jeans, an open-necked shirt and a zip-up brown leather jacket. Very Starsky, I thought, although, personally, I'd always preferred Hutch. The waiter showed us to a table in the corner by the window.

'Hope this is okay...by the river...' he said, as he shuffled his chair forward.

I looked out over the stretch of thick black water, sprinkled with lights that rocked and dipped with the flow of the river. Behind me was Tower Bridge, lit up like a golden gate to a fairy-tale castle. As I took in the view, it sent me straight to another time. Luke's sixteenth birthday - he'd wanted us all to go to London to celebrate. We'd done the usual tourist spots - living in Norwich, it was hardly our first time - but the memory that sticks most wasn't the glittering crown jewels or the changing of the guards. It was the moment when Tower Bridge started to open and I saw Luke's face. Never have I seen such rapture sweep across someone's features. I wish I'd had a photograph of that moment, although it would never have matched the quality of the one inside my head.

'I love the Thames,' I said, defiantly. 'Nothing's going to change that.' My eyes swept the room. 'Lovely place.'

'I can recommend the lobster.'

I shuddered. 'Too fine a line for me, I'm afraid... alive one minute and dead the next.' I winced. 'Sorry, I'm not usually this morbid.'

He nodded. 'I know. Cases like this,' he waved his menu towards the river, 'They can get under your skin.'

'Isn't this against the rules?' I said.

'What? Talking about the case?'

'No, taking me out to dinner.'

'You're helping us with our enquiries.' He said it with a wry smile on his face.

'And you're helping yourself to my garlic bread,' I said.

I liked the way his eyes went sideways, like a young boy pulling off a coin trick he's been practising for weeks.

'I want to ask one question and then I don't want to talk shop after that,' I said.

'Fire away.'

'Any leads on the latest woman you found at Battersea Bridge?'

He put down his knife. 'She's been identified by her parents. Another strangulation, but, the post-mortem showed she hadn't had a termination.'

'Oh. Nothing to do with me, this time?'

'Let's hope not.'

I felt my shoulders drop.

'What was her name?' I ground my teeth, hoping it wouldn't be familiar.

'Lindsey Peel. White woman, in her mid-twenties. Ring any bells?' I ran the name through my brain's data-bank. Nothing. 'PM showed she'd been in the water only about an hour, but was killed several hours before that. Strangled. So, it's pretty much the same MO, but no pregnancy or termination, so she wasn't a client at Fairways. We know that much.'

'I'll check my list of private clients, just in case.'

Brad's starter arrived: chargrilled baby squid in tomato and chilli sauce. Suddenly I wasn't hungry.

'It might be useful, if you can bear it, to see the body...' He took a mouthful of squid. His stomach was obviously made of stronger stuff than mine.

'Yes, of course.' I stabbed an olive in the dish with a cocktail stick. 'I'm getting used to dead bodies by now.'

'It's just that...we hope not, but the way things have been going, you might know her, there might be some connection.'

'Yes. I understand.' I put the stone on my side-plate and watched it roll into the middle. 'So, let me get this straight. There have been three women murdered, strangled, so far, each one under a different bridge, all found in the water?' Brad nodded with his mouth full. He looked like he hadn't eaten for days. 'Pamela Mendosa, twenty-eight, white American, had a termination at Fairways, although I never met her. Then poor Aysha Turner, black girl, only fourteen...she'd also had a termination and I'd met her.' I toyed with a chunk of meat, but left it on the plate. 'Then, this third woman, Lindsey Peel, white, mid-twenties, no termination.'

'All the same MO,' said Brad, helping himself to more salad.

'And the only other link, so far...apart from the bridges...is me. My clothes on the first, a handkerchief with my initials on the second and of course getting messages beforehand for all three.'

'I'm afraid so...and beyond that, we're struggling. I have to admit, we have no suspects. Forensics hasn't come up with much. We're in the dark on this one.' He hesitated, dabbing the napkin over his lips. 'I shouldn't be telling you this.'

It was like trying to prise terriers from a fox, but we eventually managed to talk about something else. Tentative personal questions did indeed make it feel like a first date. He told me he was divorced and regretted having no children. He liked motor-racing and playing cards; rummy was his favourite - and anything Mediterranean. I was right about him having the look of an Italian waiter: his mother was from Puglia in the boot-heel of Italy. 'My father's not Italian,' he said.

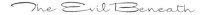

'I didn't think Madison sounded like it was from that part of the world.'

'He's from Hartlepool.'

Ouch. 'Not quite so...idyllic.'

He smiled. 'They run an olive grove now near Mum's home town.'

I found the way he struggled to find the right words compelling, likewise, the way his eyes were always a single crease away from laughter. It made everything else blissfully recede for a while.

I told him about Andrew and my work. I told him my chicken ragu was delicious, even though I barely touched it. What I didn't tell him was that butterflies were playing havoc with my digestion all evening. It was partly to do with the case, but more to do with being close to him.

I still wasn't sure if this was the beginning of something personal or a one-off thank you from the Metropolitan police for the contribution I'd made. I knew which one I wanted it to be.

He asked for the bill and I willed the waiter to get seriously side-tracked.

'So – if you hadn't become a psychotherapist, what then?' he said, sliding the mint from its wrapper.

'I was keen on the idea of forensics, as it happens, but I failed chemistry GCSE, so that put paid to that.'

'What were you good at, at school?'

'I loved the trampoline – those few seconds when you're in the air, thinking you can defy gravity - sublimely free.' He looked at me wistfully as if he knew what I meant.

'What else?'

I felt honoured. No one had taken this much interest in me in a long while. 'I was a bit of a whizz at synchronised swimming – don't laugh – a real natural, apparently. I had a hip injury when I was seventeen, so that had to go.'

'I can't imagine you at seventeen,' he said enigmatically.

Afterwards we walked along the riverbank until we reached the underground station.

'My nearest Tube station is Putney Bridge,' I said. 'District line.'

'I live near Elephant and Castle. The other way. Northern Line.'

I hooked a strand of hair behind my ear. 'Right then.'

He looked down at his boots. 'I forgot to mention. Can you bear one last thing about the case?' he said.

'I think I can just about manage it.'

'Our SIO told me there was something found on the woman at Battersea Bridge, but it wasn't anything personal.'

'What was it?'

'She had a book in her pocket.'

'A book?'

'Yes. A children's book, *The Secret Garden*, ever heard of it?'

I felt a wave of vertigo wash up my body and thought my legs were going to fold away underneath me. Brad grabbed both my arms.

My voice was a hoarse whisper. 'This person, this killer really *knows* me.'

'What do you mean?'

'That book...as a child...it was...' I leant into him, unable to make my legs straighten.

'What?'

'It was my favourite book...'

He guided me into an upright position against the wall, but didn't quite let go. 'It's a popular book. It could simply be–'

'Don't tell me it's a coincidence.' I hugged myself. The temperature seemed to have dropped ten degrees. Suddenly I didn't want to have anything to do with Bradley Madison, this case, London - any of it, anymore. I wished I'd stayed in Norwich. Or gone to Spain with my parents. 'Someone knows that book held a special place in my life. When Luke, my brother... died...I was twelve...that book saved my life... it was...'

I couldn't stay coherent any longer. I let go and fell into him allowing my tears to soak into his shirt. His arms were strong and safe and I sobbed; full-body sobs as he stood firm and didn't say a word. I was grateful for his silence. No attempts at comfort, no flinching with embarrassment. Then he put his arm around me and led me to the main road. We caught a cab and the next thing I knew, we were in my kitchen.

'I'm so sorry about this,' I said, clutching a batch of wet tissues.

He reached across the table with another hankie. 'Don't be. Someone out there is taunting you. And the police. Someone has chosen specific ways to make a connection with you, not just the messages you've been sent, but also the link with Fairways - the terminations, the clothes, the handkerchief and now the book.'

I pressed my fingers into my scalp. 'I've been trying to work it out.'

'We need to run through a kind of potted history. Look into everything in your background.' He took out a notepad from his jacket pocket. 'I know we've asked you about this already, but we're going to need to rake over your past in even more detail.'

'You're a policeman again, then?'

'And also a friend.' He started drawing a smiley doodle on his pad. 'I can be both.'

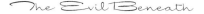

In my current situation, having a friend who was also a policeman was no bad thing. He turned to a fresh page and I was suddenly aware of the disparity between his levels of vitality and mine.

'Listen,' I said, putting out my arm. 'I don't think I can do this now.'

My body felt like it had been through an assault course and my mind was scattered all over the place, like a jigsaw someone had dropped. I was finding it hard simply to get my eyes to stay open. 'Can we possibly do this tomorrow? You could come back for breakfast...'

He folded the book away.

'You're right. It's late. Will you be okay on your own?'

Tempting though it was to suggest he stayed, I didn't have the energy to go through the inevitable coy two-step required in debating whether the sofa, the blow-up mattress or the floor in my room would be more comfortable. And digging out a fresh toothbrush and clean towel. And explaining how to flush the loo so that the handle didn't fall off. All I could think about was my head slumping into my pillow without any consideration for anybody.

'Yup. I'll be fine.'

'Let's get a fresh start tomorrow. I need to be at the station at the crack of dawn, so how about we meet near there? There's a place called Café Fresco almost opposite the police station - is eight o'clock too early?'

'No problem.' He was already walking towards the door. 'I'll try to remember to bring my brain with me,' I said.

Shepherds Bush police station is only a few minutes' walk from Hammersmith Tube, so I left the car behind. From my limited knowledge of Italian, the name Café Fresco implied there would be tables outside, but I was mistaken. Just as well. The establishment was on a busy road with a narrow pavement and the relentless stampede of traffic scorching past meant we wouldn't have been able to hear ourselves think, never mind speak.

Café Fresco had a large plain window and the kind of hard-to-push door you find in dry-cleaners. There were round aluminium tables on which stood grubby plastic tubs of salt and pepper. Instead of a vase, each table had a dish of sugar. I didn't want to look too closely, but there was definitely a cigarette butt embedded in the first dish I passed.

I found a table in the corner, squashed between an old electric fire and a stack of toilet rolls. I was trying to find a clean patch on the table on which to lean my elbows, when Brad walked in. His cheeks were flushed and his hair tousled as if he'd just got back from an invigorating hike. Didn't he ever get exhausted? Didn't cases like this gradually wear him down? It made me feel weak and inadequate by comparison, until I remembered he'd chosen this line of work. I hadn't chosen any of it.

He waved and pointed to the menu behind the counter. I managed to convey my order for an espresso.

'Thanks for coming. I've got about half an hour.' A waiter brought over two warm apple turnovers with our drinks. 'These are good, believe me,' he said, taking a bite and sending a puff of icing into the air. I tried mine. At last. Something good about this place. I licked my lips and thanked him.

He pulled out the same notebook I'd seen the night before and I realised from his official tone that we were going to get straight down to business. No time for small talk.

'I want you to think very carefully,' he said. 'We've got Hammersmith, Richmond, now Battersea Bridge - can you think of *any* connection to you?'

'I've gone over and over it. There's nothing.'

'We've got to look at the slightest odd thing, the tiniest anomaly. Is there anything you can think of in the last few months that's been out of the ordinary, disturbing? A person? An incident? However insignificant...'

'Okay...'

I hesitated.

'Go on...'

'I've got a weird client, a bloke...I'm not sure, but he might have been following me...'

'Following you?'

'I can't be sure. It's difficult when it's a client. They're often a bit odd if I meet them on the street.' I was thinking about the way Mr Fin looked like he was feigning surprise when I caught up with him in the park. 'People sometimes feel awkward, embarrassed...you know...and it was only once.'

'His name?' His voice was reproachful, now.

'It's confidential...I don't think I can...'

He folded his arms and sat back. 'I think it's gone beyond that, don't you? Three women have died.'

'Okay. But I'll need to speak to him first. I'm seeing him later today - then he's all yours.'

'Phone me as soon as you've seen him.'

'There was also that nasty bloke at the demonstration I told you about.'

'We've had nothing back yet on that e-fit you did for us. It's been in all the papers. We're going to step that up.' He scribbled something down and underlined it. 'Someone must know who he is.'

'It still doesn't explain how someone knew about *The Secret Garden*...and there's also the handkerchief.'

'Who knows about your middle name?'

'My middle name?'

'Yes. The initials *J.L.G.* on the handkerchief. Are you in the phone book?'

I stopped to think. 'Ah – of course. I'm listed as J. L. Grey.' I laughed. 'So that's not such a mystery, then. Anyone could have gone out and bought a handkerchief with those initials on it.'

'And the book? Who would have known about *The Secret Garden*? Presumably it wasn't your personal copy we found?'

'No - I don't have one. I keep meaning to replace the battered paperback I used to have.' His pen was poised over the page waiting for me to elaborate. 'My parents know it was a special book to me. My aunt, Libby. Perhaps previous boyfriends - you've already got their names. Andrew, possibly.' I also gave him the names of tutors on my psychotherapy course and my previous therapists; people who knew a lot about me. He put down his pen and yawned.

'Sorry - early start. Okay, I've got more possible leads. That's something.'

'They're all suspects?'

'We've talked to your friends and colleagues already, of course, but we've got to step things up now.' He took a final swig of coffee, but it must have been cold by then. 'The SIO wants the name of everybody you've known right from the year dot.'

'Crikey...'

'Not now – go home and make a list - nursery, neighbours, schools, teachers, friends, college - do it year by year, everything...' He gave me a pained look. 'I know it's going take time, but we can't afford to let anyone slip through the net.'

'Okay, if it might help...'

He slipped his notebook into his pocket.

'Good.'

'Thank you,' I said.

He looked surprised. 'For what?' He got up and swung his jacket over his shoulder. Starsky again. I was starting to go off Hutch.

'For putting everything you've got into this... for taking me out to dinner last night, getting me home, mopping up my tears,' I followed him to the exit. 'For not treating me like an idiot...'

He held his arm against the door frame and I ducked under it. I caught the leathery resin smell of his jacket and recognised a trace of woody after-shave. I took longer to come out the other side than I should have done.

'It's just my job... plus, *certain* parts...' he said, tipping his head to the side, 'have been a pleasure.' I managed a smile. 'Call me later when you've seen your client. We're going to have to talk to all of them, so be warned...'

As I walked back to the Tube I made a decision. I knew Brad wouldn't approve, but I needed to do some investigating of my own. One question was all it would take.

eleven

I didn't need to push open the letter box to know that Scott Joplin was playing at fifty decibels louder than was healthy. There was no point in ringing the doorbell. I went around the back. A smell of linseed oil and pancakes met me as I climbed the fire escape. The door was wide open. A notice for Andrew's next exhibition, tacked up with a single drawing pin, was flapping in the breeze. Nottingham, in a few days' time. Something heavy dropped inside my chest, as I realised I would play no further part in Andrew's future. The kitchen was empty, so I walked through into his studio.

It was the perfect place to paint. A previous owner had knocked down at least three walls to create a spacious living area, which now housed only two home-comforts: a sofa and a rocking chair. Andrew had pulled up the carpets and sanded the floor and everything about the room was devoted to and stained by paint. There were two easels, on one of which hung a dripping pair of jeans. Stacks of oil canvases, most with their backs to the room, leant against the walls. The centre piece was an oil drum, alongside a trestle table covered in opened and unopened tins of paint. In front of the iron staircase that led to the upper floor hung a skeleton from a hook. Someone had wrapped a scarf around its neck.

I found the hifi system under a cloth and turned down the volume.

'Andrew?'

No reply.

It had been a while. There would be at least three months' worth of new paintings here that I hadn't seen. Andrew had always kept me up to date with his work. He was like a young child, eager to show me how well he'd done at school. He'd often talk me through his ideas, his starting points, the way his pictures developed and the meaning of the finished canvases. I liked the psychology of it, the way it revealed Andrew's inner world.

I moved over to one wall and began tipping back the canvasses. They always reminded me of De Kooning: something savage and surreal in them, driven by a fascination with colour. Andrew said he'd developed his own personal iconography, using dream imagery. 'I can do primal as well as fairy-tale,' he'd said to me once, as if describing different flavours of ice-cream.

The recent pictures were in a pile near the staircase. I flipped the first one round. It was dark, mostly purple, with streaks of black. I stood back, hoping the extra distance would allow me to make out what it was, but no matter which way I tilted my head nothing was distinctive. Dismal and disturbing were the words that came to mind. I looked at the back to see if Andrew had given it a title.

Shadow in the water

Before I could take in the meaning of the small phrase written in pencil at the bottom, I straightened up. It was the smell of whisky which alerted me. I spun round.

'About to make off with a masterpiece, Ms Grey?' said Andrew, chewing the end of a thin paint brush.

I wasn't sure if he was joking. He had a steely look in his eyes.

'Sorry, I did shout.'

'I was on the phone,' he said. 'What brings you here?'

His words were sliding into each other.

I turned to the pictures. 'This is...interesting - these a batch of new ones?'

'They're not for sale. Leave them alone.'

I tried to tip the first picture towards me again, but he used his foot to push it back against the pile.

'Not for sale,' he said. He stood in front of the piles of pictures and put out his arm, like a policeman stopping traffic. I took the hint and moved away.

He sank into the sofa and the paint brush fell on the floor, rolling under his seat. He sniffed and made two attempts to get his foot to rest on his knee.

I wanted to leave, but I'd come here specifically to find the answer to a question. I'd know if he was lying. I knew the way his eyebrows became hyperactive whenever he tried to fob me off, usually about his drinking.

'How have you been?' I said.

He threw his head back. 'What do you care?'

I was about to perch beside him on the edge of the sofa, but decided against it. 'I do care, Andrew. You know why things didn't work out between us.'

His response came back in a sing-song imitation of my voice, 'Because, *Ander-wew*, there are three of us in this relationship... and I can't...'

'Well, it's true. Listen to you.' I picked up an empty bottle of Scotch - there were several to choose from - and waved it at him. 'It's not even lunchtime. How can this be helping?'

'You don't understand.' He lurched forward and I stood back, thinking he might be about to throw up. 'It helps *everything*. It never lets me down and it never judges me and it never walks out.' He was looking up at me, but kept blinking as if he was trying to make my face come into focus. 'I'm not the enemy, Jules.'

'You've never been the enemy. Not to me. Only to yourself.'

'Don't go all self-help-guru on me.'

'Don't change the subject.'

'Is this what you came to say?'

I took a deep breath. 'No.'

I didn't know how to introduce the question - the one question I'd come all this way to ask - so I came straight out with it. 'Do you know the name of my favourite book?'

'Your favourite book? What kind of question is that?' He laughed. 'I thought we were having an argument.'

'I know it's a strange question, but–' I rubbed my forehead. 'Just, yes or no?'

'What's it worth?' He managed to get his unco-ordinated limbs out of the seat. I stayed by the window and in a flash calculated how many steps it would take me to get to the door.

'Never mind,' I said.

Hoping his brain would take longer than normal to register, I moved fast, but I'd only taken three steps, before he blocked my path. I'd underestimated him. I had to turn away to avoid drowning in his whisky-soaked breath.

'Not going without a goodbye kiss, are we?'

'Don't, Andrew.'

The sing-song voice again, 'Don't, *Ander-wew*.' He grabbed both my wrists and pushed them behind my back.

'You're hurting me.' I wriggled. He laughed and pushed his face into my neck, holding my hands firm.

'Stop this. I'm going to have to fight back, if you don't let me go.'

'Fight back then. See if I care.' He was drooling now and trying to fix his lips onto my mouth. I jerked my head away and simultaneously lifted my right knee. It landed somewhere soft. Andrew doubled over, letting out a high-pitched squeal.

'I did warn you.'

I got to the door and started down the stairs. I heard scuffles behind me, but didn't turn round. I felt sick that it had come to this. As I opened the back gate, I heard him call out.

'Your favourite book is about a snotty little girl, just like you, who thinks she can change someone's life by planting a few daffodils.'

I let the latch on the gate drop and didn't look back.

When I got home I was still fuming. Underneath the anger, something else was simmering. Every connection between me and the dead women, Andrew knew about. My favourite book, my new job at Fairways, my middle name, my email address, my phone number. Even the clothes that went to the charity shop. I hadn't mentioned it to the police, but he'd been there the day I'd cleared out my wardrobe. I remembered him moaning, 'Not those', when I dropped the ankle boots into the bin-bag. I was trying to shake the thought away, but it wasn't going anywhere fast. Could the killer possibly be Andrew? Was this killing spree a deranged angry reaction to our break-up? Had I failed to spot the signs of a psychopathic serial killer?

As soon as the questions made it into the rational part of my mind, I dropped them like hot coals. It was unthinkable. Andrew had lashed out at me a few times; he'd cornered me like he'd done today, but he wasn't a calculating murderer. He'd have to be drunk to do anything stupid and by then he wouldn't be able to think straight. Not like the killer, who was incredibly smart with his cryptic clues and his ability to leave the bodies in public places, without ever being spotted. Andrew wasn't capable of that.

Was he?

Mr Fin arrived at 2pm on the dot. He managed to look taller and thinner every week. He sat down and averted his eyes.

I wanted to get it over with. I plunged straight in with my I-have-to-tell-the-police-about-you speech. 'Before we start today, Mr Fin, I'd like to...'

He was crying.

'I'm sorry,' he said. 'I don't think I'm going to be coming back after today.'

'Oh.'

'I don't think you can possibly understand me...'

'Right.'

'I think I need to see a man. I can't talk to a woman. I should have realised before.' He pulled out an offensive-looking handkerchief and blew into it loudly.

'You seemed to be...' I was going to say *doing quite well*, but realised it sounded patronising. 'You managed to talk...a bit...about yourself.'

'Yes, but it wasn't real. It was all crap...to get you to like me.'

'To get me to *like* you?' *How far off the mark can anyone get?*

'Yeah, I thought if I was kind of, distant and a bit difficult to pin down, you'd like it...like me...that's what my mother always used to say...women like men mean and hard, she said.'

'Your mother?'

The tears started up again. 'She's passed away.'

'Oh.'

'So, you see, I'm going to end it here and see someone else.'

'Well, that's fine, if that's what you want.' I certainly wasn't going to argue with him.

He slid to the edge of the seat. 'It's nothing personal,' he said. 'Women just...I can't...it's always been difficult.'

'Well, if you think a man could help you with these issues, I think that's a good decision.'

He stood up. He half-offered me his hand, but by the time I'd got to my feet, he'd pulled it back. He fiddled instead with his few remaining strands of hair.

'I'll go now,' he said.

'I wish you all the best, Mr Fin,' I said as I opened the door for him. Once he'd gone I went to my bedroom window and waited until I saw his wiry figure cross the road. Then I phoned Brad to pass on his details.

'Only, you mustn't tell him you got his name through me,' I said. 'I didn't get the chance to mention that you were going to be in touch with him. He could see it as a breach of confidentiality. He could sue me.'

'Unless he's the man we're looking for,' said Brad.

'I somehow doubt it.'

'How come?'

'Can I ask you something?' I swapped the phone to my other hand.

'Sure.'

'Were any of the women raped?'

'No. The pathologist said there was no evidence of anything sexual. No interference, no semen, nothing.'

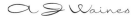

'I know Mr Fin has got problems with women - that's obvious and I know that could easily be a reason for wanting to hurt them, but I wonder if someone like that wouldn't also go for a sexual angle, a sexual attack?'

'He doesn't fit the profile, you mean?' I could hear the faintest whiff of sarcasm in his voice.

'Brad, I know I'm no expert in this, but I think someone of Mr Fin's type, if they were going to harm a woman, it would be sexual. He's probably never had a proper relationship. He doesn't know how to seduce a woman in the usual ways. He's frustrated and angry and I think sex, for him, would play a part in an attack.'

'Okay, we'll bear that in mind. But, he might have been following you. You said he freaked you out.'

'I know, but I don't think it's him.' I was picking at the bits trapped inside the woodchip wallpaper beside the window. 'How did he get the bodies down to the water without being seen?'

'By car to the nearest point? By carrying them to a boat over his shoulder in a fireman's lift?'

'What I mean is, he's tall, but he seems so frail. I don't think it's an act. He struggled to pick up his newspaper from the floor today. I don't think he could possibly be strong enough to lift anything remotely heavy...not a dead body.'

'Okay. But we'll still have a word with him. See how he reacts. Don't worry, I won't mention you. We'll find a pretext.'

'Thank you.'

'By the way, I wondered if you might take a look at some of the reports.'

'Reports?'

'From a professional point of view. What you said about Fin makes me think we could do with your expert knowledge to try to get inside the mind of the killer.'

'Isn't that the job of a proper profiler?'

'The SIO doesn't believe in it. No scientific validity, she says. We have other methods.'

'Such as?'

'We have a database of every distinctive feature in serious crimes, such as rape and murder. For example, if a murder contains a highly uncommon element, something evident in less than five per cent of killings, it gets stored in the file.'

'What sort of details?'

'Cutting off the victim's hair, putting objects in the mouth, ears, vagina or anus, sticking the lips together with superglue...' I groaned. 'Washing the victim down with bleach...that sort of thing.'

'So you'll have tried to get a match for *leaving objects behind belonging to another person* and *dressing the victim in another person's clothes*,' I said.

'We've done all that - in various permutations - and there are no matches.' He dropped his voice, as if afraid he might be overheard. 'I thought if you could take a look at the details...see if anything strikes you...any psychological patterns.'

'Is this above board?'

'Not exactly, no. But if it helps us find this bastard - frankly, I don't care.'

I had to admit he had a point. He wasn't the only one who wanted to use every available method we had at our disposal to find this killer. 'Okay. I'll try.'

'Brilliant. I'll email the report. Ring me back when you've read it.'

Twenty minutes later I rang him back.

'I've had a quick look at it,' I said.

'And?'

'I feel like I could have more or less written it myself - I know so much about this case, far more than I'd like to.'

He made a sympathetic noise. 'I know you'll need time to take it in, but does anything strike you straight away?'

'Not yet - just the sexual aspect I mentioned.'

'You think the killer is probably someone who *doesn't* have sexual difficulties or self-esteem issues around women?'

'Yes - I'll get back to you if I find anything else. How about you - any progress?'

He huffed into the mouthpiece. 'We're working flat out over here. I've got three DI's working alongside me now and we've rounded up officers from all over London. Place looks like rush-hour at Oxford

Circus. Problem is a complete lack of witnesses and CCTV has given us very little to go on, so far.'

'I wondered about that.'

'There are a few PTZ cameras in the centre of Richmond, but none on the bridge. The nearest one is outside the wine bar on the run up to the bridge, on the town side.'

'What's a PTZ camera?'

'One that pans, tilts and zooms, hence the acronym. Crafty little things - but there are none near enough the water.'

'And Hammersmith?'

'Similar story. There are various private cameras outside the pubs on the Hammersmith side of the river, but none on the other side where the body was found. None on the bridge itself.'

I sighed. 'I'd thought CCTV would have been really helpful.'

'People have an exaggerated view about how useful they are in solving crime. Less than five per cent of crimes in the UK were solved by CCTV last year, according to our national reports.'

'Crikey - I didn't realise.'

'So we're back to any other leads we can get.'

'There is something else,' I said. 'The killer is obviously highly intelligent and well-organised. He wanted the bodies to be found. Do you think he might even contact the police claiming to want to help with the investigation? I've heard of that happening before, when killers want some sort of credit for what they've done.'

'Yeah – we've got everyone on the lookout for that.'

I heard voices in the background and chairs being dragged across a floor. It sounded like they were preparing for yet another meeting.

'Just one more thing,' I added.

'Go ahead.'

'Actually, no, it's nothing.' There was something I wanted to check first.

'Sure?'

'No. It's fine.'

'Let me know if there is *anything* you think of that might be useful, no matter how insignificant it might be.'

'Absolutely.'

I didn't tell him I had a bit of breaking and entering to do, in order to tie up my own line of enquiries.

twelve

I had to wait until Sunday evening before I could be sure he wouldn't be there. The flyer on Andrew's back door had said the exhibition in Nottingham started on October 19th and knowing him, he would have gone up the night before to 'sink a few bevvies', as he would have innocently put it.

With any luck the spare key would be in the same place. Before I went up the fire-escape, I checked for any lights at the front and squinted through the letter box. There was post on the mat on the inside, left uncollected from yesterday. Good sign. The back gate was unlocked as usual, so I slipped through and climbed the iron staircase. I'd remembered to wear trainers to avoid making any noise, but it wasn't necessary. People in the area knew me. They'd seen me come and go from Andrew's flat often enough. I just needed to act normally. *Don't look round, don't look furtive.*

The stone hedgehog sat amongst a hotchpotch of plant pots on the top of the steps. I lifted it up and pulled out the key. It was a simple Yale. Andrew didn't have any sophisticated security measures. He always said a burglar would never steal his paintings, anyway, and that was all he cared about.

I wanted to set my mind at rest and if Andrew wasn't going to give me permission to see his new pictures, I was going to have to get a sneak preview myself. If Andrew was telling the truth and the latest ones weren't for sale, then it was unlikely he'd have taken them to Nottingham.

I'd brought a torch, but realised a flickering beam of light was going to look more suspicious than simply putting the light on. I needed to make sure I didn't move anything. I didn't want Andrew knowing someone had been in.

The pile of new canvases behind the sofa had been covered with an old sheet. I'd need to put things back exactly how they were. I'd brought my camera, so I took a picture, so I could exactly replicate the way he'd draped the cloth once I'd finished. Paranoid, I know, but I wanted to be careful. Events had taken such a sickening turn in the last few weeks that I didn't want to draw any unnecessary attention to myself.

I took a look at the first painting in the pile; the one I'd seen a couple of days before, *Shadow in the water*. I wanted to look at it again. I wanted to know what this latest batch of paintings was about. I knew Andrew put a lot of thought into his titles and they often revealed some deeper element to the picture.

Mostly black and purple, it didn't look like any recognisable shape. Purely abstract, which was new for Andrew. I pulled the second one out. Again, it was largely murky. Oil pigment in dark greens and black had been liberally spread over the canvas. These weren't the colourful, exuberant pictures I'd come to associate with Andrew's work. Perhaps, he was going through a morose phase. Perhaps, it was his way of dealing with our break-up. I checked the title:

Stranger on the riverbed

Something ice-cold crawled down my spine. River, water, darkness. This didn't feel good at all.

I looked at several more pictures and then thought I heard a noise coming from outside.

Someone slammed the gate.

'You can come up if you like, I won't be a minute.'

It was Andrew.

I'd shut the front door and had the spare key in my pocket, but it was too late to switch off the light. I stuffed the sheet over the pile of paintings and crouched down behind the sofa.

A key rattled in the lock and someone came in.

'Left the bloody light on,' said Andrew. 'Just wait here.'

Footsteps went up the spiral staircase. I could see another pair of feet waiting in the hall.

'Got any beer?' A male voice, unfamiliar.

'In the fridge,' shouted Andrew.

The feet backed away into the kitchen and I remembered to breathe.

Andrew came hurtling down the stairs and went into the kitchen. I heard more footsteps outside; it sounded like there were three of them now. I couldn't hear what they were saying, but Andrew seemed to have found what he had come back for. I heard the sound of a can fizzing open, then another and I wondered who was driving. I was starting to get pins and needles in my legs, squatting on the floor.

Andrew laughed and then footsteps came my way again. *Just switch the light off and leave*, I silently begged. A figure crossed the room.

'Not bringing all these then, Andy?' A different unfamiliar voice.

'No. I've got enough in the van. These aren't ready yet.' Footsteps came closer to the stacked paintings and therefore also to the sofa. I froze.

'What time are we meeting Mel?'

'Ten o'clock,' said Andrew.

'Better get cracking then. It's a good two and a half hours.'

'Yeah. Okay.'

The footsteps left the room and the light went off. Then I heard the front door close and the sound of footsteps on the back fire-escape. Then the back gate. I let out a long breath and propped myself up on the back of the sofa. Close shave.

It was only once I was half-way down the street that I realised I'd forgotten to take any more photographs. Some shots of the pictures and especially their macabre titles could have been useful, but I'd missed my chance. There was no way I was risking going back now. As soon as I was within sight of the Tube, I took out my phone.

'Did you get my list of names?' I said. It wasn't what I'd rung to say.

'Yes,' he said. 'Everyone you've ever spoken to in your entire life, I hope.'

I didn't laugh. A silence hung awkwardly between us.

'This is...a bit difficult,' I stuttered.

I told DCI Madison about the pictures.

'Right. We'll run a more detailed background check on him.'

'He knew about *The Secret Garden*... he knows a lot about me. And he's been...how can I put it?' I rubbed my left wrist, glad Brad wasn't there to inspect it. 'We split up because his drinking brought out an aggressive side in him.'

'He hurt you?'

'More emotionally than physically, but yes, you could say he laid more than a finger on me.'

I heard the beginning of an expletive followed by a muffled grunt, then silence. When he spoke again, he spoke slowly and deliberately, doing his utmost to stop himself erupting.

'Why the hell didn't you say something before? You keep doing this.'

'I can't believe it's him, Brad - really - he doesn't fit the profile at all.'

'Who else should we know about? Who else have you forgotten to mention?'

'No one. I'm sure that Andrew–'

'Stay away from him.'

I told him I'd decided to take a trip over to Cambridge to see my aunt, to get out of London, so that wouldn't be difficult.

My Aunt Joan was always known as Libby. It was some family in-joke about the way she'd always wanted to be a librarian, although with her cropped red hair and penchant for tartan miniskirts, she never came across as a typical librarian type - if there was such a thing. Like my mother, she'd been born in Cambridge, but unlike her, she'd never left. Never married either. She wasn't the sort to sit about in the Mediterranean sun, so hadn't shown the slightest hint of envy when my parents left for Spain.

I found her swinging in a hammock in the garden, the following afternoon. So much for my idea that she didn't bother with the sun. Maybe she was starting to change her mind.

'I've got the barbeque out specially,' she said. It was the middle of October and the sky already had hefty clouds brewing in the distance.

'Good idea,' I said, trying to hide my reservations.

'Come here and talk to me,' she said.

I put my bottle of wine on the patio table and sat on one of the chairs next to the hammock.

'Drive over, okay?'

'Light traffic. No trouble, really.'

'Should come over more often.'

Libby had started early with her hints about how little I saw of her. It was unfair, because she never came to London. I'd invited her several times to the theatre and for concerts, but she always turned me down.

I didn't bother to respond.

'Garden's still looking good,' I said.

It wasn't, but I knew it was her pride and joy. With no husband, children or pets, plants had become the little darlings in her life.

'How's life in the big smoke?'

'Hectic,' I said.

'Counselling going well? Lots of customers?'

'Yes. Always plenty of unhappy people in the world, Lib.'

'This a social call or do you want something?' She'd never bothered too much with common courtesies. 'It's always good to see you, but I did also think I might draw on your great wealth of knowledge.'

Turn up the flattery, it usually did the trick.

'Pour me a glass of wine and sweeten me up,' she said. 'You can light the barbie while you're at it.'

I could see my visit was going to come at a price. Libby had never been one to turn down the chance to let someone else do the work. In that respect, she was the total opposite of my mother. Mum wasn't happy unless she was expending her last ounce of energy helping someone. Libby's virtue was that she didn't beat about the bush. If I was going to get straight answers from anyone, it would be from her.

Once we'd shared half a bottle of wine and tried a few burnt chicken wings, Libby asked me what I wanted to pick her brains about.

'It's about the fire.'

'What, *the* fire?'

'Yeah, Luke's fire.'

Libby swung down from the hammock and joined me at the table. 'What do you want to know?'

'Just what you remember. What happened.'

'You know what happened. The fire started in the kitchen. It was an electrical fault with the toaster. Place went up about two in the morning and poor Luke dodged the firemen and went back in to find Pippin.'

It sounded so straightforward.

'Were there ever any doubts about how it started?'

'No.'

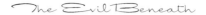

Something about the speed of her answer didn't ring true.

'Were there newspaper reports at the time?'

'I'm sure there would have been something in the local rag.'

'Can you give me access to the news archives in the library, so I can check?'

Libby hesitated. 'It won't do any good. Why are you raking all this up again, now?'

'Just want to know for sure.' I wasn't going to tell her that someone who claimed to be psychic had said the fire wasn't an accident. Anything to do with the supernatural had Libby turning her nose up in disgust. 'Can I take a look tomorrow?'

'I can't get you access tomorrow.' She brushed some crumbs off her skirt and I realised she was avoiding my eyes. 'We've got meetings all morning... and then an inspection.'

'But, the library can't be closed, surely.'

'Well, no...not closed...but it will be difficult for me to get you into the archives.'

This wasn't like Libby at all. It was starting to sound like a large dose of fobbing-off and she had me completely thrown. I didn't know whether to come straight out with what I thought or play along.

I chose diplomacy. 'Never mind,' I said.

I had another avenue to explore.

When I went to bed, I caught my image in the free-standing mirror in Libby's spare room wearing the long washed-out t-shirt I used as a nightdress. I stroked the hem and pressed it into my body. Luke's t-shirt. The only one of his to survive the fire. I often wore it when I was away from home. It was one of few remaining means I had left of holding him close.

Even though it was nearly twenty years since Luke died, there were times when I saw glimpses of him in my mind's eye as if he had only just walked out of the room. Vivid, bright scenes that filled up the white screen inside my head, flickering like home-movies. The unruly dark hair he refused to keep short, the dimples he loathed that gave him a touch of impudence, the recent walnut swelling in his throat that he was coy about. A grumpy, witty, intelligent, lazy sixteen-year-old - all manner of contradictions bundled up inside him. For years, he'd been the big brother I doted on.

I turned away from the mirror. At times like this the enormity of the loss hit me hard and afresh - not just losing Luke, but losing the family we were then. From the day of his death we each pulled away in different directions in order to cope. Instead of rallying as a family, it was as if we stood in separate corners of a room facing away from each other, not daring to look round in case we came face to face with more grief than we could bear.

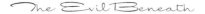

Libby had left for work before I was up in the morning. She'd left a note:

Let's meet for lunch at 1pm at The Anchor. It's on Silver Street. C. U. there.

I went downstairs in my dressing gown and pulled out my laptop. I searched for 'Norwich local newspaper' and came up with two. I copied down the addresses. If I was quick, I should be back for our 1pm lunch date.

The roads were fairly clear and I arrived at my first stop, the *Norwich and Norfolk Gazette* at just gone 9.30am. The offices were small, with a reception desk just inside the front door. It smelt like a hairdressers. I tried to locate the source of the peroxide aroma, but it must have originated behind the scenes, from part of the printing process.

Posters of the paper's high-points were laminated and stuck on the walls. The hot-air balloon disaster of 2004. The Duchess of York's visit in 2007. Delia Smith saves Norwich City F.C. in 2005. Top stories.

A man appeared behind the desk, his sleeves rolled up.

'Can I help?'

'I'm a journalist in London,' I said. 'I'm looking into a story from 1990. Do your archives go back that far?'

'1990 is before our time, I'm afraid. We set up in 2001. Nothing further back than that.' He can't have missed the crestfallen look on my face. 'You could try *The Norwich Echo*. They've been around since the fifties. Their archives are at the Local Studies Centre. They might be able to help.'

I thanked him, my shoes squealing on the linoleum floor, as I spun round.

The Local Studies Centre was located in a much older building, which also housed an overflow of old books and periodicals from the public library. I climbed the steps and waited inside a dark foyer. A porter appeared with a parcel. He ignored me. Then a woman with glasses propped on her head came out of a rear door.

'Are you being seen to?'

I repeated the same spiel I'd delivered at the first place.

'You'll need a Norwich library card or a pass,' she said.

'Oh.' Stumped. 'How do I get a pass?'

'Have you got your journalist ID?'

'Ah. You've got me there. You see, I'm freelance... on a commission for...*Country and Home* magazine. I'm not really attached to any particular paper.'

I surprised myself at how easily it slipped off my tongue.

'Haven't you got anything showing you're a journalist?'

I made a show of looking in my bag, but I was running out of momentum. I put my empty hands on the desk. 'I'm really sorry. I don't think I have. You can take my credit card as assurance if you like, is that any good?'

'We don't operate like that, I'm afraid.'

I was about to turn away, when an idea occurred to me. I looked in my bag again, hoping I'd been less than my usual tidy self, lately.

I found it. 'Will this do?' I said, flattening down a creased sheet of paper. It was the email sent to me by Brad, that I'd used to view Aysha's body at the police mortuary in Wapping. 'It shows I've been authorised by the Metropolitan Police to investigate.'

Thank goodness I'd been preoccupied lately. Normally a note like that would have been 'filed' away by now. She took one look at the police logo and handed it back.

'If anyone asks, I wasn't the one who let you through, okay?'

She pushed a white card into a slot and the turnstile clicked and let me pass.

I walked down a dim corridor until I got to a large oak door. As I entered, the smell of furniture polish was so strong I could almost taste it. There was no one else in the room. Glossy oak tables ran in rows down the room and tall pull-out racks of recent copies of local newspapers lined the walls. Everything before January 2009 was on microfilm. I put my bag on a table and flicked through the boxes, searching for 1990. I pulled out the reel for the relevant year and slotted it into the machine, then scanned the dates in January. I was looking for anything after the 18th, the day our house went up in flames.

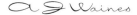

Then there it was:

> *Tributes have been made to a young boy who tragically perished in a house fire, as his name was officially released by police. Luke Grey, 16, was killed when a fire broke out in his family's detached home in Thornwell Drive, Norwich, in the early hours of Thursday, January 18th. Mr Anthony Grey and his wife, Melanie, who both suffered no injuries, described their beloved son as 'cheeky and fun-loving'. They also have a daughter, Juliet, 12, who was uninjured in the blaze. Luke Grey was taken by ambulance to Norfolk and Norwich University Hospital, but was pronounced dead on arrival. Fire chiefs confirmed investigations into the cause of the devastating blaze are still continuing, but they have no cause at this stage to suspect suspicious circumstances.*

Maybe Libby had been right: the report looked straightforward. Perhaps Cheryl had got her psychic wires crossed. I decided to check the records for

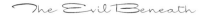

the next few days to see if there was any follow-up report, once the police had made a full investigation. I came across a small piece on page seven on the following Monday. As I read, I could feel small hairs on the back of my neck start to prickle:

> *Following an investigation into the fire at a family home in the early hours of Thursday, 18th January, police and fire chiefs gave the following statement: "The fire started in the kitchen," explained DCI Molliner, "but we are concerned about the speed at which the fire took hold of the rest of the building."*
>
> *Luke Grey, 16, who died in the fire, had returned to the property to rescue the family dog. "We have clear procedures at an incident of this kind," explained Colin Spencer, sub officer at Norwich fire station. "Sadly, the boy broke through the front line of fire-fighters and re-entered the property without our consent."*
>
> *DCI Molliner concluded with the following: "Our investigations are on-going," he said, "as we are yet to be satisfied about the cause of the blaze."*

I then searched the frames every day, for the following week. I scanned each page on the machine, my pulse pounding in my head, but I found nothing more. I went through the pages again, together with all the papers from the week after that. I drew a total blank.

I sat back and let out a loud sigh, just as someone else came into the room. It was nearly 11.30, so I quickly made copies of the relevant frames on the special microfilm copier, grabbed my things and left the building.

Libby was already inside The Anchor, sipping a port and lemon. I got my own drink and joined her by a window.

'Had a good morning?'

'I went to Norwich.' I pulled out the copies of the two reports.

Libby clicked her tongue. 'This just upsets people,' she said.

'The second report says the police weren't happy about the way the fire started...'

'We can't do anything about it now.'

She waved a bag of cheese-and-onion crisps at me. I shook my head.

'Do you remember any of this? Was there ever a follow-up investigation?'

'Nothing else came to light. It was a tragic accident, Jules.'

I prodded my finger on the second clipping, still not convinced. 'Something wasn't right. You said it was the toaster. There's no mention of that in the report.'

'The newspapers probably turned away anything that came up later as old news. The police must have done an investigation. Nothing ever came of it. Case closed.'

'What about Mum and Dad, would they know more about it?'

Libby rounded on me. 'Don't go digging all this up again with your parents.' Her eyes were wild. 'Don't you dare upset them all over again. It's over. Luke's gone. Just leave it.'

I stared at my hands in my lap and let it drop. For the moment.

When I waved goodbye after lunch, I knew I wasn't giving up that easily. I still had one more card up my sleeve, but I needed Cheryl to help me play it.

thirteen

I'd just managed to get into the scorpion position when the doorbell rang. I was furious. It had taken me months of yoga practice to develop enough strength to hold the position and I'd finally achieved it. I was tempted to ignore the bell, but it rang again and broke my concentration. I rolled on to my yoga mat and stormed down the hall.

It was Brad. He took one look at my red face and upside-down hair and burst into laughter.

'Sorry,' he said. 'Bad time?'

I waved him in, before the whole street saw me in my pink velour leisure suit. 'Just trying to get relaxed,' I said, sounding anything but. My Wednesday morning had involved two very odd clients and a *no show*, and I was in need of my yoga fix.

'I wanted to keep you in the loop...I was passing.'

As I rounded the back of the sofa I kept my smile hidden from him. I wasn't falling for the *just passing* routine. I put the kettle on and handed him a mug of coffee.

'I don't mean to pry, but what were you doing before I arrived?'

I dragged my fingers through my hair trying to force it into shape and cursed the velour suit. I sat down so he'd see less of it.

'Yoga. I'm not very good.'

I looked down and froze. I'd left a copy of *The Lovers Guide to Tantric Sex* on the coffee table in full view. I stood suddenly to make sure his eyes didn't drift in that direction, and leaned awkwardly against the back of the sofa. He shifted round to look at me.

'I'm really here about Lindsey Peel, the third body we found at Battersea Bridge. You'd better sit down.'

How I hated those words. He patted the space I'd just vacated. As I returned, I slipped a newspaper over the yoga book, making it look like I was clearing space for any notes he might produce.

'She didn't have a termination at Fairways, but we know she worked there.'

'Shit.' I felt like the air in my lungs had been sucked out of me. I sank back into the cushions. Why did I ever bother being pleased when I saw this man? I should know by now that some dreadful news would always follow him like a bad smell.

'She was a cleaner. You didn't know her?'

'No. I've never done the early morning shift.'

'I've brought a photograph. We know who she is, so there's no need for you to see the body.' He pulled the picture out of his pocket. 'But just in case you recognise...her clothes...or...'

I reluctantly took the snap. I recognised the aluminium trolley from the mortuary. The victim was dressed in a green skirt with a brown polo-necked jumper, under a khaki parka. She looked neither soaking wet, nor distressed. Her clothes appeared unruffled, her pale face serene, as if she'd simply fallen asleep in the wrong place. I tried to hang on to that belief, but it barely lasted a second, before the cruel truth of the situation took over. Like the others, she'd probably been strangled and dumped like a discarded bag of rubbish.

'No. These aren't my clothes.' I said. 'And I don't recognise her.' It was something. 'But it's another Fairways' connection...' All my energy was slowly being sapped from my body.

'Yeah. We've been interviewing everyone who works there. Nothing so far. We're still waiting for some comeback on the e-fit of the guy who threatened you at the demonstration. Zilch, as yet.'

I dug my heels into the carpet, staring at my bare feet.

'We also traced Aysha Turner's last movements,' he continued. 'The night before she was killed, friends said she'd gone to meet someone in Putney.

We don't have a name. They were meeting at the Duke's Head by the river, so we're checking that out.'

'She was right next to the river ...'

'The post-mortem put time of death at between two and six on the morning of October 6th, so she could well have been killed in that area and then taken down to Richmond Bridge...partly by car, perhaps partly by boat.'

'It's a long way. Someone must have seen something. There are always lots of people down at the riverside in both Putney and Richmond, even late in the evening.'

'We're banking on that. Forensics found size ten footprints - flat bog-standard shoes without any visible tread - at the scene at Battersea Bridge, but no DNA. Nothing from Richmond Bridge crime scene, as far as I know. The guy must have been really careful. Probably wore gloves, a hat, a long jacket without any wool... to prevent loose fibres, flakes of skin or hair from being left around.'

'Smart guy. Who the hell is he?'

'We spoke with your Mr Fin. Odd chap isn't he? He has alibis for all three murders.'

'I knew it wasn't him, even though he gives me the creeps.'

'Anyway. That's it on Operation Chicane for now.'

'Is that the name of the case?'

He looked bemused. 'You must have missed that meeting.'

'How did you come up with that name?'

'It's nothing complicated. We have an approved list - neutral words that we choose from.'

'Just random?'

'Pretty much - we use the next word on the list as long as it doesn't have any coincidental connection to the case. Every UK police force is the same. Anything from exotic fruit to islands off the Scottish coast.'

He stood up.

'So it could easily have turned out to be Operation Hedgehog or Operation Hard-boiled-egg,' I said.

He gave me a wry look that said: *I'm glad you've still got your sense of humour.*

'Our SIO would like to see you, again, by the way. She was hoping for later today, if that's okay with you.'

More grilling. 'That's fine. I've passed my shifts at Fairways to another counsellor this week.'

'Good thinking. I was going to suggest you keep away from there, for the time being.' He turned at the door and put his hand on my shoulder. 'Fourish okay for you?'

'Yeah. I'll be there.'

My mood had sunk rapidly again, but I could feel the heat of his hand through my top, long after he'd gone.

Borough Commander, Katherine Lorriman was a carbon-copy of the figure I'd seen a fortnight earlier, only this time there was a slash of scarlet on her lips. Perhaps today she'd had a lunch date.

I was led by a male officer through narrow corridors, weaving through a constant stream of preoccupied staff, to her office. I'd obviously been upgraded from the drab interview suite. We passed the main incident room. It looked like the trading floor at the Stock Exchange. With three woman dead and no sign of an arrest, this case had certainly turned into a huge operation.

The first thing that struck me about the SIO's room was the absence of plants or feminine touches. No trace of perfume in the air, no photos, no trinkets - there wasn't even a painting on the wall. Instead, it was stacked high with boxes beside grey filing cabinets. Entirely functional, stark and uninviting, giving nothing away except that this, in itself, told me something. This woman took her job extremely seriously, she probably didn't have much of a home life and what personal life she did have, she kept poles apart from her professional one.

I was relieved when Brad joined us. It made me feel less like an errant pupil brought before the headmistress.

'We're dealing with a smart and devious killer, here, Ms Grey,' she said, without any opening welcome. 'Most perpetrators take souvenirs of murders away with them,' she continued. 'It would appear, in this case, that the killer is doing the reverse.' She put both her hands on the desk in an emphatic gesture. 'He's leaving objects behind that have a personal connection...to you.'

Her tone was on the verge of implying it was my fault again.

'At the moment, the obvious connection is Fairways. Two of the victims had terminations there and one worked there. And you work there. It could simply be some anti-abortionist getting on his high horse - perhaps this guy who threatened you.'

Brad took over.

'We're checking through all the lists of known anti-abortion activists in London,' he said. 'We're looking at footage of previous demonstrations from the last few years. It's a massive job. We're also sending out officers to speak to ring-leaders and other clinics who've had threats in the past.'

'I understand that DCI Madison has been going through your personal background and family history to see why you're being targeted in this way,' she said.

'I spoke to my parents to check if they had any links to London,' I said. 'They've never spent time or worked here. I'm the only relative who has ever lived here. My father laughed when I asked if he had any enemies. Nothing at all from them, I'm afraid.'

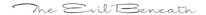

'Is there anything else we haven't considered?' she said. 'Any small thing, even if you think it may not be relevant?'

'From your days at University - your psychotherapy training?' added Brad. 'Fairways, Holistica?'

I told them I'd been asking myself these questions every minute of every day. I still didn't have any answers. We went over details, facts and speculations, but effectively the interview was over. The SIO didn't offer me any coffee. She didn't even thank me for coming. There were no words of reassurance either, although I'm not sure anything would have helped. There was a killer out there, with belongings of mine and an intimate knowledge of my life. It would be hard to frame that in a way that didn't sound like I was in danger.

Brad led me out towards the main entrance. Now we were on our own I had to ask one more question.

'I know it sounds a bit dramatic, but do you think I should go into hiding?'

Brad paused, acknowledging the difficult position I was in. 'We've been talking about your safety. We're going to give you round the clock protection.'

'Really? What does that mean, exactly?'

'It means you'll have officers assigned to keep an eye on you...at home and whenever you go out... to check you're okay.' Images of an unmarked car crawling along the pavement beside me, came to mind. 'They'll be with you during the day and check you're safe and sound at night.'

'It might be best to curb my frantic social life, then, or they won't be able to keep up.'

As if.

He smiled.

I wondered, now that other officers were in the picture, if Brad would stop dropping by from now on. Why couldn't he have been allocated the job of supervising me? I wouldn't have minded him checking to see if I was 'safe and sound' when I turned out the light. I ran with the ensuing fantasy for a second or two, then decided to save it for another time.

As we reached the door, I asked one final question.

'Do you have any leads at all, so far?'

'It's slow.' He breathed a hollow sigh. 'We need to track down the guy who threatened you. We've got extra surveillance at Fairways in case he shows up again. We're going to talk to Andrew again. A couple of your clients have been cagey. We're still trying to track down various people on your list - your former college tutors...'

I pulled a face. It wasn't sounding hopeful.

True to his word, I got a call from a female officer at around seven o'clock that evening.

'I'm WPC Penny Kenton,' she said. 'I've got PC Zak Nwoso with me. We're just across the road in a blue Astra.'

I crossed the bedroom and inched back the curtain. I could see a couple in plain clothes sitting inside a dark car.

'It's best that you don't acknowledge us at any time, unless you need help.'

'Okay.'

'We'll keep popping up all over the place, I'm afraid, but just try to carry on as normal. We don't want anyone else to know we're right on your tail.'

'Thank you.' I didn't know what else to say.

'Are you safe now? Everything locked up?'

'Yes.' I felt like a five year old. I half-expected her to ask if I'd brushed my teeth.

'We'll be staying around until the morning. Keep a mobile phone switched on by your bed and if there is anything, anything at all that you're concerned about, call this number immediately, okay?'

I said I would and rang off.

Sleep did not come easily that night, but I wasn't surprised. Nobody knew what was going to happen next. Nobody knew whether I was in any danger or not, except for the killer himself, of course. If only I could get inside his mind.

I was tempted to make sure someone was staying with me each night for the rest of the week, but I didn't know who I could ask. It was too complicated to ask Andrew, and after finding the weird paintings recently, I preferred to keep my distance. All the other friends I might have asked lived in different cities. When I woke to go to the loo at about 3am, I couldn't resist checking the street below. All was quiet and, sure enough, the blue Astra was still there. Even though I had others looking out for me, I still felt I was going to have to get through this all on my own.

When I woke the following morning, the blue car was lying in wait ready to keep tabs on my every move. This was how it was going to be from now on. Penny had called to say two new officers were taking over that day. PC Ralph Ferriton and PC Ron Alderidge. I was going to find it hard keeping track of everyone. I felt more secure on the one hand and strangely violated on the other. With my phones and email being tapped too, not much I did was going to be private for some time.

When I flicked through the notes for my first client, I realised how tired I was. My therapist had suggested I take some time out from counselling, but I couldn't afford to. I was already turning away work at Fairways. When you're self-employed, you can't take leave and get paid for it. I'd lose money hand over fist if I took a break. I'd then be reduced to a life stuck in my flat, twenty-four seven, or walking the streets with a blue Astra glued to my backside. Not an option.

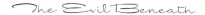

Lynn was the first to arrive. We launched into the same material as before. Lynn's son being bullied. Lynn following her son to and from school. The boy, refusing to allow any intervention.

'This must be so frustrating for you,' I said.

It was certainly frustrating for me - there was so little room for me to help her. 'What has been better, this week?' A psychology trick; try to shift to the positive.

'Nothing. It's just the same.'

'How is your son?'

'Billy's been quiet. Withdrawn. He goes to his room and plays with his transformers.'

'Transformers?'

'Those cars and animals that you turn into robots.'

It sounded terribly old-fashioned in an age when every kid's world was dominated by Xbox and Wii.

'Does he have many friends?'

'Not really. It's hard for him. He doesn't join in, doesn't mix much. The other kids...if they're not bullying him or laughing at him, they just ignore him.' An unfortunate whine was ever-present in her voice. It didn't make me warm to her, but I did feel a well of compassion towards her unfortunate son.

'What else does he do?'

'He draws and paints pictures. He's into Power Rangers and he likes collecting things. He wants to know how things work. Like engines and electricity...'

She paused. 'He's good at science,' she said, out of the blue.

'That's excellent.' Something positive, at last. 'Have you met the science teacher?'

'Yes. Mr Slade. He seems okay. He seems to be able to relate to Billy.'

'Any chance Billy might be persuaded to talk to Mr Slade about the bullying, do you think?'

She was straight down on me like a ton of bricks.

'No, No! He won't involve anyone at the school. The teachers...the headmaster...nobody!'

Why wouldn't she just consider it? Try talking to the boy about it, again? Keep gently prodding away at him, to get him to see sense?

I was forced to find another way. I wasn't convinced she had much of a support network, but I asked the question anyway. 'Have you talked to any of your own friends about this situation?'

She looked down. 'I don't really have anyone.' It sounded like both mother and son were awkward types who didn't mix well or make friends easily.

'How long have you been in the area?'

'Only since the beginning of the year. I don't go out much, except to work. I'm a part-time secretary in a company in the city. And I drive a mini-bus for Billy's school. To try to keep close to him. I'm not good at socialising.'

That much was obvious. Lynn's whining tone and dejected body-language smacked of being a victim.

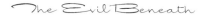

People didn't find that attractive. I tried something else.

'Do you go to a gym or a club?'

'I go swimming,' she said.

'Do you know people there? Anyone you get on with?'

'Not really.'

'It might be worth talking to other people you can trust, other mothers, about this kind of thing. Parents' groups, perhaps. I can find some websites for you about coping with bullying. There will be other people who've been through situations like yours.'

'I thought *you* were going to help me.'

'It's very hard, Lynn.' I set my pen down on the table beside me. 'The person who needs most help is your son and you tell me that he won't accept any intervention at the moment. It's hard for me to do anything constructive.'

'He won't come to these sessions.'

'That isn't how this works I'm afraid. Anyway, I'm not trained to work with children. How old is Billy again?'

I knew I had it in my notes somewhere, but I didn't want to look away.

'He's fourteen.'

'There should be an educational psychologist attached to your son's school. You could see if they could help him. Which school does he go to?'

'He doesn't want the school involved. I thought I'd made that clear.'

We were going round in circles and I couldn't find a way out.

As I was turning things over in my mind, she asked to leave the room to use the toilet. When she had gone I looked through my notes again. Was there anything here I could use as a lever to make some progress?

I was scanning the first page, when I came across Billy's age. I'd written it down in our first session. Lynn had said he was thirteen. Today, she'd said he was fourteen. That was odd at first, until I realised there was a simple explanation. He must have had a birthday during the last few weeks. No real mystery there. As I continued to read, however, I noticed another inconsistency. Lynn had said the head of her son's school was a woman, but today she had referred to *the headmaster*.

A strange thought suddenly struck me; *Was this some sort of Münchausen by proxy - some attention-seeking syndrome? Was Lynn fabricating the whole story? Did Billy even exist?*

As I read further, I realised places, dates and names seemed to have changed over the weeks I'd been seeing her. Before I could decide what to do, she was back in the room.

Right from the start, I'd had an odd feeling about this woman. I couldn't work it out; all I knew was that something about the whole story didn't ring true.

I asked for the date of Billy's birthday.

She answered immediately. 'April 12th. He's thirteen.'

Right. No recent birthday.

Lynn cleared her throat. 'He'll be fourteen in six months' time.' Her arms were now folded. She was on the defensive. 'Why are you asking me this?'

'I'm sorry.' *Make it my fault - claim to be baffled. Make it seem like I am the one messing up.* 'I thought you said he was fourteen. I was starting to get a bit lost.'

'You do think bullying is wrong, don't you?' she said. 'You do think bullies should be punished?'

'I think everyone involved needs to know exactly what's going on first, but yes, I agree that bullying is entirely wrong.'

She looked smug, like she'd won an unexpected victory.

When she left, I had to admit it: I hadn't a clue what was going on. My only conclusion was that I was going to have my work cut out reading up on both Münchausen syndrome and compulsive lying.

fourteen

Cheryl didn't own a mobile phone and when I called her home number there was no reply. I knew she lived in Chelsea, but I didn't have her address so I couldn't even turn up unannounced on her door-step.

I knew Holistica was open in the evenings, but I wasn't sure if Cheryl would be working there that day. I rang and spoke to Clive. He said Cheryl had already left. I knew it was policy not to give out home addresses even to colleagues so I lied. I said I'd left something at her place - in Chelsea - when I'd last visited and I'd forgotten to write down her address. Half-an-hour later, I was standing at the entrance to her apartment block.

A smart man was just leaving and held the door for me, so I didn't need Cheryl to buzz me inside.

'Fancy see you here?' she said, as she opened the door, although didn't look the least bit surprised to see me. Perhaps her psychic sense had already told her I was on my way. She led me to a small sitting room that smelt of incense and contained heavy blocks of Egyptian-style furniture. A mosque-shaped mirror hung over a huge chest and the compact space was over-stocked with soft furnishings and silk cushions; everything in the room appeared to have a tassel attached to its corners.

There was an awkward silence between us. She knew why I was there.

She noticed I'd spotted a photograph of an aeroplane beside the door.

'I used to be a pilot,' she said. 'Squadron Officer in the Women's Royal Air Force, before it merged with the RAF in 1994.' She must have seen my eyes stretch wide. 'Loved it. The freedom up in the skies. I highly recommend it if you've never tried it.'

I told her I hadn't - and that it wasn't top of my list of new hobbies right now.

'I'm a "feet firmly on the ground" sort of girl,' I said, 'unless you count trampolining.'

She invited me to sit. She looked pensive. 'I'm more of a head in the clouds sort, but I imagine you've already worked that one out.'

I decided to cut to the chase. 'Your psychic gifts, you mean?'

She didn't answer. 'I'm glad you've come – I knew you would, eventually.'

'I wanted to hear what you had to say.'

'It's not always easy,' she said softly, 'because sometimes I have information that could be useful for someone and yet, it could also be upsetting for them.'

Her eyes moved away from mine too quickly and instantly I knew this was going to hurt.

'You mean, my brother...what you said...about it not being an accident.'

'It could stir up a hornet's nest. Are you the sort of girl who prefers to paper over the cracks?'

My stomach churned. My eyes met hers. 'I need to know.'

'I thought so.' She made a bridge with her fingers. 'I'm certain it wasn't an accident.' Her words were slow and deliberate.

I decided to tell her about visiting the archives of *The Norwich Echo*. I explained how the newspaper report mentioned an ongoing investigation and then hadn't printed anything further.

'What did the reports say, exactly?'

'That the police were concerned about how quickly the fire had spread and they didn't know the cause.'

'I'll tell you what I see. Is that what you want?'

'Yes, yes, please.'

My mouth went dry.

'I've been getting images, when I'm with you, of a family home. It had a yellow front door, right? Detached house, with a garage on the right side, big tree on the left?'

I gulped. She was spot on. Those details had never been mentioned in the newspaper reports.

'There was someone else in that house. I can see someone opening windows downstairs. It was winter, wasn't it?'

'Yes, January.'

'Why would someone open windows if it was cold?' she asked, running her finger along the hieroglyph design on the chair arm.

Why indeed, I asked myself, wondering where this was going.

'Do you remember much about that night?' she said.

I nipped my lips together. 'I was twelve. It was nearly twenty years ago.'

'What do you recall?'

'It's a blur. My memories are mixed up with what other people have told me and my own nightmares, so it's hard to be clear.'

'Have a go.'

'I remember we'd been out somewhere. All of us as a family, earlier that evening. I do remember it being cold. I was wearing a thick coat and gloves.' I closed my eyes and felt the prickly wool of the scarf tickling my neck. 'The lights were all out. I didn't know why that was. I remember Dad had a torch and I couldn't read my book that night because none of the lights worked.'

'A power-cut?'

'I don't know,' I said, pensively.

'What else?'

'The next thing I knew we were all outside and I saw the flames ripping through the kitchen window. Other windows had been blown out. Then the firemen arrived. We were huddled together, all four of us. They gave us blankets.' I ground to a halt. 'The next bit is difficult.'

'About Luke?'

Cheryl put her hand over mine.

'Yes. I don't remember seeing him go. One minute he was there with us and the next minute he'd disappeared. My Mum was screaming and people were shouting and pointing to the front door. The firemen were angry.' I felt tears roll into the crease beside my nose. 'I didn't see him again.'

'Why did he go back inside?'

'For the dog. Pippin died as well.'

I thought about Pippin; the scruffy mutt that Luke cuddled all the time. He never barked at anyone and always smelt of sweaty trainers left out in the rain.

I looked up. My tears made Cheryl's face look like she was behind frosted glass.

'The images that keep coming to me, Juliet, are to do with the kitchen. I see boxes beside the oven. Boxes that shouldn't be there.'

'Boxes?'

'Boxes, crates, containers of some kind.'

'Anything else?'

'The lights being out. I've seen that too. The house was in total darkness one minute and up in flames the next.'

'Perhaps there was a power-cut, like you say. Why, otherwise, would my dad be using a torch inside the house?' An image from that night suddenly came to me. 'And candles. Yes. Dad went into the cellar and brought up a box of candles. I remember now. We lit them in the sitting room before we all went to bed.'

A sharp pain ran up my throat. 'It wasn't the candles, was it?' Cheryl took hold of my hand with a firm grip. 'Was it our fault?'

'I honestly don't think so. Really. That's not what I'm getting at all. It's something else...something disconcerting. About the boxes in the kitchen and someone else having been in the house. The windows being open.' She placed her hand on her chest and nodded. 'That's what's been coming through to me. That's all, I'm afraid.'

I let out a heavy breath.

'Thanks for telling me. It makes me want to look into it more. I knew there were pieces missing and I want to find the answers.' I got up, ready to go. 'Can I ask you one more thing?' I said. She nodded and I perched on the chair arm.

'I'm not sure where to start,' I said. 'You know that picture of Battersea Bridge I asked you to look at last week?'

She stiffened. 'I've been keeping up to date with the murders. Dreadful.'

'You don't pick up anything about...me...at all, do you?'

She hesitated. Bowed her head. 'No.'

'Only, obviously, I'm nervous about the whole thing. Terrified, actually.' I tried to smile, but my chin started to wobble instead. 'I've been targeted... receiving these awful messages and I feel...helpless.'

She put her hand on my shoulder.

'I don't pick up anything negative around you,' she said. 'I'm not getting much coming through about it at all, to be honest.'

'I know I mentioned it before, but the day after the first woman was found, you said you knew she hadn't drowned. You were right. She'd been strangled. They all were. I wondered if perhaps you knew... more than–'

'I had a feeling, that's all - but it wasn't connected to you. I'm sorry if I scared you.'

'But, you'd *know*, wouldn't you - if I was in danger?'

'I can't say. It's not an exact science, Juliet. I'm sorry.'

I was grateful for her sincerity. She could easily have claimed to be more certain in order to look impressive. Cheryl's stare was fixed on the floor. 'I haven't picked up anything at all to suggest you're... at risk.' She paused. 'Not yet, certainly.'

After I'd left, I had a sudden pang of doubt. Was Cheryl really psychic? Was it all a well-crafted show? Did she know certain facts because she was involved in some way? And if she *was* genuine, was she holding something back? I'd watched her body-language and met her eyes when we said goodbye. Her gaze didn't waver, but I still wasn't entirely convinced. Neither did I feel filled with reassurance at Cheryl's choice of words. When I'd asked whether she thought I was in danger, her caveat 'not yet' had sent a chilly tingle, like an icicle, down the back of my neck.

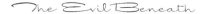

When I got back to the flat, there was an envelope on my doormat. It was from Andrew; an invitation to a prize-giving ceremony the following evening, in Holland Park. One of his paintings had won first prize. As I read his untidy handwriting, I felt a wave of sadness. He wanted me to be there.

It was tempting to allow nostalgia to bend the truth, to usher the good memories to one side and pretend that was all there was. I pulled myself up short, however, and remembered the harsh reality of the matter. Andrew couldn't control his drinking and had been physically abusive towards me. Nothing had changed in that regard; my experiences during the last week ago had told me that. I couldn't afford to let nostalgia colour my judgement. Especially now that there was the smallest chance Andrew could be capable of far worse.

Nevertheless, I weighed up the idea of an evening of glamour with flowing champagne, versus a night in, watching *Dumb and Dumber*. It didn't take me long. What harm would there be, turning up for an hour or two in a crowded room full of well-wishers? Andrew couldn't do anything with all those people around. Maybe I'd find out something useful.

Leighton House was now a museum, situated in a leafy area of West Kensington. As I entered, there was a strong smell of lilies and beeswax. My heels clacked across the polished floor and I was half-expecting one of the attendants to ask me to take off my shoes.

It was an amazing place: huge galleries full of large pre-Raphaelite oil paintings and gilded ceilings. I was taken aback by a sunken pond at the centre of the ground floor surrounded entirely by turquoise Islamic tiles and marble columns. Breath-taking.

I was escorted upstairs to a large hall where the ceremony was to take place. Chairs were laid out in rows and there were three easels at the front, each one holding a picture covered with a cloth, set up for the grand unveiling of the prize-winners.

It wasn't long before I saw Andrew. He was wearing a crisp white shirt with puffed sleeves and a wide open collar, framing a scarlet cravat. His shirt was hanging loose over a pair of dark red velvet trousers. He looked like a Renaissance prince. Just like Andrew: overstated and romantic. I watched him explain something to a couple, waving his arms around and scooping back his floppy fringe and I knew I still hadn't got him out of my system.

Someone tapped the side of a glass and we took our seats.

From the start, it was clear the proceedings were going to drag on well into the evening. Various chairmen of sponsoring companies took their turn to pontificate, followed by top-bods in the art world bootlicking them in return. I stifled a yawn and started looking around at the other people who had turned up tonight, entertaining myself by trying to imagine what they did for a living. There was a woman with long blonde hair that reached her lower back. I wondered if she was as attractive from the front. A model? Too obvious. A Personal Assistant in a fashion company? Maybe. I moved along the line, missing out the bald head and the middle-aged permanent wave. Suddenly I gasped. The woman sitting in front of me turned round with a disapproving stare. I stared right past her, my eyes latched on to someone far more interesting.

I recognised the chiselled face, the reddish skin-tone, the long side-burns and mousy hair. The guy who had threatened me at the demonstration was sitting two rows in front of me. I slid my hand into my bag for my phone. I had to get a message through to the police station to let them know he was here. I fumbled about trying not to look conspicuous and then it hit me. I'd swapped my usual handbag tonight for something light and sassy. My phone was probably sitting on the kitchen table. I could have kicked myself.

The ceremony was reaching its climax and the audience broke into applause, as the cloth on the picture in third prize was pulled free, revealing the canvas beneath. I'd hesitate to call it a painting. It was what I could only describe as *loud*; splashes of bright orange and crimson with black lines carved through it. A woman in a tie-dyed tunic walked forward and shook the hand of a man in a suit.

I kept my eyes on 'demo-man', hoping he wouldn't turn round. If he did, would he recognise me? Did he have a personal interest in targeting me or was I simply a face representing Fairways?

I missed most of the rest of the ceremony. My mind was on overdrive trying to work out why 'demo-man' was here and whether I could find out who he was. The next minute, Andrew was taking the applause and holding an envelope in his hand. I was so busy staring at the back of the mystery man's head, that I hadn't seen the unveiling of Andrew's prize-winning picture. All of a sudden, people were turning in their seats applauding, some smiling, others looking me up and down. *What was going on?* I squirmed in my seat, trying to work out why I had suddenly become the centre of attention and then

I saw it. Andrew's painting. It was a nude portrait of a woman.

I felt my bottom lip go slack and the room suddenly went blurred as though we were all underwater. It was me. Naked.

I wanted to stride over and land a sharp slap across Andrew's face, but that would have drawn even more attention to myself. Being in the spotlight was the last thing I needed right now; I certainly didn't want 'demo-man' singling me out.

The applause continued and people were getting to their feet, starting to break ranks. I stood up as elegantly as I could muster, but in the melee, lost sight of the figure I'd been painstakingly watching all this time.

I needed to get to the front and speak to Andrew. I didn't care about the painting right now, I'd have words with him about that later. What I needed to know was if he knew the man I'd recognised. I had to find out who he was.

I slipped to the end of my row and from behind a pillar, tried to scan the room. 'Demo-man' was one of few men at the event not wearing a suit and tie, so I was quickly able to dismiss large numbers of people. I checked everyone at the drinks' table, those already moving towards the exit, those dotted in groups in the centre. I was about to give up when I spotted him at the far side, talking to a woman with a loud voice.

Andrew had now become the star of the show and I had to fight through the fawning mob to get anywhere near him. I was worried that before I reached him, he'd be swept away by some sharp entrepreneur offering him a celebration supper. I pushed further forward. Eventually there were two bodies between me and him. I could hear Andrew thanking people, acknowledging their praise. Then a man moved away and I was standing right in front of him.

'Jules. Really glad you could come.' He put a hand on my arm, but he didn't attempt to get any closer.

'Don't push it.' I nodded towards the canvas in front of me. 'We need to have a conversation about this, sometime.' I glanced at the painting at close range. There was no doubt about it, it was an uncannily good likeness. A tad on the flattering side, to be honest.

'I think it's too late for that now,' he said, sheepishly.

I managed to guide him behind the easels, away from a group of people still waiting to speak to him. 'Listen. I know this is weird, but I need your help.'

'Huh?' He frowned.

'Do you remember the guy I mentioned, who threatened me at Fairways? The guy at the demonstration?' I could see him trying to make the cognitive leap between basking in his current glory and a conversation we'd had several weeks ago. 'Sorry to do this at a time like this, but he's here...I've seen him and I wondered if you knew who he was.'

Droves of people were already drifting towards the door. I knew it was too late now to borrow Andrew's phone and call the police; by the time they got here 'demo-man' would have been long gone. Andrew put his weight on one leg and brought a hand to his hip. His face was blank.

'Jules. This isn't really–'

I grabbed his wrist. 'He's a police suspect. It's really important.'

'Well, where is he?' He looked over my head.

I turned gingerly, trying to stay behind the easel. 'See the older woman in the yellow dress?' I watched his eyes travel across the room.

'Okay, yeah, I've got her.'

'The man nearby with tatty hair, long side-burns, wearing a brown jumper. Can you see him?'

'I think so. With black jeans?'

I took another look. 'Yes, that's him. Do you know him?'

'He doesn't look familiar.'

'Go a bit closer.'

He made a path towards the woman in the yellow dress, who seemed delighted he'd come over to speak to her. As he said a few words I saw him send his eyes over her shoulder. He came back, shaking his head.

'Never seen him before. Don't know who he is.'

I cursed. 'Okay. Thanks, anyway. I'll let you get on with your celebrations.'

As I turned to go, he grabbed hold of my little finger.

'A few of us are going over to Covent Garden later. Fancy coming?'

'I'm working, tomorrow,' I said. 'Thanks anyway.'

I started to pull away again, just as the young woman with long blonde hair was trying to get Andrew's attention. She was, indeed, decidedly pretty from the front.

'Someone wants your autograph,' I said, raising my eyebrows.

'See you,' he said and blew me a kiss. I turned and tried to locate the mystery man again, but I'd lost him. I did a full circuit of the hall, but he'd disappeared. Damn. I could have alerted my minders as soon as I left the building. Now it was too late.

As I stepped out into the cold, I felt a shiver flutter down my spine, but it wasn't anything to do with the weather.

fifteen

I spotted the blue Astra as I left Leighton House. I was starting to feel sorry for WPC Penny and her side-kick, Zak, spending their lives trying to keep up with me. We'd set up a system right from the start, whereby I sent a text message whenever I knew I was going to be on the move. It made things easier for them. I'd only had two days of it, but I was already getting tired of the cloak and dagger pantomime. Given that I didn't have my phone, I went over to the car to tell them in person that I was going home, even though it was officially 'against the rules'. I was tempted to ask for a lift, but that would have pushing things a little too far.

When I got back, I was restless and unnerved after seeing the man from the demo and then losing him again. I'd gained nothing from my trip over to Andrew's prize-giving except humiliation. I had no real information to pass on, but I rang Brad anyway. At least I could tell him the guy they were looking for was still in London.

'I was just about to ring you,' said Brad. 'I've had some more details through about Andrew Wishbourne.' There was a hesitancy in his voice and I knew it wasn't going to be good news. 'Did you know he's got a history of GBH?'

My silence answered his question.

'He had a twelve-month prison sentence for whacking someone with a golf club,' he continued. 'We're bringing him in again for questioning.'

I put my hand over my mouth.

'Juliet, you still there?'

'Yes, sorry. Bit of a shock.' I told him about my evening.

'Nice try,' he said. 'I've got to go...been called to an incident.' I could hear the sound of sirens in the background.

As I dropped the phone into my lap my front doorbell rang. It was Jackie wanting to borrow my hair-dryer.

'Mine's been bust for weeks,' she said. 'I've got to get to work and it's too cold to go out with wet hair.' I held it out to her. She glared at me. 'What's happened? You look awful.'

I could feel my hands shaking as I handed it over.

'It's Andrew - that guy I used to go out with.' I told her what Brad had said.

'It's a long way from GBH to murder,' she said.

'You have to start somewhere.'

'That's a terrible thing to say.'

'I know.'

'Maybe you're right,' she said, with regret. 'I didn't know him. .'

'He only let other people see what he wanted them to see: the jokey, fun-loving, pie-in-the-sky, Andrew.'

She fiddled with the plug. 'You can't tell what people are capable of, can you? There are always news items on the telly where neighbours of paedophiles say: *Oh, he was such a nice man.*'

I handed her the nozzle for the dryer that had dropped off as she was talking.

'I didn't even know he played golf,' I said.

When I woke the following morning, all I wanted was to get out of London, away from the murders, away from Andrew and even Brad. I didn't have any clients, so I sent a text to my minder - WPC Wendy Morrell this time - to tell her I was heading off for Norwich.

Thornwell Drive was a leafy residential street; the kind you find in any prosperous city. I hadn't been back here since I left home for University, in 1996; the same year Mum and Dad moved to Spain. Dad's bronchitis had been getting worse for some time, but I think they'd been waiting for me to finish my growing up before heading to warmer climes. I also think they couldn't bear to stay in that fateful house any longer.

I wondered what the odds were that the same neighbours would still be living there, thirteen years later. I remembered Mr Knightly at number sixteen. He would have been in his sixties when I'd left. He could be long dead now. There had been a young family on the other side in the 1990's. They had a noisy dog and one of the children played the recorder, badly, all the time. Everything would have changed.

I turned the corner and parked at the top of the street. I texted WPC Morrell to tell her there were some coffee shops down the road and to the right, but I didn't know if she would take up the offer. She was on her own today; her partner had been called away to an incident and they were short on replacements. Cutbacks. I felt awful leaving her to sit in the car, hour after hour. I couldn't imagine I'd be in any danger on this occasion, so far from the scene of the murders.

I took a few steps down the road and was hit by that strange dream-like feeling of returning to a place one once knew inside out. Like cheating time. It felt as familiar as if I'd been here only yesterday and yet it had existed purely inside my head, mutating into memories that were less and less accurate, for over a decade.

The road seemed narrower than I remembered it, the houses closer together. Details had changed, like the white picket fence, which was now a brick wall at the front of what used to be Mrs Lorne's house and the post-office had turned into an all-night convenience store. But, the smell of the air was the same, the way the sunlight fell across the camber in the road, the edges of the paving stones, the leaves caught in the grille of the sunken drains - everything else was how I'd remembered it.

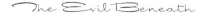

I wondered who was living in our house, number eighteen, and if they knew our history. I wondered, even though we'd had the whole place redecorated, if there were still charred marks on the walls and a lingering smell of smoke.

I came to number twenty and rapped the bronze knocker against the door. A dog barked, but it was a yappy sound, not the deep-throated one I remembered. The figure of a woman appeared through the bobbled glass and she opened the door, wearing rubber gloves. A terrier was trying to squeeze past her. She picked it up.

'I thought you were the plumber,' she said.

'Sorry. Have you a minute?'

The dog was alternating between yapping at me and trying to lick the woman's face. 'Not if you're selling something. What is it?'

I could hear water running in the background.

'Did you want to turn your tap off?'

She looked flustered, like she'd completely forgotten what she was doing. 'Hold on.'

She shut the door, then returned without the dog.

'I used to live next door,' I said. 'My name is Juliet Grey. We lived here until 1996. Were you here then, by any chance?'

'I'm the cleaner, I don't live here.' She softened a little. 'They've only been here a few years. 2006, they moved in, I think.'

She didn't tell me who 'they' were, but she'd told me all I needed to know. I said I was sorry to bother her and turned away.

My next hope was Mr Knightly, who had lived the other side. I remembered him as a jovial sort, always stopping to chat when he met us on the street on his way back from the corner shop. He'd lost his wife during the time we'd lived there and I flashed back to images of her funeral. We'd been to the wake at his house and the smell of lavender came to mind. I remember Luke dropped a vol-au-vent, by accident he'd said, down the back of the record player. A vinyl of Frank Sinatra had been playing. That was before death had touched our family. Mr Knightly brought round trays of stale cucumber sandwiches and dry chicken wings for days, afterwards.

He came to the door wearing tartan slippers. He recognised me, once I'd given my name and he extended a crinkly hand. It was cold and flaky. He looked much the same, except he seemed smaller, thinner and one eye was partly closed. As soon as I started speaking I realised he was hard of hearing. Luke used to call him 'Sprightly Knightly', because he was always dashing off somewhere. He owned race horses and was usually either down at the stables or at the next race meeting. Looking at him now, I didn't suppose that 'dashing' was part of his lifestyle anymore.

There was no smell of lavender like I'd remembered, instead, an odour of burnt cabbage was coming from the kitchen. He led me in that direction, where I had interrupted him eating a boiled egg. There was a cross-hatching of toasted soldiers on the side of his plate. He asked if I wanted lunch, but the room was heaped with dirty pans and opened cartons and looked like it would have failed the least stringent of hygiene tests. I said I had someone waiting, which was true, if you counted poor Wendy in her car.

He guessed it wasn't a social call. I asked if he minded me asking some questions, while he finished his lunch.

'It's about the fire,' I said.

'I had a funny feeling it might be.'

'A few new things have come to light.'

'It was a long time ago,' he said. A dribble of egg yolk made its way down his chin.

'I know. Nineteen years. Do you remember the night it happened?'

'Oh, I remember it, all right. Hard to forget something like that.' He rubbed his buttery hands down his trousers and pushed the finished meal away.

'Someone said there might have been a power-cut. Does that ring any bells?'

Mr Knightly screwed up his eyes, as if watching a scene in great detail.

'I remember looking over at the house, because our electrics were fine. Your curtains were drawn by then. You'd all gone out to the pictures, because... that's right...you had no power.'

What he said snagged my memory. I'd forgotten we'd gone to the cinema that evening. It made sense, given we had no light or heating. Luke had suggested it. 'If we're going to have to sit in the dark,' he'd said, 'we might as well have a decent film rolling.'

Luke was clever and cheeky like that.

'Do you remember anything about the windows?' I kept it vague. I didn't want to give him a leading question.

He rubbed his stubble. It sounded like he was scraping the edge of a matchbox.

'They were open, weren't they?' he said.

'Really?' I said.

'Come to think of it, it would have been odd in January to have the windows open, but they definitely were. I can see it now. In the lounge and the other downstairs rooms. Not the upstairs.'

He had the effortless, but radically diminished recall of the elderly; he could have told me the tie he wore when he got married, but wouldn't remember where he'd put the oven-gloves, a few minutes ago. Thankfully, the period in question still had firm roots in his brain.

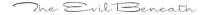

'Did you tell the police...at the time of the investigation?'

His good eye was stretched wide open.

'I don't know if I did. I don't think I realised until later. It had all blown over by then.'

A piece of the puzzle the police never got to hear about. It was starting to look like Cheryl's suspicions could have some justification.

'Having the windows open must have made the fire spread,' he continued. 'The police said that, didn't they, that the fire spread quicker than they expected?'

'That's right.'

'The lights were off, so maybe none of you saw the windows were open. Your parents don't remember opening them? Maybe there was a gas leak.'

'I need to check with them. Might someone else have got into the house, do you think?'

'Your parents kept a spare key under a plant pot at the front. We all kept keys hidden like that, under plant pots, under the mat, in those days. In case any of us were away and needed plants watering or milk taking in. It's different now. No one leaves keys around like that anymore.' He sent his eyes over my shoulder, his head tilted to the side, as if remembering times when life was simpler and safer. 'Everyone's far more security conscious these days,' he said.

I flashed back to finding Andrew's key so easily, under the hedgehog by his back door. Not everyone, I thought.

'Do you remember anything else, Mr Knightly? This is very helpful.' I had the feeling I might be losing him.

He smiled and I saw that he'd forgotten to put his false teeth in. Or maybe he didn't bother with them anymore.

'I'll make us some tea, shall I?' he said.

'Why don't I make it?' I said, standing up. Less chance of food poisoning, I decided.

'I've got something that might help,' he said. He disappeared as I rinsed two cups in boiling water. He came back with a photo album. I could see this wouldn't be a short visit, but his observations could be very useful and I felt sorry for him.

The album opened with his wedding to Maisie and we travelled through days at the races, days at the seaside and holiday snaps from abroad. There were a few pictures of our family; times when we had played in Mr Knightly's garden for a change. One shot showed Luke and I doing somersaults on the grass with Maisie holding a jug of lemonade.

'You didn't have any children?' I said.

'No. We would have liked to, but it didn't happen. None of the special treatments then that you can get now to make babies.' He chuckled.

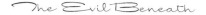

He turned the page and there was Luke again, standing on his own, bare-chested, holding a pitch-fork. He looked about twelve. My stomach turned over.

'He came and helped me down at the stables now and again. Your Luke came round that night and borrowed one of my torches. It was the last time I saw him.'

There had certainly been a power-cut, then. An isolated one that had only affected our house, by the sounds of it. Why hadn't this ever been mentioned in the newspaper reports?

A silence hung between us. I wanted to be on my way, but as we were only half-way through the album, I knew I couldn't get up and leave. I didn't want a trip down memory-lane, right now. I couldn't bear to see more pictures of Luke, but I also didn't want to be rude. I tried to loosen my clenched fists under the table.

There were a few pictures of me on one of Mr Knightly's ponies. I'd completely forgotten he'd let us ride them. Then there was a picture of Luke and I with someone I didn't recognise.

'Who's this?' I asked.

He leant closer. 'That was your babysitter. You would have been about nine, Juliet. What was her name, now?' I wasn't sure it mattered, but he was determined to remember.

'Mrs Smith...no, Mrs Jones...something like that... not terribly memorable,' he said. 'Do you remember her? Had a son about Luke's age. Bit of a funny lad.'

'I don't remember,' I said. As I looked at the woman's face, there was an inkling of recognition, but nothing solid. She wore a gold badge on her cardigan that caught the light.

I asked to go to the loo before I left and took the opportunity to have a quick look over towards our old house from his spare bedroom window. I couldn't see the kitchen from there; the point where the fire had started. Our lovely lawn had been turned into half-decking, half vegetable patch; the swing and sand-pit long gone.

When I left, Mr Knightly was still gazing at the album. It must be tragic to know that everything of value in your life lies in the past, in a place that's been and gone - leaving only a handful of six by four images to hold on to.

As I walked back to the car, I realised I'd never known his first name.

Wendy fluttered her fingers by way of acknowledgement as I approached my car, but we didn't speak. I sent her a text with the words:

Home, James.

Another weekend was looming large ahead of me. I was in one of those restless moods, when I didn't know what to do with myself. I didn't feel like having company, nor did I fancy being on my own. I was disturbed by my trip to Norwich. The cause of the fire was turning into a gruesome mystery. I didn't want to open up old wounds, but the only way to check whether either Mum or Dad had opened the windows that evening, was to ask them. If they hadn't, it meant something very serious indeed. In the light of Mr Knightly's comment about leaving the front door key under a plant pot, it wouldn't have taken rocket science for someone else to have got into the house. If someone had deliberately opened the windows, maybe they also had something to do with the fire. But, why?

My mother picked up the phone. I could hear jolly guitar music in the background.

'Darling, we've got friends over. Just mixing the sangria.'

It sounded idyllic. I didn't want to spoil their fun, but I felt I had no option.

'I'll make it quick, Mum, sorry to have rung at a bad time.'

'It's never a bad time when it's you, dear,' she said.

'I went to see Mr Knightly, today. The man who used to live next door to us.'

She hesitated and I heard a hoot of laughter in the background.

'Whatever did you do that for?' There was a different tone in her voice now: cold and wary.

'I won't go into details, but there seems to be some confusion over what happened with the fire.'

'Some confusion? What do you mean?'

'About how it started. About the house.'

Mum's voice was suddenly muffled, as though she was holding the phone to her chest. I could make out her voice telling someone where to find the brown sauce.

'I can't go into that now,' she said. 'We're in the middle of–'

'I know. Listen. I have one question. Just one. Is Dad there?'

'Is that the question?'

I brushed off her sarcasm. 'It's about the windows in the house that night. Did either of you open the downstairs windows, the night we went out to the pictures.'

She didn't say anything. I heard someone start to sing.

'No. It was the middle of winter and the heating had gone off. Why would we open the windows?'

'That's what I thought. Can you ask Dad?'

She held the phone to her chest again and I could hear her calling my father over. There was a short exchange between them.

'No,' said my mother. 'He says the same as me. Everything was off; the lights, the heating. No one opened any windows. What is this about?'

I didn't want to disclose Cheryl's psychic notion that the fire hadn't been an accident. I knew that wouldn't go down too well.

'There are some points about the fire that don't add up, that's all. I just want to make certain. I want to be able to explain it all in my own mind.'

'Don't go stirring things up, Juliet.'

'That's exactly what Aunt Libby said.'

'Well, don't. I can't go through all that again.'

Silence. 'I've got to go,' she said, and the phone went dead.

sixteen

Later that day, I went to the phone-box outside the deli, to make the call. I knew the police had been tapping all my means of communication; my emails, landline and mobile phone and I didn't want anyone listening in to this one. These days, I was having to stop and think before everything I did, everything I said - and it was driving me nuts. Every conversation with Brad, for instance. I had to remember to call him DCI Madison, for a start. I had to keep the conversation strictly business-like. I didn't want to get him into any trouble. I also had to be careful about what I said to Jackie about the case. I wasn't, after all, supposed to be discussing it with anyone.

Whenever I left the flat, I had to think about how I would get to where I was going and whether Wendy, Zac, Penny, or one of the other officers assigned to babysit me, would be able to follow. I had to remember to text, so they'd get a head-start. I was starting to feel like I should have a ball and chain around my ankle. Precautions here, filtering what I said, there - I was fit to burst. It went entirely against the grain for someone impetuous, like me.

'I want to ask a favour,' I said.

'Go ahead.'

'I wondered if you could access some police records for me.'

'Woa,' said Brad. 'Is this about Andrew?'

'No. Not him. It's about a house fire in 1990.'

'I don't understand.'

'My brother was killed in a fire at our house, when we lived in Norwich. I did mention it to you, briefly. Well, I've been talking to various people and the cause of the fire is starting to sound very sketchy.'

'Are you on your mobile?'

'No, I'm on a public payphone. Your mates should be out of earshot.'

'Who have you been talking to?'

'I checked the newspaper reports from that time. They said the fire spread quicker than it should have and that a full investigation was underway, but there were no follow-up reports.'

'Could be that the paper didn't bother to print anything else. Old news. Especially if no suspicious circumstances came to light.'

'It's not just the newspaper.' I said. 'I spoke to an old neighbour and he remembered our house being affected by a power-cut and our downstairs windows being open. I asked my parents and they said they didn't open any windows.'

'You *have* been busy.'

'Anything to take my mind off what's been happening here.'

'I take your point.' He let out a loud sigh. 'I'm not sure I can access those kinds of records.'

'Oh.' It came out weak and small, like a child. I hadn't meant it to.

'It's outside my jurisdiction.'

'Right.'

'And I could get into serious trouble.'

'I understand.'

Silence. I decided to give it one last shot. 'It was January 18th, 1990.'

'Why do I get the feeling I'm going to do it anyway?' he said.

'Maybe it's something to do with your loyalty to justice. Or perhaps, it's my irresistible powers of persuasion.'

'Okay. Look, I'll put out some feelers. I can't promise anything.'

'You're a gem. Thank you.'

He hesitated and I was expecting him to say he had to go. 'You busy this weekend?' he said.

'Not especially.'

'I might pop over...if that's okay.'

'What will your officers think? They'll be on my doorstep watching you clock in and clock out.'

'I'll send them home and take over for a while, if that's okay with you.'

It was very okay with me.

'Is that entirely above board?'

'I'm the policeman. Let me worry about the protocol, eh?'

My hand was shaking when I hooked up the receiver, but for once, it wasn't out of fear.

He was early. As I opened the door, I couldn't help checking up and down the street. Sure enough, the blue Astra had gone.

'I made her day,' he said, 'giving WPC Kenton the evening off. Means she can go to the cinema with her boyfriend.'

I wanted to say that just by showing up, he'd already made mine.

'It will only be one minder from now on, by the way,' he said. 'Our finances are stretched to the limit.' He laid his jacket on the back of the sofa. 'Something smells delicious.'

I'd spent so long trying to decide what to wear that I'd nearly messed up the chicken supreme altogether. The onions had frazzled to cinders and the chicken hadn't defrosted in time. I'd managed to salvage the situation by slipping some garlic bread into the oven in the nick of time.

In the end, I'd settled for pale jeans and a simple white blouse, which already had a splash of basil oil down the front. It had been too late by then to do anything about it.

'Just a small glass, I'm driving,' he said, as I poured out the Pinot Grigio.

I had to stop my face from falling. Not what I wanted to hear. Right now, with doubts about the fire and nothing to reassure me about the rising toll of local murders, I could have done with his company until dawn. It wasn't about sex - just having him in the flat would have been enough.

I handed him the glass and leaned against the sofa. I was exhausted already and the evening hadn't even begun. Since the police had discovered that the third victim, Lindsey Peel, had worked at Fairways, I'd been waking up at regular intervals during the night, soaked with sweat and gasping for breath. I'd felt hands around my neck, water gurgling into my lungs. I was supposed to be in bed, but instead I was spending all night in freezing water, fully clothed, kicking against the tide, fighting to keep my face out of the water, fighting to get to the shore.

In each dream my legs started strong, but quickly turned to jelly. I would look down and see useless numb tree trunks instead of legs. I couldn't swim. My body wouldn't float, I couldn't scream. I was sinking towards the river bed, dropping away from the surface, falling, falling - watching detritus drift past my face.

In the past three days, I was sure sleep hadn't claimed me for one minute. I couldn't even take a bath these days; I couldn't bear to lie in the water.

As a result, my need for comfort and protection had escalated sharply. Being on my own every night was tortuous. I hadn't told anyone - not even my therapist, and I wasn't about to disclose it now.

I excused myself to stir the sauce, then took the chair at the far end of the sofa, curling my feet underneath me. There was a yawning gap between us.

'How are things going?' I asked.

'On the case you mean?'

'That, and...you.'

'There's not much "me" at the moment. Up to my neck with interviews, trawling through statements, briefing meetings, reporting back to the SIO.'

'Not going well?'

'You'd think that with three murders in the middle of London, we'd have evidence jumping off the pavements at us.'

'Do you want to talk about it?'

'I think, more to the point, do you?'

'It's weird. I don't want to talk about it or even think about it, but I need to. It's with me every second of the day, anyway, and I need to keep trying to make sense of it. I'm greedy for any fresh information, even though a huge part of me doesn't want to know.'

'I can understand that. I'll try my best to keep you in the loop.'

The oven-timer pinged. In contrast to Cheryl's exotic apartment, my dining area had an old wooden table with a placemat under one leg and a couple of chairs my father had rescued from a skip. I brought through the garlic bread.

'We're looking at the dates of the murders,' he said, 'to see if there is a pattern: September 20th, October 6th and October 12th.'

'Are they all the same day of the week?'

'No. A Sunday, Tuesday and a Monday.' He crunched into a chunk of crusty bread. 'So far, the gaps have been sixteen days and then six days.'

'Doesn't sound like much of a pattern,' I said. I tried to remember not to speak with my mouth full.

'We're looking at the weather conditions and the tides. Seeing if there's a link there. The Thames is tidal as far as Teddington.'

'Yeah. Derek told us.'

'It seems that the killer made sure the bodies were all in the water around high tide. Fast running water, of course, makes recovering any forensic evidence extremely difficult. DNA, hairs and fibres - everything gets washed away.'

'Did they travel?' I said, swirling my glass, watching the way the liquid rocked from side to side. 'What I mean is - did the victims stay in the same place in the water until they were found?'

'I think so. Pamela's coat was hooked to a tree, but we can't be sure if that was accidental or if the killer deliberately made sure she wouldn't travel. My hunch is the latter.'

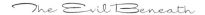

'Because he wanted to make sure I saw her...'

'The killer sent you to a specific spot at a designated time: Hammersmith Bridge at dawn. A body could travel considerable distance with the tides coming in and out, so we have to assume he wanted to make sure she stayed in place.'

I put down the chunk of garlic bread I'd broken off. My appetite seemed to have temporarily taken a walk around the block. 'What about Aysha and Lindsey...were they...hooked..?' I stopped. The word sounded degrading, insulting, as if they were inanimate objects.

'Aysha was embedded in the reeds in the bank at Richmond. Our experts think it would have taken a greater force than the tide to shift her. We can only assume the killer placed her there and knew she wouldn't travel.'

He pointed to the last piece of bread with a questioning look. I offered my palm to indicate he should take it. He seemed to have the remarkable ability to eat heartily while discussing the most unpalatable subjects. Probably years of practice at separating the two. 'Lindsey's shoelaces had been tied together and they were caught around a tree stump. Probably to do the same thing - keep her in the spot where he wanted her to be found.'

He took a sip of wine and rolled the stem between his fingers.

'And there's no pattern about the timings, other than they occur at high tide at whichever bridge he chooses?' I said.

He made a sucking sound with his lips. 'The dates aren't particularly remarkable, tidally speaking.' He ruffled his thick dark hair with his fingers. It looked soft and for a second I wondered what it would smell like. 'Basically, the killer has two choices of high tide every day, around six to seven hours apart. The tides shift by about half an hour each day, so, for example, a high tide at 2pm on one day, would fall at about 2.30pm, the next day. And there's a delay between the bridges.'

I was struggling to keep up with him

He sat back. 'High tide at London Bridge gets to Richmond Bridge an hour later. It's about a twenty-minute difference for Battersea and forty minutes for Hammersmith Bridge.' He stretched out his arms interlocking his fingers and making them crack. 'It tells us he's calculating and smart. He's not acting on impulse.'

'And he knows something about the Thames, the tides.'

'Exactly. So far, he's made sure the bodies get to the river at the time of high tide for whichever bridge he's chosen. Always undercover of dark - a night-time tide.'

'Is he a skipper on a riverboat, perhaps?'

'Or someone who works in the Port of London authority. Or the UK Hydrographic Office...or the Royal Navy. We have to look into every possibility.'

I sucked in air. 'What a nightmare.'

He sat forward and rested his elbows on the table. 'Shall we change the subject?'

'Yes, please. Ready for a supremely cooked chicken?'

It wasn't hard, this time, to find other things to talk about. He asked me about my training to become a psychotherapist and I asked about what he usually did on his weekends off. By then, I'd had several glasses of wine and he had switched to sparkling water. After the dessert, a tour de force lemon sponge (although I say so myself), we went back into the sitting room. I didn't want to offer him coffee. It would feel like I was introducing the end of the evening - and then he'd be on his way. I poured myself another top-up of Merlot.

After I turned off the spotlights and switched on the table lamp, I came up behind him. He was sitting with one ankle propped on the other knee. I caught sight of the triangle of bare flesh under the folds of his open collar and I wanted to touch it, explore it, feel the warmth of it. When you're no longer sober, moments when you notice a contour, a movement, a perfume, can become imbued with sexuality. The desire to touch can become instantly compelling. Before I knew it, I'd slipped my hands inside the top of his shirt and around his neck. He didn't move. I bent forward and gently nipped his ear lobe with my front teeth. Then he moved, but not in the way I was hoping for.

'Juliet, I really don't think...'

'I know, I'm sorry.' I withdrew my hands.

'You've had a lot to drink, you're vulnerable...'

I didn't want to hear the I-can't-take-advantage-of-you-in-this-state speech.

I moved away and switched the television on. It was half-way through the late news.

'Still friends?' he said.

'Of course,' I decided it was better for me not to sit next to him. I moved to the comfy chair.

The next item was about the case. It was everywhere. We couldn't escape it. A senior officer was explaining that there was no evidence of drug abuse linking the three women and that they came from very different backgrounds. I wondered what little Aysha Turner, a black teenager from a high-rise estate in Brixton, had in common with Pamela Mendosa, a rich American woman in her late twenties. Except, of course, the abortion clinic. None of the news' reports so far had mentioned the link all three women had to Fairways. Thankfully, they'd never mentioned me, either. I could do without a gang load of press hanging around my door. It was bad enough with my appointed minders.

'It makes us sound completely inept,' said Brad, staring at the screen.

Indeed, the item didn't come across brimming with confidence about the police finding the killer any time soon. It was more a desperate plea for someone to give themselves up.

I switched it off.

I could see he was upset.

'I feel so useless,' he said, banging his fist on the heel of his cowboy boot. 'We've interviewed sixteen hundred people already, asking when they last saw the women, where they worked, their backgrounds. All that. We've been through two thousand hours of CCTV footage around all three bridges, looking for a boat or a car that pulls up or anything unusual.'

'I hadn't realised how many people would be involved in something like this.'

'It's a massive operation, we've got about eight-hundred officers and staff on the case - and we've got this much.' He made a circle with his thumb and finger.

He plumped up a cushion and sank further down into my chair. Then he patted the space beside him.

'Listen, about before. It's not that I'm...not interested...' he said.

'It's okay. No need to explain.'

'The timing isn't right, that's all - you're tipsy and scared and right now, I fit the bill as your knight in shining armour. Just because I'm here...'

'It's fine. I got a bit overwhelmed. Brought my usual tough-cookie guard down for a few seconds, that's all.'

'Is that how you see yourself?'

'Look at that. Hard as steel.' I flexed my bicep and laughed.

He leant over and squeezed my arm in a let's-be-mates kind of way.

'You're lovely,' he said. I didn't know what to say to that.

Eventually we had coffee, I put some music on, we talked some more and by then it was getting very late.

The next thing I knew, there was a beam of light from the window trying to scorch a hole in my face. It was morning. I ran my tongue around sticky teeth and made several attempts to sit upright. I was on the sofa - and I wasn't alone.

Brad was curled up next to me. His mouth had dropped open and each breath caught at the back of his throat with a tiny tick. I had pins and needles in my arm and a hangover so fierce my head must have spent the night inside an industrial strength can-crusher, but I didn't care. I'd slept. For once, I felt like I'd actually had some sleep.

I tried to recall the way the evening had ending. I'd made us a hot drink, we'd had a Bailey's, we'd listened to music, he'd looked at his watch and said he'd have to go any minute - and then...nothing...it went blank after that. In the end I'd got exactly what I'd wanted. Not passion into the small hours, not earth-shattering sex, but the warmth of another body, another soul, who was almost as angry and frustrated as I was.

His eyelids fluttered and he moaned.

'What time is it?' he said.

I told him. He swore and grabbed his jacket.

'It's Sunday,' I reminded him.

'The case doesn't close, I'm afraid.'

At the door, he pressed a mobile phone into my hand.

'Police property, look after it.'

'No tap on this one?' I said.

He touched the side of his nose. 'Spot on, Doctor Watson.'

Then he was gone.

Jackie was loitering in the hall with a coy smile on her face when I went to check if there was any mail.

'New man?' she said.

'Er...no, not really.'

'Not over that other guy yet?'

I wanted to tell her it was none of her business, but unfortunately I'd gone and made most of it her business during the last few weeks.

'Is there anything more about him? After the police discovered his GBH record?'

'They haven't arrested him, if that's what you mean.'

She grabbed hold of my wrist and pulled me inside her flat, insisting on making me a cup of tea. I shouldn't have done, but I filled her in on the latest about the murders. In spite of her wary approach at the beginning, the whole business had piqued her interest and she wanted to know every detail. Tragedy is exciting when it is happening to someone else. Although I knew her reasons were morbid, I was glad to have her on hand as a make-shift confidante. At least she asked sensible questions and didn't look the type to go gossiping about it as soon as I'd gone.

'Apparently, Andrew was playing at a local golf club and someone ran a buggy over his foot,' I explained. 'He'd been drinking. He lashed out at the driver and broke his nose, his wrist and three ribs. The guy also had lasting kidney damage. Andrew was inside for a year, but I haven't asked him about it. It was eight years ago, long before I met him. I'm not supposed to know and it's hardly something he's going to let slip, is it?'

'Do you think he's...involved with these killings?'

'No way. I just can't see it. What does he know about the tides?'

Jackie was staring into the fireplace. Tony must work all hours of the day and night. Since the incident with the burglar, I'd never seen any sign of him.

'But what about those nasty paintings you found and all the personal links to you that Andrew would know about?' she said.

'I can't see how Andrew would know the Richmond Bridge was widened in 1939. He doesn't even know what day his bins get collected. Besides, *he* was the one pushing me to call the police after the text messages.'

'Have they checked his alibis?'

'I don't know.' I was sure he'd be hot under the collar about the way the police were treating him. Raking over a past that might be murkier than it seemed.

'You should stay away from him.'

'I intend to, but if he wants to find me, it wouldn't be difficult.'

'Hard for anyone to try anything with Lara Croft and her gang on your tail.' She tipped her head towards the window.

'You noticed,' I said.

When I went back up to my flat, I thought again about my embarrassing encounter with Brad. It was all wrong. I was a gibbering wreck and I'd probably lost all my sense of judgement. Besides, I didn't have the energy for a relationship. No - it was a stupid mistake.

My thoughts drifted back to Andrew. Was it wishful thinking that he wasn't involved? How well did I really know him? A wave of nausea swept through my stomach as I reached to close the curtains, staring out into the shroud of darkness closing over the city. The charge of GBH had certainly been a shock, but how much more was lurking under the surface, yet to be discovered?

seventeen

The police station was a hive of activity when I turned up the following afternoon. Brad had left a message to say he wanted us to meet - check if there was anything we were missing.

I sat in the reception area, trying not to get in anyone's way, as men carrying diving equipment and two dog handlers with German shepherds came into the building. Operation Chicane must have been severely stretching resources. A door opened and I saw Brad's hand waving me through.

'Had the divers down again,' he said, 'by London Bridge.' A shot of adrenaline flew up my chest.

'False alarm,' he said. 'Thank goodness.'

The incident room had so many desks it was difficult to find floor space to weave our way through. We approached a white board at the end with three photographs at the top. Written underneath in black pen, were the names of the three victims, together with their dates of birth. Lines radiating out from the pictures reached other words: the names of the bridges and the times and dates when the bodies were found.

Then I came across the list of objects found on the bodies and saw my own name, up there with the rest. I felt my knees go to jelly and stumbled. I pretended I'd nearly tripped over a box of envelopes, but Brad wasn't taken in. He was standing behind me and knew I couldn't take my eyes away from the board. I felt a subtle nudge in my back that was either an expression of concern or a shove to keep me moving.

We reached his office and he shut the door behind me.

'I thought it would be helpful to get our heads together,' said Brad. 'I could do with some fresh input.'

'I wanted to apologise again,' I said, looking away, 'for last night.'

'Me too.' I wasn't sure what he meant. Sorry it had happened? Sorry about the way he reacted? I wanted to ask more, but he pulled out a batch of files and cleared his throat to indicate the matter was closed.

He offered me a seat and was talking before I sat down.

'Studies show that a high percentage of serial killers live within an "offence circle",' he said. 'That is, their home is at the centre of the attacks. But, the area's too wide - Richmond, Hammersmith and Battersea.'

'Only about half of south London,' I said.

He sat back and looked like he was waiting for me to be the one doing the enlightening, not the other way around.

Silence. 'Anything more from a profiling point of view?' he said, eventually.

I glanced at my notes, switched into professional-speak. 'There seems to be no violence in the three cases, other than strangulation, which was quick and precise.'

Brad rocked in his chair, mulling it over. 'The killer wants the women dead, he doesn't want to torture them,' he concluded.

'Yeah. It would seem that the killer gets no pleasure in taunting the victim through aggression or pain. There are no defence wounds, no tissue under the finger nails - and I understand the river wouldn't necessarily wash away material if it was trapped.'

He nodded. 'If the murders were so straightforward, perhaps the killer wasn't new to strangulation,' he suggested. 'Maybe, he'd had practice in another context.'

'Like someone who works in an abattoir, perhaps? Or a game-keeper, a farmer, a poacher?'

'Someone who knows how to kill an animal and has no qualms about moving up the evolutionary chain?'

'Or even someone used to working with dead bodies? A mortuary assistant? A pathologist?' I suggested. 'And because there's no apparent sadism and he doesn't appear to enjoy the killing itself, it suggests it could be for a higher purpose, such as retribution, revenge, making a point. I get the strong feeling it's not *personal* - not about the individual victims themselves.'

He narrowed his eyes. 'But it's personal about *you*,' he said.

'Yes, but, the victims themselves are incidental. I think it's more about what they represent. In this case, the abortions are a likely motive. Apart from the link to Fairways Clinic, the only other thing I can see those women had in common was a small frame.'

He read his notes. 'Pamela, the American, weighed under eight stone. Aysha Turner was five foot and underweight. Lindsey was four foot eleven.'

As he spoke, I remembered seeing Aysha's body on the trolley at the mortuary. She'd looked like a doll. I remembered the photos on the incident board - Pamela and Lindsey, in spite of their womanly curves, were both tiny. Suddenly, there was a nasty taste in my mouth. I didn't want to dwell on the fact that I was the same build - Pamela had been wearing my clothes, after all.

'The point being,' he said, 'that the women could be easily lifted and carried.'

There was a sharp rap on the door and a young WPC came in with a tray of coffee and biscuits. She laid it in the middle of Brad's desk and asked if there was anything else we wanted.

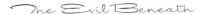

It seemed wrong to be indulging ourselves; drooling over chocolate-chip cookies while discussing the final horrible moments of people's lives. I saw Brad consider taking one, but I think he must have come to the same conclusion I did.

'What about the connections with the river?' he asked. 'Anything there?'

'He seems to know the river well,' I said. 'He could have had access to tide tables - perhaps works in that field. I agree that he made sure they stayed in one place in the water. He wanted them to be found at those exact points by the bridges.'

'It's very specific...' He was rattling a pencil between his teeth.

'The bridges have some significance for him. I'm sure of it.'

He was sitting forward looking like he was poised for the good news. I didn't want to tell him there wasn't any.

'And because there's no sexual angle, you reckon he's sexually competent, perhaps married or with a partner?' he mused.

'Possibly your average family man with kids,' I said, with distaste.

'You're right - there is often an everyday ordinariness about serial killers; they don't always stick out like a sore thumb.' He turned to his notes. 'There was a spate of railway murders in Bradford in the mid-eighties.' He grimaced. 'One of the two killers, John Weston, was married with three children.'

I shuddered. I tried to imagine being the wife of someone like that; bringing up three kids together and never knowing that your husband was capable of such despicable acts. You share a pizza, bath the kids and then he pops out with his mate and strangles someone.

He looked at his watch and I knew there was nothing else.

'We're on the look-out for someone who claims to want to help,' he said, as he walked me back to the main entrance. 'The SIO thinks, like you, that these crimes have all the hallmarks of someone who needs to be appreciated, someone who wants to know first-hand how the case is going, who wants to revel in the ingenuity of his crimes.'

He turned to me and looked like he was going to scoop my hands in his, but changed his mind. 'Thanks for coming.'

'I'm sure I'll be back,' I said, without relish.

I left him to his next meeting and made my way home.

Nothing happened for the next two weeks and it was a welcome reprieve. I wondered if maybe it was all over. Perhaps the killer had finished what he had set out to do; perhaps he'd had a car accident and was lying immobile in intensive care or had fled to the south of France. I didn't care, I was just glad to walk out of the flat without that heavy feeling of dread about what might happen that day. I'd even started to switch on the evening news without getting a lump in my throat every time. I'd stopped looking out for an unmarked police car. I wasn't sure if anyone was still tailing me or not.

Brad kept me up to date with the case, but there wasn't a lot to report. No DNA had come to light. A few fibres had been isolated, but nothing to match them with. He hadn't turned up at my door and we hadn't been on another date. I put it down to him being too busy, but maybe I was kidding myself.

I returned to Fairways and carried on with clients at home although Brad suggested it would be wise not to take on any new people for the time being. None of us wanted any more nasty surprises. No weird messages had turned up on my phone or email. Things felt like they were almost getting back to normal.

Brad rang one night as I was getting ready for bed.

'Sorry, I haven't been in touch, lately,' he said.

'It's okay. It's good in a way, means nothing awful has happened.'

'We're still in the thick of it.'

'Anything useful? Any suspects?'

'We've got an ID on the man who was aggressive towards you at the demonstration.'

'And?'

'His name is Reginald McGuire. Ring any bells?'

I thought for a moment. 'No. Why would he have been at Andrew's presentation?'

'Perhaps they knew each other. We haven't found the guy yet.'

'Andrew said he didn't know him...but...' I tried to recall Andrew's response when I'd asked him if he knew the man. He'd sounded sincere in his denial, but there'd been so much going on, I hadn't been scrutinising his face. His lies had fooled me before.

'Anything else?'

'There's Andrew.' His voice sounded grave and I didn't know if I wanted to hear what he had to say next. 'We've questioned him. He doesn't have strong alibis. He doesn't own a car, but that doesn't mean he couldn't have borrowed or hired one.'

'What will you do?'

'There's no DNA. We've checked his flat and there are no fibres that match the ones we found.'

'Good.'

'We've started a painstaking examination of the victims' hair. Lots of debris from the river was caught up in their hair, of course, but someone had to get pretty close to strangle them. Maybe, just maybe, they left behind a tiny piece of evidence. We're going through every microscopic fibre. If there's a match to Andrew Wishbourne's clothes, or anything at his flat - we'll have him.'

I stared at the phone as if it had just bitten me. 'Do you really think it's him?'

'It's got to be somebody. Like we said before, the perpetrator could be an ordinary, everyday guy.'

I thought back to the morning I'd rung Andrew from Hammersmith Bridge and dragged him out of bed. He'd seemed genuinely shocked by what had happened. He didn't seem to be play-acting. I would have known. I know I would.

'I don't think it's him. It can't be. He doesn't know anything about bridges or the tides...'

I got into bed and wrapped the duvet around me with my free hand. I didn't want to discuss it any-more. I just wanted to go to sleep. For a long time.

'You didn't know he played golf...or had been inside for a year...'

'It's not him. I know it isn't.' I couldn't talk to him anymore. 'Sorry, I've got to go,' I said, disconnect-ing the line before he could utter another word. I switched off the volume altogether. I didn't want to talk to anyone any more. I'd had enough.

All my sensible brain cells were telling me it was a bad idea, but the following evening I had to go back to Notting Hill.

Andrew's lights were on and as I got closer, I was desperately trying to work out what I was going to say. He opened the door with a tea-towel in his hand.

'This is unexpected,' he said, 'and rather late.'

He turned away, but left the door open.

The Killers were playing. The irony of it didn't pass me by. I hoped he didn't have company.

'Is this a social call?' he said.

'I've been speaking to the police,' I said.

'Are you a suspect, too?' he snorted.

Andrew moved a pile of books from the sofa and I sat down. I looked around for a half-filled glass or bottle of whisky, but I couldn't see one.

'Coffee?' he said.

When he left the room, I stayed where I was, tempting as it was to look again for more mysterious pictures like I'd discovered last time. He handed me a mug and put his own on the floor. He caught me staring at the pot of coffee. 'I'm on the wagon,' he said.

'How long?'

'Couple of weeks. Actually, thirteen days and...' he glanced up at the clock on the wall, 'six hours.'

'That's really good.' I felt genuinely heartened. At least I knew which Andrew I would be conversing with tonight.

'The police gave me a grilling about the three deaths under the bridges.'

'I know.'

'I don't have watertight alibis, as far as they're concerned.' I was tempted to ask him exactly what his alibis consisted of, but that would have made me sound suspicious, too. 'What do I know about how fast the Thames flows?'

'Is that what they asked you?'

'I said I'd painted the river. They wanted to see the pictures. They searched my flat. Bloody nerve. Raking over my past like I'm some piece of rotting meat.' He got up and pulled out a stack of canvases. 'I don't think you've seen these,' he said.

I hoped my cheeks didn't give me away.

'Are they the ones you said weren't for sale?'

'Yeah. They weren't finished.'

He turned the first one round. I recognised the background as being one of the dark, unsettling paintings I'd found with disturbing titles. But there was something different about it, now. Andrew had added detail at the front; reeds and trees and the light had been changed. He'd lifted the colours at the back and added a sunrise. There was a water-vole tucked behind a log. It was an entirely new picture. Nothing sinister about it at all.

'It's...lovely,' I said. 'It's very different from your usual style.'

'Grant, you know, my mate at the gallery, said there might be some scenic work going in the West

End. They're doing Wind in the Willows. I wanted to see what I could do.'

'Did you give it a title?' I asked, knowing the title I'd seen had nothing remotely pastoral about it.

He flipped it over. 'I originally called it "Stranger on the riverbed",' he said, 'but now it's "All along the Backwater".' He laughed. 'I hate compromising my style, but I need the work, Jules.'

'The original title is a bit gruesome,' I said, tentatively.

'I was drunk when I did the first version. I was feeling pretty shitty after we'd broken up.' He stared at the coffee in his mug. 'To tell you the truth, I was a tad on the suicidal side.'

'Oh, God,' I said.

He ran a finger along my thigh. 'It's okay. I'm all right now. I'm off the booze, for a start.'

I didn't want to turn this into a counselling session. 'What about the others?'

He pulled out the remaining canvases from the stack. They'd all been transformed into idyllic waterside scenes with titles to match.

'The painting, the nude that won the award...' I said, trying to shift the mood. 'It was a terrific painting. I'm very flattered, but you should have asked my permission...and you should have warned me.'

He picked at a shred of paint under his thumbnail.

'Is that why you've come? To give me a bollocking?'

I shrugged. I couldn't tell him I'd come to check out his reaction about the sinister paintings; to run my own 'tests' about whether I thought he was lying about the murders.

As I finished my coffee, I weighed up what I knew. He'd altered the paintings, but had he done so because he knew they might incriminate him? Except, why tell me the original title? He didn't need to do that. He didn't know I'd seen the earlier versions; he could have claimed they'd never been anything other than picturesque tableaux.

Ultimately, however, one fundamental factor swung it for me. If I was a murderer and the police were closing their net around me, I wouldn't be on the wagon. I'd be even more dependent on alcohol to stave off the fear of being found out. I could tell from his skin and his eyes that Andrew had been off the drink for days. That didn't ring true for someone with a string of killings to hide.

'The portrait wasn't designed to win you back, if that's what you're thinking,' he said. I wasn't sure if he was joking or not. 'Listen, I've got work to do.' It didn't sound like an apology was forthcoming. He stood and picked up my mug.

'I know it isn't you,' I said.

'Sorry?'

'Who attacked those women and–'

'Thanks for the vote of confidence.' His flat tone wasn't without irony.

'I'm really glad you're not drinking. It makes a big difference.'

'I'm doing it for me,' he said, as he held open the front door.

'That's brilliant. That's the very best reason.' I swiftly planted a kiss on his cheek and left.

When my phone rang the next evening, I recognised the number as my parents' in Spain. My mother's voice was aiming for bright and breezy but didn't quite make it.

'What's wrong?' I asked.

'Tony was speaking to his friend, Ricardo, today. He'd seen an English newspaper report about some awful...murders in London.'

'I wondered if you might hear about it.' I couldn't believe it had taken them this long.

'Why didn't you tell us? You know we don't often look at the English papers over here.'

'There's not much to tell.' I didn't want to worry them. They'd been through so much with Luke, I didn't want them to be fearful about their one remaining child.

'The papers said the murders were by the Thames, not so far from where you live.'

'Yes, but, the police think the murders were linked to abortions, Mum. The women had been in the early stages of pregnancy. They're not just random killings. You mustn't tell anyone that.'

I cringed at slightly bending the truth, but my heart was in the right place.

'Your father wants us to come over.'

'What for?'

'Just to make sure everything is all right.'

I knew this meant she would want to check up on my life-style; who I was hanging out with and whether I had a boyfriend. She'd want to make sure I had better locks everywhere. Probably even suggest a burglar alarm. I'd end up having to make promises, like never going out on my own after dark, always catching a taxi instead of waiting at bus-stops, making sure someone always knew where I was. That sort of thing. There was so much about my life she didn't know about. Like Andrew (and his criminal record) and Brad. Like my work at Fairways.

Like my personal connection with each of the murders.

'There really is no need,' I said. 'Let me speak to Dad.'

As soon as she passed over the phone, I knew she, not Dad, was the one with the idea about coming over. Dad and I agreed that he should spend the next few days trying to convince Mum that travelling half-way across Europe wasn't going to help protect their daughter any better than she could protect herself.

As soon as I put down the phone, the mobile on loan from Brad broke into a rendition of *Cagney and Lacey*. It was the first time it had rung and took me by surprise.

'Hi,' said Brad.

'Did you choose the ring-tone on this phone?' I said, laughing.

'Is that a crime?'

'It's superb. I like it.'

'You okay?'

'I'm really sorry I was rude - the other night when you rang. I think I'd reached tipping point.'

'No problem. It can't be easy when someone you know is a suspect,' he said. 'Any chance we could get together?'

'To talk about Andrew?' My stomach reacted as if I was in a lift and it had suddenly dropped a couple of floors.

'Not really - for an up-date.'

For one second I thought he said *date*, instead of *up-date*.

'Have you got any news about the fire?'

'Not much. A few things to tell you about the case, too.'

'Okay. When and where?'

'I thought a takeaway pizza...tonight, your place, if that's not too presumptuous.'

'I'll need to ring and cancel Orlando Bloom,' I said, 'but I'm sure he'll be fine about it.'

'Who?'

I didn't bother to answer.

'See you later.'

eighteen

'How did you know gerbera were my favourites?' I said.

'I'm a detective.'

I went into the kitchen for a vase. Brad had brought the pizzas with him that Sunday evening, together with a bottle of wine and a bunch of flowers. That's what I call pushing the boat out.

I brought the orange flowers through and put them on the table. 'Seriously. They're lovely, but not an obvious choice.'

He walked to the wall and pointed to a photograph. It was taken on my twenty-first birthday and in the background was a vase with the very same flowers.

'Observant, or what?' I said.

'When was this?' he said, pointing to a photograph of Oxford winning the boat race.

'That's Chiswick Bridge - 2008.'

'Ever done any rowing?'

'Not really. Went to the Lake District once, down some rapids. Bad experience, actually.'

'That will need to go in my notebook. Tell me about it later.' He was staring at the pizza boxes.

'What about you?' I said.

'Nah. Can't swim. Never been tempted, but my brother used to row at University.'

It was nice to hear Brad wasn't good at something for a change. Not that he was arrogant, just that he had air of all-round competence about him that was a tad unnerving. Failings brought him down to my level.

We opened up the pizzas. Brad tucked straight in. Probably his first proper meal of the day. When he stopped for a breather, I asked him about the news he had for me.

'It's not great,' he said. 'I got the fire reports sent through from 1990 and frankly, they're messy and incomplete.'

'What does that mean?'

'Shortly after the fire at your house, a large warehouse went up on the outskirts of Norwich. All resources were temporarily diverted to that and it looks like your fire got sidelined due to lack of fresh evidence. There were gaps left in the report. It's inconclusive. I'm really sorry.'

I felt my body sink. I'd had a lot of hope pinned on this. I wasn't sure there was anywhere else to look to get to the truth.

'Thanks for trying,' I said. 'Am I allowed to see what you've got?'

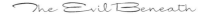

'No,' he said, with his mouth full. 'I shouldn't even have got hold of the report.'

'There must be something in the files that can shed light on the cause of the fire; to indicate whether it was deliberate or not?'

He reluctantly pulled out a manila file from his rucksack.

'Can I accidentally photocopy that?' I said.

'No way.' He held it behind his chair out of arms reach. 'There's no mention of windows been open, but there is reference to the fire spreading quicker than expected. It says there were signs of flammable substances in the kitchen.'

I was on my feet. 'Like petrol, you mean?'

'Hang on a minute,' he said, flapping his hands to get me to sit down.

'It doesn't mean it was arson. There are lots of everyday substances kept in the home that could accelerate a fire or explode. Camping gas and fire-starters for barbeques...butane, propane...even aerosols, paint-thinners, nail-varnish...'

'I see what you mean.' I was trying to picture our old kitchen, travelling with my minds-eye along the shelves and inside cupboards, to get a feel for what we used to keep there. I could see boxes of washing powder under the sink, bleach, fabric softener and a cupboard where Dad kept the odd can of paint, brushes, cloths, perhaps a bottle of white spirit. Not much that would accelerate a fire, in my view.

'Two cooker rings had been left on,' he said. 'Looks like a tea-towel may have been left on the rings.'

'What?'

I leant over and this time he let me see the typed report. I read the section he was referring to.

'That doesn't sound like my mother at all. I can't imagine her *ever* leaving a tea-towel on top of the cooker.'

'It might not have been her.'

'I can't see any of us doing it, either. Mum was really strict about that sort of thing. I grew up being overly cautious about dangers in the kitchen, switching things off...electricity...'

He squeezed his lips together in an expression that said: people make mistakes.

'The report mentions a power-cut,' he said.

'Yes - that rings true with other people I've spoken to. It's why we left the house and went to the cinema.'

'It's easy when there's a power-cut to forget that appliances have been left in the "on" position. Maybe your mother had been cooking before the electricity went off and in the confusion, forgot to switch off the rings.'

He was right, of course. Maybe, for once, my mother hadn't been so careful. There was also another explanation.

'It might have been someone else,' I said. Air made a hissing sound against my teeth, as I drew a breath. 'The same person who left the windows open...to fan the flames...'

'Deliberate, you mean?'

I nodded.

'It's a possibility.' He tapped the pages. 'No more information was added to the report. No more details about the flammable substances or the cause of the power-cut.'

'Can the investigation be re-opened?'

'Not without some concrete new evidence. It's nearly twenty years ago.'

'My Aunt Libby said it started with the toaster,' I muttered, mostly to myself.

He closed the file. 'I'm sorry. I feel responsible, somehow. We've let you down. The investigation should never have been left like that.'

I poured another glass of wine and I tried to put my niggling concerns about the fire out of my head. After all, Luke was gone. Nothing we discovered now would bring him back. We moved in the sitting room and I put on a CD of film music by Ennio Morricone.

This is snazzy,' he said, twisting his mouth to one side. His tone was seductive; deliberately so, I thought. This man was teasing me. I leant over the back of the sofa.

'I've got a blow-up mattress,' I said. 'You can stay, if you like.' I knew he'd already drunk too much wine to drive himself home and he knew it too.

He yawned loudly. 'Sounds dangerous.'

'It's more comfortable than the sofa - trust me.'

He stretched and slid to the front of the seat. 'That would be great - sure you don't mind?' he said.

I switched up the lighting and rubbed my hands together.

'One pillow or two?' I'd also switched off the flirting and gone into practical mode. I wanted to make the boundaries clear. I didn't want him to think there was any other offer tonight. Not because I didn't want to invite him into my bed, but because I didn't want to do anything we'd regret later. Especially after last time. Things were going too well for that. If the occasion eventually presented itself sometime, it would be when neither of us were too drunk or too tired to think straight.

As I handed him a glass of water, I asked him what time he needed to be up in the morning.

'I've got an eight o'clock briefing on the case. I'll try not to wake you. Have you got a spare alarm clock? I'm not sure I can trust my watch.'

I went to fetch a small spare clock from the kitchen. Once the bed was inflated, he sat on it, testing the tension with a couple of bounces.

'I don't want to find you using this as a trampoline in the early hours,' I said, wagging my finger at him.

'Spoil sport,' he said, stroking the duvet. 'I haven't slept on one of these since Dave Rockman's eighteenth birthday. We were stuck in a caravan in South Shields.'

'A story for another time, perhaps,' I said, heading for the bathroom.

When I crossed back through the sitting room we both said a prim *goodnight* to each other, but I didn't fail to see the knowing glint in his eye. It was as if we both knew things would change between us, soon enough, and tonight was a necessary part of the game we were playing. I closed the door of my bedroom with a sigh.

I'd set my alarm early too, because I didn't want to wake up with that empty deflated feeling knowing he'd gone. Besides, I wanted to know what he looked like over a bowl of cornflakes.

At 6.45am, I pulled on a thick towelling dressing gown and crept into the darkened sitting room, edging past the crumpled mass on the floor, trying not to look too closely. What I really wanted to do was stand over him and watch him sleeping, see how his face fell when it was relaxed, hear the kinds of sounds he made when he was breathing deeply, but I didn't want to risk being caught.

All that was visible above the duvet was a bundle of dark hair, as if a small kitten was curled up on the pillow, but the room was thick with the woody, musky smell of him. I used the bathroom as quietly as I could and came back to find his bare arms outside the duvet and his eyes open.

'Morning,' I said, cheerily. 'Coffee, tea?'

He squinted. 'Black coffee would be great,' he said, his voice gravel-like with sleep.

I opened the curtains a little and went into the kitchen. When I came back, he was already dressed and was folding away the bedding.

'House-trained too,' I said. 'Very impressive.'

'It's all show, actually. My flat is in a terrible state.'

He sat at the dining table and I brought out coffee, cereal and several slices of thick toast. He helped himself to lashings of marmalade on granary followed by a large bowl of cereal. Only then did he sit back and look at me. I felt self-conscious in my dressing gown when he was already fully dressed, but at least I'd brushed my hair.

'Thank you,' he said, rubbing his abdomen. 'That was just right.'

'You don't normally have breakfast, do you?'

'How did you work that one out?'

I laughed. 'I'm a psychotherapist, don't forget.'

'Now I feel like I'm under a microscope,' he said. He suddenly got up and bobbed down to look in the mirror beside the kitchen door.

'Sorry - I didn't bring a comb,' he said, trying to flatten his unruly hair with his hands. 'I'd better get going.'

I took the dishes into the kitchen as he gathered up his jacket and car-keys. When I returned, he was leaning against the back of the sofa with his legs crossed at the ankle.

'Your clock's fast,' he said. 'I've got a couple more minutes.'

'What will the briefing be about?'

'New evidence...didn't I tell you?'

'No...'

'You remember we were getting a special team in to sift through every possible fibre caught up in the victims' hair?'

I nodded.

'Most of it - and there was about five pounds worth of twigs, reeds, dead fish, shells, that kind of thing - belongs to the river,' he said. 'But, they've isolated some tiny fibres - PEVA - polyethylene vinyl acetate, to be precise, from Aysha's hair. It's found in lots of things - ski-boots, fishing rods, shower curtains. And, they've picked up something we've identified as a polymer wax with PTFE, from Lindsey's.'

'What's that?'

'Polytetrafluoroethylene,' he said, articulating every syllable, like a child learning a new language. 'I only remember it, because I was explaining it to the guys yesterday. It's a waxy substance and the original properties stay the same, even after it's been in water.'

'What's it used for?'

'It's in a number of products, but it's often used in car polish - although, we've got nothing to match it with, yet.'

'Car polish...well, that's something.'

'We need an absolute match. Could be the women got it in their hair, if they were pushed against the side of a car - or from the floor of a garage or shed.'

'This business of matching evidence sounds incredibly hit and miss. I'm surprised anyone ever gets put behind bars - not unless you actually catch a criminal in the act.'

He yawned. 'It's tedious and time-consuming.' He checked his watch and I knew it was time to go. As he got to the door, he turned. 'We got Charles Fin in again.' 'Mr Fin? Why?'

'We had a query over one of his alibis. Said he was with his mother for all three dates, but his neighbour said she was in hospital.'

'His mother?' I said, rubbing my temples. 'I'm sure he told me his mother had died. Not that long ago, I think. Hold on.'

I rushed to find my counselling notes. Flipping through the pages, I found Mr Fin's file and pulled out the sheets.

'Yes, here it is,' I said. 'He said his mother had told him to "play hard and tough" if he wanted to attract women.'

'Did she now?' He folded his arms and smiled at the floor.

'Then he said she'd passed away.' I ran my finger down to the spot on the page. 'He didn't say when.'

'Something weird going on there, then.'

'Mr Fin certainly drives a car,' I said, as Brad opened the flat door. 'When I saw him at the park, he was getting into it.'

He turned back, keeping his eyes lowered.

'Andrew isn't ruled out yet,' he said evenly. 'Still no alibis.'

'Andrew is so vague about everything. He probably *does* have decent alibis, he just hasn't thought it through. Surely, he's a million miles away from the right profile. He's too scatty and disorganised. He can only just about turn up on the right night for his prize-giving ceremony.'

'It's not just Andrew, we're interviewing more people connected with the demonstration and anti-abortion groups.' He tapped his watch. 'Got to go.'

He gave me a quick wave and left.

I suddenly realised I'd been playing at being bright and breezy and now I was alone, tiredness made my body slump. I was tempted to go back to bed. I slipped off the dressing gown, slid under the duvet and was about to close my eyes when something we'd just talked about started niggling at me, like a finger prodding at my shoulder. Phrases began replaying in my mind like a stuck record. Then it hit me. I kicked off the duvet and reached for my private phone; the one Brad had lent me that wasn't tapped.

'Why didn't you tell them?' I said.

'I don't know. They didn't ask directly.' Andrew's voice was slow with sleep, but he didn't sound like he had a hangover.

'I'm going to tell the police. It's not fair them hounding you.'

'Do what you like, Jules, I'm going back to sleep.'

I knew Brad was probably in the car on his way to the briefing, but at least I could leave a message. Ten minutes later, the *Cagney and Lacey* theme burst through the silence.

'I realised something important after you left,' I said.

'Go ahead.' I could hear the jangle of phones ringing in the background.

'Andrew can't drive.'

'Okay...'

'Well, it can't be him, can it? He hasn't got a car. *And*, he doesn't drive.'

'Yeah - but it doesn't mean he wasn't with someone who does. There could be two people in this together.'

I heard my voice fall flat. 'I hadn't thought of that.' There was an awkward hiatus. 'There's something else,' I said, tightly. 'You said the footprint you found at one of the bridges had no tread - so it can't be Andrew. He lives in trainers. Even used to try and sleep in them.'

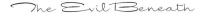

He didn't sound convinced.

I sat on the edge of the bed and considered the fact that Charles Fin and Andrew were both back in the picture. In my view, neither of them fitted the profile which meant one thing. The real killer was still out there and the police hadn't got anywhere near him.

nineteen

When I saw the first name on my list of appointments that day, it sapped what little get-up-and-go I had left. The sessions with Lynn Jessop weren't going anywhere and I was tempted to consider bringing them to a close.

True to form, Lynn launched into another diatribe about how bad the week had been and how upset she was about Billy, before I'd even closed the door. Maybe the most useful part for her was being able to off-load. Sometimes that was enough for people, especially when they'd exhausted all their friends, having repeated the same woes, time and time again. Not that Lynn seemed to have many friends. Strange woman.

Since our last session, I'd done some homework and consulted Richard, my supervisor. He'd been overseeing my work at Holistica since I came to London and I trusted him completely. Every therapist has to have a supervisor, no matter how experienced you are, but Richard never met my clients.

He was an invisible presence overseeing my work; a gate-keeper, a third eye making sure I was working ethically and not missing anything obvious.

He told me more about *Münchausen by proxy*: a syndrome whereby an adult carer fabricates symptoms or actually causes harm to their child in order to convince others, including medical practitioners, that their child needs medical intervention. He explained how the behaviour was designed to gain sympathy and often a sense of empowerment at maintaining the deception. He warned me that Lynn could be abusing Billy as part of the condition. If that was the case, Lynn's GP and social services would have to be involved immediately.

Richard advised me to start suggesting to Lynn that we might need to get other professionals on board and if she refused, the last resort was to breach confidentiality and speak to her GP. In line with common practice, I'd taken down her doctor's details when we started our sessions, so I knew where to start. I just wasn't sure yet if I was dealing with compulsive lying, *Münchausen by proxy* or whether Lynn, in her distress, had simply got her dates mixed up. It was too soon to say and Richard advised me to tread carefully.

Lynn was still waving her arms around, spittle forming at the corner of her mouth as she ranted about the latest episode of Billy's bullying.

'I wondered if you had a photograph of Billy, Lynn. I'd like to get more of a sense of him. Perhaps something in your purse?'

She folded her arms and looked wary. Richard had suggested Lynn's response might indicate whether Billy actually existed or not. At least we could start ruling things out.

'Why?' She narrowed her eyes.

'To see who he is. Feel a bit closer to him. A school photo, perhaps?'

'You won't take them away?'

'No. Of course not.'

She reached down to her bag and pulled out a folder. She tipped it out and a bundle of pictures spilled on to the low table between us. I tried not to look surprised.

'How many do you want?'

I leaned forward and shuffled through them, handling them carefully, respectfully. There must have been about twenty photographs, many of Lynn holding or standing beside a young boy, others of the boy on his own, at different stages from baby age upwards.

'This is a comprehensive collection,' I said. 'Which one is the most recent?'

She moved straight to a six by four portrait showing the boy wearing a blazer and stripy school tie. 'This one was about two months ago,' she said. The boy had thin wispy hair just like Lynn's and looked awkward posing for the camera. He was averting his eyes away from the lens, but making a brave attempt at a smile. I thought I saw traces of Lynn's features in his broad nose, wide-set eyes, bulky chin.

'He looks proud, here,' I said, handing back the photo. 'When did the bullying start?'

'About six months ago,' she said. 'He's a good boy,' she added, as if I'd indicated otherwise. One thing was for sure. The boy existed and he certainly looked like he was Lynn's son. She had a full record of his life in pictures and as she was in so many of the shots herself, it was hard to imagine she'd got hold of pictures belonging to another family.

'Has Billy seen a doctor recently at all? About his injuries from the bullying?' I wanted to steer us towards the medical side of things. Find out if the boy was fit and well. He certainly looked okay in the latest photo. She sniffed as if I'd started talking about something offensive.

'He's fine.'

'Has he seen a doctor lately, Lynn? It's quite important.'

'Yes,' she snapped. She scooped the pictures possessively back into her folder. 'He had a bad throat a couple of weeks ago.'

'Would you mind if I had an informal chat with your GP? You gave me his details.' I was on the edge of my seat, again watching for her response. If she stalled at this point it could indicate she had something to hide.

She shrugged. 'Go ahead. Billy's mostly traumatised, scared, confused - he gets a few bruises, his school bag gets trashed, but he isn't injured or anything.'

'So, he's more psychologically affected, than physically?'

'Yes, but he's not unhinged. He's very bright and he's got a brilliant memory; he can tell you the half-time score of a football match played two years ago,' Lynn said. 'Unlike my daughter who'd forget her own name even if it was pinned to her t-shirt.'

'Your daughter?' This was new. I'd never heard Lynn mention a daughter before.

Lynn stiffened, as if she'd said something she wished she hadn't.

'Yes. I have her pictures in another folder.' She was about to reach for her bag again, but I put out my hand to stop her.

'Maybe next time,' I said. I couldn't help wondering why her daughter hadn't appeared in any of the other pictures she'd shown me. Perhaps this woman had a fixation on compartmentalising things. It would explain why she hadn't mentioned her daughter earlier.

'Angela. She's older.'

'And does Angela have any problems at all?'

She laughed in a mocking tone, but didn't answer.

Our time was up and when she stood up to leave, I had the beginnings of a pounding headache. She came towards me and rested her hand on my shoulder. For a woman who exuded no warmth whatsoever, it took me by surprise.

'You're looking tired, dear - having a bad week?' she said.

'Thanks. I'm fine,' I lied. I couldn't work out if she was being friendly or sarcastic.

Her hand lingered a moment. She muttered something about our sessions being helpful. Another thing I found hard to believe. In fact, nothing Lynn had said had dispelled the feeling that she'd led me into a complex maze and left me there not knowing which way to turn. It was hard to feel anything but depleted with an edgy sense of disquiet.

Jackie came up the path just as I was shutting the front door.

'I haven't seen you for a while,' she said. 'Have they arrested anyone?' I shook my head. 'No more messages, no more attacks?'

'No. Nothing.' I crossed all my fingers. 'I really hope it's over.'

'It won't be, you know, not until they catch him,' she said, turning away.

I sighed and returned upstairs.

The time had come. I took a deep breath and decided I'd put off phoning my parents long enough.

'Listen, I know it's painful digging up the past, but–'

'You have no idea what you're fooling around with, Juliet,' she said.

'I'm not fooling around, Mum.' For once, I wasn't going to back down. 'I've been looking into the fire and spoken to the neighbours...and the police–'

'The *police*?' She said the word the way most people say paedophile.

'There are unanswered questions. It might not have been an accident.'

'This is ridiculous.' I could hear the rubbery thud of water running into a washing-up bowl. 'I'm getting your father.' She said it as if I was five and would end up with a sore backside.

'What's going on?' His tone was tired, but gentle.

'I just want the truth, Dad. I've been looking into the fire again.'

'It's difficult for your mother.'

'I know, but I need to know. I think we all do.' He didn't say anything so I carried on. 'I managed to get hold of the original police report and there are serious questions. About why the fire spread so quickly and how it started. You remember I asked you over the phone if you'd left the windows open?'

'Yes, I remember. And I remember that night in great detail and I know for certain that I didn't open any. None of us did.'

'Mr Knightly from next door - he said the windows were open.'

'Did he?' I heard him take a wheezy breath. 'Just hold on a minute.'

A few quiet words were exchanged and then what sounded like a door was closed. He came back. 'There was a power-cut,' he said. 'We'd been over at Aunt Libby's that afternoon. Got back around sixish. Your mum was in the middle of cooking and everything went off: the lights, the kitchen appliances... the heating, too, as the gas boiler needed electricity to keep it going.' He sounded out of breath. 'I reset the trip switch, but it went off again, so I called the emergency number. They couldn't get anyone out to us until the next day. It was Luke's idea to go to the cinema - *Back to the Future*, I think it was.'

The words DeLorean and flux capacitor popped into my head. Yes - he was right.

'Your mother thinks it was all her fault. A police officer came to the house a few days after the fire and told us that a tea-towel had been left on the oven. He said that oven rings had been left on overnight and that it was the most likely cause.'

'That's what it said in the police report. Poor Mum.'

'She swears she didn't do it, but when the power goes off, you forget what's been left switched on...'

'It's an easy mistake - it explains why she's been so cagey about my enquiries.'

'She didn't want it to be common knowledge that it was her fault. She's felt bad enough as it is.' He paused. 'There's something, though, that she doesn't know...'

'What? Tell me.'

'Your mother needed to get away from the house for a few days, so she went to stay with Aunt Libby. The police came back when your mother was away and said they'd found traces of kerosene barbecue firelighters and camping stove fuel, both highly flammable substances, right beside the oven.'

'Really?' Cheryl's words leapt into my mind.

'I didn't put them there of course, but we certainly kept those substances...in the shed. I asked you at the time if you'd brought them into the kitchen for any reason.'

'I don't remember that.' I was trying to recall what it was like being twelve and having that dazed foggy feeling that hung around me after the fire.

'You said you hadn't.' I bit my lip. 'Luke and I had been hoping to take the campervan over to the Lake District for a few days. Crazy at that time of year, but Luke wanted to climb Scafell Pike in the snow...' There was a long gap and I wondered if he was fighting back tears. 'I didn't ever want Luke to be blamed, but he must have been the one who brought the flammable containers into the kitchen. Silly boy...' He blew his nose. 'I didn't ever tell your mother,' he said. 'She never knew.' He drew a sharp breath. 'You mustn't tell her. It would break her heart. She knows the facts point to the fire starting because of her absentmindedness. She doesn't need to know her son compounded it by leaving dangerous substances nearby.'

'I won't say anything.' I took a moment. 'But it still doesn't explain the open windows...'

'Mr Knightly must be a doddery old chap by now. He must have got it wrong.'

It wasn't only Mr Knightly, though, I thought. I didn't want to mention how convinced Cheryl had been about it. I wasn't sure that would hold any sway with my father.

I heard my mother's voice call him. 'Hold on...' he said.

I still wasn't convinced. Call it that sixth sense again, but it still didn't feel right. Mum was always so careful and Dad said she didn't remember leaving the cooker on or draping a tea-towel over it. The thing is, I'd never ever known her do such a thing. It's like suggesting that a resolute vegetarian popped into the butchers one morning for a tasty piece of steak.

No one knew for certain, either, whether it was Luke who had brought the containers in from the shed. Surely, Luke, even at sixteen, had more nous than to leave flammable substances by the oven?

When my father came back on the phone, I asked him one final question.

'Was the shed always kept locked?'

He took his time and that in itself was the answer I needed.

'Mostly,' he said. 'There was a padlock, but if I was going in and out a lot; getting tools, tidying up and so on, I used to leave the padlock in place, but not snap it shut. That day? I don't know.'

I heard his breathing quicken.

'What is it?' I said.

'Luke wasn't...he wasn't perfect...'

'No. Of course not.' He made a little whining sound. It made me think he wasn't simply making a general comment; he was referring to something specific. Was it about the fire? Was it about something else?

'What do you mean, Dad?'

'Luke...he...'

I waited. There was a crackle on the line.

'What did you say?' I said.

'It doesn't matter.'

I didn't move, hoping he'd change his mind, but he said his farewells and rang off. I didn't want to burden him by saying just how much I missed them both. Especially the familiar comfort of my father's hugs, the dusty smell of his pullovers. But, thinking about it then, I realised that more than that I missed how it used to be before Luke died. There was a deep gully carved in my mind separating the days with Luke and the days without him. Like two parallel motorways that could never join up. Two different lifetimes. When Luke suddenly left us, it stole a huge slice of my father's sense of fun and made my mother edgy and tight. I don't know how that happened. I did, though, know one thing for sure. I wasn't going to let this drop until I'd got to the bottom of it.

.

twenty

That evening, I was all ready to watch *Raiders of the Lost Ark*, with a dish of Twiglets on my left and a glass of Merlot on my right, when the phone rang. Blasted thing. I lifted the phone from the cradle and made my hello as polite as possible.

'10.48 on November 9th,' said a male voice.

'Hello? Sorry? Who is this?' The voice was unclear, distorted.

'10.48 on November 9th.'

A banging started in my chest like a steel demolition ball.

'Is this another murder?' I said. 'Where is it? Which bridge?'

The man repeated the same sentence in exactly the same tone, as if it was on a tape-loop. I ran over to my wall calendar. Today was November 8th, so the date the voice was referring to was tomorrow.

'Please tell me. Please...' I sank to the floor, clutching the phone like it was the most precious thing I'd ever held. 'Don't go...'

There was nothing coming back to me except a faint roaring in the background. Interference? Traffic?

'Hello?' I said again, my voice struggling to get past the lump of concrete in my throat.

'10.48 on November 9th.'

That was it. The phone went dead. I laid on the carpet in the foetal position, holding the receiver to my chest. My sleeve was wet and it took me a while to realise I was crying. I was paralysed with fear and indecision. Then the phone rang again and I thought I might have a second chance.

'Detective Inspector McKinery here, Ms Grey. We heard the call come through. Are you okay?'

'Yes, I'm fine,' I lied, getting up from the floor.

'We've got it on tape and we're tracing the call. We're getting an officer over to you now. Did you recognise the voice at all?'

'No. I don't think so.'

'The officer will bring over a recording of it, so you can listen to it again,' he said. Lucky me, I thought. 'DS Broxted will be with you shortly.'

Why couldn't it be DCI Madison, the terrified five-year-old in me wanted to ask, but the DI had rung off.

By the time the doorbell rang, my head was already spinning with ideas. I'd switched on my laptop, but didn't know where to start. If this was a clue to another bridge it was damned obscure.

DS Broxted came in holding out a USB stick, as if he was offering me a cigarette. I slotted it into my laptop and we heard the recording of the phone call. We both agreed that the man's voice was muffled as though he'd held a cloth over the mouthpiece. The voice was stilted like he was reading it.

'We're getting straight on to the bridge expert,' said the DS, tucking the tail-end of his tie into his waistband for the third time. It was too short and it wasn't going to stay put, but he kept trying anyway.

'There's not much to go on, though, is there?' I said. 'It's the first time we've had a date, but there's no bridge, no location.'

'I'm taking over outside for the night shift, by the way. In the brown Volvo. Just in case.'

Just in case it's *me*, you mean, I wanted to say. *Me*, who is going to come to a nasty end at 10.48 tomorrow morning. I had a sudden thought.

'Is it 10.48 in the morning or evening?' I said, staring at DS Broxted. After all, he was trained in these things and should know. He opened his hands and flapped them about. I think he was trying to indicate he didn't have a clue. He used the loo, then left to spend a cold night with a fellow officer outside on the street. I didn't even contemplate inviting them to stay in the flat. I had things I needed to do.

First off, I rang Cheryl.

'I know it's late, but I've got something really important to ask you.'

'Juliet?' she said. I hadn't bothered to introduce myself.

'Can you come over. I live in Fulham. I'll pay for a taxi. Someone's life is in danger.'

'It's nearly 9pm.'

'I wouldn't ask if it wasn't urgent.'

I think she could tell by the resolve in my voice that I wasn't messing around.

'Give me the address.'

While I waited for her, I paced up and down the sitting room trying to get inside the killer's head. The previous communications I'd had from him had all given some clue as to where the murders were to take place. The text telling me to go to Hammersmith Bridge, the text with the measurements pointing to Richmond Bridge and the email with the old etching of Battersea Bridge. They were all bridges. Was this clue referring to another bridge? Or was it a departure from the other messages? Was he telling us *when*, instead of where? And if so, what use was that to anybody? We didn't even know if he meant morning or evening. I was starting to wear a groove into the carpet, when the doorbell rang.

Cheryl was standing beside DS Broxted. The look on her face would make anyone think she'd been arrested.

'This lady said you'd phoned to see her.'

'Yes, it's fine.' I gave a blanket 'sorry' to both parties and hustled Cheryl inside.

'This really does look serious,' she said.

I sat her down and offered her coffee. She asked for a herbal tea instead. I gave her an update on Operation Chicane and played her the recording DS Broxted had left with me. She put her hands together in her lap as if she was going to pray.

'Play it again,' she said. 'I need a candle.'

'No problem.'

I stood a large white candle on the coffee table in front of us, lit it, then turned off the light.

'Let me hold your hand,' she said.

Hers was cold, but firm. We sat in silence for a minute or so, then Cheryl started to rock slowly backwards and forwards. Her eyes began to flutter and then her head dropped down. At this stage I didn't care if she started wailing or throwing herself around. I just wanted to get information from her - anything - that might give the police a fighting chance of getting to the murder victim before the killer did, this time.

'I'm getting water,' she said. 'It's cold.'

She started a low hum that carried on as she breathed in and out. I wasn't sure if I was supposed to join in. Instead, I decided to try to focus on the message, myself. Maybe, if I stopped panicking for a moment, something might strike me, too. I closed my eyes and ignoring Cheryl's hum, I tried to see the words of the message printed in the flickering black void behind my eyes. *10.48 on November 9th*. I repeated the process, breathing deeper, trying to open up some space inside my head.

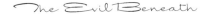

I was getting nothing at all. Cheryl was still in her trance and I started to find the humming oddly soothing. After a few more minutes, the sound came to an abrupt stop.

'I need a glass of water,' she said.

I put the light back on and went to the kitchen, picking up a notebook on the way back.

'What can you tell me?' I said, my pen poised over the blank page.

'It's definitely tomorrow,' she said. 'In the morning.' She put up her hand. 'There's something about royalty. Kings and queens.'

'Really?'

'I'm getting something to do with Queen Victoria, but it's not directly connected with her. She's not it.'

'What else?'

Cheryl let out a heavy sigh. 'I think that's all I'm going to get this evening. It's late. I'm tired. I'm better in the mornings.'

My hands were making fists. 'But tomorrow morning is *the time*. That's it. We've only got until then.'

'Juliet. The sense I get is that the time, 10.48 in the morning, is definitely correct. But it's correct as a *clue* - it's not the time something bad is going to happen.'

'You're sure?'

'As sure as I can be. The death won't happen at that time in the morning, but it will happen tomorrow, I'm afraid...later tomorrow, after dark.'

'Really?' So we still didn't have much time.

She got to her feet and I could see our meeting was over.

'Thank you so much.'

'I don't know what it means. I'm not sure if it gets you anywhere. I'll think about it again, tomorrow, and I'll call you if I get anything else.'

'Please do, that would be brilliant.' I realised I'd been squeezing her arm.

It was late by the time she left, but I knew Brad would be on duty, on high alert. I picked up the phone, but was in two minds about using it. I had nothing that was verifiable, nothing concrete, but if I didn't pass on something that turned out to be important, I'd never forgive myself.

I pressed Brad's number into the keypad.

He answered straight away. 'I hear you had another call,' he said. 'You okay?'

I cut to the chase. 'I wanted to get some information to you and for you to pass it on to the bridge expert.'

'Have you had another call? We didn't pick anything else up–'

'No.' I took a deep breath. 'My friend Cheryl from Holistica...'

'The psychic woman you mentioned?' He sounded wary.

'Yes, that one...well, she's been over here. I asked her for help with the message.'

There was a silence. 'She's been at your flat? She's heard the message?'

'Yes - what's going on, Brad? Why are you being so cagey?'

'She's come onto our radar lately, I'm afraid.'

'What?'

'Remember we discussed that the killer might be someone who takes an interest in the case, who might seem to want to help?'

'Yes - but, I've been the one to approach *her*, so far - about the etching, about the fire, about this latest message - she's never come to me.' I was stunned for a moment, until I considered that she did seem to know certain things about me, about my past. She knew Pamela Mendosa hadn't drowned, knew about Battersea Bridge, Luke's fire, my old house in Norwich. She was also well-built with big hands. 'Has she been in touch with you, separately, to try to help?' I added.

'I can't say too much now, Juliet. How much do you know about her?'

I tried to recall the few proper conversations we'd had.

'She's travelled a lot, been married twice, I think. She used to be a pilot.' I was struggling to say more, realising I knew very little about her life, apart from the few anecdotes she'd told me involving exotic places. 'Surely, you can't think she's involved?'

'She could be an accomplice. Her brother has got a checkered past. I don't think you should be alone with her.'

'*Brother?*' Cheryl had never mentioned a brother, never mind one with a checkered past.

'Look, I can't go into all of this now,' he said. 'What happened when she came over?' He sounded as though he expected her to have come at me with a machete.

'Nothing,' I said, vacantly. 'DS Broxted let her in.' I was still reeling with this new information.

'She wouldn't try anything with our guy right outside.'

'I invited her over,' I said, raising my voice. 'She was reluctant to come. She told me her...insights... about the phone call.' I told him about the royalty link and the fact that Cheryl thought the time the man gave was part of a clue and wasn't actually the time the next murder was going to occur.

'Right,' he said, stretching out the word. 'We need to bear in mind that she could be trying to throw us off the scent...'

Did the police really believe Cheryl could be an accomplice to murder?

'Surely not...' I still couldn't see her playing a part in any of this. I'd always seen myself as a good judge of character. But, I'd been caught out by Andrew recently - maybe I was losing my touch.

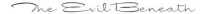

There was a long gap. Eventually, he spoke. 'I've got someone checking the tide-tables to see if high tide falls at exactly 10.48, morning or evening, at any of the London bridges.'

'The other victims were all killed during the night weren't they?'

'It makes sense, especially in London, fewer people about. But we're checking the morning tides too. He's given us a very precise time.'

'Which is the closest bridge to Buckingham Palace?' I asked.

'Westminster Bridge or Lambeth Bridge to the south. Look, Juliet, this royal idea - it really isn't worth following up.'

I tensed. 'Can you afford to dismiss it out of hand? I don't know what you think you've got on Cheryl, but you haven't arrested her, so it can't be conclusive. You could at least check out those bridges.'

'Sorry, Juliet, but we're the professionals here. Let us handle this.' His tone was sharper than he'd used with me before.

'Okay. I've told you - that's all I can do. I'm going to carrying on looking for more on my laptop. I'll stay up all night if I have to.'

He rang off. I tried to see it from his point of view. He had to be suspicious of everyone - it was his job, after all. And he couldn't afford to spend time following up fanciful whims and speculation.

I thought again about Cheryl's part in this. Had she got details of the case spot on because she was truly psychic, or because she was secretly involved? The murders seemed to be as much about me as they were about the unfortunate victims, but Cheryl had never seemed the least bit hostile towards me, so it didn't add up for me.

I put my laptop on the dining table and set my alarm clock beside it, for 7.30am. My body baulked at the hard-backed chair, but sitting on the bed or sofa would have lulled me to sleep. I made myself some strong black coffee and propped an opened packet of crunchy breakfast cereal beside me. It was going to be a long night.

There were nearly four-thousand hits in the UK for *10.48 November 9*. Cheryl insisted that the time referred to morning and that brought it down to two-hundred. Until Brad came up with something more concrete, I was prepared to trust the information she'd given me. I could backtrack if it led to a dead end. I scrolled through every one of the entries. I then added *bridge* to the mix and started wading through those. At 3am, I got up to put loud music on my headphones and did jumping-jacks on the spot at regular intervals to keep me awake.

Next thing I knew, the alarm was jangling in my ear. I lifted my head from the table and slapped my hand on the off button. My first thought was: *where am I*? The next was: *today is the ninth of November*.

I quickly dressed and splashed water on my face between more sips of black coffee. I hadn't got anywhere with my surfing last night and was angry with myself. Had Cheryl given me a red-herring or had I missed something? Returning to the royalty link, I went back to the laptop and punched in *10.48am November 9 Queen*, and scrolled through all of them. Then I tried changing the last word to *King*. I clicked from one page to the next until suddenly something caught my eye. It was a reference to Edward VII. I ran my eye along the next line.

He was born at 10.48am on November 9th, 1841.

I couldn't believe it. There it was in black and white. I thought at first I must be dreaming. *I'd found it*.

I jumped up and down, wrenching my head-phones from the computer socket and was about to rush to the phone, when I realised that all I had was a king. No bridge, just a king. I put *Edward VII bridge* into the search engine and waited.

I sat back, consternation gripping every muscle in my body. There was a bridge all right. The Edward VII Bridge - but there was a big problem. It wasn't in London. It was a railway bridge in Newcastle upon Tyne. I lifted the phone anyway and heard Brad's voice as soon as I'd dialled.

'I was about to call you,' he said. 'Derek Moorcroft reckons it's a bridge in Newcastle.'

I nearly put the phone down. Bloody Derek Moorcroft had gone and stolen my thunder.

'Yes - I'd got that far,' I said, pointedly, 'but it's not in London. It can't be right.'

'We've alerted the Northumbrian police. They'll have officers out there straight away.'

'It doesn't make sense.'

'But, none of it did anyway, Juliet. This whole thing has been crazy from the start.'

'Is that it, then?'

'We're still checking. Until we find a *London* connection with Edward VII and a bridge here, this is all we've got. Listen, I've got to go.'

He rang off without saying goodbye. It was all wrong. It had to be London. I knew it. I rang Cheryl, hoping it wasn't too early.

She said she'd been awake for an hour already, mulling over the message again.

'Any joy?' I said. 'I got as far as a bridge. The Edward VII Bridge - but it's in Newcastle.'

'No, it's not that one. It's not going to happen there.'

'Are you sure?'

'As sure as you can be with psychic information. It's going to be in London. It's going to be tonight, but not necessarily at 10.48. That was just part of the clue to the *bridge*.'

'The police are focusing all their resources in Newcastle.'

'You'll have to tell them you know differently.' I hesitated for a second. Was this a diversionary tactic? Was Cheryl trying to steer everyone away from the bridge in Newcastle, because it was the *right* bridge?

'How can I?'

'I don't know. That's the problem with the information we get sometimes. Most people don't believe it. Good luck.' She said it like she meant it.

I rang Brad back, but it went to voicemail. I tried again a few minutes later and it was the same. I didn't leave a message. I didn't know what to do.

I was fully booked that day and didn't want to let everyone down. If Cheryl was right (and all the other murders had, after all, taken place during the night), then there was nothing I could do all day, anyway.

I switched the radiator on in the spare room, made myself look vaguely presentable and waited for the doorbell to ring. It was the hardest day of my life: sitting there trying to be understanding and sympathetic when I knew someone's life was in danger and had the terrible feeling the police had gone off on the wrong track.

10.48 came and went that morning and no messages popped up on my phone.

At lunchtime, I finally left a message with Brad, saying that I thought they were wrong to focus on the bridge in Newcastle. My message fizzled out, because I couldn't explain myself; I couldn't give a valid reason for how I knew. Call it gut-reaction, intuition, ESP, whatever you like - I just knew.

After my last client, there was a text waiting for me. It was from Brad telling me that everything was quiet according to the Northumbrian police, but that they were getting police boats into the water and plenty of officers staking out the bridge. He didn't refer to my message.

I rang Derek Moorcroft as a last resort, to ask him if he could see any different angles. He told me there were royal connections with nearly all the main London bridges. He also said that high tide that day didn't occur at 10.48 at any of them - morning or evening.

'Can we forget 10.48 for a minute,' I snapped. 'Are there any specific references to Edward VII and any of the London bridges?'

I knew there were thirty London bridges over the tidal part of the Thames. That was a heck of a lot of bridges for the police to keep watch over. We had to narrow it down.

'I'm doing my best, Ms Grey. My mother's not well...and I've had problems with my computer today.'

'Then go to a library. Find another computer. I'm convinced the Newcastle bridge isn't the right place.' I was starting to sound hysterical, but I didn't care anymore.

I'm not sure who ended it, but the call was over abruptly and I was fuming.

Thankfully in the steam of the moment, another idea came to me. Jackie had once said her grandmother was a historian. I had a vague recollection that she'd written a book about some aspect of London's history. Edward VII was born in 1841. Had the old lady, by any chance, written about the nineteenth century? The odds weren't that great, but maybe she could refer me to the right person, if British monarchs weren't her field. The only problem was, I was seriously running out of time.

Jackie wasn't in when I tapped on her door, but she'd given me her mobile number and I got straight through.

'She lives in Teddington,' she said, 'I'm sure she'd love a visit.' She gave me the address.

'It won't be a sociable call, I'm afraid. Could you tell her to expect me? I need to see her - as soon as possible. Don't suppose you could come too?'

'I'm working the nightshift, otherwise I would.'

'Don't worry.'

'She's eighty...and her memory has been...how can I put it...slightly wayward in the last few years.'

'Thanks for the warning,' I said. I went outside and spotted PC Zac Nwoso sitting in a car a few spaces behind mine. I knew I wasn't supposed to make obvious contact, but I strode over and tapped on the glass.

'I'm going to Teddington, Zac,' I said, as the window slid down. I didn't add that I might be breaking the speed limit.

On a good day, Putney to Teddington would take me twenty-five minutes. That day, it took me sixteen. My right foot was barely off the floor and I cut through several orange lights and skipped a red one altogether. I hoped PC Nwoso would understand - or be too exhausted to notice.

twenty-one

I found the right avenue and pulled up outside number fifty-four. Mrs Dalton was already standing at the front door in a frilly pinafore straight from another century. It was chilly; she should have been waiting inside. I waved to PC Nwoso and pointed to the house, as I locked the car.

'Are you meals on wheel?' she said. It turned out Mrs Dalton hadn't been waiting for me.

I apologised for disappointing her and said Jackie had given me her address.

'Who's Jackie?' she said. She looked down at her bootie-style slippers as if there was something she ought to know that wasn't quite slipping into place. A grey terrier that looked like it used to be white, ducked between Mrs Dalton's legs and started barking and grabbing at my trouser legs with bared teeth.

'Bonaparte, leave the lady alone.' The dog ignored her. 'I said, *stop it*!' came the woman's voice, completely out of proportion with her diminutive size. A trait that Jackie had inherited, I noted.

The dog darted back inside and Mrs Dalton invited me to follow him, although she still clearly had no idea who I was or what I wanted.

A thought occurred to me.

'Your dog, Bonaparte,' I said. 'Is that because you are an expert on that area of history?'

'Me? No. I'm much earlier,' she said.

That didn't bode well.

She led me through the hall into the sitting room. It was like an entire exhibition from the Victoria and Albert Museum condensed into one tiny space. There were swirls everywhere: in the carpet, wallpaper, the curtains and embroidered into the three-piece-suite, all competing with one another. Every shelf held a vase or ceramic bowl with more swirls, only these were exclusively in blue and white. It was dazzling to the eye and I took a step back as we entered.

'Bit of a collector, as you can see,' she said. 'There's William Morris, William de Morgan and some of the pottery is original Wedgwood. My grandfather knew Rudyard Kipling, you know.'

I made a mental note to check with Jackie that her gran had adequate household insurance. Mrs Dalton offered me tea and when she was out of the room, my eye was drawn, amongst the mass of conflicting designs, to a cabinet on the wall. It looked like it was made of rosewood and had ivory portrait medallions inlaid into it. It was exquisite. I could spend ages in here, I decided, if I wasn't on such an urgent mission. I vowed to come back with Jackie, another time.

Having taken a sip of tea, I realised Mrs Dalton had filled the jug with condensed milk. My instinct was to spit it straight out, but I had to quietly gag and swallow, hoping she wasn't watching me. Fortunately, she was preoccupied with Bonaparte who was snuffling around her feet.

'I'm a friend of your granddaughter,' I said. 'She said you are an expert on history.'

'In my day,' she said, sitting upright with her hands folded in her lap, as though it was a press interview.

'Which era did you specialise in?'

'Roman London, dear. I wrote a book about it. I have a copy of it here.'

I couldn't hide a groan. *Shit. Completely the wrong era. This was a waste of time.* I browsed through a few yellowing pages of the hardback book she handed me to be polite.

'Did you want to buy a copy?' she said, hopefully, bending over me.

'Not today, I don't think.' Time was pressing on. I tried a long shot. 'I wondered if you'd ever studied Edward VII at all?'

'The nineteenth century isn't my period, I'm afraid. Roman London, did I tell you?'

We were about as far away from Edward VII as London is from the Falkland Islands.

'More tea?'

I declined, struggling now with how to proceed.

'You don't happen to know anything about the bridges in London do you? Their history?' Clutching at straws, now.

'Can't say I do. Did I tell you my grandfather knew Rudyard Kipling?'

'Yes. I think you did.'

I was going to have to draw this to a close. I reached for my bag.

'Did you want to see some photographs?' she said.

My heart was still on double-time, pumping fast, urging me to get moving, but I knew there was nowhere for me to go, no other avenues for me to try. I'd reached a dead end. I decided to give it five more minutes and then make my excuses.

Mrs Dalton pulled out a wooden box from under an armchair. Inside was a stack of well-thumbed black and white photographs and postcards. Her pride and joy were at the top: two pictures showing Rudyard Kipling standing beside a man she pointed out was her grandfather.

'You said bridges didn't you?' she said. She sniffed and a mist of puzzlement stole the animation from her eyes. It was like a light coming on and then swiftly going off again.

'My father was a historian, like me,' she said, feeling her way back into the conversation again. 'He didn't write a book like I did, but he worked at the London Museum when it was at Lancaster House. Around 1935, that would be.'

'Did he have an interest in the London bridges?' I asked, trying to nudge her back in that direction.

'Who's that, dear?'

'Your father.'

'Oh, him. He lived in Kew. There's a picture here.'

She flicked through photos deeper in the box, her mind still able to recall how she'd mentally catalogued them. 'Here it is.'

It was a photograph of a man proudly holding a little girl on his shoulders at the end of a bridge. There was bunting behind them and crowds of people. She turned the picture over to read what was on the back.

'This was 1903, when Kew Bridge was opened. It was the third one. Too much traffic, so they had to build a new one. This is my grandfather again, with Doris, my mother. She would have been three-years-old, then...'

I let her carry on in her Tinker Bell voice until something she said made me sit bolt upright.

'Can you say that again?' I said.

'The king opened the bridge. Edward VII. My grandfather met *him*, too.'

'Edward VII opened Kew Bridge?'

'Yes. In 1903. It was known as the Edward VII Bridge for a while and then everyone went back to calling it Kew Bridge.'

I got to my feet and the dog leapt up, barking again.

'Mrs Dalton - you have been fantastic.' I leant forward and gave her a bone-crushing hug. 'Thank you so much. This has been really helpful. I've got to go.'

I ran through the hall and out to the road, my hand inside my handbag trying to locate my phone.

'It's Kew Bridge,' I shouted to PC Nwoso, as I waited for Brad's number to connect. Zac's forehead creased into a concertina of bewilderment.

'Brad. Listen. Edward VII opened Kew Bridge in 1903. It was known as the Edward VII Bridge for a while. The clue I was given was just the time and date of Edward VII's *birth* - it's the link to a *London* bridge we've been looking for, it has to be the one.' I'd said it all in one breath and was nearly doubled over, leaning on the car door.

'I'll check with Derek Moorcroft. You could be on to something. We'll need to get the times of high tide for the rest of the day at Kew. Good work, Juliet.'

My watch said it was gone 8pm. It had already been dark for several hours. I only hoped we weren't too late.

When I pulled up on a side-road close to Kew Bridge, I knew straight away that something was wrong.

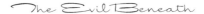

There were too many people about. Many of them were holding long-lens cameras.

'Get these bloody reporters out of the area,' shouted an officer in uniform. 'The killer's going to spot them a mile off.' A group of his colleagues across the road started wading into the crowd. 'Get a move on!' he screamed.

He turned round and saw me. 'You! I don't know who you are, but move your car. Clear the area. This is a police operation.' He flapped his arms as though he was under attack by a swarm of bees.

I did as I was told and parked a couple of streets further away. By the time I came back, the crowd had thinned out, but it was still far too busy for an ordinary Monday evening. I spotted Brad talking to a group of officers and they, in turn, started speaking to people individually. The ones holding the cameras began nodding and moving away. Brad walked towards me.

'What a disaster. The press have got hold of it. It's a hive of activity up here and we need everything to look as normal as possible.'

His radio crackled and he clipped an earpiece over his ear. He listened for a moment, then stepped forward. 'Get everyone off the road, now. Speak to them one by one, DC Blake, don't try and herd them like cattle!'

Brad turned to me. 'The SIO is on her way...she'll do her nut if she sees this.'

'Is it best if I go?'

'See that place over there?' he pointed to a café in a short row of shops. 'Go and wait inside. I'll join you when I've sorted this mess out.'

It was a typical greasy-spoon: chequered table-cloths overprinted with the rings left by mugs of builder's tea and brown net curtains that hadn't been cleaned since the smoking ban. Customers and staff all had the same worn faces and no one seemed to notice the upheaval on the bridge. The menu-board read: *Bubble and Sqweek* in red felt-tip. The wonky block-capitals sloped down to the right, as if the letters had gradually got too heavy. The flickering fluorescent tubes and piped muzak vied with each other for the most irritating feature award.

I didn't trust the coffee, so I asked for a mineral water and sat by the window. The bridge itself was made of grey stone in three sweeping arches, lit from above by lantern-style streetlamps. The café bell tinged and Brad came in. He asked for the manager and had a quick word with a short, plump man bound in blue aprons. He came over to my table.

'We're clearing the all-night café and putting plain clothes officers in their place,' he said.

'That'll be a treat for them.'

'We've got boats on the river and divers at the ready, with officers at each end of the bridge. There's a helicopter if we need it. I think we've got everything covered.'

'When's high tide?' I looked at my watch.

'3.02 - five hours away.'

'The next woman could be dead by now,' I said, stabbing my finger into a pile of spilt salt on the table. 'He gets them into the water when it's high tide, but–'

He leant forward and pressed his finger over my lips. 'Shush. That's not helping.'

'Sorry,' I said. 'Can I treat you to a coffee?'

'I can't stay long. Remind me to take you somewhere nice when this is all over.'

It sounded flippant. I didn't want to read too much into it. 'Listen, before I go, I wanted to fill you in on Cheryl Hoffman and her brother.'

'Good. I'm still struggling with that.'

'Cheryl and Leyton Meade were born in America. He's a couple of years older. He was a platoon leader during the Vietnam war and in 1969 he was indicted for war crimes during the My Lai massacre, but never charged. There was a massive cover up involving twenty six soldiers, many of whom were officers, but only one was ever convicted.'

A high-pitched croak slipped from my mouth.

'Hundreds were killed,' he continued. 'Mostly women and children.' He lowered his head. 'Beaten, raped and tortured.'

I gripped the collar of my coat. 'And Cheryl's brother was part of that?'

'Never convicted...but, from the reports I've seen, it looks like there was some vigorous brushing under large expanses of carpet going on - if you get my meaning.' He pulled a creased sheet out of his pocket. It was a grainy photograph printed from a computer. 'I wanted to show you this. See if his face rings any bells. It's from a few years ago.'

I stared at the picture. It looked like it had been taken in a steamed-up bathroom, but I could make out a stern face with a thick moustache. He reminded me of a character in a play by Chekhov.

I shook my head and handed it back. 'Okay - so how does he fit in?' I said.

'Cheryl came to the UK with her mother when she was six years old, but Leyton stayed with his father. He's lived in the US mostly, but like Cheryl, he's travelled a lot - arrested several times for domestic violence, assaults, one case of kidnapping - but unbelievably, he was never ever charged with anything.'

'Must have had a cracking lawyer.'

He lowered his voice again, even though no one else looked remotely awake, never mind interested. 'Get this - all the attacks were against women and one of them, in 2008, had undergone a recent termination.' He flared his nostrils. 'Leyton came to the UK, arrived in London, two months ago.'

'Did he now?' I trailed a teaspoon across the table cloth. 'Plus,' he continued, 'Cheryl also came to us recently offering to "help".'

'I see. We did say we should be on the lookout for someone doing just that.' I tapped my fingers against my temple. 'But where's Leyton and Cheryl's connection with me? She joined Holistica a few months before I did - I've never met her, or heard of either of them, before that.'

He shrugged. 'Early days. We're delving into their family history to see what we can find and we've got surveillance on Leyton Meade. He's renting a flat in Stockwell.'

A voice came over his radio and he got up to leave.

'You think he could be here?' I said, grabbing his sleeve at the last minute. 'Let's hope so. I'll see you soon. Blend in.'

I sat there for a further two hours, sipping water and trying to read an abandoned *Metro*. Sure enough, there was an exchange of clientele in the café. The faces and apparel changed. Not a shabby raincoat in sight.

I felt stupid and lost sitting there, but I knew going home wasn't an option. I wouldn't sleep; I'd pace up and down, holding my phone with one hand, dipping the other into a box of Crunchy-nut Cornflakes. At least the food here was so unappealing I wouldn't be tempted to comfort eat.

Brad reappeared after 11pm and crouched down beside me.

'All's quiet,' he said. 'Everyone's in place - we just have to wait.'

His cheeks were rosy, but he looked edgy. I could only assume that the adrenalin was keeping him going.

'I've been thinking about what you told me,' I said. 'Leyton Meade would be in his sixties - at best - if he was old enough to be an officer in charge at Vietnam.' He nodded. 'Isn't it a lot to expect a sixty-year-old to manhandle a dead body - even if the victims had small frames?'

'He could be working with someone else - besides, Sylvester Stallone was still playing Rambo when he was sixty-one. I'm not saying Stallone's the norm, but Leyton's a chunky bloke. I'd say he was fit enough.' He leant forward. 'We've just had a useful piece of forensics.' I envied his ability to remain chirpy in the face of the ominous uncertainty hanging over us all. 'Aysha had scuff marks on her clothes, on one of her shoulders.'

'Scuff marks?'

'Made by a zip, apparently. Also, we've found fibres now in *two* of the girls' hair - that PEVA, I told you about - it's a match for a certain type of body-bag. It looks like the killer put the women in body-bags after he strangled them. In each case, the pathologists noticed that body fluids were concentrated in patches, consistent with being wrapped up, before being left in the water.'

'Body-bags?'

'We're trying to identify the exact make...see if it's a common type used in mortuaries and funeral parlours in the area. It could be a useful lead. Leyton Meade, aside, the killer might be an undertaker.'

'Or anyone could have bought them on the net,' I said.

'Little Miss Optimism today, aren't we?'

I felt sick and knew it was nothing to do with the rancid smell of black-pudding.

Brad soldiered on. 'It helps explains why the bodies were so free of contaminating evidence.'

'Any more on Charles Fin?'

He got up from his haunches and winced, pulling over a chair instead. 'He's an attention-seeker, that guy. He was leading us up the garden path giving his mother as an alibi. You're right, she died a couple of years ago.'

'So, he's still in the frame?'

'At the time of the first murder, he was at a women's wrestling match, the second, he was refereeing a women's football tournament and for the last...wait for it...he was at Lou-Lou's massage parlour in Soho. We've crossed him off the list.'

I smiled to myself. Cheeky Charlie Fin. Surrounding himself with women all this time.

'We're going to knobble him for wasting police time,' he said. I had the feeling he'd been wasting mine, too. I wanted to ask about Andrew, but

I thought Brad would have said something by now, if he'd been cleared. The plastic clock above the counter said it was 12.20. We stayed there, sharing a forced idle chatter as the minutes ticked by and the nervous tension settled on my skin like a jungle sweat. At 1.10am, Brad switched up his radio, plugged in the earpiece and then beckoned me outside.

'I need some air,' he said.

'Where do we go?'

He led me to the river path and we started walking slowly away from the bridge. The water was coming in by now, but black and almost invisible except for the occasional ripples that flashed white when they caught the street lights. A swirling fog was descending, wrapping itself around us.

'That's not going to help,' he said, peering back at the bridge.

I remembered seeing small rowing boats left chained into the mud banks along this stretch. I'm sure many were left there for months, going through their tidal ritual of being set free into the river, then pulled back down in the mud again. I couldn't see any of them under the smoky whitewash, but I knew they were there.

Brad had said there were police divers on boats, but I couldn't see or hear any of them, either. It was like staring into a pot of grey tar, as we walked further away from the street lights. I could hear the water, inexorably making its way in. I wondered what it might be bringing with it; whether soon a cry or a whistle would shatter the quiet and a mound of wet clothes would come into view under the bridge.

Unexpectedly, Brad took my hand. It was warm, solid and it wrapped right around mine.

'You're freezing,' he said. 'Do you want to go back?'

'No. I'm just scared.'

He guided my hands into his pockets. 'I'll have to go in a minute. I need to be by the bridge, making sure there are no last-minute hiccups.'

I admired his optimism; the term 'last-minute' implied nothing terrible had already happened. 'You can come as well. Can't leave you out here on your own.'

We turned and retraced our steps, then wandered over the bridge. We must have looked like lovers lost in the solitude of a romantic stroll. We stood leaning over the cold stone. There was no one else on the bridge now, just the odd passing car. When we got to the other side, an arm came out of a bush and offered Brad some night-vision binoculars. He climbed down to the water's edge and pulled me after him. After he'd done a 360 degree check himself, he let me try them. Through the lenses, the river turned lime-green and I could see black outlines around branches and several sets of steps leading into the water. I could also make out two short piers and the boats I'd known were tethered to the bank were bobbing around, innocently.

'Where are the police boats?' I asked.

'They're well-hidden, in banks and behind trees.'

'I can't see any of them.'

'Good,' he whispered. 'Hopefully, the killer won't spot them either.'

Without the special night-vision lenses, the fog was dense now, like clouds that had accidentally slipped down from the sky. I held the binoculars to my eyes again and thought I saw something. I stood upright, squinting, wondering if it was just the hazy mist creating shadows. *No, I was right.* In the distance, in the middle of the river, something was breaking through the white billowing curtains and floating towards us. *Oh, God, No! Not a body.*

I had to hand back the binoculars. 'What is it?' I hissed, trying to keep my voice down. 'What's in the water?'

He waved me away and took several steps closer to the river. From nowhere a huge search light came on, like the ones you see on Hollywood film sets. Other lights came on, one by one, forming clusters in the water, as officers started switching on their torches. An officer directed me away from the water's edge and I moved on to the bridge, unable to take my eyes off the shape that was heading our way.

Men in wading gear were entering the river, but the current was flowing fast now and they were forced to stay near the bank. Several divers formed a little reception party to meet the shape as it drifted towards them. I could now see what it was. A small wooden rowing boat.

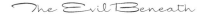

The violent pounding, as my blood bolted through my body, didn't ease up. I squashed my scarf into my mouth, shivering in spasms. *What's inside the boat?* I said, over and over to myself, pacing from side to side.

I strained to see over the edge of the bridge, dodged around, trying to get a better view, but the divers were in the way. *Was there a body inside? Had we been too late, after all?*

Everything was taking longer than it should. I could hardly bear it. My vision began to swim around the edges and I had to grab hold of the bridge. I checked my watch - it was nearly 3am. High tide was due at 3.02. The timing was spot on.

The officers dragged the boat on to the bank and I could see now what was inside.

twenty-two

I looked down into the shadows of the boat, hardly daring to allow my eyes to settle on what was inside. I saw the curve of the bare planks, running under the seat; the clean lines of the wood. *What else?* I edged closer trying to survey every inch as the divers steadied the boat on the grass. They were leaning over it making it difficult to see. I moved to get a different angle, but figures still blocked my view. Officers were shaking their heads. In shock? I couldn't see.

Then the officers cleared away. There was nothing there. *Where was she? Did I miss something? Had the police removed the body already?* Not trusting my initial examinations I went right down to the grass. Sure enough, no shapes or shadows. Not even an oar. Or an empty crisp packet. Nothing. The boat was completely empty.

I was ushered away so I returned to my original vantage point. I leant with my back against the crusty bridge for support, questions leaping back and forth in my brain like the filaments inside a plasma ball. *Had we prevented a murder? Or was the boat part of the plan? Was the killer trying to tell us something?*

Men were dragging the boat up the ramp and away from the river. I could see Brad waving instructions to two officers and then the boat went out of sight behind parked cars.

'There's nothing in it,' he said, jogging towards me, 'but we're taking it to forensics, in any case. We've all got to resume our positions and stay put - it doesn't mean it's over.'

My stomach turned like a flipped pancake. He left me on the bridge and a woman came over asking me politely to make myself scarce. I went back to the café, my body dripping with exhaustion following hours of mounting trepidation.

It still wasn't over.

The clock said 3.20am. The tide would be turning now and anything in the water would start flowing the other way. There was no body under the bridge. *Didn't the killer always leave them in position at high tide? Surely that meant it was over?*

Against my better judgement, but driven by necessity, I ordered a coffee and watched the waitress prize open a large tub of instant. The best thing I could say about it was that it was hot. I spoke to a few of the plain clothes officers, started a crossword and then rested my head on my folded arms for a few moments. I thought about how Brad and I had walked along the river together like a courting couple. Did it mean anything, other than to provide convenient cover so he could check out what was going on?

And what did it mean to me?

I flashed back to the moment he cupped his hot hand around mine and the warmth flushed through my body again.

The musak faded in and out and so too did images of Brad, the river, the bridge. With no awareness of the passing of time, all of a sudden it was getting light outside.

The clientele in the café was changing again and the stiff white shirts and moleskin jackets went out into the street. It was 7am. The fog had gone.

'You missed a stunning sunrise,' said Brad, leaning over me. I could see he was running on overdrive; his shoulders were sagging and a prickly shadow was etched around his chin. The manic look about his eyes made me wonder how long it would be before he slumped into a heap.

'Anything happened?' I said, my mouth gluey with sleep.

'Everything's fine. But, we've taken a man in for questioning; a guy with binoculars we found loitering near the bridge, but there's nothing in the water.'

'Leyton Meade?'

'No - a younger guy.' He had the same look Andrew had when he'd received his prize; wide-eyed and triumphant. There was no woman tied to the chains under the bridge. No body facedown kissing the water. 'Time you got home and had some sleep,' he said.

'You sure? Is it all over? Did we prevent it?'

'It looks that way. We're getting the boat to forensics and we've got the guy at the station. Something's going to come of this. I just know it.'

I was too tired to share his elation and dragged myself back to my car.

I felt like I'd only just got my head down on the pillow, when the phone rang. I hauled my heavy body up, shocked to see the clock said it was 2pm.

'Don't you ever sleep?' I said.

'It's the adrenaline,' said Brad, trying to suck back a yawn. 'Keeps everything switched on. We're questioning the man we picked up at Kew. We wondered if you might recognise him. Any chance you can get over here?'

Moving was the last thing my body felt like doing. Getting up, getting changed and driving to the police station felt like nothing short of a miracle.

'I'll be there in half an hour,' I said.

On the way, I remembered the fretful dream I was having before Brad's call. I was back at the house in Norwich, twelve years old, standing in my pyjamas leaning against the doorway to the kitchen.

I was watching as Luke brought boxes and containers in from the shed through the back door. He was stacking them beside the oven. Boxes which had words like 'butane' and 'propane' on them with yellow drawings of flames on the side. He stacked box after box until they reached the ceiling.

Then he held up a red checked tea-towel and draped it carefully over two of the rings on the oven. I was trying to call out to him, but nothing came out of my mouth. I tried to move towards him. I wanted to snatch the tea-towel away from him, unplug the oven, drag the boxes away from it. I was fixed to the spot, already able to smell smoke, felt it curl into my nostrils, soak into my lungs. The last image I had was Luke smiling, unable to take his eyes away from the tiny flames starting to pucker into life on the oven rings.

I don't know where the dream would have gone after that. I was only grateful that the phone had rung when it did and dragged me out of it. It left me with the same feeling I'd had when Dad had spoken to me: that same sense of disbelief that either Luke or my mother could have been so stupid.

But, what did I actually have to go on? What proof was there that the fire was anything other than a tragic accident? Only the word of an old man who thought he saw the windows open. I clung to that one outward sign that things were not as they seemed, because I knew - I just knew - that the fire was deliberate. It meant someone wanted to hurt our family then, twenty years ago, just as someone was trying to terrorize me now.

The massive downside was that I didn't know how I was going to get any further with it. The police report was incomplete and inconclusive and everyone personally involved with the fire, apart from me, wanted to forget all about it.

An officer at the desk was expecting me when I got to the station. I was led through to a small room, no larger than a cupboard, alongside an interview room. There was a two-way mirror and I watched Brad get up, switch off the tape-recorder and leave the room. Moments later he came alongside me.

'How's it going?' I said.

'He's very weird. Not quite all there.' He tapped his head. 'Name is William Jones. He's thirty-three. Ring any bells?'

I tossed the name around in my mind but no lights were coming on.

'Not yet...'

'An officer has just taken him to the bathroom. When he comes back in, get a good look at him.'

'Okay.' I swallowed hard.

'We're going to run a voice-scan to see if it matches the phone-call you had. By the way, it was from a public phone box. Somewhere in Kennington.'

I sat with my knees together on the only chair, a wooden one that folded flat, feeling like a school girl about to recite a difficult poem in Greek.

'I'm going back in,' he said. 'See what you make of his voice, see if there's anything about his movements, his behaviour, that's at all familiar. Think big, not just people you know now. Think back to all the stages of your life you told me about before.'

I nodded, chewing my thumbnail, and saw Brad re-enter the interview room, followed by another man, a demure looking woman, a police officer and another plain-clothed woman. I assumed the latter must be the social worker Brad said the solicitor had insisted upon.

'So, tell me again Mr Jones, what were you doing by Kew Bridge, last night?'

'Out and about. Nothing wrong. I haven't done anything wrong.'

Brad gave the man's solicitor, Ms Kemp, a weary glance. She was sitting high in her chair, as if pressed against it by a strong wind. Her red hair was pinned up in a severe chignon and a neck scarf was tied too tightly under her chin. If only she'd relax a little, I thought, she'd almost be pretty.

The man Brad was addressing looked agitated. His face was plump with no visible facial hair, making him look anywhere between twenty-five and forty. His hair was mousy and so thin his pink scalp was visible and his dark eyes shifted around the room as if he was following the path of a blue-bottle. There was something naïve and inexperienced about him; it was the way he avoided any eyes in the room and ran his fingers up and down the table, as if he was practising a few bars of a piano piece, over and over. My psychotherapist's instinct told me straight away that he probably had some form of autism. Must be the reason Ms Kemp had called in the social worker.

He was wearing a sweat shirt with *David Bowie* printed on it, with grey combat trousers and he plucked the skin on his neck as he spoke, repeating the same statements again and again. I closed my eyes and listened to his voice. It was distorted and wiry through the loud-speaker in my little box-room. I couldn't honestly say whether it was the same voice I'd heard on the phone or not. I hoped the voice-scanner would be able to do a better job.

'What time did you get to Kew Bridge?' asked Brad.

'Six minutes past ten.'

'That's very precise.'

'That's the time it was.'

'And how did you get there?'

'On the number two bus from Brixton, number nine from Hyde Park Corner and then the number 391, then I walked. I haven't done anything wrong.'

Pluck, pluck, pluck went his fingers at his neck. He had the look of someone permanently connected to a mild electric current.

'That must have taken you ages.'

'One hour and forty-two minutes.'

He hardly blinked and was finding it hard to make eye contact with Brad. It was as though he was talking to himself. Awkward, childlike.

'And why did you go to the bridge?'

'Out and about,' he said, again. 'Nothing wrong.'

'But why there? And why so late?'

Ms Kemp suddenly spoke, her voice cutting through the stuffy room like cheese wire. 'Don't harass my client, DCI Madison.'

Brad caught her eye and paused to take a breath.

'Okay, Mr Jones - just tell us why it was you went all the way over to Kew Bridge that night.'

'I like the buses.'

'And what did you do, when you got there?'

'Watched the people. Trip out. Nothing wrong.'

'Okay,' said Brad. 'Let's leave it there for now.'

He jerked his head to one side indicating that the solicitor, standing officer and social worker should leave the room with him. William Jones was left on his own. Brad joined me. The two women must have been hustled elsewhere. 'I want to see what he does on his own,' he said.

'I've wracked my brains, Brad. I really don't think I've ever met him. He doesn't ring a bell in terms of any of my clients, or anyone from the demo...or anyone from University or Norwich.'

'Nothing at all?'

I shook my head, wishing I could say otherwise.

'We've taken his fingers prints. He's got a scar on his thumb, so if there's anything decent from the boat, we might get a match.'

We watched Mr Jones as he shifted from one position to another in his chair. He started untying and retying his shoelaces.

'Do you think he's got attention deficit disorder?' he asked.

'Definitely some sort of autism, I'd say. Possibly Asperger's Syndrome.'

'Asperger's...' said Brad, jutting out his jaw. 'Interesting...' Mr Jones started putting his hands down on the table in a repeating pattern. Right, left, right left, like an animal pawing the surface. 'He's certainly got a nervous tic,' he said.

'Might mean he's just nervous...not necessarily guilty,' I said. 'Where does he live?'

'A flat above a shop in Brixton, he told us. We're checking his details.'

'Does he drive? He said he went over to Kew on the bus.'

'He said that he doesn't have a car or a licence. We're checking that with DVLA.'

'Poor chap. He looks completely out of his depth.'

Brad sighed. 'I hope this isn't another big fat red-herring.'

'What happens now?'

'I want to get a search warrant for his flat. The SIO will need more than this, though.'

'Shall I go home?'

'Hold on a minute.'

He went out to the main incident room. A woman was clutching a phone to her chest, beckoning Brad over to her with wide swoops of her arms. He was out of breath and looked excited when he joined me again.

'He used to work in a funeral parlour! He could have easily kept hold of a few body-bags.' He tightened his hands into triumphant fists.

As we crossed back through the main incident room, Katherine Lorriman, the Borough Commander, launched herself towards us like a missile.

'What's this about a search warrant?' she said.

'He lives alone...he's got no decent alibi.. I want to get in there and see what he's hiding.'

'Being a loner is not a good enough reason and you know it,' she hissed, wagging a finger at him. 'We've got nothing on him. I thought we were looking for someone really smart - he keeps repeating himself. Looks like he's a few sandwiches short of a lunchbox, if you ask me.'

'Juliet...Ms Grey...thinks he's autistic. The psychiatrist will be able to tell us more. I'm expecting a call any time now.' Brad shifted his weight to the other foot, rapping his pen against his palm. 'He used to work in a funeral parlour, would have had access to the body-bags...he was at the scene, acting suspiciously.' I could see his jugular vein working overtime inside his collar. 'We need to get into his flat. We've got nothing else.'

'Why was he at Kew Bridge?'

'A "trip out", he said.'

She drew her lips together as if she'd tasted something sour. 'Can't you do better than that? It's too vague.'

'We're having to tread very carefully, ma'am. We don't want to push him over the edge. He seems very fragile, vulnerable...and his solicitor's a real... hardliner.'

'Who is it?'

'Melody Kemp.'

She let a thin whistle escape her lips. 'Enough said.'

Brad drew his hands to his hips. 'The warrant?'

'Okay. Be it on your head, Madison' she said, undoubtedly knowing that the responsibility would always fall, lock, stock and barrel, back onto hers.

Clip, clop and she was gone.

'I've got to get this done,' he said.

I went back into the booth alongside the interview room and watched William Jones again. I wanted to see what he got up to on his own before I left. He had pulled the two chairs together and was now standing on them, rocking from one to the other. He looked bored and frustrated, like a child having been sent to his room. Had the police tracked down a parent or guardian, I wondered, someone who was keeping an eye on this man?

I'd never had a client with Asperger's, but I knew from my training that those with the syndrome became agitated when their routine was interrupted and I was witnessing such a situation right now. William was now standing on the table and I was starting to get worried that he was going to harm himself. I was just about to go for help, when Brad went into the room accompanied by the others. He asked William to get down from the table and he did so, without any shame or embarrassment.

Brad spent a few more minutes with him but nothing new came to light.

'I don't think we should leave him in there alone again,' I said, when he came back to the adjoining room. 'He was getting very antsy.'

'I'm on to it,' said Brad. Sure enough, the social worker went back into the room and sat down opposite William Jones. The uniformed officer stood by the door, his hands clasped in front of him.

'You were right,' said Brad. 'The psychiatrist called me before I went back in. William has Asperger's,' he said. 'Come to my office and we can talk to him on speaker-phone.'

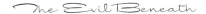

We weaved back through the main incident room and sat either side of the box at the edge of Brad's desk.

'I've worked with children and adults with this syndrome' said Dr Mountfield, his voice echoing as if he was inside a church. 'They're often very bright, but have problems with basic social skills like small talk, eye-contact and empathy. They retain facts and figures, but they find it hard fitting in.'

'Are they killers?' asked Brad, squinting as though a bright light was being shone into his eyes.

'No more and no less than the rest of the population,' said the psychiatrist. 'Not unless there's also schizophrenia or psychopathology involved. Or substance abuse. There's no evidence of that, so far, with Mr Jones, but we'd have to do full diagnostic tests to be sure. I can arrange that.'

'Is there any connection between Asperger's and criminal behaviour?' asked Brad.

'No. The moral development of adults with Asperger's is often impaired and they don't see the consequences of their actions, but there is no clinical evidence of violent acting-out, as a result. They're more likely to be victims than offenders,' he said. 'They are often suggestible. Their naivety and vulnerability make them easy targets.'

'They often find it hard to lie, I believe,' I said, refusing to let Dr Mountfield take all the kudos.

'Yes - they tend to deal with actualities. Metaphors and idioms go right over their heads.'

'Difficult for them to find suitable jobs, I imagine,' said Brad.

'A funeral parlour sounds about right,' said Dr Mountfield. 'He would have a nice rapport with the dead, I'd say.'

'There's one more thing that could be useful,' I said. 'Asperger's sufferers are collectors, aren't they?'

'That's a common trait,' said the psychiatrist.

Brad was on his feet. 'All the more reason to get round to his flat as soon as we can,' said Brad.

twenty-three

Unfortunately, there was no place for me in the search of William Jones' flat, so I spent Wednesday morning with supervisees at Holistica, trying to fool myself into thinking everything was normal. I kept checking my phone for a message from Brad, but it was blank. I was waiting for a breakthrough, some ultimate discovery that would signal that this monstrous case was heading towards closure. It had gone on far too long and I felt like I'd been emotionally wrung out weeks ago.

When I'd finished my sessions, I noticed from the appointment book that Cheryl had no one booked in. I'd bought her an apricot croissant during my coffee break, so now was the ideal time to hand it over, before I left for my afternoon clients. It was a safer bet than leaving it under Clive's dubious custody.

I tapped on the door of her consulting room and hearing no reply, tentatively opened it. I stalled, realising she wasn't alone.

'Sorry,' I said, backing out.

Cheryl beckoned me in. 'It's okay,' she said. 'Leyton's just leaving.'

The broad man sitting beside her didn't give the impression of doing anything of the sort. He was leaning back on a fold-out chair that under his great weight looked like it was made for a child. He didn't look anything like the man in the tattered photograph Brad had shown me of Cheryl's brother; he was clean shaven for a start, and there was nothing austere about his face.

'This is Juliet Grey,' she said. 'You remember I mentioned her to you?'

Leyton clambered to his feet and gave me a gracious smile, resting a puffy hand on my shoulder and reaching out the other. It was warm and his flamboyant gesture reminded me of the sincere manner of a particular uncle I adored when I was little. Leyton was all crumples and smiles, but once he'd got his balance and stood tall, his shoulders went back and I remembered what Brad had said about him being in the armed forces until he retired. His deportment confirmed it.

'Leyton Meade at your service,' he said and a waft of lemony freshness enveloped me. He talked to me as if we were old friends and told me about all the tourist attractions he'd visited since he'd arrived in London, two months ago.

Cheryl had her arms folded and breathed heavily from time to time.

As Leyton spoke I recalled the rest of my conversation with Brad; the catalogue of heinous crimes Leyton Meade had allegedly committed, but for which he had never been convicted. I was trying to assess whether this man was capable of those violent assaults - beatings, rape, torture - and whether he could be involved with the bridges murders. He was certainly big enough, strong enough, mobile enough to lift the bodies and his hands would have no problem wrapping around a neck twice the size of mine. But was Leyton a killer?

Psychologists claim that everyone is capable of murder, if pushed to the limit. What do you look for when meeting a potential killer? What are the warning signs? Characteristics such as over-control, a sense of entitlement, an impulsive temper, jealousy and possessiveness are the commonly known triggers that can tip people over the edge. I decided I would need to see Leyton under stress to be able to make any sort of judgement. As it was, he appeared to be as convivial and playful as an oversized teddy bear.

Cheryl looked at her watch. 'I've got a client, Leyton,' she said.

'Okay,' he said, jovially. I knew for a fact that she hadn't. He got to his feet. 'I'll have to take leave of you two lovely ladies.' He shook my hand again and turned to Cheryl, who avoided any contact and reached over to open the door.

'I'll be in touch,' she said, in a matter of fact way as he left.

'Sorry to barge in,' I said. I handed her the white paper bag. 'Thought you might like this - you said the other day you were partial to anything with pastry.'

She peered inside and licked her lips. 'Perfect,' she said. 'Thank you.'

'Your brother seemed charming,' I said, hoping to probe a little into why there had been such a tense atmosphere between them.

'Yes,' she said. I saw her arms stiffen as she spoke. 'Isn't he...just?'

The clock behind Cheryl's head said it was two minutes to one and I realised I had to get back home for my clients. When I left the room, I was cross with myself: I'd missed several opportunities with both of them to dig deeper.

During the afternoon I had two clients who were making progress - and then Lynn Jessop. In most cases, counselling helped turn people's lives around, but there would always be the odd exception, like Lynn, where it barely seemed to scratch the surface. In cases like hers, I felt lost and de-skilled.

Lynn looked more tired than usual when I opened my front door. Her iron-coloured eyes fixed on mine straight away; they were heavy and hard with contracted pupils that made me think of a stag beetle.

Before she launched into another catalogue of concerns about Billy, I wanted to check the number she'd given me for her GP. I'd tried to reach the surgery and only got as far as a recorded message saying that the number had been discontinued. I wasn't quick enough, however. Before I could take a breath, she was off.

'They've been dunking him in the water...trying to drown him,' she said, spitting the words at me as though it was my fault.

'I'm so sorry,' I said. 'What happened?'

'I followed Billy after school again and they came after him. One boy in particular. They forced him down to the water...knee in his back...banged his head... pushing his face under...' Her sentence gave up the ghost. 'They laughed. I didn't know what to do.'

Tears were tipping on to her cheek and I leant over with the box of tissues.

'Is Billy okay?'

'I took him to A&E. Concussion. They couldn't say if there would be any permanent damage. They kept him in a day or two.'

'This is really serious, Lynn, did you report it? Would you recognise the boys?'

'I can't always be there. He won't talk about it.'

'But, did you tell the police?'

'They won't do anything. I've reported it before. I told you. I know who the ring leader is now. He should be punished.'

'Is he at the same school as Billy?'

'No. But I've seen him before. In the neighbourhood. I know his name.'

'Won't the police follow it up? Talk to the school, his parents?'

'*You*, of all people, should know that doesn't happen.' Her sudden sharp tone took me aback. It was as if, again, she was accusing me of being part of the problem.

I knew before I said it that I was overstepping the mark. 'I know a decent police officer. I could talk to him about this...confidentially.' A look of horror shot across her face, but I carried on, anyway. 'Whereabouts do you live, Lynn?'

'No. That's not going to work.' She continued to shake her head. 'They'll tell the school and Billy will get all upset and hate me for it.'

'But Billy is getting seriously hurt. Doesn't he want it to stop?' She gave me a pleading look. I didn't know what it meant. 'I know I shouldn't be suggesting this,' I said. 'I'm a psychotherapist, not a social worker, but this has been going on–'

'No. You don't understand.'

'Understand what? Tell me...I want to help.'

'You can't. It's too late. It's far *too late* for all that!'

She was on her feet, punching out those final words in my face, before she yanked open the door. I opened my mouth but nothing came out. As her stomping footsteps faded away down the corridor, the door handle was left swinging out of its socket; she'd pulled it right off.

I flopped back into the chair, flummoxed. I heard the front door slam and went down to lock it. I was done for the day in more ways than one.

There was a note on the mat. Lynn had trodden on it, on her way out. It simply said: *Outside*. I recognised the writing. I opened the door and found Brad leaning against his car with his ankles crossed.

'I was just passing,' he said, smiling in a way that indicated we both knew he was fibbing.

'Is everything okay?' I said.

'It does get to that stage, doesn't it?' he said. 'When every time you see a policeman you assume something awful has happened...'

'Sorry...it's just...'

'Bad day?'

'Not my best - are you coming in?'

He nodded. 'I'm off duty for once.'

'Hot chocolate?' I suggested, as I slammed the flat door to shut out the cold. I needed something warm and soothing.

'Love one,' he said. I liked the way he settled himself on the sofa without being invited. 'Wanted you to know the latest.' He patted the space next to him. He looked smug. I could only assume there'd been an arrest. 'Good news and bad news.'

'Did you go to Mr Jones' flat?'

I flopped into the space he'd indicated, faintly warmed by his hand.

'No obvious evidence of the victims, but we've sent various fibres to forensics. Nothing there about Fairways, nothing yet about you. But, we found two folded body-bags in his wardrobe.'

'Really? Anything else?'

'The voice scan is a match. It *was* him who left the last message over the phone.'

'Wow - that's brilliant.'

The elation on his face faded.

'Downside is his shoe-size is nine and we're looking for size ten - we checked all this shoes - so that's not good. Plus, his hands are too small to have made the marks on the victim's necks.'

'It's not him?' I sank back, let my face fall into my hand.

'He didn't do it, but it looks like he could be working with someone who *did*. An accomplice who is pulling the strings. The psychiatrist says Jones is a follower; he's highly suggestible, he'll do what someone with influence asks of him.'

'And this someone is the actual killer...' I sat up.

'Presumably. We're pretty certain now that the bodies were driven down to the water in body-bags, then put in a boat, perhaps a fair distance away from the bridges. Forensics says the fibres of PEVA we found are a match for the same type of body-bags as the ones William had in his flat - same colour, same material, same make.'

'So you've got him,' I said.

He put his hand up.

'Not exactly - the *type* of body-bag is the same, but we haven't got the *actual* body-bag he used and we know William *isn't* the one who strangled the victims.'

'Is it enough to arrest him?'

'Not yet. The only real link is the body-bags and his message. The boat that turned up at Kew Bridge had been stolen from the river bank near Hammersmith, but there are no matches for William's prints.'

'You've let him go?'

'For now, but he's under strict surveillance. We're hoping he'll contact the other guy.'

'Leyton Meade?'

'Don't know yet. He hasn't put a foot wrong it would appear, since he's been in the UK.'

'I've met him,' I said. 'He was with Cheryl at the clinic.'

'And?'

'He seemed incredibly sweet - but Cheryl certainly had a problem with him.'

'I wonder what that's about,' he said, pensively.

'Was William's flat obsessively neat?' I said.

'Stacks of magazines, backdating to 1990. Everything arranged in odd ways. His dinner plates were set out for the whole week side by side, with the knives and forks already in position.'

'How weird...it does fit with Asperger's, though.'

'And we found lots of handwritten sheets with figures in columns and hand-drawn maps, diagrams of circuit boards, newspaper clippings...we're looking into those.'

'It's not enough - but you seem pleased.'

'We're on to something. At last. And this hot-chocolate is great. And I'm off-duty.'

I noticed that he'd said that twice now.

I put some music on and asked him if he wanted to stay for supper. He accepted without any reservations. Spaghetti bolognaise wasn't much, but the bottle of Chardonnay helped it go down. We managed to steer ourselves away from the case and he talked about his childhood; how his father had been in the navy and met his mother at a barn dance in Italy, how he'd persuaded her to move to England.

I took a sip of wine and stared at the glass. 'But, with a father in the navy, how come you never learnt to swim?'

'I fell in an outdoor pool when I was four and panicked. I hated the water after that. I knew Dad was ashamed of me. A Commander in the Royal Navy and his son can't even swim.' He frowned. 'He tried everything to try to get me in the water again - special navy trips, swimming pools, the seaside - but I couldn't do it.'

I could picture him as a four-year-old boy floundering, out of his depth in the water, swallowing, choking, going under. I squeezed his arm and he put it around me. He seemed engrossed in his past and it was almost as if he hadn't realised he'd made such a decisive move. It felt natural to be wrapped against him.

'How did you get out that day?'

'We were at a neighbour's house and the dog started barking. The neighbour jumped in and pulled me out. I was unconscious and they got me to hospital. It gave my parents a real scare.'

I thought of Lynn Jessop's son; his head pushed under the water by cruel, malicious boys. I nearly mentioned it, but remembered the look of horror on Lynn's face when I'd proposed the idea.

'You mentioned an incident in the water, yourself,' he continued. 'The Lake District, I think you said. I'm not sure when we ran through your history that I got down the full details, in the end.'

'Oh, yeah. I forgot to tell you about that. It wasn't a big deal. It was a school trip and our dingy went the wrong way around some rocks. We ended up in rapids and the two other girls in my boat fell out. I managed to save them, that's all.'

'That's all?'

He tipped my face up towards his and gently rubbed my chin.

'They had life-jackets on. They would probably have been okay, but there was no one else around. We were the last boat to go through.'

'And you jumped into the rapids and got them both out?'

I'd always seen the incident as trivial in my mind, but now that I was explaining it, I realised that it was probably a life-threatening situation.

'There were two of them. Emma Brockley was in my class at school, I swam towards her first. She admitted she wasn't a great swimmer once we were on the water. She was nearest to me and I suppose, because I knew her, it was instinctive to get her out first. The other girl, Angie, was sixteen, in the year below me. She didn't seem to be doing anything to save herself once she fell in. She bobbed under the water a few times before I could haul her back into the dingy.'

Brad made a noise like a steam engine. 'Flippin' heck, Jules...'

I gave his cheek a tender peck. 'It's only because you can't swim that it seems a big deal.'

'You're right...saved two girls' lives...no big deal...'

His skin smelt a dizzy mixture of cocoa, faint spice and fabric softener. He pulled me to my feet, both his arms around my waist. Those lagoon-blue eyes were playing havoc with my breathing.

'I wanted to apologise,' he said, smoothing loose strands of hair away from my forehead.

'What for?'

'For being such a dork...the other time...when you...'

'It's okay...I was probably too emotionally charged.'

'And what about now?'

'What do you mean?' He ran a finger along my neckline and something hot and compelling burst into my bloodstream. 'Shall we do this properly?'

I didn't need to stop and think. I didn't need to consider Andrew, anymore. I was free and I was ready. This man; half Italian waiter, half airline pilot (but really a detective) was filling my veins with urgency, making the muscles behind my knees go soft. It made what we were going to do next seem as inevitable as a bomb exploding, once the fuse has been lit. Which, by now, it well and truly had been. Right there, right then. Unstoppable. Everything about me; my weak limbs, my dreamy eyes gave him his answer.

He pressed his mouth against mine, at first hesitantly and then as I responded, with more pressure, his tongue searching inside, exploring, caressing. We moved, joined as though in an inelegant three-legged race, through into the bedroom. There was no time to put on the light or draw the curtains. We bundled straight onto the bed. I could feel his hands making their way under my jumper, urgent, pulling at my blouse. I started wrenching at his shirt, smoothing my fingers over the thicket of dark hair on his chest. I pressed my face into it, breathing in the musky oil of his skin and ran my tongue down to the top of his jeans.

At that moment the phone rang. Rude and abrasive in my ears.

'Ugh...' I said.

'You going to get that?' he muttered between kisses.

'Do I look like I am?'

We both heard the answer-phone take over and would have ignored it had a man's voice not filled the space in the sitting room. We both froze as the voice reached us.

'Oh, God, no,' said Brad, clawing his way to the edge of the bed.

I followed him into the next room and we both stood staring at the phone, as if it was a deadly reptile we'd never seen before.

The voice was the same muffled monotone as before. William Jones.

'Are you ready to take me down? Clean and close to the edge?' came the voice.

'What the hell does he mean?' I said.

'Shush!' said Brad.

'Are you ready to take me down?' the voice repeated. 'Clean and close to the edge?'

'Should I pick up?'

'Yes. Now.'

'Hello?' I said, my voice fragile and small. Brad squashed his head against mine, trying to listen in. There was a silence the length of an inhalation and then the voice repeated the two questions.

'Mr Jones? Is this another..?' I whispered into the mouthpiece.

The phone went dead.

'Bloody hell,' said Brad. 'What on earth does it mean?'

'Another clue?' I said.

'What kind of a clue is *that*?'

'There's no date, no place, there's nothing.'

The phone rang again and I answered straight away. It was the police saying they'd heard the call and had recorded it. We both sat on the edge of the sofa staring into our own murky visions of what could happen next.

He slapped his hands onto his thighs. 'I've got to go. They'll buzz me any minute.'

'I thought you were off-duty.'

'Not now,' he said. 'I'll make sure we get another officer back outside straight away.'

He grabbed his coat and disappeared, leaving a delicate kiss brushed across my lips.

twenty-four

I don't know how long I stood there in my bare feet after Brad had left, my jumper around my neck, my blouse half-open. I noticed one button had been snapped off during our brief, but unfettered moment of passion. The clock said 11.30pm. I wasn't the least bit tired. I stomped into the kitchen, infuriated by the interruption to our special moment, but also angry and bewildered by the ridiculous clue we'd been given. *Was it really a clue to another murder? How on earth were we going to prevent this one?*

I poured boiling water on to a bag of camomile tea. We couldn't even be sure we had prevented a murder at Kew Bridge. Nothing appeared in the water, but perhaps there was still a body lying in hiding somewhere. Maybe that's why the latest clue had come along so soon afterwards. Just two days after Kew.

If we *had* managed to prevent the latest murder, it would make sense that the killer would raise the stakes by making the already cryptic clues even more tenuous. Was it really William Jones? Jones with someone else?

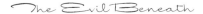

I took a sip of tea and tasted bits, like saw-dust, in my mouth. The teabag had burst. I poured it down the sink and wandered into the sitting room, automatically gravitating towards my laptop. It had helped in the past, but this time? The clue consisted of two silly random questions. My search engine wasn't going to be able to pin anything down from those, surely. I didn't even bother to punch in the message. There was no point.

Instead, I emailed everyone I could think of, asking them if they could think of any link, however weird, between *Are you ready to take me down?* and *Clean and close to the edge?* I didn't give the reason, just said something vague about a competition. I expected to receive some puzzled responses as a result, but I didn't hold out much hope that they were going to lead anywhere.

There was nothing else I could do. I went to bed.

First thing on Thursday morning, I phoned Cheryl and told her about the latest message.

'You were so helpful last time, Cheryl, do you think we might–'

I was interested in her response. If, in some way, she was involved with her brother, she might try to throw me off track - although the royal connection she'd come up with after the last message had eventually taken us to the right bridge. I still wasn't ready to condemn her.

'Say the questions again,' she said.

I heard her breathing, then she said she was picking up nothing at all. 'It's sometimes like that. Sometimes there's no connection, nothing happens. Nothing at all.'

'But, if we could meet - sit together, like we did last time...'

'I'm not getting a thing, Juliet.'

'I could get the recording of his voice. You might be able to–' I didn't care that desperation was oozing from my voice.

'You can't switch these psychic powers on and off, Juliet. I'm sorry. I'll call you if anything comes to me.'

She cut me off and I sat holding the handset in some vain hope that I'd misheard her and she was on her way over. The room suddenly felt hollow and I was acutely aware of being alone. *Was Cheryl telling the truth or was she deliberately holding back this time?*

I knew Cheryl had no appointments at Holistica that day, but I had one supervisee I had to see. Feeling isolated and burdened with the excruciating pressure of stopping another murder from taking place, I was pleased to turn my attentions somewhere else. I caught the Tube - I couldn't trust myself to drive.

Clive had dyed his hair pink, looking as if he'd been in the same wash as his red t-shirt.

'Nice,' I said, realising as I said it, that it sounded half-hearted.

'I know, I know. Supposed to be "burgundy",' he said. 'A friend did it. Never trust amateurs.'

There was no one waiting in the reception area and Clive was keeping himself busy by painting his toe-nails black.

I had a thought. Clive was an off-the-wall sort of bloke. It was worth a try. 'You wouldn't happen to know a link between "Are you ready to take me down?" and "Clean and close to the edge?", would you?'

Clive let out a little laugh that sounded like a Pekingese sneezing. I took that as my answer and turned to go, but he spoke before I got to the stairs.

'It's obvious,' he said.

'What is?' I said.

'Both of them.'

'I'm sorry, Clive, you've lost me.'

'They're both songs.'

'What are?'

'Those phrases: "Are you ready to take me down?" and "Clean and close to the edge?" - they are both song titles...by the Federal Jackdaws.'

I could feel my face twisting into a something resembling a gargoyle.

'*Federal Jackdaws*? What on earth..?'

'Yeah. I saw them in concert last year. Bloody good they are too. "Are you ready to take me down?" was a single; came out earlier this year, and "Clean and close to the edge?" was released ages ago. 2003, I think.'

It didn't make any sense. What did this band, the Federal Jackdaws, have to do with a London Bridge or the river Thames? I found myself sitting down on the edge of one of the chairs.

'Are you okay?' he said. 'You've gone a funny colour.'

I thought that was ironic, coming from him. He got up, after rolling up the legs of his jeans to avoid smearing his toenails, and brought over a plastic cup of water.

'It's not what I expected, that's all,' I said. I rang and left a message for Brad, hoping it would mean something to him.

'Why do you ask? Pub-quiz?' asked Clive.

'They don't have any link to a bridge in London, by any chance, do they? Those songs, or the Federal Jaybirds...'

'Federal *Jackdaws*, if you don't mind.' He made a little 'humph' noise. 'A London bridge? Sorry - I can't help you with that one.'

After seeing my supervisee, I wandered out into the street in a daze, wondering what Brad and Derek Moorcroft were making of this one. It had started raining and I ducked into the doorway of a closed shop to call Brad again. His team had also got as far as the Federal Jackdaws, but had no other leads. He was as incredulous as I was.

'We're looking for an expert on this Indie band,' he said, 'to see if they have any connection to any London bridges.'

'It seems so obscure,' I said.

'Yeah, but hasn't that been the theme of this case?'

It started to rain harder. I didn't have an umbrella and the underground station was a few streets away. 'There's more bad news, I'm afraid...with William Jones,' he said. I waited. 'Apparently, he was in his flat all yesterday evening and didn't use either his mobile phone or his landline.'

'Are you saying the call I had last night wasn't from him?'

'The call was made from a coin-box near Waterloo station, but it wasn't him. *But*,' he emphasised the word, 'it could have been his voice.'

'Sorry?'

'We've got specialised spectrographic software that picks up unique features of a person's speech. Things like pitch, tone, cadence and vibrations in the larynx. It's not a hundred per cent accurate, but the voice analyst says it's close enough to identify Jones as our caller - only the voice was slightly distorted this time, as though it was played from a tape-recorder.'

'So, it *was* William Jones' voice...recorded beforehand, you mean?'

'Looks like it.'

'He's one step ahead of us every single time. Can't you just arrest him, on the basis of a voice-match?'

'Nothing happened at Kew, remember. The previous messages you got were in text. We can't attach his voice to those.'

I drifted out from the doorway, not caring now that I was getting soaked.

'But the two phone calls I had were threats. He called me, threatening to kill someone.'

'No. He didn't. He left a few words, that's all. A cryptic clue. No mention of killing anyone.'

I moaned.

'There's something else,' he said.

Why did I always hate it when he said that?

'It looks like the killer was on to us at Kew Bridge.'

'Really? How do you know?'

'Forensics checked out the boat that drifted towards us. It looked empty, but, as well as grit, debris and sand, they picked up two hairs in the bottom, deliberately left for us, it would seem.'

'And?'

'You remember giving us DNA samples, early on, so we could screen you out of any evidence we found at the crime scenes?' I held my breath. 'Well...

the hairs we found in the boat...' There was a silence and I thought I'd lost the line.

I squeezed the phone. 'What? What about them?'

'They're... yours, I'm afraid.' As he spoke, my arm went limp and my bag fell to the pavement. I swore. I couldn't trust my legs to continue walking, to hold me upright. I staggered inside the next doorway and rested my head against the wet brick. *My own hair. How up-close-and-personal can you get? Left where the body was supposed to be.* My bag was soaking wet. My head was spinning. I let the wall take the weight of my whole body. I could feel myself sinking down onto the soggy doormat.

'Juliet...are you okay?'

I was crouched in a ball. 'Not really...'

'Don't worry, you're not a suspect again.'

I rallied suddenly. 'I should think not!'

'We're more concerned about what it means.'

'How on earth did the killer get hold of my hair?' I cried. A van roared past, sending a cascade of water on to the kerb.

'Where are you?'

'Near Holistica. On foot.'

'Is one of our officers tailing you?'

I glanced up and found the blue Astra waiting at the kerb. 'Penny's right here.'

'Good. Make sure you don't lose her.'

'I'm going home,' I said, forcing myself to my feet. I was tempted to hail a lift from the WPC, but knew that was against the rules, so I broke into a jog until I got to the underground.

The flat felt cold and unwelcoming when I got back. Dark and hostile, like a place I barely knew. I ran into every room with clenched fists checking for an intruder. I looked in the wardrobes, under the bed, behind the doors. Nothing, but still I didn't feel safe.

I needed to keep busy, so I made a sandwich for lunch, but put most of it in the bin, then popped downstairs to see if Jackie was there. There was no reply. I didn't want to be left on my own all day with four walls bearing down on me and the knowledge that the killer had somehow managed to get close enough to grab a handful of my hair.

I picked up the hairbrush in my bedroom and glared at it. There was another one in my bag. There were hairs on my pillow. I wanted to scream.

My life didn't feel like it belonged to me anymore; bit by bit, it was being dismantled by this monstrous killer. Fragments of who I was were gradually being taken from me. Personal momentos from my life were being removed and placed on the bodies of dead women. I felt naked, stripped, like someone was slowly peeling away my skin. Everything was slipping away; my privacy, my dignity - my sanity.

I walked back into the bedroom. The blue Astra was in place across the road. At least I wasn't quite alone.

I switched on my laptop and took a look at several sites about *The Federal Jackdaws*. I couldn't find any mention of London or any songs with a London bridge in the title. I knew Brad and his team must be doing the same; I wished I could have been with them. I started running through play-lists on video-sharing sites, but many were only short extracts. I moved on to downloading lyrics and listening to full-length videos and suddenly I found something. Seconds later Brad was on the line.

'We've got something,' he said.

'So have I,' I shrieked. 'The *Body-Snatchers* track,' I said, jumping in before he could say any more.

'That's impressive,' he said. 'There are eight of us here working on it and only one of you.'

'Blackfriars Bridge,' I said, triumphantly.

'Ditto. Pitlock has searched every line of their lyrics and that's the only bridge mentioned by name.'

'Then it has to be there, surely. That has to be the bridge.'

I was on my feet, but Brad's words were slowing down instead of speeding up. 'There could be something else we haven't got to yet; something in one of their interviews...' he said. 'Perhaps one of them lived near a London bridge sometime, maybe they were on a bridge when they wrote one of their songs...'

'I've just heard the song - it's all about dead people!'

I could visualise the broad red and white arches of Blackfriars Bridge, with its white criss-crossed ironwork and gold rosettes set into the red beams. I could see the green-black river rushing underneath it and I knew we had to act on this.

'You've got to get William Jones in again, question him about it,' I said.

He took his time. 'It's all conjecture at this stage.'

'But, talk to him, interview him, break him down. He's fragile, get him to tell you what the plan is - we need a date. We have no idea when the next one is due to take place.'

'Blackfriars is in a very busy section of the Thames. There are always people about. There are a fair number of security cameras. It's an ambitious project to get a body down there, in the water, without being seen - even at night from a boat.'

'He's managed it before! At Battersea Bridge. And the police can't be on high-alert every single day until Christmas. We need a *date*.'

'I know. You're right. But, we don't even know if it's definitely Blackfriars Bridge.'

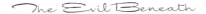

'Get him in. Please. Speak to Jones again or let me do it. If he has, or thinks he has some personal connection with me, perhaps I can surprise him and catch him off guard.'

I could hear his pen rattling between his teeth.

'Okay. Let's go for it. I'll speak to the SIO.'

twenty-five

William Jones seemed less agitated this time. He knew the room, knew DCI Madison and had a sense of how things worked. The five of them sat in silence around the black shiny-topped table: Brad, Jones, Melody Kemp and the social worker, whose name nobody seemed to know. Poor woman looked like she'd been hanging around for hours. An officer stood by the door.

'It's Thursday, November 12th and the time is 8.30pm,' Brad said into the tape-recorder. Nothing moved except the spool of the tape. I was tucked away in the adjacent box-room, crouched on the floor, my hand over my mouth. I wasn't alone this time. Cheryl was with me. I'd let her have the only chair.

Brad had told me that Cheryl's alibis were squeaky clean for all the dates in question, but as long as her brother was still in the picture, Brad still had her on his list of potential suspects. It was certainly unorthodox to have so many 'civilians' wandering around the police station, but he'd suggested we could kill two birds with one stone and keep a close eye on Cheryl while also interviewing Jones. Part of my job was to check out how she reacted to what was going on in the interview room. So far, she'd not done anything out of the ordinary. She'd come along with me without any apparent reservations, although she'd complained in the car about the way the police had been harassing her brother.

She certainly hadn't reacted when she first saw William Jones through the two-way mirror, but Brad said he had something up his sleeve for later on.

I was getting cramp crouching on the floor in the small room, so I swapped to a kneeling position. Cheryl had her eyes firmly fixed through the two-way glass. A beat in the distance started pumping out of the speakers in the top corners of the interview room. I recognised it from earlier: the Federal Jackdaws' song, *Body-Snatchers*. Cheryl and I watched Jones' reaction. He started bobbing his head.

'Do you know the tune?' asked Brad, smiling.

'It's a good song.'

'You know it?'

'Yes. Federal Jackdaws.'

A brief glance passed between Brad and the solicitor.

'Do you know the words?' asked Brad.

'All the words. I know all the words. All the songs.'

'That's amazing. You know every song they released?'

'Yes. All the words.'

'Do you know the first line to this song?'

'Yes.'

'And which bridge is mentioned, Mr Jones?'

'Blackfriars Bridge.'

Jones jutted his chin in and out to the beat. The music faded and he looked around him, disappointed, trying to work out why the music had stopped. He sat still and started plucking at his neck. It was already red-raw with friction.

'What do you think?' I whispered to Cheryl. I was hoping, like before, that she'd use her psychic skills to discover something none of us knew.

Cheryl stared at the scene through the glass. 'I'm not sure, yet.'

She dropped her head and closed her eyes. I let her get on with her own inner process; I, for certain, couldn't take my eyes off what was happening in the adjacent room.

'Do you know someone called Juliet Grey, Mr Jones?' Brad asked him.

'No. I don't know her.'

'You haven't met her?'

'No.'

'Do you know who she is?'

There was the briefest of hesitations before he answered. 'No.'

'Have you seen her at all?'

'Done nothing wrong.'

I could hear an edge in his voice now, his words came out slightly quicker, clipped, coated in a brittle layer of nervousness. I remembered what I'd told the others about people with Asperger's often finding it hard to lie.

'Tell us about Blackfriars Bridge,' said Brad.

'What do you want to know?'

'Anything at all that you can tell us about it.'

'Toll bridge at first. 995 feet long, made of Portland stone with nine arches, opened in 1769. Current one was opened in 1869 and is 923 feet long and 105 feet wide.' He carried on as though reciting from a catalogue. Brad stopped him.

'Okay. That's fine. You know a lot about it.'

'All the bridges,' he said.

'You know a lot about all the London bridges?'

'Yes. Nothing wrong.'

'Do you remember what happened at Hammersmith, Richmond and Battersea Bridges, Mr Jones?'

'Yes.'

'And what was that?'

'Ladies dead,' he said. 'Saw it on the news.'

'I know we've talked about this before, Mr Jones, but did you touch those ladies? Put them inside black body-bags?'

'No.'

'Do you know what body-bags are?'

'Yes. Used them at the funeral parlour. For dead people.'

'Do you have any body-bags, Mr Jones? Did you keep any for yourself?'

Jones looked down at the table. The police had taken away the bags they'd found at his flat as possible evidence. I wondered if he might be thinking he was being tricked.

Without warning, Ms Kemp broke the silence. 'My client is tired,' she said. The sound was hoarse and breathy, as though her voice-box was being squeezed through a pasta maker. Brad glared at her.

'We'll take a break as soon as your client has answered the question,' he said. He turned to Jones again. 'Did you keep any body-bags for yourself?'

Mr Jones was chewing at a fingernail that had long since tried to retreat behind the cuticle.

'Mr Kain said I could,' he said.

'Mr Kain?'

'Funeral director. My boss.'

'Okay. And why did you want to keep them?'

'For my mother.'

'For your mother?'

'For keeping her long dresses clean.'

'Are you sure about that?'

'Yes. Party dresses. Posh. Expensive. Keep them nice. Nothing wrong.'

Brad's sigh said it all. Disappointment, frustration, exasperation. It dripped from him like sweat. He sneered at Ms Kemp.

'Okay, we'll take a break there,' he said.

I heard Brad shouting at an officer outside the door. 'Get me the report. I want it now. I want to know exactly what Kain said about the body-bags. And let's get Mrs Jones back in - and what happened to tracking down his father?'

He came in to join us. Cheryl still had her eyes closed. I put my finger to my lips to make sure he didn't disturb her. Brad ignored my instruction.

'What do you make of it?' he said, his voice riddled with sarcasm. His presence was weighty and cumbersome in that small space. It was like putting a bull in a broom cupboard; energy crackled from his teeth, his eyes, his bare arms.

Cheryl lifted her head, opening her eyes.

'It's Blackfriars, alright,' she said. 'But there's something else. Something different.'

'And what's that?' said Brad, rubbing his forehead.

I squatted down beside Cheryl and made my voice soft. 'Something different?'

'I'm not sure, yet. Something underground,' she said, slowly, as though she was watching a slideshow click from one scene to the next in front of her wide, blank eyes.

'Are you saying the victim isn't going to turn up in the river, like the others?' Brad's tone was hard, dismissive..

'I don't know,' said Cheryl, her eyes half-closed now, as if she was straining to hear something in the distance.

'Well, that's helpful,' he said and stormed out.

I bit my bottom lip and stood up as the door slammed.

'He's under a lot of pressure,' I said. 'Don't take it personally.'

'It's okay,' said Cheryl, shaking her head. 'I'm used to hostility when it comes to anything psychic.'

I leant against the narrow sill under the two-way mirror. 'When you say it's something underground - could that be the Tube station?'

Her face brightened up. 'It's possible.'

'I'll go and check on a map - see how far the Tube is from the bridge itself.'

I left Cheryl and went into the main office.

Brad was standing by the incident board, staring without any focus. He looked like he was somewhere else; a place where he was trapped and scared and starting to panic. I wanted to touch him, stroke his face, squeeze his arm, press some comfort into him. I tapped his shoulder.

'Anything going on with Ms Hoffman?' he said.

'I haven't picked up anything about her responses that concerns me.' Apart from the fact that Cheryl seemed to 'know' things, she hadn't done anything to raise my suspicions. 'She thinks the Tube might be important,' I said, hoping to drag Brad back into a world where there were still answers, still hope. 'We need a map.'

Brad pulled one out from a row of reference books and flicked through it.

'The Underground is right at the end of the bridge,' said Brad. 'Maybe he's going to kill the next victim down there.'

'It would be odd - for him to change his methods,' I said, pensively. 'He has some reason for leaving the bodies in the *river* under the bridges. It has some significance for him.'

'But, maybe, because the last one at Kew didn't go to plan...maybe he - they - have decided to change the plan,' he said.

'I'm not sure. I really don't think the way they're killing them will change. It's very precise. It's a ritual. This guy, for certain, won't be happy about changing that.'

Cheryl joined us. 'Just remembered,' she said. 'Blackfriars Tube is closed...for months and months. They're upgrading the mainline station.'

'So that's that, then,' said Brad, looking smug . 'It won't be in the Tube.'

'We're back with the bridge again, then,' I said.

'But we know it isn't Mr Jones doing the actual killing,' said Brad. 'We know his hands are too small.

The marks on the necks of all three women show the same. It isn't him.'

He didn't seem to care that Cheryl, someone he still regarded as a suspect, was within earshot.

'But he's got to be heavily involved. His knowledge of the bridges. The same make of body-bags. Turning up at Kew...the voice-match...' I said.

'It's not enough.'

'We need a date,' I said. 'You've got to ask him about when the next murder is planned to take place.'

'Easier said than done,' said Brad. He wandered off towards the coffee machine.

I drew up behind him. 'Let me talk to him,' I said. 'It might throw him off guard. If he is involved, he'll know who I am. He might let something slip.'

He rubbed his day-old stubble, staring at the plastic cup filled with a milky grey substance that looked nothing like coffee.

'Okay,' he said. 'But first let's get Cheryl Hoffman in there. I want an impromptu meeting between them to see how Jones responds to *her*.' He held a finger up close to my nose. 'And when Cheryl leaves, it will be your turn. But, you *must* follow my lead to the letter – okay? No going off on your own track with this, got it?'

'As if,' I said, turning away.

We reconvened outside the interview room and I saw Brad have a quick word with Cheryl. She nodded and followed him into the room, while I went into the small adjoining one. Ms Kemp had stayed with her client.

'Do you know who this is?' said Brad, as Cheryl walked in.

I saw nothing in Jones' face to indicate he recognised her. He stared at her as if he expected her to do something. Cheryl sat down.

'This is Cheryl Hoffman,' said Brad. Jones continued to stare. 'Do you know this lady?

'No,' said Jones, clearly, without hesitation.

'Do you know her brother, Leyton Meade?'

Brad and I both had our eyes trained on William Jones, but he didn't flinch. Didn't twitch. He simply looked confused.

'No,' he said. He looked at Ms Kemp, hoping for some direction. She gave him an encouraging nod.

Brad pulled a sheet out of a file on his desk.

'Are you absolutely sure you don't know this man?' He turned to the tape and said, 'I'm showing Mr Jones a photograph of Leyton Meade.' I could see from this distance that it was a much better image than the one he'd shown me at Kew Bridge.

No reaction. Jones shook his head.

'For the machine, please, Mr Jones.'

'No - I don't know him.' he said, in a bored tone.

Brad signalled to Cheryl and she left the room. Seconds later she joined me next door.

'Your turn,' she said.

I walked in and sat down.

Brad asked the same question. 'Mr Jones, do you know who this is?'

William lifted his eyes and instantly dropped them back down to his finger nails.

'No,' he said.

'Do you know what a lie is, Mr Jones?' said Brad.

'Course I do. I'm not thick, you know. Stop treating me like a mental person.'

Ms Kemp glared at Brad.

'Okay. Sorry,' he said, making a bridge with his fingers on the table. He opened his mouth to say something else, but I was too quick for him.

'I'm Juliet Grey,' I said. 'I wanted to ask you about the dates of the recent murders under the London bridges.' I wasn't quite following our plan, but I couldn't help myself. Brad sank back as though someone had hit him in the chest. 'Shall I call you William or Mr Jones?

'William.'

'Good. You said before that you know the dates of the recent murders, William?'

'Yes.'

'Can you remind us again?'

'September 20th, October 6th, October 12th and November 9th.'

'Are they special dates?'

'They're when it happened.'

'When what happened?'

He looked up and for the first time since I'd been observing him, he let his eyes engage. With mine. They locked on for a least a second; searching, scared, uncertain.

'When the women...' he said.

He stopped. I felt a flash of victory tear through my rib cage.

'But, no one was found at Kew Bridge on November 9th,' I said. 'There was nothing on the news that day. Nothing in the papers. Why is that one of the dates?'

William looked down at his nails, across to the tape recorder, down at the floor. His fingers went to his neck. Pulling, plucking at the skin on his neck again.

'You're confusing my client,' said Ms Kemp, raising an eyebrow in my direction as if it was a lethal weapon.

I leant forward, ignoring her. 'Why is November 9th one of the dates, William?'

'I went to the bridge,' he said.

'Yes. You went to Kew Bridge on November 9th. The police saw you there, didn't they?'

He nodded.

'Did you go to the bridges on the other dates; on September 20th and October 6th and 12th?'

'That's when the women were killed,' he said.

'That's right. But were you there as well, William? At the other bridges - Hammersmith, Richmond and Battersea - on those dates?'

'Those are the dates when it happened,' he said. 'Water... bridges.'

Ms Kemp slapped her hand on the table. 'You're harassing Mr Jones,' she said. She turned towards William and whispered something to him. He nodded.

I took a breath and sat back.

I could see Brad lean forward out of the corner of my eye. He was about to say something, but I hadn't finished. I put my arm out, desperate to stop the juggernaut from running us all over. William was staring at the table. I sent my eyes swiftly around the room, exhorting them all with my gaze not to jump in with anything at this point. I knew exactly what I wanted to say next, but I needed the silence first. It was a crucial moment of power; an apparent vacuum fizzing with energy. Everyone froze as if I'd pressed the pause button on a DVD player. Not even Ms Kemp twitched.

'When's the next date?' I said. Matter-of-fact, with no great weight or emphasis. 'The next important date.'

'Soon,' he said.

'You know when it will be?' I said, slowly, quietly, gently.

'I know when it was,' he said.

'You know when it *was* when something happened?' I said. 'Something to do with the water and a bridge?'

'Yes. Bad things.' He stroked his hair, as if soothing himself after a frightening incident.

'And when *was* that?' I said, 'The next date when the bad thing happened.'

'November 15th,' he said.

I did a quick mental calendar check. I could almost hear us all doing it, simultaneously. It was the twelfth, today. The fifteenth was this coming Sunday.

'November 15th?' I said. 'That's when the next bad thing happened - you sure?'

'Yes. Never forget. No need to write it down.' He pointed to his head to indicate where he was storing all the dates when something bad had happened.

'And these bad things...the bad things that happened...they happened to you?' I asked.

'Yes.' He answered straight away. Clean, straightforward.

'And they're connected with the water...under bridges...on the dates we've mentioned?'

'Yes.'

I sat back again. 'Thank you, William. That's really helpful.'

Brad leant over to switch off the tape-recorder and we left the room.

As soon as we got into the corridor, he rounded on me. I braced myself.

'I've got to hand it to you.' he said, a broad smile transforming his face. 'That was something.'

I was holding my chest. I felt like I did on the day I ran a ten-kilometre race with a head-cold. The floor was starting to roll like waves in the sea; the walls were pulling me towards them. Brad grabbed a chair just in time. I sank my head between my knees.

'Well done, girl.' Cheryl was at my side, her hand stroking my back.

'Let's not get too ahead of ourselves, here,' said Brad, chewing his lip. 'He knows the dates of the murders. And where they took place. So he reads a newspaper...'

'He knows the case inside out,' I said.

Brad looked like he was about to rest his hand on my shoulder, then dropped it. 'We've got a date, but it's still not conclusive. Jones hasn't owned up to anything, yet.'

'He's using the same dates that have some significance to him in his past,' I said, ignoring Brad's scepticism. 'Dates, when something traumatic happened to him.' All of a sudden, I needed to be outside. The room was stuffy, stifling.

'Let's give Juliet some air, shall we?' said Brad, who must have seen the way my face was rapidly going grey. They walked me outside into the car-park.

I leant against the wall and took some deep breaths. 'I should have asked him if it was Blackfriars Bridge,' I said. 'We need to know for sure if that's the right place.'

'No,' said Brad. 'If we mention Blackfriars again in that context, he'll think we know too much. He... they...will change the plans.'

I mulled it over. 'Maybe you're right.' I turned to Cheryl. 'Did you pick up anything else?' I said, straightening up. The duplicated blurred shapes around me were gradually returning to form only one of everything.

'Nothing apart from this underground feeling at Blackfriars Bridge. But I can't put my finger on it.'

twenty-six

I woke up at 6am the following morning with a pervasive sense of gloom. Two days to go. Everything was in the hands of the police now; they had a date and a location and there was nothing I could do. I tried to go back to sleep, but my body felt like it had been hooked up to a caffeine-drip all night.

The two clients I had booked in for the following day had cancelled, but I had to get out of the flat. I couldn't spend the day doing ironing or watching false smiles on daytime television. I wanted to be sealed within a crowd of people, doing something normal and every day. Besides, it was Friday, 13th. I'm not normally superstitious, but with so many awful things happening lately, I didn't want to be on my own fretting over what fate might decide to add to the mix.

I ran through a list of places I could go. The National Gallery seemed about right: ordinary people, distraction and nowhere near any bridges. I pulled the curtain aside in my bedroom and spotted WPC Penny

Kenton inside the car across the road. She must have drawn the short straw again. I texted her to say I was catching the Tube from Putney Bridge to Trafalgar Square, and left without any breakfast.

I thought about the information the police were now working with: Blackfriars Bridge, November 15th - and realised how flimsy it was. Deduced on the basis of a pop song and the word of a disturbed man who the police knew wasn't even the killer. What if we'd got it horribly wrong? What if William Jones was feeding us red-herrings? What if another woman was going to die because the conclusions we'd come to were wrong?

I reflected on Cheryl's sense that there was something underground in connection with the impending murder. It couldn't be the Tube, because that had been closed for months, but was there anything else underground in that area? Or was that a red-herring, too?

Surely, there were too many coincidences for William not to be involved, but I wasn't sure he had anything further to tell. Presumably, whoever William was working with, had sense enough to realise he would be a liability if questioned by the police. The less he knew the better.

Brad's main concern was that the plan might change. William had only mentioned Blackfriars Bridge in the context of the song by the Federal Jackdaws, so he may not have felt he'd given that piece of information away. But William *had* revealed the next date, although he'd done it in the context of explaining how all the dates had been relevant for *him* in the past. Given his mental condition, maybe William wouldn't *know* that he'd let something slip.

My view was that William certainly wouldn't want the date to change. To him the dates were sacrosanct: they were significant for their link to something traumatic in his past and he wouldn't want to shift to a different date that had no meaning for him. A change of date would only be in question, of course, if William had told his accomplice that the fifteenth was out of the bag. My instinct was that he hadn't.

It was pouring down and there was a biting wind as I hit street level at Trafalgar Square. I pulled my coat around me and re-wrapped my scarf, keen to get inside.

I trawled round the galleries, trying to transport myself into a world of high art and aesthetics. I went up to level two, towards the paintings from the end of the nineteenth century. I drifted from room to room and tried to focus on the paintings, but stopped with a jolt every time I came across a picture of a river with a bridge. There were plenty of them: Canaletto, Monet, Turner. I was standing in front of one by Millias, when I recognised the figure who drifted into my field of vision. I knew the soft corn-coloured curls tucked inside his collar, the scuffed hems at the bottom of his jeans.

He hadn't seen me and was gazing at the picture. I watched him tip his head on one side, taking in the scene. It was *Ophelia*. A Pre-Raphaelite portrait of a woman lying in a stream. Just before she drowns.

I saw the look of melancholy on Andrew's face change into an expression of fascination and delight and found myself starting to wonder if he was responding to the quality of the oil technique or the imminent fate of the subject.

Abruptly, to block the direction in which my brain was heading, I stepped forward and tapped him on the shoulder.

He said how good it was to see me.

'You too,' I said. My eyes sought out Penny, to give her a nod of approval. 'How have you been?'

'Good. Very good. I'm still off the drink. Going to AA meetings regularly, now. Done some new paintings. Got some work in a gallery in Oxford. Yeah, pretty good. And you?'

Life had moved on for Andrew and I realised mine had remained stuck fast in the cement of uncertainty and fear.

'Pretty much the same,' I said, trying not to look at the picture.

A woman came up beside Andrew's shoulder. I saw her shyly take hold of his hand.

'This is Genevieve,' he said, lifting up their inter-linked fingers so I could see they were a couple. 'She's a photographer.' She had long blonde hair, was a good four inches taller than me with a cavernous cleavage tucked under the fur neckline of her coat. It looked like the same woman I'd seen at his award ceremony. Andrew had clearly reverted back to type. I could image a few more nude portraits emerging out of this relationship.

'Hi,' she said, 'you an artist, too?' Her French accent was strong and sexy.

'No,' I said. 'But I do appreciate art.'

She showed no signs of recognition at my name. It would appear that Andrew hadn't mentioned me. We made polite conversation, before I looked at my watch and said I had to go. I watched their heads lean together as they moved into the next gallery.

By now, my concern over the way in which Andrew had been transfixed by the painting had been overtaken by more complicated emotions. I felt flat and angry. Andrew really had moved on. But it wasn't the new girlfriend that disturbed me, it was something else. I blindly made my way to the exit. Then I realised why I was so upset. The gorgeous Genevieve was getting the Andrew I had always wanted; carefree, fun, but above all, sober. The timing had been wrong when the two of us had been together and the sober version of Andrew hadn't been available, except in tantalisingly short bursts.

I ran down the steps of the Gallery, not caring whether Penny was keeping up or not. It was raining hard and I didn't bother to pull up the hood on my anorak. Getting wet and cold was fitting, given how desolate I felt inside.

On the way back, I had a call from Brad. He wanted to meet, but he didn't say why. He'd suggested the pub by the river in Putney, so at least I could have a drink. It was about all I was fit for.

The Duke's Head was swamped with Friday evening commuters in their blue pin-striped suits and pink shirts, so we took our pints outside. The picnic tables on the patio were full, so we wandered over to the path overlooking the water. The pub was literally ten meters from the river.

'Is this your night off?' I said, innocently.

'Only a couple of hours. Then I'm back on again.'

I didn't want him to see my disappointment. I could see he had other things on his mind. 'Things are moving,' he said.

'Tell me,' I said, huddling into the lining of his coat like a child. I was glad the pub was too packed. The cold outside drew us together.

'We've been looking into the possibility of an underground aspect to Blackfriars Bridge.'

'Really? You're taking what Cheryl said seriously?'

'We're covering all avenues, that's all. We would have done it anyway.'

'Is Cheryl off the hook now?'

'We're still keeping a close eye on her. The SIO thinks killers of this kind - the smart ones - often want recognition for their brilliance, but they can end up shooting themselves in the foot by giving away too much information. She says they thrive on the risk of staying one step ahead of the police. Could be that Cheryl is playing that game. She could be in on this with both Jones *and* her brother.' He ran his finger down my nose. 'Or she could be genuine, like you say.'

'I hope so,' I said, the chill forcing me to press further under his coat.

'Did you track down Jones' parents?'

'We'd already spoken to Mrs Jones to find out more about his condition and his whereabouts, but we got her back in again to ask about the body-bags. She confirmed William's story, but says she's only taken them to keep him happy. She said it was far too morbid to keep her dresses in them. The funeral parlour let him have old stock, apparently. She didn't have a lot to add, to be honest. Says none of the dates William mentioned mean anything to her.'

'And his father?'

'They split up years ago and he's remarried, living in Dorset. Couldn't throw much light on William.

Says he hasn't seen his son for years and that's corroborated all round.'

'So we're left with William's date and Blackfriars Bridge. What else is underground in that area? The Tube is closed, right?'

'Yes. But we've discovered something else. I don't know how much you know about the city, but much of it is built over old rivers that have gone underground.'

'It vaguely rings a bell. The underground rivers of London...I saw a programme about it once.'

'The Fleet is one of those hidden rivers. It goes underground near Hampstead Heath station, then stays buried under the streets until it comes out right under Blackfriars Bridge.'

My jaw gaped. 'The exact spot...'

'We've had an officer following the last section over-ground and there are places where you can stand over a manhole cover and actually hear the river running underneath it.'

I grabbed his collar. 'Oh my God, Brad - it makes sense! An underground river ending at Blackfriars could be the place.'

'There's a problem as far as we're concerned,' he said. 'Once the Fleet gets to Blackfriars, it's become part of the sewage system.'

'Ooh – not so good.' I stared blankly at the water. 'Hold on a minute - so far the bodies have deliberately been left where they would be found. Wouldn't something as bulky as a body get trapped out of sight, down there?'

'That's the big question. We've talked to experts and they reckon with enough heavy rain, the cast iron floodgates inside the Fleet's outfall would open up, causing it to overflow and a body would be swept out into the Thames.'

'So, it fits - if there's enough rain.' I looked up at the sky that over the last few days had been tipping water down at regular intervals. 'How much rain is heavy rain?'

'The Met Office says this could be enough.'

'How would someone get down to it?'

'That's the issue. We talked to Thames Water and we've had our guys over at New Bridge Street. The best access to the sewer is in the middle of a busy road. You'd have to stop the traffic. There's no way anyone could get down there without drawing considerable attention to themselves.'

'In theory, though, could a body be dropped down a manhole into the sewer?'

'Yes. It's wide enough. Then it would gradually make its way towards the floodgates.'

'What are you going to do? It's Saturday tomorrow and then Sunday is the big day.'

'I'm going down with a team tomorrow to take a look.'

'Into the sewers? Wow...' I stood back, animated again. 'Can I come?'

What was I thinking? The words came out of nowhere and as soon as I uttered them I realised how childish and incongruous they sounded. Me – miss prim and proper – literally mucking in and getting myself filthy? Understandably, he gave me his characteristic you're-talking-gibberish look. 'No way,' he chuckled.

I rested my hands on the wooden rail and stared out across the choppy black water. The Thames looked relatively clean, but I knew it harboured risks of E coli, salmonella and hepatitis. What would the sewers be like?

'I need to know if we've got it right,' I said earnestly. 'If what William told us adds up to another wretched victim – down there under the bridge.'

'You'd get to hear about it soon enough.'

'Yeah, I know,' I huffed. 'On the side-lines - waiting. I feel so useless. My life's been completely taken over by this lethal game of catch-up and I've been powerless to do a thing.' I turned to him, took hold of both his hands. 'I'm caught in the middle of it and yet, I'm always at least one step behind. Can you understand?'

'Sort of.' He withdrew his hands and turned to the water too, the breeze lifting his hair into thick tufts.

'Come on, Brad. When am I ever going to get another opportunity to get knee-deep in...a London sewer?'

'Not a chance.'

'Why not? I've been really helpful, so far.'

'I can't deny that, but this is different. It'll be disgusting.'

'Not suitable for a woman, is that what you're saying?'

'No...it's dangerous. If we don't get the timing right and the water rises too fast, it's going to be panic-stations down there. It's a police operation. You're not trained.'

'And you are?'

'I'm a police officer. You're a psychotherapist. Which one do you think has a better chance of doing a good job?'

'Excuse me. Who's the good swimmer around here?'

He opened his mouth and closed it again. I leant into him.

'In any case,' he pointed out, 'what exactly do you think you would you do if we caught whoever it was, in the act – or found a body?'

I sighed. 'I've no idea. I just need to *know* – that's all.'

'Subject is closed, okay? The answer is no. I'm serious.'

My irresistible charm wasn't going to work this time.

I felt his phone buzz against my hip and he pulled away from me, nodding his head in response to the caller.

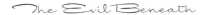

'What is it?' I said.

He closed his phone, his face grave. 'Andrew Wishbourne. We've found an old pair of flat-soled brogues in his outhouse. Size ten. '

I didn't hesitate. 'Andrew's a size eight-and-a-half.' I was trying to imagine Andrew in brogues. It just wasn't him. I'd only ever seen him wear trainers. 'They must belong to someone else.'

'I've got to follow this up.' He buttoned his coat and left. I walked back home, a deep crease cut into my brow.

It was Saturday, 14th. I'd barely slept: dreams of deep tunnels, thick brown water and putrid darkness came and went in waves. I kept waking up, and despite the danger Brad talked about - and the inevitable stench – I knew I had to be there. This entire sinister web was woven around *me* – I was at the centre of it, no one else. I couldn't stand aside now that we had a date and a location.

Besides, it was *doing something*. Sitting about waiting was going to be far worse. I'd done enough of that.

I knew it would start to get light at around 7am and although Brad hadn't told me exactly what time his crew were heading over to Blackfriars, common sense said they'd do it early, before the traffic started to build up.

Before I'd gone to bed, I'd tapped on Jackie's door to ask a favour. Although I'd hardly ever seen him, I knew Tony was a mechanic. Jackie beckoned me into the kitchen and started delving into the wash basket.

'This is his spare,' she said, holding it up. The boiler suit was crumpled and spattered with oil and paint. 'It's not very clean.'

'That will be perfect. Where I'm going it's not going to matter.'

'You really going down a sewer?' she said, as if I'd told her I was going to walk off the edge of a cliff.

'Don't tell anyone,' I cautioned. 'I'll give it a really good wash...twice...with disinfectant, afterwards. Tony will never know.'

At 5.30am, I climbed into the grimy boiler-suit. Infused with the sweat of a strange man, it felt unpleasant, with an inappropriate intimacy. Thankfully, it was going to be cold outside, so I had every reason for wearing layers of tatty clothes underneath, to keep Tony's suit from touching my bare skin.

Tony was only a little taller than me, but portly round the middle and once I'd fastened the buttons up the front I looked like the Michelin Man. I gathered in the excess material under a wide belt at the waist and it looked marginally better. I put a pair of rubber gloves in my rucksack and pulled on my hiking boots. I scrunched my hair back under a clip and added a woolly hat, partly for warmth, but mostly for some semblance of disguise. I didn't want Brad to spot me a mile off and have me escorted from the scene before I'd got anywhere near the sewer. My first problem was getting past my police protection. For the last few days, Penny had been my shadow practically around the clock, but I'd noticed that a new officer, sitting in a Ford Focus across the road, had taken over from Penny late last night. The whole plan would be scuppered if I didn't get the next bit right.

From my bedroom window I could see the dark red estate, about ten meters away. The driving seat looked as if it had been set in the recline position and I sincerely hoped that the constable had lapsed in his duty and fallen asleep. At the front of my flat, there is a low wall, about six feet from the front door. I slowly opened the front door, squatting down, then slipped out keeping low inside the wall. I didn't dare look over the top. I heard no sound, except a passing van. I followed the line of the wall around the corner. Being the property on the end of a row, there was a side gate. I slid through it and scurried down the side street away from the main road. My mini was parked a few cars down.

I got in, holding my breath and checked the main road through the rear-view mirror. Nothing stirred. Begging the car to start first time, I turned the key and slowly pulled out, driving through the back streets in three sides of a square, before joining the main road further up. I was now too far away to see if the PC was on the move, but after a few minutes there was nothing behind me, so I took that to mean I hadn't been spotted.

When I got to New Bridge Street just after 6.15am, it looked like a serious incident had taken place. Around ten officers were organizing the traffic, putting signs and orange cones in place to clear two of the four lanes that led to Blackfriars Bridge. I parked in Bridewell Place and loitered on the corner of Tudor Street. There were a surprising number of ordinary people about: delivery men, street cleaners, staff appearing for their early shift at the Grand Plaza Hotel and shop assistants from an all-night convenience store, sharing a cigarette on the pavement.

Nearer the bridge, a group of men stood on the kerb dressed in waterproof suits and there was bundle of what looked like waders, hard hats and heavy rubber gloves, beside them. It was a major operation. At this point, I knew it had all been for nothing. I'd never get down. There were too many officials about and my collar would be snatched the moment I stepped out of line.

It felt safe enough to get a bit closer, as officers and onlookers had started to group together at the road-side. I was able to pick out Brad, already suited up with thigh-high waders and a lamp attached to his hard-hat. He was signing something on a clip-board.

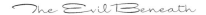

It was only when I started to look for them, that I realised how many manhole covers there were embedded into the ground. I wandered along the kerb and started to read, for the first time in my life, what was written on these cast-iron sheets. Some said BT or Thames Water, others had cable companies inscribed on them or the words 'street management'. That was without considering the fire-hydrant covers, coal-holes and gas covers. All of them doorways to hidden underworlds to which I'd never given much thought.

I looked up and things were starting to move. A manhole cover on the pavement had been levered open and a team were clustered around the hole. I moved closer. It was easier than I expected, as the bunch of onlookers was swelling all the time. I overheard an official explaining to a police officer how the main sewer tunnel was under a manhole in the middle of the road, with a fifteen foot drop into the water and no ladders beneath it. The crew were going down one nearby used for cleaning, with iron steps.

It was dawn by now and the city was coming to life. Car horns were tooting, traffic officers were adding more orange cones. I overheard someone ask if there had been an accident.

I crept as close as I could to the group of guys from Thames Water, making sure there were always figures blocking Brad's line of sight in my direction. I didn't recognise any of the police officers and hoped they would return the favour. I was stalling now, not sure what to do next. Was I really going to try this? Wouldn't it be enough to wait on the surface out of harm's way, with everybody else?

No. I'd come too far to be a bystander.

I was suitably dressed in Tony's boiler-suit and Wellington boots, but the men poised to go underground were togged up in considerably more protective gear. If I tried to make a move in the direction of the manhole, I'd stick out like a sore thumb.

It was no use. There was no way I was going down.

I was about to turn back when I overheard one of them say that the crew was a person short.

'One of our guys, Limmington's, got a stomach bug,' said a broad man wearing a Thames Water bib to a police officer. My heart-beat shot up a gear.

'I think we all will after this,' said the officer, pulling on a pair of waders.

The broad man strode over to the hole and started lowering himself down. Brad was behind him, tightening the fastenings on his gloves and hard hat before he disappeared underground, followed by two others.

I had to act now, but without the right protective gear I knew I wouldn't get far.

I kicked at a small chunk of gravel on the pavement. I should have paid more attention to where the protective gear had come from. A man shouted an instruction to a colleague and when I looked over, I noticed the back of the Thames Water van wasn't quite shut. I narrowed my eyes, trying to remember if I'd seen waders and bibs being pulled out of there. It was the obvious place. Surely it was worth a quick look.

I looked back towards the hole in the pavement. The last man in the team was about to go down. If I didn't get over there soon, I'd not only lose track of which way they'd gone, but also draw too much attention to myself.

I marched over to the van, giving a winning smile to the man leaning against the side and without hesitating, pulled open the rear door. Inside, a spare set of waders, gloves, a Thames Water bib and hard hat lay waiting for me in the corner.

This was my chance.

I had to take it.

twenty-seven

The key was to be quick and look completely confident. I began pulling on the spare pair of heavy waders as the last figure was disappearing under the pavement. My pulse was bolting like a runaway train. I didn't know what to expect down there, but I knew it wasn't going to be pleasant.

At the same time as the crew going down the manhole on the pavement, what looked like abseiling equipment was being set up by another team of police officers over the manhole in the middle of the road. There was a lot of activity. I hoped none of the officers left on the surface was keeping close tabs on exactly who was supposed to be involved in the operation. On the other hand, why would anyone actually go out of their way to surround themselves with excrement?

Complete with rubber gloves, bib, hard hat and headlamp, I stood up and stepped over to the hole.

'Oi! What do you think you're doing?' The young officer was straight on to me.

'Thames Water. We're a person short. I'm part of the backup.'

'I don't think...' He looked around, hoping to find someone more senior to consult. Teams from traffic division, the Met and Thames Water were scattered in all directions. It wasn't clear who was in charge.

'You don't think I'd *choose* to do this, do you?' I said, sitting down, dangling my legs inside the hole. 'I'm in flipping reserve.' I straightened my bib, grabbed the torch and sighed, trying to look like my Saturday morning had been ruined.

'Okay, love. Rather you than me,' he said, moving out of my way.

I'd been lucky. A more experienced officer would have been reaching for his handcuffs by now.

I switched on my headlamp, swivelled round and began backing down the ladder. My legs were shaking and I urged them to keep me upright. I couldn't believe I'd actually done it. I was convinced I'd never get this far. There was an offensive smell at first, but then I either started getting used to it or it dissipated. It certainly wasn't as bad as I thought it was going to be. At the bottom of the ladder there were steps leading into the main tunnel. I climbed down those and stepped into the water. It was knee high. I was glad I'd swapped the wellies for waders. There was a roaring sound echoing around the high walls. For a second I froze. *What on earth was I doing down here?* I'd naively talked myself into this situation and hadn't a clue how to handle it.

I quickly caught up with the back of the group. Thankfully, Brad was second in our group of six, right at the front, so he couldn't see me. I'd expected it to be cramped so we'd all have to stoop, but I was struck by the sheer size of the space. The tunnels were about fourteen feet high; broad elegant arches built with neat Victorian bricks that towered above me. Far from giving the impression of a mouldy dungeon, it reminded me of a cathedral. That thought didn't last long. One glance at the brown water reminded me of what I was dealing with.

I said hello to the man in front of me, giving only my first name. Colin was from Thames Water and must have assumed I was part of the team from the Met. He didn't seemed phased either by my last minute appearance - or by the fact that I was a woman.

'Limmington's got a stomach bug,' I said. My voice echoed, but I still had to shout above the rush of the water.

'So I heard. They dragged you down, instead?'

'Yup. Short straw.'

The roaring got louder and we reached the point where the waters of the Fleet form a small waterfall into the low-level intercepting sewer.

'I should be at the back,' said Colin, 'then I'll lead when we retrace our steps.'

I pressed myself against the sticky wall to let him come past me. A police officer was ahead of me now, together with another Thames Water official, before I could see Brad's helmet.

'Over there,' said Colin, pointing into the distance, 'even on a dry day, the flow is too fast to stand up in. When there's a storm, there's the most ginormous howl as the wind surges through the tunnels. Then the water comes thundering through, filling up the chambers to the roof.'

'To the roof?' I wished he hadn't told me that. I looked up trying to imagine what would happen to anyone who didn't get out in time. Visions of being swallowed up by this foul liquid flashed before me. My eyes started to water and I almost lost my footing.

'If it does rain hard, how long before this whole place fills up?' I asked, trying to sound matter of fact.

'Around twenty minutes. That's all we get. You can see why we have to be highly tuned to the changes in the sounds, down here.' He tapped his radio. 'Plus, we've got guys on the surface who'll let us know if there's been rainfall on higher ground.' I squeezed the torch hard with both hands through my protective gloves as if it would afford some kind of protection against an imminent flood. 'It didn't rain much overnight,' he continued, 'that's the only reason we can get down here. It's always touch and go. This time yesterday and it wouldn't have been safe.'

I watched the putrid fat floating on the surface of the water like concrete blocks. 'Have you ever had to swim in this stuff?' I asked, before realising I didn't actually want to know the answer.

'Sure - occupational hazard. But no one is going to get wet today. We're all very safety conscious and we've done our homework.'

I was glad the light was so patchy. I'm sure my face would have given away my rising terror as we waded along the passages, further away from our point of entry. I knew Brad couldn't swim and the idea of taking a dip didn't much appeal to me, either. I tried to distract myself by focusing on what was ahead. We came across a pair of crusty old boots, a spade and an old lantern which stood in little alcoves in the wall. I half expected a figure to step out of the darkness.

We turned corners to find more expanses of arches; passageways going left, right, branching off into smaller horse-shoe shaped tunnels. It reminded me of catacombs I'd visited in Rome and I found my thoughts dragging me towards the idea of death and its murky underworld. In the flickering light of our torches I kept seeing movement out of the corner of my eye; shadows coming at me in the shape of skulls; feeling breath brush against my face, making me turn sharply. My hands were shaking and I almost dropped the torch.

After a few minutes, the passages converged and the arches soared upwards with five, even six extra layers of bricks. Even though there was more space, I suddenly felt hemmed in. I was stuck down here now; they wouldn't let me go back on my own. I swallowed hard, taking down the bile taste that had saturated the air. I wasn't feeling so good; nausea was beginning to bubble inside my throat and everything was starting to spin. Even though I could see the others ahead of me - solid strong men - I felt acutely alone; a gate-crasher, isolated on that thin ledge, so close to the poisonous water.

A thought bubbled up from nowhere. There was no record of me being here. It was the perfect place for an 'accident' and there was only one person who might have expected me to muscle in despite the warnings...Brad. What if he'd given me all the details deliberately to entice me into this situation? Had he lied about not being able to swim?

Come on! I shook my head in a bid to talk some sense into my addled brain. Brad was one of the good guys; I was just being jumpy. Everyone becomes a suspect when you've had no decent sleep for weeks and your stress levels are going through the roof.

Without warning, a deafening bang shook the tunnels. Instinctively, I grabbed Colin's arm. *Slam, bang* - it came again.

'What's going on?' I cried. Gold coloured globules began falling from the roof.

'It's okay. It's only the flaps opening. There must be a boat passing on the Thames. It sends waves back up the tunnel, forcing the floodgates to open and slam shut.'

The mention of the Thames made me remember why we were down there. Either to find a body or prevent a murder. Nobody knew which.

I could see the torch beams ahead of us as officers searched the alcoves and shadowy caves. The next victim was due to be found tomorrow under Blackfriars Bridge, having passed through these tunnels - if our supposition was correct. Less than seventeen hours from now.

I managed to bypass my absurd qualms about Brad and thought instead about William Jones; meek, troubled and awkward. I wondered what part he played in this abhorrent series of murders under bridges. Brad said his hands were too small to have strangled the women, but I wondered if he'd carried them, or held them down, or somehow, in his own oblique but structured way, selected them.

Someone from the front of the group shouted to us. They must have found something.

'Steve says we need to go back.' said Colin, his ear pressed to his radio. 'There's just been a downpour in North London and it won't be long before this place starts filling up.'

'But DCI Madison wanted to get as far as the floodgates,' I said. 'I know he wanted to check the whole area.'

'Not today, he won't. We've got to move. NOW!' He turned round and took the lead. I wasn't going to argue. I quickened my pace, forcing my legs against the water. Colin was right, there was an immediate change in the atmosphere. The wind was fuller and the noise in the distance was turning into a low rumble. The air-quality shifted and ominous gusts of fetid wind whipped past us. I retched into my rubber glove at the sudden increase in stench. The water level had already risen an inch or two and thrusting my legs against it was making my thighs ache.

The floor beneath us was slightly concave and with the quickening flow, I was having to focus on staying right in the centre to make sure I didn't lose my footing. In the next two minutes, the water climbed to within three inches of the top of my rubber waders. Suddenly this didn't feel like such a good idea anymore.

Ahead of us, I could see a cone of light radiating from street level, looking like a scene out of Star Trek. Only about twenty meters to go. It wouldn't come soon enough. The water was surging and swelling, getting harder and harder to push against. Without warning a weight fell against me from behind and I staggered forward. Like a domino, I fell against Colin in front of me, but being of sturdy build he barely shifted. He came to a halt and turned round.

'You okay?' he shouted, above the increasing roar of gushing water.

'Yeah. Someone slipped,' I said, 'but we're okay.'

'Sorry about that,' shouted the man who had fallen against me. 'I'm PC Craig - Jack - by the way. I thought I was going to be down for one horrible moment.'

Colin was beckoning us all to move faster. 'Where are the last two?' he shouted over me. He must have meant Brad and the man with him. They had pulled away from the rest of us on the first leg of our search.

I didn't dare look back. I couldn't risk losing my balance. Colin flipped a switch on his radio. 'Come on, guys,' he said. 'Let's not hang around.'

We reached the ladders and Colin started to climb. Once he was out, it was my turn. The water was gurgling fast now, wanting to take me with it. I stuffed the torch in my pocket and just as I placed my foot on the bottom rung, I heard a cry from behind me and twisted round. Jack had lost his balance again and this time he fell, splashing facedown into the gushing mass. The water was rapidly rising and he started coughing and spluttering.

Colin was almost on the surface, out of earshot. I'd lost my footing and air-cycled madly, trying to find the rung again. Once I was secure, there was no question in my mind. I had to go back. I retreated down the ladder and waded back into the main tunnel. The water was now up to my armpits. Brad and his mate, behind us, had still not emerged around the final bend.

Jack was trying to stand up, but the torrent of water got the better of him. I didn't hesitate. I waded further in and reached out to grab his arm. He was thrashing around and I couldn't get a firm grip. I shuffled a couple of steps further in, the water reaching my chin. There was no other thing for it, I had to start swimming. *For goodness sake, don't get this dreadful stuff in your mouth.*

I clamped my lips shut and thrust hard with my legs, managing to get as far as Jack's head. He was trying to keep his face out of the water and I reached over, grabbing him around the shoulders. I dragged him onto his back and started kicking furiously again, back towards the cone of light.

Then I saw it.

It shot out from behind the entry ladder and lodged against Jack's shoulder. It was the smell that gave it away. A putrid rotting smell that was even worse than the stench that belonged in the sewer.

'*Shit!*' I screamed, trying not to get water in my mouth. '*It's her. She's here.*'

An arm came from nowhere and flung itself around Jack's neck as if in a drunken greeting. The hand was black and curled like a claw. Jack reared up when he realised what I was shouting about, his eyes bulging, his mouth twisting into a petrified grimace. He flinched and tried to pull himself out of the corpse's path, but in his struggle he ended up sending his head under the water and gulping down more mouthfuls. He sounded like he was choking now in between terrified blubbering sounds.

Getting Jack out was my priority. I had to work the bloated corpse loose, tugging at the hood of the jacket, to pull it away. The body had the pliability of rotten fruit and felt like it was about to break apart. The jacket, zipped up at the front, was probably holding it together. Thankfully, I was too preoccupied with Jack to see her face. Suddenly she surged forward, as though she was in a rush to be somewhere.

Once Jack was free, I did my utmost to keep him afloat, thrashing with my legs and my free arm, fighting the fierce thrust of the water, to reach the ladder.

Eventually I reached something solid. I bundled Jack up the concrete steps into the shallow water at the base of the ladder, just as Colin was coming back down again, wanting to know what was taking us so long.

'Jack's been in,' I shouted, hurriedly, 'and the body's turned up.' I pointed to the dark shape fast disappearing away from us.

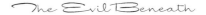

Jack leant against the ladder and threw up as Brad and his colleague emerged around the final bend, the water now nearly reaching their shoulders. I waved at them on tiptoe and pointed frantically at the shape in the water, watching it bob and rock and career towards them.

'They've got the message,' shouted Colin, 'But, we're getting out - right now.'

At this stage, the ledge at the base of the ladder was fast filling up. The roar was deafening and we had to communicate in signals from then on. Colin helped me drag Jack, once all in white, now in nothing but brown, up the ladders.

I hesitated when it was my turn to climb out on to the surface. I wanted to wait to make sure Brad got out safely, knowing he and his colleague also had the corpse to contend with. Colin, however, grabbed my arm and hauled me out, taking my brief halt as a sign of flagging energy.

'You alright?' he said, out of breath.

'Yes. Fine.' I tore off the gloves and sank down to the pavement. Two police officers in abseiling kit were crouched over the hole with torches. Colin joined them.

'Are the last two okay?' I croaked. 'Have they reached the ladder?'

'They're on their way out,' cried Colin, straightening up. 'You did a good job there,' he said, patting my shoulder.

'What about you?' he said, squatting down beside PC Craig. The constable responded by vomiting again, narrowly missing Colin's boots.

Jack looked terrified, bedraggled and filthy. I looked down and realised I must look the same. Bystanders started backing away from us, repelled by the smell. Colin and several police offers were instructing them to move back even further, knowing that something far worse was on its way.

A man from Thames Water handed me a towel and a bottle of water to pour over my face and hair. Jack, who had by now got to his feet, was being sick again.

'He's swallowed a lot,' I said to a paramedic who was on standby. 'He's going to need some treatment.' I was constantly watching the hole in the pavement, waiting for the moment when three shapes, instead of two, broke the surface.

'What about you?' she said.

I ran the clean water over my lips. 'I didn't take any down,' I said.

'Wash your mouth out with this a few times...' She handed me a bottle of grey-coloured liquid. 'And you'd better come to the hospital, just in case. Don't want you picking up any E. coli infections.' She handed me some antiseptic wipes to clean my face.

An officer from one of the police vans brought over a folded grey blanket and left it beside the manhole. Another carried over a barrier wrapped in orange tarpaulin and erected it around the opening in an attempt to provide some element of dignity for what was to follow.

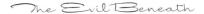

There was a hush all around. Then I saw the top of a white helmet and Brad's colleague came out first. He was dragging the dark dripping bundle, craning his neck away from the smell. A horrified gasp rippled through the crowd. Brad followed, the same strained and exhausted look on his face. They laid the body down inside the makeshift enclosure and a paramedic laid the blanket over it. I didn't quite cover her face. Her puffy skin was purple and waxy. It looked like she'd been down there for several days.

A team sprang into action and the body was quickly shifted onto a stretcher and taken out of sight into the back of an ambulance.

I was exhausted and still had to remove all the gear I'd pinched, but all I could focus on was the smell that was still lurking in the street. The unmistakeable gangrenous stink - way beyond the sticky sweet smell of a dead rabbit. I had a feeling that this final trace of her – whoever she was - would be with me for many weeks to come. It seemed even more of a tragedy that this was the only thing I knew about her.

I turned round just as Brad was walking away from the ambulance. He saw me instantly, a look of confusion, then anger, consuming his face. Confirmation that he hadn't known I was there.

'What the hell do you think you're doing,' he said, pulling me by my arm away from the others.

'Did I break the law?' I broke free, rubbing my bicep.

'What?'

'Did I break the law?'

He stared at his boots unable to meet my gaze, his hands on his hips, bearing his teeth.

'You hampered a police operation,' he said, his eyes wild with fury, his damp hair curling with perspiration.

'Did I hamper it?'

'Well...I don't know...but if you were down there, you were a liability. I should arrest you.' He leant towards me, waving his rubber glove in my face. 'You *shouldn't* have been here.'

'DCI Madison?' A man wearing a Thames Water bib was calling him and Brad turned away. I stripped myself of the gear I'd borrowed and made my way over to the second ambulance.

It wasn't until later that afternoon, when word must have got out, that Brad phoned.

'I heard about PC Craig,' he said. He sounded contrite, but a touch of belligerence was still loitering in his voice.

'Oh.' Nonchalant. No big deal.

'He said you saved his bacon.'

I laughed. 'That's nice.'

'It was still a *very bad idea*.'

'I know. I couldn't help myself.' I decided to move on. 'Was there any sign of William or...Leyton Meade...Andrew..?'

'No. We're waiting for an ID on the body. Definitely a young female.'

A short silence followed.

'Is PC Craig all right?'

'Bruised ego, but apart from that, he's fine. Craig was on our list as a good swimmer,' he said. 'I don't know what happened to him.'

'Water's like that. It's unpredictable. He slipped and started to panic.'

'You're making a habit of this.'

'Of what?'

'Rescuing people who are drowning.' I didn't make the connection. 'Those girls you saved in the Lake District,' he said.

'Ah. Yes. You see, I'm a pretty useful person to have around. I'm surprised they let you go down, given you're not a swimmer yourself.'

There was a brief silence, long enough for me to grasp that he hadn't told the team. Or he'd lied.

'I think perhaps we're both guilty of a misdemeanour,' I said, allowing the slightest hint of smugness to flavour my voice.

'No point, I suppose, in getting you to promise that nothing like this will ever happen again?' he said.

'You're right. No point.'

He sounded like he was going to say something else.

'What is it?'

'Not sure I should mention it.'

I tutted. 'Come on, Brad. Put me out of my misery.'

'It's Andrew.' His voice was clipped.

'Oh, no. What's happened?'

'Looks like there's a connection...between Andrew and William Jones.'

I couldn't speak for a moment. 'I don't understand. How?'

'Andrew has been teaching at an evening class. A painting course. William is in his group.'

I could feel my face snap back to the expression of dread that had been its natural position all day. I stared at the carpet unable to move. *William was in Andrew's painting class. They knew each other.* I thought again about Andrew's gruesome pictures of the river. I'd thought that had all been explained. Now I wasn't so sure. I didn't hear Brad end the call.

twenty-eight

I stayed in on Saturday night, watching vacuous DVDs. I kept going to the window to watch the rain. Images of the underground passageways I'd walked along filling up with more and more water played on my mind. Visions of the corpse looming out of the darkness. I traced the wobbling course of the rain drops, as they made their way down the glass and wondered if the police had found out by now who the victim was.

It was the early hours of Sunday when I finally got to bed. As soon as I sank my head down I knew I couldn't sleep. My body was exhausted with the emotional turmoil, but when I closed my eyes all the lights were still on and my brain was firing on all cylinders. *Who was the dead woman? Could we have prevented it? Would there be another creepy connection with me?*

I had an awful sense of foreboding in the pit of my stomach that felt like rotting fish. I went to the kitchen to fetch a bucket and stood it beside the bed. I couldn't trust the soup I'd had earlier to stay where it was.

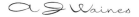

I tried picturing sheep, but they wouldn't come out to be counted, one by one. Instead they huddled under a tree, refusing to budge. I let them be. I couldn't blame them. I hadn't known dread like this - ever - in my entire life. I didn't expect sheep to save me at a time like this.

I listened to the occasional passing car, hissing in the rain. It was 3.15. I didn't want to be in the dark, so I put the bedside lamp on and then, restless, I got up to make a cup of tea. Sometimes just hearing the kettle come to the boil is comforting, but not this time. I sat on the edge of the bed and breathed into the hot steam, hoping it would somehow scorch away the evil. I finally put out the light at nearly half-past four.

Sunday came and went. I heard nothing. Then Monday morning came round again, dragging itself out of the dawn; heavy, dull and still drizzling. The last thing I felt like doing was listening to other people's problems, but I had a full day of clients and feeling grim didn't seem a good enough excuse to let them all down.

Once I got into the swing of things, I didn't feel so bad. There really is truth in the notion that focusing on other people's problems tends to make your own retreat for a while.

At the end of the day, there was a message waiting for me from Brad.

'Can you come into the station, first thing tomorrow?' he said, when I rang him back. 'There's something I'd like you to see.'

I didn't have enough energy to ask what it was about - no doubt it would involve the recent victim - so I just agreed and tried to make myself eat something.

On Tuesday morning, Brad led me to the incident room, his shirt crumpled, his sleeves rolled up. As I followed him, I caught the same musky aroma I'd noticed when we'd embarked on our short-lived intimate moment, which now felt like months ago. I wondered if Brad had forgotten all about it, by now. He'd certainly not referred to it, but then he did have rather a lot on his mind - and I had to admit, some of my actions probably hadn't helped.

We stopped at the white board dedicated to Operation Chicane. Another photograph had been added to the three already up there. It was hard to tell whether the disfigured shape was a person or an inanimate bundle of sodden clothes. Beside it was a small snapshot from happier times, showing a teenager with braces on her teeth, her hair tied back into a ponytail.

'Suzanne Mahoy, seventeen,' he said. 'Been dead about five days, according to the post-mortem.

We think she was the victim intended for Kew on November 9th. Recognise her?'

I forced myself to look at the smiling face and leant against the nearest desk, shaking my head. The place had filled up even more since I was last here: plastic crates and boxes of files were stacked in every corner and there was a heightened buzz of activity.

'We think she'd been in the sewer for several days,' he said, stretching his arms over his head. He invited me to sit on a spongy typists' chair; the kind you pump up and down, but I preferred to remain on my feet. 'Must have got the body down long before we went over there. Witnesses said there were gas works on New Bridge Street on the twelfth, on the exact spot where we got access to the sewer, but British Gas says no work was scheduled to take place there that day. They did admit, however, that equipment - red barriers and the like - had been stolen a few days earlier from a nearby street, but they didn't report it. Happens all the time, apparently.'

'She was down there all along...'

'Yeah. We found some frayed elastic attached to the belt of her jacket. She'd been tied - perhaps to a tethering ring set into the brick - just upstream from the ladders we went down. Killer must have hoped that, with the rain and the high water-flow down there, she'd eventually break loose and head towards the Thames on the fifteenth.'

'We found her on the fourteenth. He must have got his calculations wrong by at least twelve hours,' I said, cynically.

'There must have been more rainfall than he - they - thought. The weather was one thing they couldn't control. And they hadn't banked on us getting down there.'

He dragged his hands through his hair. It was lank and could have done with a wash and he seemed to have extra folds under his eyes. He must have been at the station all night.

'It's still a considerable achievement to pull off.' Brad yawned and didn't bother to hide it. 'Jones might have mental problems, but from the papers we found in his flat, he's got an amazing brain.'

'Where was he?' I said.

'Didn't leave his flat all night. Went to the corner shop this morning...'

'Nothing to pin it on him, then?'

'Bugger all...sorry, been a long night...day...' He looked confused as though he had no idea what time it was. 'Your "Demo-man" alias Reginald McGuire is back on the radar, though. That's not his real name. He's also known as Damon Hartnell and has a record for assault on...wait for it...women who've had terminations.'

'Really?' He tapped one of many loose sheets lying on his desk.

'He was in Paris earlier this year outside an abortion clinic and allegedly punched one woman and was verbally abusive to another, but he wasn't arrested. We know he's been an agitator in Ireland and has been at various Pro-life demonstrations up and down this country. Problem is, we can't find him.'

I let my shoulders drop with a heavy sigh. He'd made no mention of Andrew, but I knew that didn't mean he was out of the picture. I couldn't handle any further setbacks, so I didn't ask.

'You wanted me to see something.'

'Yeah. You can't see the body. It's badly decomposed and–'

I put my hand up. 'I know - can we stop there?' I'd already spent a night seeing images of the victim; her skin puffy and transparent, and starting to peel away. For once I wished my imagination wasn't quite so sharp.

He reached across his desk for some photographs. 'Suzanne was strangled like the others,' he said. 'Dead before she got in the sewer - pathologist says there wasn't enough water in her lungs or stomach to suggest she drowned. And, like the three others, she'd had a recent termination - at Fairways.'

That link again.

He handed me a batch of photographs. I flinched.

'It's okay. These are just pictures of her clothes, that's all. Like before, we wondered if there was anything familiar.'

I carefully checked each print. The girl's clothes had been dried and laid on a white table; a thin zip-up jacket, a single green glove, jeans, a black t-shirt, black bra and matching panties. My first thought was that it wasn't much for a wet November night, forgetting that she may have been killed on a dry day earlier in the week. I didn't recognise any of it.

'And then there was this.' He handed me a sealed plastic bag containing a small white card. It had been scuffed, the way paper disintegrates when you've put it by accident through the washing machine.

It was the size of a business card. I held it closer until I could make out a few letters on the front.

'It says "Odeon", I think,' I said.

'Yeah, that's what we think. We've also been able to work out a couple of other sections; one is "Future", the other looks like it might be "Derby Street".'

I dropped the plastic bag and took a step backwards, colliding with a filing cabinet. I had that horrible feeling: the one when you look up and realise your purse has been stolen or walk in the front door and know you've been burgled. That nasty cocktail of shock and despair that made the pit of your stomach collapse. 'It's a cinema ticket...from Norwich.' I grabbed hold of it again. 'Look here...these numbers...it's a date.' I squinted, unable to believe what I was seeing. 'It's from...1990.'

'What the–'

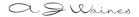

'The killer knows about my past. He was *there*,' I said. This stupid, vile game was turning into a never ending torment.

While Brad stabbed about on DS Markeson's desk, trying to find the file to replace the ticket, I leant against the desk, not trusting myself to stand unsupported. I glanced down at the cascade of overlapping sheets. There were pages and pages of handwritten numbers in columns and others that looked like complex diagrams of electrical grids. I was about to ask if I was free to go, when my eyes fell on another page. I stared at it in disbelief, my pulse throbbing in my temples.

This can't be happening.

'Where did this come from?' I asked, my voice sounding like it was being dragged over sandpaper.

Brad turned round. 'Oh, it's the pile of papers we picked up from Jones' flat. Tide-tables for the Thames and pages of calculations about boats and speeds. It doesn't mean anything to me, I'm afraid, but our technical guys say it's high-level complicated stuff.' He glanced up at my face and must have noticed my ashen colour. 'You okay?' He pushed a chair into the fold of my knees and I gratefully slumped into it.

I held up the top sheet. There it was: the hallway with stairs on the left and the sitting room first right; the dining room second right, leading to the breakfast room and then the kitchen. I pressed it against my chest as if it was a photograph of a long lost relative.

'It's mine,' I said.

The home where we were all happy, until the fire swallowed Luke up.

'What is?'

'This plan. It's the layout of our old house in Norwich.'

Brad dropped the folder he was holding. '*Your house*?' he said, pressing his fingers into his forehead.

'Yes. And look at it.' I held it up. 'It shows the power points and the position of basic appliances. It's about the fire, isn't it?'

'Let me see.' He prised the page out of my hands and flattened it out on the desk. 'You sure this is the plan of *your* house?'

'William was involved with the fire...' I whispered. My voice didn't sound like mine anymore. It sounded flat, distant, disembodied.

He repeated his question, the way policemen do.

'Yes, I'm sure,' I said. 'Every detail. The exact location of the rooms, the fuse-box under the stairs... the fridge, the cooker - everything.'

'Oh my God,' he said. He squeezed his eyes shut and looked dazed for a second, then called to an officer sitting at a desk by the window. 'I want all the records of Jones' history, where he used to live and when,' he said. 'And I want it now.' He turned to me. 'We've missed something huge,' he said. 'You don't have to stay. This might take a while.'

twenty-nine

I wasn't sure if I could cope, sitting in the police station unable to do anything; squashed inside this manic bee-hive, but not part of it, wondering what other nasty shocks might be in store for me. I checked my watch: only 10.30am. The rest of the day felt like it was going to be an ordeal.

I felt like someone had punched me hard in the face and I was trying to see though a blanket of stars: blinding, flashing, blurring my thinking. This new discovery was taunting me, teasing me, but felt slightly out of reach. Two entirely separate tragedies were merging together. The fire that killed Luke and the deaths of these women - there was a *link*. And that link was William Jones: a man I'd never met, who was two years older than me and had Asperger's. I was trying to complete a circuit but, pull as hard as I might, I couldn't get the two wires close enough to touch each other. I needed to be somewhere on my own to try to process what all of this meant.

I caught the Tube back to Putney Bridge and walked along the river. Thoughts battered around inside my head like hailstones, as I tried to figure out what had happened over the past eight weeks since that dreadful first text message in September. I needed to focus on the facts, not speculation or assumptions.

For a start, what did I know? William Jones had a plan of our old house showing the power points, main appliances and the fuse-box under the stairs. William Jones had been at Kew Bridge and had given me the date of the last murder. I'd never met him before the police interviews. The dates were significant to him, due to some traumatic incidents in his own past. But he wasn't the killer: his hands were too small, his feet were too small and he didn't drive, but he did have lists of tide-tables for the Thames in his house and spare body-bags that were a match for fibres on two of the victims, at least.

What other facts were there? On each body of the victims, something belonging to, or connected with me had been left and each of the women had strong connections with Fairways; three having had a recent termination there and one working as a cleaner. I worked there. Another link.

Who would have known my favourite book was *The Secret Garden?* How could this person have got a handful of my hair? And who on earth could have got hold of one of our cinema tickets from the night of the power-cuts, nearly twenty years ago - the night Luke died?

I could feel a frown burrowing into my forehead as I fought to get it all to make sense. It was like dragging parts of a buried skeleton to the surface, but not knowing what it was going to be. Then, for some reason, I had a flashback to my visit to Mr Knightly. His tartan slippers, his missing teeth, his photo album. There was something I wasn't seeing, floating just out of my grasp. Someone wearing a badge - a gold badge - with coins dangling together.

As soon as I headed back towards my flat my phone rang.

'Where are you?' said Brad, his voice breathless, sounded like he'd been running.

'Near home, why?'

'William Jones has given us the slip.'

'Shit.'

'You still got Penny with you?'

I looked up and saw Penny, sitting holding a half-eaten sandwich on a bench near the road.

'Yes - she's here.'

'Make sure you keep her informed about where you are,' he said. 'I'll let you know once we've caught up with Jones. And by the way,' He cleared his throat. 'Thought you'd like to know - Andrew Wishbourne's last-minute alibis have just checked out.'

Finally - some good news.

'On October 6th he was on a train to Derby,' he said. 'And on the 12th, he was causing a fuss in an all-night café in Notting Hill. Someone remembered him because he was...drunk.'

'Sounds about right,' I said. I didn't bother to add that since then, he'd gone on the wagon. For all I knew he could have fallen off it by now.

'And those shoes we found - the size tens - they belong to the next door neighbour. Andrew lets him leave stuff in the outhouse, as he doesn't have a shed of his own.'

I felt an internal cheer sing out loudly inside me.

When I got back home, there was a message waiting for me on the answer-phone. It was Lynn Jessop, sounding apologetic, checking to see if I'd found a set of keys. She said she lost them around the time of our last session.

I went straight to the spare room and took a look around. There was nothing on the floor. I checked behind the cushion, inside the tissue box. I was on the verge of phoning her back, when I decided to check down the side of the comfy chair. Sure enough, I came across a key-ring with three keys attached to it. They looked important.

'Thank you *so* much,' she said. I'd never heard her sound so gracious. 'They must have slipped out when I last saw you.' I heard a rush of traffic in the background.

'Where are you?' I said.

'I'm not far from where you live,' she said. 'On the embankment opposite Bishop's Park - my daughter's having a rowing session. I'd drop round, only she needs me to be here to let her back into the boathouse.'

I didn't hesitate. I knew it would shed more light on Billy if I could meet another member of the family and the idea of coming across Lynn's daughter in this off-hand way sounded too good to be true. It wasn't exactly orthodox practice, but I was running out of ideas when it came to supporting Lynn.

'I need to come over that way to go to the supermarket,' I said. 'Tell me exactly where you'll be and I'll be over in about half-an-hour.'

I sent a text to Penny to tell her the starter motor on my mini was still playing up and I was going over the bridge on foot. Once I'd been shopping, I sent another message to say I was heading down to a boathouse by the river. She tailed me in the car, but I lost her for a while as I cut down to the Thames through a pedestrian walkway and she had to take the long way round by road.

There were several boathouses facing the boat ramp, just along from the Duke's Head, where I'd met Brad for a drink on Friday night. It was around 3.45pm and the light was fading, so most of the boats had been hauled out of the river by now. It looked like the tide was edging its way out. I found the second boathouse, walked around the side and tapped on the door. Lynn appeared straight away and invited me inside.

It was like a warehouse, with wooden racks holding upturned boats from floor to ceiling and rows of lockers at the back. There were stepladders for reaching the higher boats and trolleys of paints and waxes for keeping the boats in tiptop condition. My heels clacked on the dusty granite floor.

'It's very kind of you to drop off my keys,' she said. She pushed the side door shut behind me and locked it. There was a strong sweet gluey smell; a mixture of rubber and marshmallows.

The lighting was poor inside, even though the doors at the front were wide open. I looked up and saw several swinging sockets where light bulbs used to be. She smiled and held out an opened bag of sweets. I understood now where the sugary smell was coming from.

'Angela is going out for another session on the water before it gets dark,' she said. I looked out towards the embankment and saw a lone figure climbing into a boat. 'Come and say hello.'

We walked down the ramp towards the river. Lynn's daughter was considerably older than Billy. She was busy leaning into the boat adjusting the footplate, but she looked up.

'Hi,' she said simply with a distracted smile and returned to securing the oars. There was something familiar about her lank mousy hair and broad chin, but I put it down to the family likeness to Lynn. 'She'll be back soon,' said her mother. 'We can talk more then.'

As Angela expertly pushed herself away from the bank and glided straight into her rowing rhythm, I was disappointed that our meeting had been so brief. I hadn't had the chance to get a sense of what she was like and it wasn't appropriate, as Lynn's therapist, for us to stand around and chat while we waited for her to come back.

'I'd better go,' I said.

'Why?' she said sharply.

'It gets in the way of our therapeutic relationship.'

'I didn't realise there were *rules*.' She strode off towards the boathouse.

'I'm sorry,' I said, catching up with her.

Her face softened a little. 'I understand,' she said. 'But, my session is due in a couple of days and there's no one else here,' she beckoned me inside, as if she owned the place. 'How about we have it now, if you've got time?'

She pulled the doors shut as if the matter had been decided.

'That's not really–'

'We could go upstairs. There's a private room overlooking the river. No one will disturb us,' she said. 'We can stop when Angela comes back. I'll pay you just the same.'

'I don't think–'

'I want to tell you more about me...my life,' she said.

Her words were music to my ears. That's what I'd been hoping for with Lynn all along after weeks of facing a closed book. I came to the conclusion that it could do no harm to talk privately upstairs until Angela returned. We might start getting somewhere, at last.

Lynn locked the main doors to make sure we weren't interrupted and I followed her upstairs into a cosy well-furnished room, with a huge window looking out across the Thames.

'This is only for committee members,' she said, pulling two seats together.

I rested my hands in my lap. 'So - what is it you'd like to tell me?'

'This place is like home to me,' she said. 'I was supposed to be selected for the double skulls at the Seoul Olympics in 1988. We were all celebrating and then I saw my name wasn't on the list.'

My eyes shot wide open. 'You were that good? At rowing?' Lynn had told me she swam regularly, but I had no idea she'd ever been Olympic standard at anything. This woman had once been strong and powerful. I'd seen before how life's setbacks could break people so that their entire demeanour was affected.

'That same year I was told I couldn't have any more children, due to the punishing amount of training I'd put myself through. No one tells you it messes up your reproductive system.' She stroked her abdomen as if there was a child inside. A child she was waiting for. Something about the way she touched her stomach sent a chill around my legs, as though someone had opened a door.

I gulped audibly, hoping she hadn't heard. 'Lynn - that was two devastating disappointments. How did you cope?'

It wasn't what I was thinking. I was thinking that here was a woman still visibly grieving for that loss, over twenty years later. I was wondering who had paid the price for those two major setbacks in her life. The room felt like it was shrinking, the air getting heavier with something I couldn't explain.

She didn't answer. Instead I caught the trace of an expression flickering across her face. If I hadn't been studying her I would have missed it. The slightest tug of a sly, self-satisfied smile. As if she knew something I didn't. In that moment I knew Lynn was a woman who had first-hand knowledge of reprisal. She was a woman who knew how to hold a grudge.

Lynn pointed outside to Angela's boat barely visible in the dusk. She was skimming the water away from us at speed.

'Do you remember her?' she said, her eyes now watery and deep.

'Remember her?'

'Yeah. You were at the same school. '

'Were we?'

'Back in Norwich. She was in the year below you, but you met on a school boating trip once. Silly girl - she was a terrible swimmer back then.'

Visions of the Lake District leapt into my mind; the dinghy tipping up in the rapids; the two girls from my boat who fell in the water. One of them called Angie. *Angela.*

My head was buzzing. I was quickly trying to piece things together: the Angie I'd dragged out of the water in 1995, was Lynn Jessop's daughter.

I gave a quick smile. 'Angela - yes I do remember...' My brain was somewhere else whirring fast, matching things together. Norwich. Angela went to my school there. Lynn used to live there. My mind shot back to Mr Knightly and the way he assiduously pointed out the people in his photo album. People from my past. I had a vision of a gold badge catching the light...

'We lost the baby, you know.' She sniffed. 'After the accident in the Lakes. Don't know if you knew Angela was pregnant.'

'No. I didn't. I'm so sorry.'

Her arms were folded now. I noticed she hadn't offered any acknowledgement that I'd saved her daughter's life. She didn't look like she was going to, either. She was defiant. Angry. Angry, with *me* for some reason.

'Angela will be here shortly,' I said, casually. 'I'm afraid we'll need to draw our session to a close and go downstairs.'

'Angela is a long way away,' she corrected with a forced smile. 'She won't be back for some time.'

I found myself on my feet, overwhelmed by an acute sense of impending danger. At the same moment, an image finally burst through into my conscious mind. In that instant I knew what was trying to reach me. The gold badge. They weren't coins - they were rings. Five of them. The Olympic symbol. A shoal of goose-pimples came to life along my arms, sending the hairs upright.

The horrible truth was settling around me like fast-acting fog. The items that belonged to me that were left on the bodies in the river - Lynn had access to them all. It was Lynn who knew my favourite child-hood book was *The Secret Garden*. She'd read it to me when I was nine years old. Our baby-sitter. She must have come across a cinema ticket the next time she baby-sat after the fire and slipped it in her pocket. She was the link to my past.

Lynn must have been there when the women went into the water.

Before I could react, Lynn slipped past me and locked the door, dropping the keys into her pocket.

She knew.

'You killed Angela's baby...in that boat accident.'

'What? No - I saved Angela's life!' I caught a flash of venom in Lynn's eyes. Something she had said earlier was tugging at my sleeve. To do with the words she had used. *That was it.* When she described Angela losing the baby during the boating accident, she'd said *we lost the baby* - not, *she*, her daughter, but *we*, as though Lynn had some claim to the unborn child.

'You saved your little friend, first, then as an afterthought, you decided to bother with my daughter.'

'It wasn't like that,' I broke in. Images of that day, when the waves tipped our dingy upside down into the rapids, were flicking one after another through my memory, like a DVD on fast-forward. 'The other girl, Emma Brockley...she was nearest to me when the dinghy went over. It wasn't about choosing Angela second - it was about getting them *both* out.'

Lynn ignored me. 'I didn't care that Angela was only sixteen when she first fell pregnant - in fact, you might say I encouraged it. We would have raised the child together,' she said. 'It would have been our family.' Lynn's face fell and she rounded on me. 'But *you* put a stop to that. You killed our baby.' She wagged her finger at me, getting closer. 'And it wasn't just the *one* baby you killed.' I could hear the blood pumping in my ears and my hands starting to sweat. 'You just don't get it do you!?'

She stamped her foot and I flinched, convinced she was about to land a punch right in my face. 'Angela lost another one last year. Another dead baby because of you. It was all your fault. Doctors said it was because of the way she lost the baby in the accident and she'll *never* have a child.' She took hold of my shoulders and shook me violently. 'Do you know what that's like? *She'll NEVER have a child!* You've robbed me of my grandchildren, my future. You can't get away with that.'

It wasn't until that moment that I realised the level of danger I was in. Lynn saw me as someone who had not only killed her daughter's unborn child, but ruined any future hope she had of having grandchildren. She was pathologically obsessed with continuing the line of her family.

'That's why I had to punish them...those slags...three of them who killed their own babies... and the other one who worked there, in that disgusting clinic, like you. It was easy to slip in on your days off, hang around and follow the ones who came out of the operating block looking fragile, clutching a post-op leaflet. None of them deserved to live.'

The impulse to grab a chair and fling it out of the window crossed my mind, but even if I managed to break the glass, there was no way down. We both stood staring at each other, poised like two open doors in a lift about to slam shut.

'The police know I'm here,' I said, my voice hoarse, catching in my throat.

'I know. Nice girl. I said hello.'

I was blinking hard. *Shit.* Poor Penny. Lynn must have caught her off guard. I hoped she wasn't badly hurt.

The awful realisation that nobody knew where I was and nobody would dream of coming here to look for me, spread through my body, like poison. My first thought was to try to appeal to Lynn, but I could think of no point of entry. It was like staring at a Chinese puzzle box with no idea which tiny piece would slip aside, so I could open it. How could I possibly sway this woman who was so adamant in her cause. How could I say *sorry*, for not saving her daughter first? It would sound hollow and pointless to this woman who had decided I'd destroyed her life.

'I wasn't alone,' she said. 'Let's go downstairs. I'd like you to meet someone else.'

She unlocked the door, grabbing my arm with her other hand in a vice-like grip. She was so strong she almost lifted me off the floor as she dragged me on to the landing. As we got to the bottom of the stairs, I heard another set of footsteps and jerked around.

William Jones stepped out of the shadows.

thirty

William didn't say anything, simply stood and stared at the floor, plucking at the skin on his neck. He had just reduced the odds of me getting out of the boathouse in one piece by half.

'William...' I said, still trying to get it all to fit inside the same frame.

'Juliet...this is Billy,' said Lynn, curling her lip.

The truth suddenly crashed over my head like a collapsing chandelier. *Billy. William.* Billy was William Jones, the son she'd talked about being only thirteen. I couldn't believe how short-sighted I'd been. When I first met William, I should have realised that the boy Lynn had been describing to me, week in and week out, was suffering Asperger's, the same condition. Perhaps then I might have realised that she was actually talking about the *same person*, transported back in time.

I was still trying to process what difference it would have made if I'd made the connection sooner, when Lynn took a step closer to me and started prodding her finger into my shoulder. I pulled away and took a swift look around. There were no windows. The side door was sturdy, solid, as was the large double door leading on to the riverside.

I tried to work out how many steps it would take to make a dash for one of them. How many vital seconds. But, what was the point? Once I got there, all I could do was scream. The doors were locked, Lynn had the keys in her pocket and she had Billy at her beck and call. Lynn was taller and broader than me. In our sessions, she'd appeared vulnerable, with her low self-esteem giving me the impression of impotence. She was, in fact, a lot fitter than I'd given her credit for. I wouldn't stand a chance; I had to think of something else.

'The dates were special to him,' said Lynn. 'Those dates we chose for the women under the bridges were when he was bullied. His head was pushed under the water when he was thirteen, just like I told you. It started in September 1989... then twice in October and twice in November. Do you remember what you were doing then, Juliet?'

I couldn't work out what she was getting at. I was finding it hard in the current circumstances to send my mind back twenty years. I must have been eleven. It was the year before Luke died.

'I don't see what–'

'We decided to use the same dates - and Billy loved the idea of using his knowledge of the tides on the Thames. He knew them all backwards.'

The five dates. September through to November. The dates Billy had been bullied and the same dates the women were strangled.

'I drive a school mini-bus,' said Lynn. 'Plenty of space for a small boat when you remove a few seats.'

She looked over to Billy, as if hoping to share some of the glory, but he continued to stare at the floor, a forlorn look on his face.

'No one was going to bother with two people rowing on the river, even after dark,' she continued. 'Sometimes we left a body-bag in the boat for a few hours and came back to it later - we were versatile.'

So that's how they'd done it. It sounded so simple. They probably hadn't even got their feet wet. I remembered the boats I'd seen moored on the mud banks at Kew. Benign, unremarkable. Many had tarpaulin or bin bags left inside. Even if a body had been left in their boat for an hour or two in broad daylight, no one would have suspected a thing.

'And that's what this has all been about?' I said. 'Retribution, because Angela lost any chance of having children - and you lost the chance of carrying on the family line?' It probably wasn't such a good idea to challenge her, but fury was starting to cloud my judgement.

'You're missing quite a lot here, dear,' said Lynn. She sounded breezy and cheerful as though she was about to bring out tea and cakes. 'Come on, Billy, tell her...she needs to know.' She opened her arms towards him as though he was the star guest.

He cleared his throat. 'He did it.'

'Who did what?' I said.

'He was the bully. Luke. He was the one who pushed my head under the water. 1989. Deep water, like high tide.'

I stared at him. *What was he saying?* He must have got it wrong. My sweet Luke. Our special boy. *A bully? No way.* I felt myself sway and the boathouse started to pulsate in and out before my eyes. *It was ludicrous. Not Luke.*

'Luke was at the school down the road,' said Billy. 'Him and his friends - they used to come after me. Luke was the leader. Hated me. I know the dates. Never forget. Mother saw it once.'

Billy showed no signs of malice, he was simply stating the facts. All the malice was being manufactured and shouldered by Lynn.

'Yes. It's true,' said Lynn. 'That's why Luke had to pay.'

Without any warning, my knees went weak and I dropped to the floor.

'Luke...' I whispered. My mind blanked out for a moment and then was flooded with snapshots of my brother. Luke smiling, Luke laughing - then Luke burning, fighting to find a way out of the house. I started hyperventilating until Lynn kicked my foot hard and I began silently weeping instead.

'The fire was very clever and undetectable,' she said, rubbing her hands together; in control, enjoying every moment. 'I knew your house. I'd babysat for the two of you a number of times.' She glanced across at Billy. 'Poor boy had head injuries following Luke's bullying sprees - he's never been the same since. I reported it, of course, but the brain scans were clear and with Billy having Asperger's anyway, it was difficult for the neurologists to see any difference in him. But I knew he was scarred for life.' She sniffed loudly. 'So, we had to think of something else. The fire was a stroke of genius. Billy worked it all out, didn't you, darling?'

Billy shuffled from one foot to the other. He didn't look like he was particularly enjoying himself.

'Billy has always been a whiz with circuit boards and electricity. Your family were all out that afternoon, so Billy found the key under a plant pot by the front door, I mean...' She tossed her head back to emphasise the stupidity of such a hiding place. 'He caused the power-cut. If a fuse is too low it will blow, so he replaced some 13 amp fuses with 3 amp ones. You came back and sure enough the power went off. No one would think to check individual fuses. Your father probably tried to reset the trip switch, but it would all have blown again. Then, when you were all safely tucked up in bed, Billy went back in again and replaced the fuses and switched the power back on. Opened a few windows. Just a little breeze to fan the flames. It was dark, nobody was going to notice.'

Except Mr Knightly, I thought, who unfortunately didn't do anything about it.

'My clever boy switched on two rings of the cooker, just like we agreed.' She waved her arms in his direction, full of pride for him. 'He laid a couple of tea-towels over the cooker and left some opened cartons of flammable liquid beside it, from the shed. Anyone else in the family could have done that. No real evidence, you see.'

She was tapping her foot on the floor. I knew the only reason she was telling me all this was because she didn't intend I'd be around much longer to repeat it. I wondered which bridge they'd chosen for me. I gulped at the thought of it and found my mouth as crusty as charred wood.

'It was a magnificent blaze,' she went on. 'We could even see it from Donnington Street. We came over, of course. Anything to help. Couldn't believe it when Luke ran inside after the dog. We'd have been happy just to see your house burn down, but taking Luke with it - that was an extra bonus.'

I was still on the floor, holding my knees tight to my chest in a bid to protect myself. I felt sick and had started shaking as if overcome by fever. Everything was moving too fast. I wanted to make things go into slow-motion to give me a chance of holding on.

'And that's about it, I think.' Her voice was light and gleeful. In spite of the low lighting, Lynn's pupils had shrunk to a pin-prick and her irises had turned a vibrant metallic colour, as though the pigment was being lit up from the inside.

'But why now? Why wait twenty years?' I was desperate to keep her talking, spin things out, but I knew I was running out of time.

'I thought about coming to get you years ago, after Angela lost her first baby, but by the time I'd worked out a plan, your family had moved to Spain. I thought you'd gone with them. Besides, although you'd killed one child, I thought then there would be more.'

She grabbed a handful of my hair, pulled it hard, forcing my head back. I knew then how she'd got hold of the hair that had been found in the boat at Kew. Clever. I should have realised at the time. Lynn had reached out in a session just once and touched my shoulder. It was completely out of character. I should have known she wasn't the touchy-feely type.

She kept a firm grip on my hair. It felt like it was on fire. 'After Angela lost another baby last year and we knew there would be no more children - well, that was it.' She ran her hand under my chin, slicing the air. 'Where ever you were, I was coming for you. Billy isn't fit to be a father. Our family will die out, killed off by yours.'

There was a pause when all I could hear was her rasping breath, then she gritted her teeth. 'Last year, I did a little bit of checking and - lo and behold - you were living in London. I decided we'd move here. I made it my life's work to spin my magic and see you terrified, to watch you slowly buckle as the women died one by one and the one link to them all was you. They were fair targets - they didn't value the gifts they were carrying, whereas Angela and I... we didn't have any choice in the matter. Neither of us could be mothers again.'

I could see she was done with talking. 'Where's the body-bag, sweetheart?' she said. My stomach lurched and I felt a heaviness pressing down in my bowel. Billy bent down, rolling out a black shape like a sleeping bag on the floor beside me. Lynn grasped my arm.

Like the flick of a switch, I remembered the rape alarm in my pocket. I made a grab for it and removed the pin. A terrific squeal broke out around us. Lynn made a swipe for it and knocked it to the floor. I tried to go after it to kick it out of her reach, but within seconds she had ground the small box to a pulp with her heel and the noise fizzled out. She was still gripping my arm.

'Pathetic,' she said, laughing. 'Is that the best you can do?'

She shook me. I felt like a rag doll. 'You were meant to be the fifth body, to be found on November 15th, but the police were on to us at Kew on the 9th. We had to keep that one and use it a week later at Blackfriars - but you'll round things off nicely. Five special dates - five sacrifices.' She reached out and stroked Billy's hair. 'Now then, Billy. You know what to do. You hold her down and I'll do the rest.' He leant into her hand before kneeling down to unzip the body-bag. It was a well-practised gesture. They knew this next part off by heart.

I had to think quickly and I had to think like a psychotherapist. I couldn't afford to be distracted by panic. If I couldn't reach Lynn, I had to reach Billy. I had to find a way to climb into Billy's head. After all, that's what I was supposed to be good at: thinking on my feet, finding ways to connect with people, encouraging them to trust me. *What had Billy revealed to me in the brief time we'd spent together in the police interview room? What could I use to get me out of here?*

'Billy, you don't have to do this,' I said, calmly, gently. I couldn't be sure how strong a hold his mother had over him. Did he blindly follow her every instruction to the letter? Did he ever make decisions on his own?

Lynn dragged me to the body-bag and kicked my legs out from under me. I fell forward with a thud on to the granite floor and let out a yelp. She swung me onto my back in one swift, effortless manoeuvre and Billy knelt over me pressing my arms into the floor. The pain in my wrists when I'd fallen was making me dizzy. My knees felt like they were splintered and I could feel dribbles of blood running down the inside of my torn jeans. My fingers felt something gooey on the floor and I thought at first it was blood, but then noticed a bottle of Boatsheen, standing on a rack, above me. It must have been the waxy substance the police had found in the victims' hair. Now it was going to be in mine.

Inexplicably, time became dreamlike and elasticated. Billy was holding me down and Lynn was putting on a pair of gloves, spinning things out to allow my terror to escalate. I began to think of all the things that were left undone: I wouldn't be able to say goodbye to Mum and Dad or tell them the truth about the fire. *Mum, you didn't leave the tea-towel on the oven rings. You weren't to blame. Dad, Luke didn't bring the flammable containers into the kitchen. He wasn't to blame.* I couldn't die now. I couldn't die without them knowing the truth. I had to find a way out of this.

My eyes darted around me in a futile bid to try to find something I could use as a weapon, but I didn't have time. Lynn kicked my shin hard, then knelt down, her face right next to mine filling up all the space with a blurred leering image. I wriggled and kicked out, but I was trapped under Billy and my arms were going numb.

Come on, think. There has to be something. Use your knowledge, Juliet. Use your experience. My mind kept being tugged back to Billy. He was the weak link. So far, he'd followed Lynn's instructions, but he hadn't hurt me. He hadn't acted independently. He was my one final unexplored point of leverage. I *had* to win him over. *Think. Pull it together.*

I knew there was one difference between the other women they'd killed and me - and that was we'd already met at the police station. We'd spoken. We'd made a connection. *A connection!* Suddenly, an idea came to me.

'Billy, do you remember me?'

He looked confused.

'Do you remember you were in a room and there was music playing? You remember the Federal Jackdaws, Billy?'

His face brightened up. 'Yes.'

'Which song is your favourite?'

'COME ON, Billy, let's get this over with,' said Lynn, her hands closing in around my neck. Instead, he straightened up and sat back on his haunches.

'*Special People*, he said.

Without his weight on my shoulders, I was able to work my hands free.

'Billy!' screamed his mother.

'Oh, yeah,' I said. 'I like that one, too. How about *Body-Snatchers*?' I'd been cursing that song for days; it had been jangling over and over on a loop inside my head. I now had all my hopes pinned on it saving my life.

Billy took hold of his mother fingers and pulled them away from my neck 'In a minute, Mum,' he said.

Here goes. It was my final hope. My last chance to try to swing things in my favour. I started singing the song, hoping with all my might that he'd recognise the wobbly, breathy sound; hoping he'd respond, even if it only bought me more time. He started bouncing his head.

'BILLY!' shouted Lynn, she tried to make his hands press down on my arms, but I had twisted round and was clapping now, my legs still trapped under him on the floor. Billy ignored her. His irises were floating under his eyelids and he was rocking now to the beat. He saw me clapping and joined in. At least he was now doing something else with his hands. Lynn got to her feet, pulled my hair out from under my head and stamped her foot on it. I cried out in pain and stopped clapping.

'No, Mum - good song,' he said. He stretched upwards. He was trying to make her clap and she flapped him away. She wasn't having any of it.

'Stupid boy - what are you doing?!'

She shifted her foot from my hair and knelt down, sliding her hands around my neck again in one slick movement. She meant business this time. Her vice-like grip was crushing my windpipe. I started gagging and kicking my legs, writhing like a beetle. I was slapping my hand on the floor, barely able to breathe, but desperate to keep the beat going.

Billy took hold of his mother's hands and tried to prise them from my neck. At the same time, I shoved her hard. The combined weight of the two of us was enough to push Lynn aside and I managed to wriggle out from between Billy's knees. Lynn shook herself lose and instantly gave Billy a hard slap across the face.

'Leave him alone,' I shouted. I started running towards the stairs, desperate to find some place of respite until Angela got back. I had to pray that she wasn't part of this murderous campaign, but I had no way of knowing. Lynn was already right behind me, lashing out with well-placed fists on my shoulders. I turned to fend her off, but she bundled me between two boat racks, trapping me so she could punch me as hard as she liked. I was helpless: she was too big and strong for me.

'Get the keys from her pocket,' I screamed at Billy. 'Get the door open.' I was trying to break free as Lynn continued to batter my face, chest and solar plexus. I bent away from her, my head down, trying to protect myself and suddenly she landed a solid punch in my spleen. I felt an excruciating pain in my side and hit the floor again. Lynn was on top of me ready to smash my face into the floor. She'd pulled my arms behind my back so I had no way of defending myself. I held my breath, waiting for the searing pain I knew would shoot through my front teeth, as they crunched against the hard surface. I waited. Waited.

Nothing happened. Instead, there was a kafuffle behind me and next thing I knew, Lynn's head crashed down beside mine pressed to the floor. Billy was on top of her holding her down. He'd left the keys on the floor beside me. I struggled to my feet and rushed to the front door.

I ran out down to the river, still clutching the keys, desperate to find a passer-by. Angela hadn't returned, but a boat was heading towards the embankment. I rushed up behind two men walking a collie dog, but before I opened my mouth, I saw Brad followed by three uniformed officers, sprinting my way.

'In there, quick,' I shouted, dragging his arm.

They disappeared into the boathouse and I left them to do their job. I collapsed against a wall, breathing hard, wiping blood from my face. I was shattered.

Lynn and Billy both emerged a few moments later, their hands behind their backs, already cuffed.

'She planned it all... the fire...the murders...everything,' I croaked.

'Okay, guys, you can take it from here,' said Brad. The three officers led them both towards a police van parked on the boat ramp.

Brad stared at my battered face and mottled neck. 'Hell - you look dreadful. Are you okay?' He took his handkerchief and wiped the blood from under my nose. A female police officer came up to me, holding a blanket.

My stomach churned as I conjured up an image of the sodden bundle of clothes being regurgitated from the sewer, as though from the belly of a giant whale. I knew it could have been me.

'Lynn's daughter, Angela, is out there on a boat,' I said, pointing to the river. He turned and squinted into the distance. 'I'm not sure if she's involved or not.'

'Get two men onto the water,' shouted Brad to a group of officers emerging from a squad car that had just squealed to a halt beside us. 'Take a couple of these boats, guys, quick as you can.'

Angela, however, was rapidly steering a path towards us.

'What's going on?' she said, innocently, as she drew alongside us in the water. I let out a sigh of relief. One of the officers started explaining to her what had happened as she climbed out of the boat. Even though there was barely any light left now in the sky, I saw the way her jaw fell and the colour blanched from her face. What she was hearing was definitely news to her.

'How did you know I was here?' I asked Brad, refusing to let go of his arm.

'WPC Kenton hadn't done her usual timed check-in. We knew where her last position was and when our officer found her tied up, she managed to tell us what had happened.'

'Is she okay?'

'She was left gagged in the boot of her car - she'll have a headache for a day or so, but she'll be okay. She said you'd been heading for one of the boathouses.'

'Where's a knight in shining armour, when you need one?' I said.

'I was almost there,' he said, defensively, 'give or take a few minutes.'

'Is that right?'

'It's always *almost*, with us, isn't it?' he said, giving me that sideways look that still managed to set off fireworks inside my stomach, even in my condition. I bent forward still catching my breath, my entire body aching from the attack. 'Always taking things into your own hands, aren't you?'

I rolled my eyes at him and burst into tears.

epilogue | two weeks later

Brad was waiting by a fountain in Trafalgar Square. It was a bitter November evening again, but for once, I didn't feel the cold. We'd planned to go to the *Beatles to Bowie* exhibition at the National Portrait Gallery, have supper in Soho and then...who knows? We hadn't planned the rest.

We had both had our own separate debriefing about the case; me, through my therapy, Brad as standard procedure at work, but we still felt a need to talk about it. Besides, it was what had brought us together.

'Did you find out any more about that aggressive guy I spotted at Andrew's presentation?' I said. 'The one who went for me outside Fairways Clinic.'

Brad had his arm around me, holding me close. 'Reg McGuire, aka Damon Hartnell, is a real troublemaker. He was in a cell in Spain on two of the murder dates.'

'What was he doing at Andrew's ceremony?'

'Had fingers in many pies, apparently. He was a Pro-life agitator only in his spare time - his main career was in fraud and fencing stolen art. He was there to get some inside information about an auction coming up at Christie's. There were plenty of top art people there, including their head of sales for contemporary art.'

I tutted. We were silent for a while.

'What about Leyton Meade?' I said.

'We watched him for days, but he didn't put a foot wrong. He's gone travelling again.' He sucked air through his teeth. 'I'm sorry about Cheryl - there was something about her that made my skin crawl.'

I laughed. 'She unnerved me too, with the details she knew at times - but she only ever wanted to help.' He slipped his fingers inside my glove and stroked my wrist. 'I found out more about Lynn's obsession with continuing her bloodline,' I said. 'It's a pathological form of Parturiphilia, apparently - a fixation with childbirth, due to an obsession with securing the genetic line. Her sense of outrage at failing to do so was so great it convinced her to kill in revenge.'

'I hope that won't make her unfit to plead.'

'I very much doubt it. She knew exactly what she was doing. Where ever she ends up - I hope it will be for life.'

'If only we'd made the link between William Jones and Norwich, sooner,' he said, rubbing his cheek. 'Lynn moved around a lot and she alternated between Jessop and Jones at various times. We lost track of him. We should have made the link to you and got to Lynn before–

I pressed my finger over his lips.

'Don't–'

In the two weeks since Billy and Lynn were arrested, I'd gone back to Norwich to try to find some closure. It was great going places now without a police car on my tail. I had a newfound sense of freedom and tremendous relief, knowing it was all over. I went to tell Mr Knightly that it was thanks to his observations about the windows being open, that the seeds of doubt about the fire had been sewn in the first place.

'It's not often at my age that you get to make a difference to people's lives,' he said. 'In a *good* way, I mean.' He pulled a large grubby handkerchief out of his sleeve and blew into it. I noticed his pullover was on inside out. 'I'm sorry about Luke, but I'm glad you know what really happened - and people are going to jail for it.'

He asked if I'd like to see more photos and I said I'd be delighted. We went through every shot, this time. I was glad to. I gave him a big hug when I left, knowing I'd never see him again.

'What did your parents say,' Brad said, 'when you told them about the fire?'

'My mother couldn't stop crying. I couldn't get a sensible word out of her. For nearly twenty years she's been carrying the guilt of believing *she* was the one who caused Luke's death. Terrible burden to bear - about your own son. The one upside is that she doesn't need to carry that guilt anymore.

'And your Dad?'

'I have a feeling my Dad knew all along about Luke's bullying. I think he'd been trying to tell me. My Mum is in denial about it, though. She's having to reprocess Luke's death as murder - I don't think she can take the other part in, yet.'

'And you?'

I watched the bubbles in the spray of the fountain explode one by one. 'It's very sad, but Luke wasn't the angel we all made him out to be. Nostalgia had coloured our view of him. Death does that. It tends to strip away the wrongdoings.' I hid my face inside Brad's jacket. 'I've got some reprocessing of my own to do about Luke. Right now, he feels like a stranger, like everyone is talking about someone else. He was my older brother and he never bullied me.' I swallowed hard. 'Never.'

'The killers were mother and son - who would have thought it?' he said. 'How come William didn't crack under pressure in the police station? How come he didn't give the whole thing away?'

'I think everyone was so aware of his condition - and that solicitor was so fierce - that none of us asked the right questions. He was easy-led, but he had a pact with his Mum. He adores her. She must have found a way to make sure he didn't reveal anything incriminating. Perhaps made it into a game. I also think she must have told him as little as possible. She was very clever, too.' I hesitated. 'One thing puzzles me - neither Lynn, nor Billy wore size ten shoes.'

'She'd got Billy to wear shoes a size too big on the days they committed the murders,' he said. 'Just in case we managed to get any prints from the crime scene. She'd picked up a few pairs at a charity shop and then got rid of them each time. That's where she got your clothes.' He let out a long breath. 'You held up really well, you know,' he said, trailing a finger down my cheek. It sent goose-bumps into places on my body I didn't know I had. I nestled against his neck and we leant against the fountain, watching tourists, friends, families; their arms around each other, laughing, taking snaps.

'We've got some getting-to-know-each-other to do,' I said, stroking my fingers gently under his eyes, gazing into their luminous blue.

'Yup. Sounds good.'

A trilling sound came from Brad's pocket. He checked the number. I knew what was coming.

'Sorry. I've got to take this.' He held my hand distractedly as he spoke in single syllables. 'Yes...No... When..? And..? Now..?' His grip tightened and he gave me a forlorn look. 'I don't believe it. This wasn't supposed to happen. I asked for one evening's grace, but Roxland and McKinery have been called out to an emergency.' He thrust his hands onto his hips. 'I've got to go.'

'This is becoming a habit,' I said. 'Just as well I'm not the clingy type.'

'I'm really sorry. A stabbing in The Broadway Centre.'

He pressed my hands together and kissed them. 'I'll call you soon. We *will*...you know, get a chance soon, I promise, to spend some time together.'

He pulled away from me and broke into a jog towards the Tube, then turned and blew a kiss before he disappeared underground.

I sat for a while on the edge of the fountain watching the water pound into the basin, getting splashed. Water; the means Luke found to persecute Billy. Water; the substance that carried those victims and cradled them in their final resting places. I took off my glove and ran my hand along the marble, collecting a tiny droplet on my finger. I watched it dribble down into my palm. Water; that cleansing, powerful, life-giving substance.

I thought about the Thames, the lifeblood of the city.

I'd made friends with it again.

THE END

Acknowledgements

For being my very first reader and for encouraging me to aim high, I'd like to thank Mike Holmes. Also, my wonderful sister, Ruth Holmes, for being my anchor and advisor.

Thank you also to the following:

Jo Dorrell for her creative insight, unquenchable interest and humour.

My terrific agent Caradoc King, who together with Louise Lammont, Mildred Yuan and Linda Shaughnessy have given me five-star treatment in their guidance and editing expertise.

Kerry Jarrett, Anna Kiff, Helen Greathead, Chris Best, Belinda Bavin, Nigel Hartley, Jackie Brady and Sandy James for regular morale-boosting.

London sewer experts, Tim Newbury and Luke, for imparting their invaluable knowledge of the underground River Fleet.

My parents, Gordon and Mary Waines, for their unfailing support in whatever I try my hand at.

And my biggest thanks of all go to Matthew, my amazing husband. Without his unflagging support, I would not have got past first post.

~

Made in the USA
Middletown, DE
23 November 2018